HEIRS TO THE KINGDOM

A NOVEL

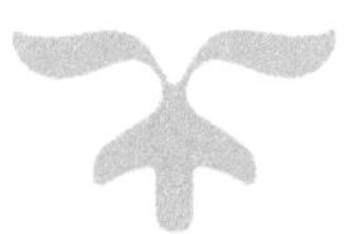

TREY RICHARDS

For Sarah, Dane, and Jenna

The dearest people in my life!

Your love moves me to action!

The world will not be destroyed by those who do evil but by those who watch them without doing anything.

~ Albert Einstein

About the Author

Trey Richards grew up in northwestern Pennsylvania and knew two things from a young age: he wanted to see the world and he wanted to tell stories. He and his family lived in Berlin, Germany for over a decade before moving back to central Pennsylvania. He currently teaches high school Global Politics, History, and Rhetoric. Heirs to the Kingdom is Trey's first novel.

Contents

The Heirs

The Heirs should never have been born.

Anthony Abbott thought about that as he pulled the last file from the hidden cabinet in his office. The official files had been requested, and it was time to hand them in. His services were no longer needed, and to keep things out of the press, any proof of his services needed to be handed over.

He carried the last file to his desk and put it on top. It was no coincidence that he had chosen this file last. He opened the computer and located the file named "The Heirs." The information in the paper files on his desk was only part of the story. The file on his computer was the whole story.

He took a USB stick out of his pocket and plugged it into his computer. He dragged the folder to the drive and watched as it copied onto the USB stick. When it was finished, he checked to ensure the whole file had been transferred. All six files were there.

Abbott had spent over forty years of his life helping women. The mothers of The Heirs were no different in that sense. What was different was who had impregnated them. Marcus Brent was himself in line to inherit his father's multi-billion-dollar business. Rumors had floated for years that maybe one day he'd have a future in politics. Abbott knew Marcus well enough to know that politics were only a starting point.

Harlan Brent, Marcus's father, had connections around the world. His business interests were to be protected at all costs. Marcus was one of his business interests. To that end, Marcus had a fixer, Elizabeth Deavers, a calculating, slender, evil woman, assigned to him. Rumors had swirled that she, like many of Brent's associates, had been blackmailed into the job. She was gifted at making problems disappear. Abbott found her conceited, constantly reminding him of her power over him. Yet, in the end, it was Abbott who duped her.

Abbott knew how men like the Brents operated, so he developed an insurance policy. He would offer each mother an alternative: to stay off the Brent Family's radar, keep their hush money, and, more importantly, keep their children. Now that Brent's promises to him had proved all lies, it was time for Abbott to light the fuse on his time bomb.

He looked through his office one last time. A tidal wave of feelings hit him at once. Yet, they didn't sway him. He was ready to make a move, which was to say, to put this information into the hands of someone who could execute his plan. One of the Heirs. He was banking on this heir having the courage that he lacked. He flipped the top file open and glanced at it one last time.

His revenge would now be in the hands of a man named Miles.

Chapter One

Miles struggled to find his shoes at the door. It was dark, and he wasn't sure which switch controlled the hallway light and which activated the neighbor's doorbell. His struggle was exacerbated by the final shots of Killapitsch, the herbal liquor he had consumed with his friends and coworkers. It was his farewell party, yet he was the first to leave. The party, roaring inside, echoed through the night, but he had things to do to prepare for his move back home to Philadelphia in a few weeks. As he went down the steps, he pondered: Was Philadelphia still home?

On the train, he sat and reminisced about the last three years of his life. Working as a professor at the American University in Berlin had been a real honor, but it paled in comparison to the life he had rediscovered here. He was twelve when they moved back to Philadelphia, so being in Berlin felt therapeutic.

As he exited the U2 train station and wound his way through the streets of Prenzlauer Berg, his head began to clear. He found his keys without fumbling as he arrived at the door to his building. In this hall, he knew which switch operated what. The one with the small light turned on the hallway light, while the ones next to the door were the doorbells of his neighbors.

Climbing the stairs to his apartment, he felt his head clear. When he reached the landing, he noticed a package leaning against his door. At that moment, he couldn't recall if he had ordered anything recently, and he was pretty sure he wasn't expecting a package from anyone.

He picked it up; it was light, and he could feel that whatever it held was quite small. He focused on the return address just as the timer for the hallway light went out. He reached over, hit the switch again, and decided to enter his apartment before reading the label.

His apartment had one long hallway with five doors leading off of it. The first door was the kitchen, which he always left open. He shut the door behind him and slipped out of his shoes, as was customary in Berlin. Taking his steps ahead, he hung up his jacket on one hook and placed his keys on the other. He walked into the kitchen and set the package on the table.

He poured himself a glass of water and drank it before picking up the package to examine the return label. It was postmarked from Philadelphia, but other than that, it didn't have a name on it. Did his Dad send him something? That wouldn't make sense since he was coming in a few days to help him move back to Philly. Curious, he opened the package and slid the contents out of the envelope. A USB stick tumbled out along with a letter. He picked up the stick and unfolded a handwritten letter, which was not signed. He shook his head, trying to free himself from the mental fog. Who could have sent this?

The letter read:

Miles,

You're in danger. On this USB are the names and medical files of six women, including your mother. You'll see why you are all special. You need to get to all of them as quickly as you can. You're all in danger. These people don't like loose ends. You NEED to act quickly!

"What in the world does this mean," Miles exclaimed aloud. He flipped the gray stick around in his fingers and looked between the USB and the letter. The ominous tone of the letter weighed upon him, and he felt his body tighten up. What could it contain that was so important? There was only one way to find out. He opened his laptop and let it come online.

Miles plugged the USB stick into his computer. A single folder appeared, and he clicked it open. There, he found his mother's name, along with five other names he had never heard before. Stacey Marsden, Ellis Baker, Hannah Vaughn, Esme Conners, and Angela Camp.

He clicked on his mother's file, and what appeared to be a medical report opened. As he read through it the first time, he wasn't sure what he had discovered. The second reading didn't make it any clearer, but he was pretty sure that his mother had endured an abortion. He shook his head and blinked his eyes, "That can't be," he said aloud. "Not my mom!" At the bottom of the form, a few neatly written words revealed it was paid for by the father of the child: Marcus Brent.

It felt like his world was being struck by an earthquake. Marcus Brent was a name he knew, and seeing it written there was a gut punch. The emotions were under the surface, bubbling up, but he pushed them back down and steeled himself to press on.

So, his mom had an abortion? It didn't make sense to Miles. Why would someone bring this up now? She'd been dead for almost two decades; there was no reason to dredge up something like this. He scrolled to the next document, which had a new patient. It read like a check-up, and at the end was an older version of an ultrasound picture. As he went through the file, he felt his body tense up. It was the date that caught Miles's eye. He scrolled back up and noticed that both the documents were dated the same: about seven months before he was born.

So, was he supposed to not exist? What changed her mind then? Confusion rushed over him; this didn't fit in with what he knew about his mother. Questions surged at breakneck speed. Was it possible that his birth father was Marcus Brent? His mom never mentioned anything about his birth father. Had she told his Dad, Simon? How long had she been involved with Marcus Brent? Did Marcus Brent know about the pregnancy? It said he paid for the abortion.

Fear began to creep into his thoughts. The Brent family had a shady history. He had stumbled upon some sketchy things in his research that made him wary of ever crossing them. It seemed like his mom may have crossed them, and he was the evidence of that.

His mind swirled and raced. Simon, his Dad, had been a lawyer and dealt with insurance fraud for multi-million-dollar companies. He would know what to do, or at least whether the threat was legitimate.

Miles grabbed his phone from his jacket and typed a message to the only Dad he had ever known:

"Call me! I need you to move up your visit."

ଔଊଚେ

Miles stood outside the baggage claim, looking through the glass, trying to catch a glimpse of his father. He had been very excited to spend time with him in Berlin during the last few days that he was here. Now, he stood there waiting for him, hoping to gain clarity from the one person he trusted in his life. Simon Trent was nowhere to be seen among the passengers unloading from the plane. Normally, Miles would have felt relaxed, but his desire to see his father had only grown over the past few days.

Finally, Miles spotted him heading towards him. He waved, and Simon nodded back.

Simon took Miles in his arms and held him tight.

"Son," he addressed Miles with a wide smile on his face, "I'm here now. We'll figure this out together!"

Simon had met Miles's mother, Betsy, when Miles was only

two years old. Miles couldn't remember a time without Simon in his life. His mother had been upfront about the situation that had led to his being born fatherless, but it was always confusing for Miles. Simon was the only man he had ever called Dad. Simon would never be anything but his father; Simon raised him. Together, they mourned Betsy as father and son, nothing less.

Miles stood in his father's embrace, wondering, What did he know? What conversations had Simon had with his mother? Had Miles missed his chance to ask his mom important questions, or was she just good at keeping secrets? He'd been so content with the life he had that it rarely ever crossed his mind that Simon was not his biological father. But if he asked Simon now, would he even have answers to the questions that were weighing on Miles?

Betsy had always brushed off questions about her past before he was born. What job she had worked as a teenager, what college was like, the normal things that he asked her, and she only gave him brief answers. The way she portrayed it, you would never guess that she was an unwed mother in a world where it was still scandalous for someone from her social class.

"I'm…," Miles spoke but paused and changed direction. "I'm just glad you're here. I don't know what to make of this whole thing."

"I know, Miles. So, let's get back to your place and take a look, okay?"

It was so typical of Simon to want to address things right

away, to have everything out in the open. Simon put a hand on Miles's shoulder, but Miles moved out from under it, focused on what needed to happen next.

"I'll grab us a taxi," Miles said.

They drove through Berlin, a city Simon had raised him in after his mother's passing. They didn't pass the tourist areas but the lived-in parts of Berlin: the old pre-war apartment buildings, bruised and never fully restored. This was the East German government's mark, with its flat, high-rise buildings, the corner cafes, bars, and bus stops that blocked traffic. Berlin had worked its way back into his blood, and he already felt extreme sadness to be leaving it behind.

As they pulled onto the street, Miles glanced over at his father. Simon was staring out the window, and there was an exhaustion in his face that he wasn't used to seeing. It struck him then that it had been nearly a year and a half since they'd last seen each other. He was reminded of the days he'd come back from summer camp or college, and Simon would comment on how much he'd grown. Now, looking at his father, Miles realized he was seeing him in a different light.

Once inside, Miles helped his father carry his luggage up to the apartment. He put the suitcase in his office, beside the bed he had made up for him. Simon dropped his backpack just inside the door.

As Simon slipped off his shoes and hung up his coat, Miles

noticed the weariness on his face. Miles said, "Let me get you something to drink."

"Water would be great," he replied, "just not the bubbly stuff, okay?"

Miles had grown accustomed to the carbonated water since living in Berlin, but he rarely kept it in his apartment. He filled a glass from the tap as his father followed him into the kitchen. Simon grabbed the glass and smiled at his son.

"So, bud, what's been going on?" he asked.

Miles rubbed his face with his hand; the stubble on his chin reminded him that he had been preoccupied these last few days. "I think it's something that would make more sense if I let you have a look at it first."

Miles pulled out a chair at the small kitchen table positioned under the kitchen window. A few pots of basil and mint lined the sill; their faint scent mingled with the aroma of the coffee that Miles poured for himself.

"I'm not even … sure how to start this … tactfully," Miles stammered with unease.

"Just spit it out—tact be damned," Simon bristled.

Miles breathed in, filling his lungs to their capacity. "Like I said on the phone, I came home from a party the other night and found a package waiting. Whoever sent it wanted to make sure it got into my hands." He pointed at the return address and label. "It's from someone in Philly. I'm not sure who the sender is. You know, I couldn't resist peeking into it." Simon gave a confirming nod, and Miles chuckled.

"There was this note with it," he said, handing the note to his father. Simon looked at it and nodded.

"Who are 'these people'" Simon asked, "and what's on that," Simon pointed to the USB stick.

"Medical records for six women."

Simon scratched his head as he listened to his son.

"That's … odd," he said, eyebrows knitting. Then something dawned on him, "Wait … was one of them your mother?"

"Yeah. And here is the part that's hard to figure out how to ask."

"Just ask, I think I can handle it."

"There's a medical record saying my mother had an abortion," Miles paused as his voice filled with emotions, "about seven months … before I was born."

"Well, that's obviously not possible," Simon blurted. "You know that, right?"

"But that's not the weirdest part."

"Oh?" Simon raised an eyebrow. "That's the normal part?"

"All six of the women have the same father listed."

Simon's eyes widened, and his eyebrows pushed up nearly to his hairline. It seemed as if he ran out of words momentarily. After minutes of silence, he resumed, "Do you… know this man, Miles?"

"Everyone who's following the news knows him," Miles's voice rang out in the air. "Maybe you should look at it yourself."

He opened up the computer, and within a few clicks, he brought up his mother's medical record. Simon leaned in to read on the screen. It displayed that the father of the aborted baby was Marcus Brent. A prominent name, especially now, as one of the top five Republican presidential candidates.

"Whoa," Simon murmured in shock. "This … this is unbelievable, Miles."

"I can't wrap my head around it, Dad. But there it is."

Simon looked up, still processing. "Did you... check this link?"

"No, I didn't see a link," Miles said, shifting his chair to sit next to his father and look closely at the screen. A string of letters and numbers were at the bottom of the page. Miles assumed they were a part of the scan. Simon moved his mouse over the sequence while highlighting it. It wasn't a hyperlink. So, he copied it before pasting it into the web browser.

A secure page popped up, displaying a plain white background with a blue banner that read "Enter Password." Dead end, Miles thought. His father typed something into the box, and boom, another file opened up. It was entirely different from the medical file.

"What did you type," Miles asked curiously while looking at his Dad.

"Your birthdate." Simon winked.

"Are you seeing this," Miles asked out loud in disbelief.

Simon's eyes grew wider. He scrolled slowly through the pages.

"What are we looking at here, Miles?" Simon kept scrolling, "What!" he exclaimed, "This is information about you! Hell, they even have my name, address, and the date we got married. This is crazy."

Suddenly, Miles's gaze fell on the last line. "What's that on the last line," he pointed to help Simon's searching eyes. "It says: Payout 1,000,000 USD?"

Simon shrugged, scrolling back through the document. "Whoever sent you this has been keeping tabs on you. It seems they know everything about you, including that you were in Berlin."

"Let me check the documents again." Miles clicked over to the next file, titled Ellis Baker. The same type of web address appeared at the bottom of the scanned medical document. If this followed a similar pattern, Ellis's child would be about two years older than him. As he examined the order of the procedures, he noted that Ellis Baker's record was dated 1978, followed by his mother's in 1980. Then, there was a gap before Stacey Marsden and Hannah Vaughn's records from 1995 and 1996. Another long gap led to Angela Camp's file in late 2006 and then, about a decade later, Esme Conners's file in early 2014.

Miles cut and pasted the website link, and once again, the plain-looking page with its blue-bannered box appeared, asking for a password. He looked at the date of birth for Ellis and entered it into the box. The little box shook back and forth, *Password is incorrect.'*

"Crap," Miles's voice broke through the sheer silence, "It wasn't her date of birth."

"Try yours again. He sent these to you." Simon suggested calmly, reacting to the frustration in Miles's voice.

Miles typed in his birth date, and the website opened to reveal a new dossier. This time, the name in front of him was Rhea Baker. If this information was correct, she was a professor of Modern Literature at Portland State. An address came into sight for what Miles assumed was her apartment, and she was single. He also found out Ellis Baker was deceased.

"I recognize this name, Ellis Baker," Simon said, leaning closer. "Put her into Google."

Miles entered her name into the search bar, and the results generated a list of websites, one of which was the obituary of a beloved children's author. "Click on that," Simon directed. Miles obliged, and an obituary came up.

Ellis Baker had passed away from cancer. She had written a book that received the Newbery Honor Award and was survived by her brother, Uriah, and her daughter, Rhea. This all checked out.

Of the six names they had, three of the mothers had died. Hannah Vaughn passed away about ten years earlier in a stampede at a bar in southern Nebraska when a fire broke out; a link to the newspaper article accompanied her dossier.

Stacey Marsden, Angela Camp, and Esme Conners were all still alive. Each file contained their children's names and what Miles and Simon assumed were current addresses. However, for Hannah Vaughn's son, it was different. A note indicated his mother's sister and husband had raised him in a remote part of Oklahoma. His last name was Sharp, and his current location was unknown, but he was presumed to be out of the country.

There was so much information to sort through. Each dossier revealed new information and aspects. Miles sat there, stunned, as he and his father tried to digest all that each new file presented to them. It sprang in his mind that his last few weeks in Berlin would be occupied with more than he had planned.

"If this is true," Simon began tentatively, forming his sentence slowly and with purpose, "the levity of this information is unfathomable. Brent is running on a massively conservative platform. This could put that into question, and you don't interfere with this family!"

"Everything a politician does is put into question, Dad," Miles retorted. "No one will care. He's charismatic, and he is pushing for changes that everyone seems to want right now."

Miles noticed that Simon's expression was of deep concern,

and his silence began to unnerve him.

"I don't think you understand. There is no delicate way to put this, Miles, but you don't fuck with the Brent family."

Miles raised his eyebrows. It was rare to hear Simon swear.

"If this is true," Simon motioned to the computer screen, "then all of these women and their children are in trouble. Brent is not going to allow loose ends. Especially not the ones that have swindled him."

"What does it matter to him that these women secretly had their babies," Miles asked.

"Nothing," Simon replied. "Which is exactly the problem. They mean nothing to him, and thus, he will take care of them before they become a problem! Miles," he paused for dramatic effect. "I've seen firsthand what these people can do. Harlan Brent, Marcus's dad, was a thug, and just because no one can prove he made people disappear doesn't mean that he didn't. Marcus and his cronies will want this cleaned up."

"Nothing here says that Brent knows about this," Miles countered. He felt the muscles in his body tense. "Maybe this is just an FYI for me?"

"You're too smart to believe that, Miles!" Simon paused for a second, "For some reason, someone has trusted you with this information."

"But why?" Miles added quickly.

"I don't know why, but I know that it requires some action on your part." He came closer and put his hands on his son's shoulders.

"Didn't you just tell me that the Brents were not to be messed with?" Miles pleaded with his father, panic rising in his gut.

"Yes," Simon sighed. "I did, but this is different."

"How?" he almost yelled.

"Miles, think," Simon took a deep breath. "If you don't do anything, they will come after you. So why not be the one who goes after them?"

"So, be killed or die trying?" Miles was perturbed.

"To put it bluntly, yes," Simon exclaimed, but then he smiled. "You have the element of surprise on your side; they will have no idea you're coming!"

"Where would I even begin," Miles sighed. Simon tightened his grip on Miles's shoulders.

"Your passion is research and investigation, Miles." He grinned, which reminded Miles of when he would encourage him as a kid.

Miles shook his head at him, knowing where this was heading.

"You become intense when you work. You leave no stone unturned. The real question isn't where to start; it's why you would want to start." Miles regained his composure as Simon talked.

"Besides the fact that I might die," Miles shot at his Dad, who nodded, more to say continue than to agree. "No matter what I find, I won't like the results." Miles paused as he wrestled with the thoughts racing through his head. Why would he want to investigate this? He had a father; he didn't need to connect with another one. His mother had kept this secret for a reason, and that alone, coupled with the amount of money it looked like she took to keep quiet, was so out of character for the discerning and purposeful mother he had known growing up. This search would unwrap boxes that had been sealed for many reasons. Miles was all for unwrapping those types of boxes in his research but not in his own life.

"Miles, there is a man out there who most sane people think is dangerous. At best, he is borderline manic-depressive. Whoever sent this to you is, one, afraid for their life, and two, hoping you'll do something about it. You don't have a choice. You gotta act." Simon's eyes were fixed intensely on Miles.

"You've always told me I had a choice," Miles retorted.

"Don't be smart," Simon scolded, "you do have a choice, but choosing not to follow up on this would be the wrong choice."

Miles tilted his head back and sighed. His Dad was right. The only choice he had was between right and wrong. Doing nothing made him the villain, even if only in his eyes, his Dad's, and the source who had sent him the files.

No one else knew he had the USB stick or that he had unlocked the files. None of these women or their children were expecting this intrusion into their lives. Was it his place to intervene?

"I need to think about this," Miles said. "I'll make a decision when I get back to Philly."

"That's your prerogative," Simon responded.

Miles got up to brew another cup of coffee to ease his racing mind.

ೞ೮ೲೲೞ೮

Having grown up in Berlin in the years following his mother's death, Miles had formed many friendships. Over the last few years, he had renewed those friendships and made more. His father's visit to Berlin was filled with visits to their family friends, dining at their favorite restaurants, and catching up with old work colleagues. If Miles had expected Simon to give him a moment of peace about his pending decision, he was sorely mistaken.

Every chance Simon got, he worked hypothetical questions into conversations with friends. He led them in a way he would never have done with a witness on the stand. He skillfully prompted them toward statements that supported his conviction that Miles should delve deeper into the matter.

In the evenings, as they returned to the apartment, Simon would reopen the files. He obsessively calculated the amounts each of the women had received for their silence. The last name, Esme Connors, stood out; her payout was the largest of the six, close to 2.5 million dollars. According to the file, she was somewhere in Mexico, and her daughter's name was Esperanza. Esme intrigued Miles, particularly because her pregnancy had come much later than that of Angela Camp, the mother before her.

Each time his Dad rehashed the information, Miles felt his mind spinning. His investigative instincts were kicking in, pushing him towards a place that he had yet to choose to go. One evening, grabbing a beer from the fridge, he looked at his Dad and said, "Please stop."

"I can't," he replied.

"Then you do it," Miles shot back. "If you're so interested in this, if you think it's worth looking into, you go to these people! You be the bearer of this news," Miles paused for impact. "It's a heavy task you're flippantly asking me to do, Dad! I can't wrap my mind around my mother sleeping with that man, let alone the fact that she then took the money and ran." Miles's voice had risen to a roar, but then it broke.

Simon looked at him. Miles's eyes brimmed with tears.

"Son," Simon rose, moved towards Miles, and put his hands on his shoulders. "I'm not being flippant. I'm being urgent. You don't think that this scares me, too? That I'm not just as miffed by how your mother behaved? Never once did I ever experience her acting in a way that led me to suspect that she was sitting on such a secret. The thing that I can't shake right now is this: you know, almost with certainty, that Marcus Brent is your father."

"I don't know that, Dad!" Miles blurted out.

"You do, Miles," Simon said in a firm tone. "Those records say so."

"We don't even know those are legitimate! Who the hell just sends a random USB to some random guy in Berlin? Who?"

"You aren't random, Miles!" Simon raised his voice, "I did not raise you to ever be that random guy. You're the guy who they trust to get to the bottom of this. That makes you extraordinary." Miles's stomach churned with trepidation.

"Stop with the build-you-up sentiment, Dad," Miles sighed, "I don't need a self-esteem boost. I need you to understand that I can't verify this, not at all."

"Then find the doctor," Simon responded in his lawyer's voice as if winning a case. "By talking with the people on this list. It's possible that one of them already knows that he is their father. Maybe one of the women can point you in the right direction and put you in touch with this doctor."

"I've already thought of that," Miles responded.

"So, you're telling me that you've already made up your mind, but you're just waiting for your heart to catch up?" Simon gave him a perplexed look. Miles shook his head, seeing his Dad acting stubbornly.

"I haven't found any phone numbers for the addresses on the list," his voice betrayed his sense of sadness at the truth of that statement.

Miles lifted the bottle of beer to his lips and took a swig. As he lowered it, he turned away from his father and left the kitchen, heading to the balcony. He stepped outside and stared at the city he had come to love. It was where he'd always wanted to live as a kid, East Berlin. There was a wall that prevented that. Now, here he sat, in the East, where a wall had once divided families and ideologies. Here he sat where a wall divided his brain and his heart. Simon came out to the balcony behind his son.

"I'm afraid I'll lose you," Miles started. Simon attempted to counter, but Miles continued. "I don't want to lose the only father I ever had, Dad! Marcus Brent can't be my dad. He's an ejaculation at best, not a dad. I'm afraid if I go down this road, it will … change us."

"I won't let it happen, Miles. You're my son. I'm your father. I sacrificed for you because I love you. I never left you, not once." Simon paused; the emotion behind his words caused his voice to waver. Miles felt tears well up in his eyes. "That won't change just because Marcus Brent may have gotten your mom pregnant. For all intents and purposes, you don't even exist to him." Simon assured him.

Miles let that sink in. He didn't have to let his relationship change with his father. It was true, but he may have half-siblings, too. It also opened doors for him to have a family; even though he had Simon and Betsy, he had always wondered what it would be like to have siblings.

"I'll do it," Miles said, regaining hope, "which I'm pretty sure you've known since the day we looked at that USB."

Simon grabbed his beer and drew Miles closer like two buddies hugging after winning a bet. They had always found strength in each other, and Miles was going to need that strength for what lay ahead.

"I love you, Miles," Simon said with the deepest love Miles had heard in a long time.

"I love you too, Dad." He responded with the same intensity.

They paused together and took in the moment. Simon sipped some beer even though it wasn't his favorite drink. "So here is what I'm thinking."

"Start with Rhea, the professor," Miles and Simon answered together. They smiled.

But Simon added, "Exactly, because…"

Miles raised his index finger in the air. "Hers is the only email I could find. I'm a few steps ahead of you, Dad." He winked as he cut his Dad off halfway through the conversation.

Simon smiled, "That's good. Because if the note is telling the truth, then you need to be a few steps ahead of whoever is cleaning or spreading this mess up."

At that moment, Miles realized that the shadows of uncertainty still loomed, but for the first time since he had opened the USB, Miles felt an ounce of hope. Together, they were ready to uncover the hidden heirs to the Brent kingdom.

Chapter Two

Elizabeth Deavers dumped the contents of the desk onto the floor. There was no need to toss the office; the files she had requested from Abbott were exactly where he'd said they would be. She did it because Dr. Anthony Andrew Abbott, or Triple A Battery, as her boss Marcus Brent called him, was fun to scare. Ever since she'd first contacted Abbott, she knew he was a pushover. Now, for what should be their last interaction, she would send him out with a message. The message was simply: *thank you for your service; you're no longer needed. Please don't contact us.*

Elizabeth picked up the eight folders, walked out the door and down to her car, and placed them in the box on the passenger seat. Dr. Abbott wasn't the only one who had helped her out in the past with Marcus Brent's messes, as she called them. Abbott was one of three doctors who had helped clear the messes. Now that Marcus had made it clear to his inner circle that he was running for the Republican nomination, it was time for her to erase the things that they didn't want anyone to find. These eight files were only part of what she needed to recover.

What was hard for her to understand was why Dr. Abbott had

been passed over for a future cabinet role in a hypothetical presidency. Abbott had always been loyal, flexible, and, most of all, discreet. Elizabeth felt jettisoning Abbott from future plans had more to do with his role in helping the current wife, number four, with her infertility issues than with his competency as a doctor. He was either too invaluable to lose to a new position, or he knew too much personal information, and that made him a liability. Elizabeth thought that through and recognized that her knowledge made her a liability as well.

Can you still be a liability if you're being blackmailed? That was the difference between her and Dr. Abbott. It was also the difference between Dr. Abbott and Marcus's new favorite, Dr. Levi. There were a lot of secrets that swirled around Dr. Levi, and those secrets had been and could continue to be leveraged for favors and privileges, and most importantly, coverups.

It's how Elizabeth ended up in this position, too. Now, with these last few assignments, her time with Brent Industries was ending. She could move on, slate clean, and live a quiet, reserved life in Napa, where she would buy a tiny vineyard and host select tastings. If not there, there was always Sedona, where she could dabble in the arts and esoteric spirituality. But as the future unfolded before her, the past rushed back.

⊗⊗⊗⊗

Los Angeles, 1983

The room was colder than she'd expected, but she also knew

this was a tactic that Brent Industries had used for ages. Make the meeting room slightly uncomfortable to help tilt the talks, whether negotiations or interviews, into their own best interest. Brent Industries was well known for this. It was talked about in hushed tones across the business world, both domestically and abroad. She had first heard of it when she was working in West Berlin in the late seventies. She found its simplicity interesting. Now, she sat here several years later, experiencing it for herself. She was fascinated by the fact that Brent Industries had called her. It wasn't common knowledge that she was moving on from her current position.

As she waited in the room the pert blonde secretary had led her to, she wondered who had offered up her name to the company. Was it Milt, whom she had worked under in Zaire for a few months? He knew her capabilities and had pushed her on toward Berlin and all of the intrigues the city held. Milt had moved on shortly after he got busted for recruiting American missionaries to relay information. It wasn't exactly legal, but it wasn't illegal either- a part of her old job she'd loved. She never was quite on the up and up, and at the same time never quite a criminal. Always, though, she was discreet and disarming, and she got the information that her companies wanted.

A middle-aged man in a brown suit with a wide striped tie walked into the room and made his way to her. She stood to greet him.

"Ms. Deavers," he began, "I'm Saul Traeger. You were referred to us by Milton Pierce."

Good old Milt, she thought, looking out for his young protege. "It's been a while since I've worked with him," she responded. "May I ask what he has referred me for?"

"Please," Saul pointed to the chair she had just stood up from, "take a seat, and I'll start. Mr. Brent will join us very shortly, but I'll start the preliminaries."

She sat down and Saul made his way around the table to sit across from her. He was a man who carried himself confidently, but she noticed an apprehension in him. Was it because she was a woman? Was it the thought that he would have his boss sitting in on this meeting? What was it that they were about to offer her? She cycled quickly through the ideas that could make a man of his standing a bit reserved.

"Elizabeth Grace Deavers, born in Appleton, Wisconsin, date missing," Saul said. "Went to Boston College on an academic scholarship." He paused, "What made you decide to leave Appleton for Boston?"

"Boston College had what I was looking for academically," she said coldly.

"I see," Saul responded, almost matching her coldness. "And what was that exactly?"

"It should tell you in my file," she said.

"Your file only contains what Milton shared with us, which

wasn't more than what I just read back to you. So, we must complete some additional personal information if you're to pursue this position."

"And what exactly is this position?" Elizabeth asked while raising her eyebrows.

"I need a woman of your talents to handle some very delicate business," a large and deep voice responded from behind her. She had heard the door open but hadn't had time to turn and see who had entered. There was no need to look now; she knew that voice well. She had heard him speak a few times, most recently in Bonn at a lecture in the Department of Commerce.

"I'm afraid that doesn't clear up the matter yet," she responded with a slight glance toward Harlan Brent as he moved toward the side of the table where Saul was sitting. Saul's face told a story, more like a warning, which was imprinted on his face. He was not at all comfortable with what was about to take place; she could tell by the way his eyes darted back and forth, and his body seemed resigned to the worst as Harlan Brent spoke.

Harlan took his place next to Saul. He was a large man. Over six feet, with shoulders that seemed to be twice the width of Saul's. His stature reminded her of the size of the buildings that he erected worldwide. Hotels, commercial skyscrapers, and foreign embassies of a massive scale. Some of which took up large amounts of land and displaced hundreds of people. He was a man who acted as though he could do whatever he wanted. As if there was no one who would tell him he couldn't just do what he pleased.

"Ms. Deavers," he said, "I have an issue that I need your help with. The tricky part is, if I offer you this job, you'll need to take it."

"I find that could be difficult for me to do," she replied.

"Well, I'm willing to talk finances first and job second, just to give you an idea of what it entails."

"If I see the financials for this speculative job, and I don't like it, can I walk out?" Elizabeth asked.

"Yes, with, of course, a few technicalities of what you can say and to whom you can say it."

"Naturally," she replied.

"Milton Pierce is a consultant for my company in matters of personal security. He suggested that you would be a perfect fit for this job.

So, Milton is consulting, she thought. And his opinion is that I would be a perfect fit for this. She pondered the pros and cons of seeing the financials for a few seconds. If they were low, it was a no-brainer, walk. If it was too high, it was more complicated. While her limits of what she would or would not do in a job were vague, she also knew that she liked setting her own boundaries, and taking up a job without knowing what exactly it entailed could push her into a position where those boundaries were set for her. The higher the pay, the more likely that was.

"I know Milton well enough to trust that if he thought this was a good fit for me, then it would be worth looking at the financials. How long would this job last?" She asked.

"That depends on you," said Saul in his smaller voice. "The hope would be for a long-term contract. The compensation would go up, depending on how involved you become with the work."

Elizabeth nodded. It was going to be a large number, which meant it was going to be a difficult job. A long, difficult job. The higher the number, the higher the boundaries and the risk.

"I understand," she replied, "I would be interested in seeing what you're offering."

Saul took out a folder and opened it. "Before I show you, you'll need to sign this form that says you cannot tell anyone what you're about to look at. You're most likely familiar with the legal language. According to Milton, you helped organize and write a few of these contracts with him in Africa."

Saul passed the folder to her, and she opened it. She recognized the phrasing and the terminology. She hesitated for a few seconds, pretending to read the document that she helped to formulate, albeit on another continent and for another reason. That's when it hit her. The reason she and Milton had put together this non-disclosure form was to help a business tycoon find a personal fixer, someone to make his messes disappear. Was Milton trying to communicate with her through this? Was she going to be guarding and covering up someone else's mess? If so, she was uniquely skilled to do so. It would be an assignment that she would excel in, just as Milt had told them. She also wondered what else he had told them. If he had been completely transparent with them, then she was going to have bigger troubles than the ones that would be created by taking this job.

She signed the form and slid the folder back to Saul; he looked over the documents. He then pulled out a second folder with a green tab on it. He opened it and glanced at it. He wanted to make it seem like he was looking at it carefully, but Elizabeth knew damn well he was playacting. He closed the folder and slid it across the table to her.

She opened it. It took a moment for her eyes to register the amount. "This is yearly," she asked, relying on her training to make her sound like it hadn't startled her to see that many zeroes. Milt had always told her to act like she'd seen it before, even when she hadn't, and that advice was coming in very handy now.

"Yes," replied Harlan Brent, "as you can surmise, it's an important job with some long-lasting implications should you fail to do it well. The remuneration is purposefully large so that you're properly motivated."

"I see," she replied. She debated for a second whether to just say yes and move on with the assignment, but her mind urged her to assess before acting. That large annual sum pointed at something fishy. Why did they not hire someone older and more seasoned? What could possibly be so important that such an amount per year would be thrown at her?

"After a few years, would the salary be negotiable?"

"If you don't fuck it up, it could be," said Harlan Brent. "The goal is to hire once and never to hire again."

She looked down at the sheet once more and collected her wits. She closed the form and passed it over to Saul. She turned towards Harlan Brent, who was looking down at her, although he was seated. She met his gaze, "Luckily, I don't fuck things up. Show me what I just committed the rest of my life to."

Harlan smirked, "Milton said you had balls of steel, but I wasn't so sure. Let's talk about my son Marcus."

Elizabeth nodded. She had heard a lot about Marcus. He was a loose cannon in many regards. His brief stint at military school was halted by an opening at the Booth School of Business in Chicago. Rumor had it that if he hadn't left for Booth, he would have been leaving with a little more fanfare. At Booth, he had applied himself again, and all the rumors had said that he would be threatened with a boycott from the family fortune if he didn't make this work. He was often reminded how many strings had been pulled for him to have a spot there, which was something he had talked about freely in the press. When he graduated from Booth, he marched back into his father's business and took a seat at the table. Uninvited.

"Parents love their children," Harlan began, "but we don't always like them. Marcus," he paused for a significant amount of time. "Well, his mother loves him. But I don't. And because I don't love him, I find it way easier just not to like him."

Harlan stared off for a fraction of a second and then continued with his diatribe, "My wife, on the other hand, adores him. She loves him always and likes him most days. What she sees in him is the kind, generous son who, at the age of eleven, sat next to her bed and encouraged her during her chemotherapy. She sees the son who dotes on her when he comes home. What she doesn't see are the reports. Reports that I deal with daily show me that he has no clue what he is doing. He has no character whatsoever. He does not have an ounce of ability that has been trained or tried by life. He is a blathering idiot."

"And yet here I sit about to hire you, Ms. Deavers, to watch after him. I don't want, need, or desire anyone, especially a child of my own, to do something that would endanger this family." Harlan's face was enveloped by a scary amount of anger as he continued, "Excuse me," he said, "not 'this family's fortune,'" but he yelled the next words, "MY fortune!"

Harlan paused again while Saul sat there resolutely looking across the table at Elizabeth. She knew he wasn't comfortable with this deal. Her hunch was that Saul had had one too many run-ins with the 'blathering idiot,' and while he wasn't ethically a fan of Harlan's plans, he understood without a doubt the grave need for it to be done.

"What do you mean by watching after him?" Elizabeth asked.

"He is in his late twenties; what sort of watching would he need?"

"You can guess, but I'm sure that you'll only begin to scratch the surface of what you'd be dealing with. Hear me on this," Harlan's voice raised in a way that didn't match his height. "You're only going to deal with his messes. You aren't going to be dealing with him. One day, he'll make a mess that you won't be able to manage, and that's when your time with us is over."

"That's fine," Elizabeth said politely as she tried to bring Harlan back to the present time and place, not expounding on everything Marcus related. "But what if I come to the point where I don't want to clean up these so-called messes anymore? Money only motivates people to a certain point."

Harlan leaned back in his chair. His pause made Elizabeth realize that he knew. He knew and would use it to coerce her into his service.

"I'm sort of a magician," Harlan began. "And I have an uncanny ability to make things and *people* disappear." He leaned forward, "Now, I'm not saying that you have something in your life that could benefit from my special talent, but women in your profession are very rare. They take risks to stand out to those who are hiring them. They aren't allowed to have weaknesses because things can go awry when they do. Does this sound familiar?"

"Stop being coy, Harlan," she narrowed her eyes to slits and spoke with a command of her emotions, "I can deduce already what is going down. My question to you is, what do you have on

Milton that made him turn on me?"

Harlan chuckled, and Saul's face revealed his unease about where this conversation was headed. Poor Saul, Elizabeth thought, he doesn't have the fortitude to deal with this level of deceit and strong-arming. Harlan saw that Elizabeth was observing Saul's reaction.

"Saul, you may be excused while Ms. Deavers and I finish up the last of these negotiations."

Saul willingly obliged, practically sprinting from the room.

"Let me guess," Elizabeth nodded towards Saul as he left the room, "plausible deniability?"

"Damn right, and what I have on Milton doesn't concern you."

"Like hell, it doesn't! We have sat on that secret for almost 6 years, and he just suddenly throws it out in a quasi-reference check? That would only happen if what you have on him is serious." Elizabeth's voice hit the walls and took over the room.

"That doesn't matter," Harlan began again, "but what does matter is that I'm willing to make all evidence of your issue disappear if you take this job."

"You don't have the power to protect me from the people who could hurt me with that information."

"You've been trained better than that. You did your research, I know. If you hadn't, you wouldn't have taken the risk of walking through those doors this morning. My ability to make things disappear forever is on the level of the great Houdini himself."

"Houdini was an illusionist. Are you sure you want to use that comparison? It's not as compelling as you think."

"You get my meaning," Harlan held back his irritation. "Can you do this job?"

"Yes," Elizabeth responded.

"Will you do this job?" Harlan asked her. "There will be mutual benefits for both of us if you do."

"I assume at this point, if I say no, I can expect the CIA to show up at my door within the week."

"You wouldn't make it out of the door," he said plainly. "There happens to be a CIA agent here today who is familiar with the outcome of your mistake. He just never seems to be able to figure out who caused the issue."

"Shit," Elizabeth whispered, "you're thorough."

"Which makes me such a pleasure to work for," Harlan retorted.

"I can't wait for the company picnic this year," she shot back.

"So, I take that as a yes," he said. "Welcome to Brent Industries, Ms. Deavers."

Harlan pressed a button on the phone near him, and a squawky voice came over the intercom. Despite the squawkiness, Elizabeth sensed a tension in the voice. Subservient and resigned to the power structure of the industry. "Yes, Mr. Brent."

"Send Saul back in," and before she could answer, he took his finger off the intercom. Elizabeth began to wonder how many people were working here under the same pretense as she was about to. As Saul timidly walked back into the room, she realized he was likely in his position because of blackmail as well.

"Well, Saul," Harlan said out loud, not breaking eye contact with Elizabeth, "Ms. Deavers has finally decided to take the position."

With that, Harlan got up and walked towards the door. He did not offer Elizabeth his hand. He opened the door and stopped before exiting. He turned towards her and smiled. It was a smile that was as menacing as it was handsome. If it was how he smiled all the time, it must have been confusing to those who were closest to him. Was he scheming, or was he genuinely happy? Elizabeth couldn't tell.

"I'm going to go work my magic," and he walked out the door.

ଔୠ୫ଓ୧

And he had. He had held up his end of the bargain, as far as she could tell. She had spent the last 45 years cleaning up messes for his foolish son. A son who, now, after years of mismanaging his father's fortune and the fortune of his second wife, had set his sights on public service. Marcus announced to the board 10 months before that he was going to seek the nomination of the political party, which he had opposed his whole life. He had an aim to become the president of the country. With Harlan now dead, there was no one to stop him.

As he made the announcement, the board sat there staring at him. It wasn't like this was a new idea. The country had dealt with other upstarts going into politics. Land barons, actors, lawyers, and real estate moguls had all thrown their hats in the ring with varied results. What was one more business despot leading this country going to hurt?

For her, it meant retirement. Harlan would have lost his shit if alive. He would have done everything in his power to keep Marcus out of the limelight. Harlan would have made her stay on, but the current staff of advisors felt that Elizabeth's presence would only complicate things if Marcus landed in office. So, they told her that she only needed to complete one last assignment. Obtain the files. There were twenty files in total, split between three doctors. She couldn't imagine what the numbers would have been if he had impregnated every single woman he had been in a relationship with.

In the thick of it, the hardest part of her "clean-up job" was keeping the wives from finding out. She could deal with the weepy ladies, begging and pleading. "We won't say anything," they would say, but it was too much of a risk. Harlan Brent was not going to be dividing up his kingdom to illegitimate heirs, and with today's legal system, it was a fight he would lose every time. Harlan had told her shortly before his death that no one would ever know how important she was to the family. She was the sole reason that he didn't have twenty different heirs staking claims to his fortune.

A month later, he died of a heart attack in the middle of a tirade directed at Marcus. The whole board of Brent Industries watched helplessly as he fell to the floor. His last words are rumored to have been directed right to Marcus, and they varied, but Elizabeth's favorite version was the one where he looked at him while clutching his chest and said, "We should have castrated you," and then died.

Stories grow with time, she thought, that was about three years ago. Interestingly enough, Marcus hadn't gotten anyone else pregnant since then.

Saul, who over the years had changed into a hardened and spiteful director of operations, had made it very clear to her that she needed to close the loop on these women. As far as she was concerned, gathering the files was enough. To Saul, it was only the beginning, and she needed to make sure that they had held up their end of the bargain.

"Really," she had said to him, "after all these years? Rumors of affairs aren't going to hurt his chances at a presidency."

"The conservative vote will care," Saul sighed.

"Then I'll clean it up," she said, "if I find they have made a mistake."

That was a lie. She knew she wasn't going to do a damn thing. Let them crawl out of the woodwork as far as she was concerned.

She knew women well enough to know that these ladies weren't going to be splashing their sins, especially the fact that they aborted their babies, all over the news.

She drove off with the final files sitting next to her in the car. She hated Philadelphia and couldn't wait to be back in Boston.

ভ৪৩৪৩৫

Elizabeth arrived in Boston, walked into her house, placed the box in a corner, and went to bed. Three days later, she had yet to begin the last task that Saul had assigned her. It would have been a few days longer if Saul hadn't contacted her.

"Where do we stand with closing the loop?" he wrote to her.

"Almost there," she texted back. She looked at the box in the corner. If there was something she missed in there, it was too late now. Her laptop contained a document that she had created in the late 80s. It was a simple list to save her in case she had missed something. The list contained the names of the women he slept with. Next to each name was the person assigned to track them for a month or two. Then there was the list of those who had been impregnated and the doctor she took them to.

Abbott in Philadelphia had been the largest group, 8 in total, because he had always been the most loyal and the most discreet. She looked through the list of names that she had recorded. The number of deceased women always surprised her. The liberal writer out in Oregon, the quiet desk receptionist in Philadelphia, the crazy blonde girl from somewhere in Iowa, the mother of five in Tennessee who didn't need another kid, especially one that wasn't her husband's. There were at least three more whom she didn't remember all that well, but she could still put a face to the name.

She had never looked into what had become of these ladies, and part of that was that she couldn't face them. Most of them felt relieved to see her and hear her pitch about the payoff for their silence, but without exception, most of them were appalled at the other part of the deal. Shouldn't it be their choice? Elizabeth never caved; she had one job: to terminate the evidence that had been created inside of them. It was never personal, and it was never a betrayal. It was a job that paid very well. It was also a job that, if not done correctly, would cost her more than just money.

Her years of working for Brent Industries had shown her just how dangerous this family could be. They were connected, but those connections were obtained through some of the darkest dealings she had ever witnessed. She could, with ease, name former employees who were missing or had tragic endings to their lives. She had been hired because she was a high-functioning sociopath. Harlan Brent had recognized this in her because he was one, too. Harlan, unlike her, just never got his hands dirty. If he did, she didn't know about it. She remembered the day he said that to her.

"Female sociopaths are very hard to hire," he said as he sat at the end of a conference desk where she had briefed him on some new developments.

"I'm not sure if that's a compliment," she replied.

"They're hard to hire because most of them already work for the government," he continued, almost as if it were a punchline and not an actual conversation about her work.

Sitting at her computer and looking at these names, she had a sense of dread come over her. What if she missed something? Was there a woman who had escaped her notice? That seemed impossible. She had so many people watching so many aspects of Marcus's life that she could not have missed anything. Her job had been way easier these last three years since he was no longer able to produce children. Wife number four had made that decision when she realized that it was her womb that wouldn't produce children and not his penis.

It had to be a coincidence. Maybe too many years of this job and being with this family. She was forever grateful that he had only ever had daughters born to his wives. The Brent fortunes would pass to his oldest, most clueless daughter. Somehow, that felt like justice being served.

She took her phone and texted Saul back.

"I've seen nothing alarming," she wrote. She sat the phone down, expecting no reply. She got up from her desk and went to the kitchen. She was only halfway there when she heard her phone ding. She abandoned her trip and went back to the phone.

Saul had responded simply with:

"Then explain this."

She clicked on the file he sent. And it took only a few seconds for her to literally feel the rug pulled out beneath her feet.

"Abbott lied," was all she said out loud.

Chapter Three

Rhea Baker walked through the campus taking in the sounds as she did and then putting them into words. The only sound that she couldn't poetically describe was that of the streetcar as it rattled its way through the campus.

Summer was on the horizon, and she had yet to decide where she was going to be spending her break. This sort of beautiful weather made her feel like staying put this summer and enjoying the Pacific Northwest for once. She also knew that feeling would last for about three weeks, and then she would wish she had booked a holiday on some remote Pacific Island.

These were the thoughts running through her head as she entered her classroom, still pondering how one would go to say, Tuvalu. She was surprised to see a man her age sitting in the upper back corner of the room. She squinted at him, but a student's question interrupted her.

"Dr. Baker," a student three rows back called to her. "Is something wrong?"

She shook herself free, smiled, and then dismissed the thought of him. When the class began to file out 50 minutes later, he reappeared. He descended from the place where she had first seen him. He was dressed in a button-up shirt with a tie, nice pants, and dressy shoes. He looked very official, and now more than ever, she was sure she knew him from somewhere.

"I always took The Handmaid's Tale as a great example of dystopian literature, I've never thought of it as being postmodern," he began. As he descended the stairs, she couldn't shake the feeling that she had met him at some point in her life.

"Well in our current political climate, especially with some of these want-to-be candidates, The Handmaid's Tale might be more prophetic than anything else," she replied kindly with a smile.

"Funny you would mention politics," he said, a little less light-hearted, "the reason I'm here is somewhat related to that."

"Oh," she replied, "why is that?"

"My name is Miles Trent," the man said to her as he moved closer to the podium where she stood.

"Trent," she seemed to recognize that name. "Wait," it came to her, "did you send me an email recently?"

"Yes," he smiled as he stopped a comfortable distance from where she stood. "Four days ago, to be exact."

"The semester has been pretty busy," Rhea smiled, "I haven't had a chance to read it. I did notice that it came from an email address from Penn. Do you teach there," she asked him.

"I'm a professor of political history there," he smiled.

"So, Ivy League," she noted with some underlying jealousy, "Nice to meet you, Dr. Trent."

"Please call me Miles," he said, "I take it you didn't read my email."

"I'm so sorry, I truly meant to get to it," Rhea sighed. She had left it in her inbox but hadn't gotten around to opening it. Her email was a constant stream of student work and faculty appointments. She was pretty sure it was buried on a second or third page of email by this point. "What can I help you with?"

"Well," Miles hesitated long enough to make her feel very uncomfortable. "It's somewhat sensitive, but," then he trailed off.

"But, what?" she asked him.

"I've a story for you…"

⋆⋆⋆⋆⋆

She was stunned, but it had to be true. Why would someone lie to her about that, especially someone in Miles's position? She sat alone at the table, waiting for the aggravated barista with orange hair to call her name. She wished that she could be able to add a shot of something stronger to her coffee because this seemed completely insane. Could it be that this man, this Miles, was the key to unlocking that one mystery of her mother? He had left her his phone number and a file.

The answer sat right in front of her. It was a folder with her name written in pencil under her mother's name, Ellis Baker. It was unreal, and Miles seemed to understand her need for hard factual data. Now, it sat in front of her, and she just couldn't bring herself to open it.

"My guess," he said to her after dropping that bomb of information, "is that your mother, Ellis Baker, has never told you anything about your father."

"Professor Baker," the angry-looking barista blared as she slid her coffee onto the pick-up counter. Rhea stood up to retrieve it, took up the folder and her bag, and decided to head to her home to read the file. As she walked, she replayed the conversation in her head.

"That doesn't make any sense. Couldn't they have been checked up on or been followed afterward," she said, asking the first question that popped into her mind. One that she noted in her mind was secondary to the fact that suddenly her mother's lack of money problems made some sense, but that wasn't something Miles needed to know about, or maybe would even care about.

"That's what I need to find out," he said. "How did these women go off the grid so as not to be caught? This is just the beginning," he said. "Once you read this, you'll have an idea of what I'm trying to do."

"I'm sorry," she stammered, "I'm really not following you. I'm sort of stuck on the fact that I may, or may not, have a brother, or maybe a few more."

"I have five names," he said, "and when I researched them on my own, your mother's information was the most comprehensive. A published and a well-known activist in her day."

"So, you're aware that she died seventeen years ago," Rhea asked.

"Yes, I'm sorry for your loss," he said with sympathy. "From what I gathered on the internet, she was ahead of her time."

"That may be the classic definition of an understatement," she responded snidely and then suddenly felt bad that she had taken that tone with him.

"My mother passed away shortly after I turned fifteen," Miles relayed, a hint of hurt in his tone that Rhea was not expecting. "These last 22 years, I've always wondered what all she would have told me if she had lived, especially about the man who was my father. I waited for years for him to show up and claim me after she died, but he never did."

"But now you know," she said as she nodded her head.

"If the information is true, then yes, I know who it is," he paused for a second. "If it isn't true, this is someone's very sick idea of a joke."

"You said there were five more, other than you; so, six in total," she asked.

"Yes, you're the oldest, by a year," he said as a matter of fact, "and if the records I have are right, the youngest is four."

"What's your proposal," she asked. "Or your mission? Maybe a better word to use."

"Basically," he said with some intensity, "I want to make sure we're all safe. I don't trust the Brents. They don't like loose ends, and if this is true, then we," he gestured at her and the folder, "are loose ends. I need to find all of us and convince us to go public. It will be harder for them to do something to us if we have come forward and made claims."

Rhea looked at him, his handsome face complemented by his light brown hair. It was his eyes, not the gravity in his speech, which convinced her. Those eyes were familiar, like looking in a mirror.

"You're the first of these children that I'm contacting," he said. "I'm not trying to be mysterious, but I feel like you should have a choice about what you do next. Once you read this," he handed her the file, "you'll have some choices to make. I didn't exactly have that choice."

"How did you end up with this information?"

"It was sent to me in the mail, postmarked Philadelphia," he explained. "It was a USB stick with a very vague and mysterious note."

"What did the note say," she asked.

"It said, 'You're in danger, etc.'"

Rhea scrunched her face up. That seemed very ominous, didn't it?

"Why would we be in danger? No one seems to know about us," she asked Miles.

"I believe," Miles shrugged, "whoever sent me this information knows that it may come out and wants to protect us.

I'm guessing he thinks we're the best shot at keeping Marcus Brent from becoming president."

"That would be doing this country a service," she scoffed out loud.

They had talked some more about the file, he answered every question she could think of. When they had finished, he left her with the information and his phone number. "Call me if you have anything else you want to talk about."

She replayed that conversation in her head again and again. Sipping on her coffee, she entered her house and set the folder down. Miles seemed like a man she could trust. She had stalked him on the internet after he had left her. He was published, had credentials, heck, his "Rate My Professor" score was higher than hers. If she could have dreamed up a younger brother, Miles would have been it.

"There has got to be a way to prove this," she said to no one. She realized as it came out of her mouth that there was a way to prove it, approximately six different ways. She grabbed Miles's card with his number on it and dialed.

He answered, and she spoke quickly, "You need to trust me," she said.

"I figured I would be the one that had to say that," he said on the other end, "not the person I'm trying to convince."

"I mean, you'll need to trust me because I've an idea that could prove if this is a fool's errand or not," she said. "Meet me tomorrow at my office," she said and hung up the phone. It was a touch dramatic and very out of character for her. She redialed the number and Miles picked up, "Sorry, that was a little abrupt."

"No problem," he said. "I'll meet you at your office tomorrow around 9. I'll bring the coffee, any special order?"

She answered him, and they exchanged pleasantries, this time, she gave him a proper goodbye. After she hung up, she googled autosomal DNA tests. If they were siblings, this would let them know. Rhea found herself hoping it was true.

Chapter Four

Miles was unsure about this course of action. A blood test would definitively confirm whether this was a red herring, but at the same time, something just didn't sit right with him. Rhea was wrapping up her presentation to him about the tests and mentioned that she knew someone at a lab who could expedite the results.

"So, I would need to stay a few more days," he asked.

"Just one, maybe two at the most," she replied. Her answer felt redundant because it was already what he assumed to be the case. "By then, I'll be finished with my classes for the spring and can be more invested."

Miles figured that staying a few days for the results wouldn't be the worst thing. It could give them more time to plot out how they would go about contacting the rest of the people on the list. The two of them could collectively do some research and decide what they would do next if they were, in fact, siblings. If they weren't, Miles thought, should he even consider moving on to any of the other half-siblings he never knew he had on the list?

"Can you think of any reasons we shouldn't do the test," Rhea interrupted his thoughts.

"Not concrete reasons, but there are questions that could lead to objections," he responded.

"Like what," Rhea asked.

"Are you going to ask everyone to take a blood test?"

"Why wouldn't we?" she countered. "Wouldn't we need them if we intend to take on Brent?"

"Theoretically, we would need *him* to agree to a blood test, and I'm not sure how we can pull that off, without at least one of the mothers going on record and saying that Marcus Brent is the father."

"That should be easy," Rhea said.

"Really?" Miles asked skeptically. "As of right now, we're sitting here as two possible illegitimate children of Marcus Brent. The keyword in that sentence is possible."

"Because we don't know for sure," she answered Miles with a sigh.

"Why don't we know for sure, Rhea?"

"Because we don't have a blood test showing that we're related."

"Look beyond the blood test," Miles said calmly, feeling that she was becoming too focused on the science and not on the practical aspects, "that will only prove you and I are siblings."

"Right," she agreed.

"That means we have the same father," Miles continued.

"Marcus Brent," she interjected.

"Possibly," Miles sighed, "but did your mother ever tell you that he was your father or even mention him?"

Miles could see that what was obvious had eluded Rhea in this situation. She was right about the blood test being important, but the fact that it would lead them directly to the front door of Brent Industries with a request for his DNA was wrong.

"Oh, Lord," Rhea sighed, "at this point, we would look a little crazy." She quietly seemed resigned to the fact that this wasn't going to be an open-and-shut case. It wasn't as simple as getting a blood test and toppling a giant; it was going to take more work than that. It was the hurdle that Miles himself had to overcome.

"So, our mothers never told us. None of our families knew about our fathers. Our only hope of having a shot at this is to convince one of the mothers who's still alive to break her deal and fess up to what happened."

"What did your mother do with her money," Rhea asked unexpectedly.

Miles was caught off guard. He didn't expect Rhea to ask about it this soon.

He had thought about that, and his father told him that she had claimed it was a family inheritance. Miles knew that *this inheritance* was what had helped him go to Brown and made their life comfortable while growing up overseas.

"She always claimed to have an inheritance. I never outright thought to ask her about it," Miles responded. "It was never on my radar. From what I believed, we had money, her family, and my father…"

"Adoptive father," Rhea's response was off the cuff, yet it hit Miles like a spear, piercing every corner of his heart and forcing emotions to surface, emotions he had tried so hard to bury.

"No, he is my father," Miles responded firmly and then paused for an uncomfortable amount of time. "He was an international lawyer and made a very good wage. I just never thought of the money. That's all I was trying to say."

"Sorry," Rhea responded. "I didn't mean to imply that..."

"I know," Miles said forgivingly. "It was different for you, not having someone to fill that role completely."

Rhea glanced out of her office window, and Miles could tell she was reflecting, however briefly, on the absence of a father. They sat in silence for a bit, and Miles felt a pang of guilt for being a realist. He admired Rhea's optimism, the idea that with one move, they could have answers, and those answers could propel them to the truth. Miles wasn't even sure why he was on this quest. Was it the truth he really needed? Did it matter to him that some up-and-coming rich boy politician had fathered children and then paid off women to have abortions to keep quiet? How many of these women would have chosen that path for themselves anyway?

"Rhea," Miles broke the silence, "why do you want to know for sure?"

Rhea looked away from her window and across her desk at him. Her eyes, which were similar to Miles's, locked onto his.

"I want to know for sure because I know absolutely nothing for sure about my father, Miles. Not one thing!" She emphasized the last statement strongly.

"And if we find out for sure, and nothing happens, he never even acknowledges you or us, will it be worth it?"

"Yes," was all Rhea said out loud, but her eyes and her face were unsure of her answer. She just wanted to know.

"I don't need to know," Miles replied, "but I also know that, for some odd reason, this information was given to me. It wasn't sent to a journalist or a group that's vetting Marcus Brent. It was sent to me, and I'm not even sure why I'm looking into this. If I boil it down, I don't like that he didn't give people a choice. He threw money at them to be quiet and to sever any ties to him later in life. That bugs me. Does it bug me enough to passionately pursue this? The jury is out. I benefited from that money. My mom screwed him over but took that money and lied about it. I feel like justice on my part has been served. Whoever the doctor was who had these files obviously gave them a choice and then covered the whole thing up."

"Which makes me ask the question," Rhea jumped in, "why would he uncover it now? What would that benefit this doctor?"

"He must know something," Miles surmised, "but what?"

"My guess," Rhea retorted, "is that this doctor thinks that

Marcus Brent can win, and for some reason, he or she does not want that to happen."

"I've thought that as well," Miles sighed, "but then why not be completely specific about this information?"

"I think whoever has sent this information wanted to reveal his duplicity."

"That's nothing new," Miles said. "His own father said as much about him when he was alive. I've done some research, and his father was not a fan of his own son."

"Here's the thing," Rhea paused, "bear with me here, but in your research, who are the people who are throwing their support behind his bid for the presidential nomination?"

"Heads of larger companies that owe him something," Miles shrugged. "Conservatives, the old moral majority, which confuses me the most."

"Right," Rhea said with raised eyebrows and cock of her head to the right as if to say *you see why this is relevant.*

"I mean, it's obvious that he is a proponent of abortion," Miles started, "but has he weighed in on his thoughts about being Pro-Life?"

"Not yet," Rhea said. "I think that he has been avoiding the questions. But if he wants to have a shot at the nomination, he will have to lean to the right on that one."

"And we have proof that he, at one point, didn't lean that way. He can just say that he used to be, but that he changed his mind."

"Have you met some of these pro-life radicals? That won't fly!"

"Those radicals don't make up a majority of voters," Miles countered. "There has to be something more here; I'm just not sure exactly what. My Dad gave me the impression that the Brent family isn't to be messed with."

"Look, Miles, we can start researching this together. We can go have the blood test done, and I've access to pretty much every library within a 25-mile radius from here. We can lay out these names and come up with a game plan."

Miles heard the hope in her voice. He felt bad that she hadn't begun to wonder what would happen if they weren't genetically related. He wasn't sure what he would do either. Was it worth pursuing this any further? He looked at Rhea, and she looked ready to charge ahead. He knew that look. It would show up on his face when he stumbled upon the address of a former Red Army Faction member or someone who marched in the streets in Leipzig in 1989. It was that drive to know more.

"Let's go and get that test," he said, "and then we can talk about what is next over lunch."

The two days it took for the test to come back turned out to be two of the most productive days Miles had ever had. At the end of it, they had a game plan in place that felt more like a choose-your-own-adventure novel than anything reliable. Everything hinged on the results.

In the meantime, they had pieced together details and ideas. They didn't have addresses for all of the mothers or the children, but they did have a handful of locations with no phone numbers or emails. Miles felt like everything he was looking at was meant to be a code of some kind, which he wasn't able to sort out. Rhea had suggested that the doctor who had compiled this list may have just been random. If you can't detect a pattern, you stop looking for one.

Rhea had begun to do some research about her mother and the possible whereabouts of Marcus Brent at the time that she was conceived. She told Miles that she had always thought that her mother was in the Andes Mountains when she was conceived but had found an article on a microfiche archive that mentioned Harlan Brent. Harlan was at a fundraiser in Portland around the time her mother would've gotten pregnant. It said that Harlan's family had attended with him. It was a fundraiser for an education-based NGO that had been helping remote villages in Bolivia build schools.

Rhea tried to research possible places where Harlan, Marcus, or both had been about nine months before Miles was born. Their names didn't show up in any of the searches around that time. Miles wasn't certain where his mother was when she met Marcus Brent. But if he had to guess, then it had to be on the East Coast.

It seemed that for every piece of information that they found, they faced six more dead ends. Rhea would have that excited look on her face as she tracked the whereabouts of Marcus Brent, but then it seemed Miles would be the one to break the bad news to her. Over and over and over again. They ended up with very little information than they already had. So, they decided to work on a plan.

Miles had decided to head to Mexico right after that visit to find Esme Connors, who, they believed, ran a surf shop near a resort. Finally, they would meet up in Philadelphia to see what they had to work with and come up with their next moves.

No matter what the test results said, Rhea was completely sold on this plan. She thought that someone, somewhere, had felt this was important enough—and dangerous enough, she added—to send it to Miles. On the other hand, Miles felt that he had done his due diligence if their blood test came back inconclusive or negative.

"What if it's not me you're related to," she said one evening over dinner. "What if it's this young man in Oklahoma? What if you're to try and figure out which ones are his kids and which ones aren't?"

"Whose kids would they be then," he asked her with a chuckle. "His Dad's? His Son-in-laws?"

"Don't mock me," she sounded hurt. "I'm just saying it's possible that this wasn't just a you-and-me thing."

"That's possible," Miles smiled at her, "but as the two oldest, my guess is if we aren't the ones, then none of them are."

"I've the rest of the summer, and if this is the end for us, I'll keep it going," she looked out the window as she ended that sentence.

"That's fine with me," he said, "I'll give you everything I have."

"Dr. Baker, Dr. Trent," she called out as she looked at the folder and looked at them. "Here are your results," she handed them an envelope. "It looks like you've paid, so that's all I have for you." Miles felt like she was holding back a ton of sarcastic sentences while giving them the results. But he wasn't concerned about a dissatisfied receptionist at that moment; she could think whatever she wanted. He knew that the information inside the envelope was about to change his trajectory, *their trajectory*, one way or another.

"I'm so nervous," Rhea said to him as they walked to the car. He knew she would say that; he knew that this was a way bigger deal to her, and if he was her brother, it would make a massive shift in his paradigm for a family. Miles knew the struggle within himself. He hadn't wanted to take on this task, but the deeper sense of justice and the oppressive guilt over the thought of ignoring the issue had pushed him forward. It was obvious at some point that the guilt motivation would fizzle out, and he hoped that he'd be finished with this whole thing by then. In his mind, it would hit a roadblock, and from there, he could wash his hands clean of the whole thing. He'd be able to look at his father and say clearly that he had tried, and it just hadn't led anywhere.

The sound of the envelope opening brought him back to the moment. Rhea's gasp confirmed what was inside.

"We're related, Miles."

That was all she said. She sat there looking at the slip of paper. Miles could see her eyes scanning and taking it in, and then she would rescan it again. Tears were welling up in her eyes, and Miles looked at her in awe. He was neither excited nor disappointed. It was a dull feeling. A feeling that had nagged at him since Berlin. He was someone's brother. He had never wanted to be a brother.

The rest of the afternoon went how he imagined it would. Rhea was continually in a state of disbelief and happiness and then back to disbelief. The whole time, it was tempered with a reminder of what the plan looked like. They had decided to head to Los Angeles first, and from there, they would split up, with Miles heading to Oklahoma and then Mexico. Rhea would hopefully go from there back to Oregon to meet the mother of Lillian. Then, they would meet up in North Carolina to talk with Angela. The hope was to convince the three mothers—Angela, Stacey, and Esme—to get on board with the plan.

What that plan was was still not fully developed.

Miles hoped they would meet in Philadelphia and stay with his Dad. There, they would put together the end game. Until then, he planned to impress upon them all that they were in grave danger, even though there was no proof that they were.

In the whirlwind of the afternoon, Rhea had already booked their flights to Los Angeles and began to put plans into motion. Their research had already given them a head start, and they had divided up the folders. Rhea stopped as Miles was standing. She looked at him in a way she hadn't looked at him since his arrival.

"You're my brother."

Miles nodded at that. He knew in his heart that what Rhea wanted to hear the most was for him to say something about her being his sister. He tried to form that sentence as he opened his mouth to respond.

"Yep," he started, "it seems that's the case." He smiled as wide and broad as he could, something past girlfriends said he did so well when he was uncomfortable with something. He could tell in Rhea's expression that she had hoped for more.

"Well, I bet your Dad is looking forward to hearing about this," she replied. He realized then that he needed to call his Dad, too. And yet, his heart broke a little because he knew he had someone to call, and Rhea didn't.

Miles waited to call until he was back at his hotel. He had laid out all of the folders on the desk. He had taken off his shoes, untucked his shirt, and sat down on the edge of the bed as he dialed his number. His Dad picked up almost immediately.

"So," he answered with a question mark hanging suspended between the two cellphones on opposite ends of the country.

"She's my sister."

He heard his Dad chuckle. Miles couldn't figure out why that would be funny. It had suddenly become a weight to him. Rhea was his sister, which meant that, most likely, everyone else on that list was going to be related to him as well. What did that mean for him? In his mind, he saw the only possible outcome of this was that he would now be taking care of five other people because they were his siblings.

"You don't seem as excited as I do," his Dad said abruptly, ending his chuckling.

"It's complicated," he answered.

"How so," he asked him.

"It just is, Dad. " He sighed. "I'm just struggling to wrap my head around this whole thing."

"Well, I can understand that. What's the next move?"

Miles relayed to him the plan that he and Rhea had set into place. He had already talked with him earlier in the week about the meet-up in Philadelphia, so most of it wasn't news to him. Miles paced his hotel room as he finished talking with his Dad.

"Dad," he interrupted him mid-sentence, "why am I doing this again?" He felt like a teenager, pleading with his Dad not to have to visit his mother's grave because it was just so painful.

"That's a question only you can answer."

Miles rolled his eyes; just like a teenager, he thought to himself. "Dad, I don't need platitudes. I need help here. Why am

I doing this? To piece together a family I never knew I had? If so, I don't need that. Am I doing this because I want to take down Marcus Brent before he can land in the highest position in this land? I've never cared. The president is a joke. So why am I doing this?"

"Six women were put into a horrible position at a fragile time. They weren't given any choice in the matter."

"And yet here I'm," he interrupted, "Here is Rhea. These ladies all chose at some point. They weren't forced to go through with the abortions."

"Marcus Brent doesn't know that. He thinks he has been able to be sneaky and keep things in the dark."

"So, what," Miles bantered back at him.

"So what?" his Dad answered as he raised his voice. "Marcus Brent, just two days ago, pulled out of thin air the most heinous secret for one of his opponents. He is a man who has always used extortion and coercion to obtain what he wants. This is an opportunity to show the world that he isn't who he says he is before he ends up in a place where he's untouchable. We've already seen how that turns out!"

Miles understood, not with the passion and the focus that his Dad had, but with an understanding of the abuse that had taken place. Was this the missing scale in the dragon's armor? Did Miles have a shot, where others hadn't been so lucky?

"I get it, Dad," he said almost in a whisper. "I've got a shot at him, especially since no one is going to see it coming."

"That's my boy," he said. They said their goodnights, and Miles hung up. Miles walked over to the mini fridge under the TV. He looked inside it and realized that there were three beers left. He popped the top off of the first one and took a swig

Miles was finishing the second beer, and he felt his head begin to spin. He never loved being drunk, but the flight was later tomorrow, so he could sleep it off. He popped the cap off of the last beer and took a big swig. He caught his reflection in the mirror. The more he studied Marcus Brent, the more he realized that there were ways that he resembled him. The range of emotions that it brought to him was unpredictable. One second, he was angry at the image in the mirror. The next, he was laughing; the next, he was disgusted. Over and over, feelings and thoughts rushed into his head. It overwhelmed him and left him shaken at the core, altogether at once.

He wasn't sure when he fell into bed that night. He was a lightweight when it came to alcohol, and three empty bottles were on the dresser by the TV. It would explain his headache and most likely explain why he was still dressed. He rolled onto his back and pulled the covers up to his chin. The evening slowly came into focus for him. He remembered very clearly addressing the man in the mirror and letting him know that he was the son he didn't want and that he was also the son who would take him down. Miles had made that his mantra. He just hoped that it wouldn't take him another three beers to recite it to Marcus Brent if he ever met him.

Chapter Five

"I hate North Carolina," Elizabeth seethed to no one. Her car was parked at the gas station, which led to the causeway onto Ocean Isle. She had spent the last two days digging into the email that Saul had sent her. It was worse than she thought.

The email was from Angela Camp. The second-to-last woman. She had sent it to Abbott, and it was cryptic, but it was something she had to investigate. She opened the file once again and read:

Doctor,

Today a letter showed up at my door! Someone knows about us! What should I do?

Angela.

That was it. She packed and was on the road within an hour. They had traced the email to North Carolina, north of Myrtle Beach. She stopped in southern Virginia for the night. Her researcher had come through. He had found a large purchase of a house by A. Camp. He even had an address.

She had arrived at the beautiful home on the island. She knocked on the door, and a little kid answered it. He looked at her, screamed, and then ran into the house. This brought a young man to the door. The house had been rented out, but the young man was not interested in providing her with the contact information of the person they rented from. People were so suspicious.

She waited around for a few hours, but she saw no one she recognized. She left the island and stopped at the gas station where she was sitting. She was here now because of what she saw that evening.

A young man, maybe 17, sat on the curb outside the mini-mart at the gas station. His polo shirt identified him as an employee. He was on the phone. She tried not to eavesdrop as she walked in.

"No, Mom," he said, "I told you that my shift was done at 7 today and 8 tomorrow." He sat silently and looked up at her as she entered. A sickly feeling settled immediately into her gut, and it took everything in her not to react to what she saw.

The kid looked just like Marcus Brent did when he was a teenager. She had seen pictures of him so many times, and the likeness was very uncanny. As she stepped through the door, she couldn't help but hear the conversation.

"Then I'll see you in ten minutes," he said. "But I have to leave as soon as I change."

The door closed behind her. She thought about how she could spend ten minutes in the tiny store. It would be hard to do without bringing suspicion on herself. She grabbed herself a drink from the cooler, all the while keeping an eye on the spot where the boy had been sitting.

When she checked out, an idea hit her. The young lady behind the counter looked to be college-age. She was phoning it in as she checked her out.

"I've a quick question," she said to the lady, whose name badge read "Tilly."

"Sure," she forced a smile.

"The young man out there, what's his name?"

She looked out at the boy and then back at her.

"Why," she asked suspiciously.

"He was just very helpful to me," she lied, "and I want to write to your manager and let him know."

Tilly didn't seem to buy her line at first, but then she smiled and said, "He was such a dear. Young men aren't like they used to be."

Tilly paused and then said, "his name is Dustin Camp." It was her grandmotherly charm that had caused Tilly to ignore the suspicion that was nagging at her.

"Thank you," she smiled as she took back her credit card. "Have a great night."

She walked out of the store and saw that Dustin was playing a game on his phone. "Have a great night," she said to him. He looked up at her, and she took in his face again. The spitting image of Marcus. She couldn't have been this lucky right off the bat.

"You too, Ma'am," he said to her with a bright smile and sincerity in his voice. That smile, those green eyes; he was breaking hearts for sure.

She walked to her car and pulled it around the station from where she could still have a clear view of whoever picked him up. It was a newer blue pickup truck. The boy stood up and smiled and put his phone in his pocket as he opened the door. The woman who greeted him was Angela Camp. Elizabeth never forgot a face.

She had gone back to her hotel that evening. There were plans to put in place. The next morning was spent doing her own digging. Angela Camp had a second house inland. A quick track of her license plate had given her everything she needed. Later that morning, she drove by the address. It was secluded, with no visible signs of security. The closest house was a quarter mile up the road. It was like Angela Camp had tried to get off the grid, and probably, in her mind, she had. It was perfect for Elizabeth.

She drove about an hour south to Myrtle Beach. There, she connected with a friend of a friend at Brent Industries, who supplied her with the equipment she needed. It had been a while since she had had to liquidate a liability. When she took the job, she was aware that it would come to that on occasion. She had learned from Harlan and Saul how to keep her hands clean, but this time, she would need to be personally involved.

At 7:45 PM, she was parked in the gas station parking lot. She could see the boy, Dustin, working inside. Her plan was simple.

She was going to let herself be seen.

To everyone else in the parking lot, it looked like someone's grandmother was fishing through her purse. Her gray hair was pulled back into a ponytail. The deep tan and wrinkly complexion gave her the ability to blend in. In the last ten years of working for Brent Industries and cleaning up Marcus's messes, her age had been beneficial. It had led people to trust her when they never should have. At 7:55, Elizabeth walked into the store.

At 8:02, Angela Camp pulled into the parking lot. Dustin was in the back, probably clocking out. Her eyes kept Angela in sight. As Dustin came out of the back of the store, she grabbed the coffee she had paid for and followed him right behind.

It was a pleasant feeling watching Angela look up with the caring eyes of a mother, seeing her son come across the parking lot, and then those eyes locked in on hers. There was no mistaking it. Angela instantly recognized her. Terror was written across her face.

Elizabeth waved.

Dustin was barely in the car when Angela whipped out of the parking space.

She pulled up her phone and watched the blinking dot drive away.

It was time to go hunting.

Chapter Six

It took them a whole day to find the bar where she was working. The young man behind the counter was suspicious of them asking about her, but in the end, admitted that, yes, she worked there. Rhea became almost instantly giddy, and as they walked away from the bar, it took everything in him to not tell her to calm down in a way that would have broken her spirit.

They would need to go back for dinner, and in the meantime, he wanted to organize his thoughts on how he had to present the information to Lillian. One of his Dad's most trusted investigators lived in L.A., and Miles wanted to visit him to get his take on the matter. Rhea was full of questions as they drove to Adam's Laurel Canyon home, but Miles had only one: how much danger were they really in?

"Oh, God," Adam said after hearing the story and looking at the documents. "This isn't good, Miles." Adam was a large man, tall and broad, and his eyes were dark in comparison to his graying hair. "This would explain why I never found out who your biological father was."

"You looked into it?" Miles asked him.

"Yes, your Dad had me look into it a year after your mother

died. He felt you should know."

"Well, now, I know," Miles said with a sardonic tone.

"Yes, you know," Adam looked at him and then at Rhea. "This isn't good."

"How so," Rhea asked him.

"I've been doing my job for decades, and I know that if my search leads me to the door of Brent Industries, I don't knock—I go the other way and cover my tracks as I go."

"What should we do, Adam?" Miles asked him in an urgent tone. This was a man he trusted. He had been a constant in Miles's life since he was a child. His childhood was full of the memory of coming home from school and seeing Adam's long overcoat hanging on a peg and his size 13 shoes at the door. There were always Gummy Bears or Chocolate waiting for him.

"Run."

"We can't," Rhea said firmly. "That would mean leaving the others out there."

"How do you know that they're going to look into this?"

"What makes you think they won't," Miles retorted.

"True, the Brents won't let information like this have any chance of landing in the news. If you won't run, what can I do?" he tossed a question at them.

"I've sent letters, actual handwritten ones, to everyone alive on the list. I tried to find phone numbers for the addresses that I had, but the only one I managed to obtain was Jennings Sharp's."

"You'd like something more concrete?"

"Yes, especially for the last name on the list, Esme Connors."

"I'll see what I can do." Adam shifted to look at Rhea now, "so you got his letter?"

"No, he found my university email."

"And what made you feel like you should be in touch with him?" he asked her.

She grinned at him and then at Miles, "I never read the email, he just showed up in my classroom one day."

Adam shook his head. He picked up the list, "I'll see what I can do."

"Thank you," Miles said to him, "and if you can, find out if they know about us."

Rhea squeezed Adam's huge hand in her tiny one, "please help us find them before someone else does."

Cঙঙঙঙেঙ

Lillian came into the bar earlier than they expected. They had already let the bartender with the dreadlocks know what they were drinking. She slipped through the back door, and Rhea almost got up to follow her, but Miles stopped her right in time. He put his hand on hers to calm her down.

The young man who had been there earlier in the day was nowhere to be seen, and Rhea was happy about that. She felt like he was too suspicious. Miles had ordered a beer, but Rhea felt like something stronger would help her calm down. Finding out that she had siblings had been exciting. But realizing who their father was made it dangerous. Those feelings were not mixing well together, and she was feeling awkward and anxious.

Tre was the name of the bartender who had brought them their drinks.

"Would you like a menu," he asked them.

"That would be great," Miles answered him.

"I'll have Lillian bring them over," he said as he walked away.

What luck, Rhea thought and was about to say as much to Miles when he said, "Calm down. We don't want to scare her off."

"I'm calm," she protested. "I'm just excited; they're not the same thing."

Miles nodded at her, and she turned to see Lillian coming to the table. She had menus and silverware in her hand.

"Good evening," she set the menus in front of them and the rolled-up silverware on the table. "I'm Lillian, I'll be your server to…" and she stopped talking. Her eyes were fixed on Miles.

"I know you," she said. "You wrote me a letter."

"I did," Miles replied, and Rhea looked at her face. Lillian looked unsettled by their presence. "I'm Miles Trent, and this is my sister, Rhea Baker."

Lillian looked at Rhea, and her eyes recognized her as well.

"That must make you Lillian Marsden," Rhea said to her.

"Yes," she said. "How did you find out where I worked?"

"A little research," Miles said.

"It's really important that we talk with you," Rhea added.

"That's what his letter said," she sounded a touch annoyed. "I'm not sure I want to know why you're here."

"It's about your father," Rhea said.

"I know," she said, sounding even more annoyed, "that's what he wrote in the letter."

"Sorry," Miles broke in, "I'm not trying to be a pain here, but do I look like a weird stalker sort to you?"

"No, but you obviously are since you literally stalked me here," she seethed at him.

Miles shrugged at her, and Rhea was confused. "That's fair," he said to her, "but hear me out."

"I don't have time to hear you out." Her voice went up a little this time. Their presence was putting her on edge.

"I'm your brother," he said.

Lillian crossed her arms and looked at them both. She nodded her head towards Rhea, "And you're my sister?"

"I'm," she said.

"Great, welcome to CJ's," she said, almost scoffing. "I'll get you my family discount on those drinks."

"Can we talk somewhere private," Rhea said to her.

"Not right now," she sighed, "I'm working."

"Do you have a break," Miles asked her.

"In about an hour and a half, I do," she said. "I can talk with you then."

"That's great," Rhea said, her heart beating faster. Miles shot her a look that she was learning meant she needed to calm down. She could tell Lillian wasn't completely comfortable with her excitement either.

"Who are you again," she asked her.

"I'm Rhea Baker. I'm a professor of modern literature at Portland State University."

The word Portland evoked a visible reaction in Lillian.

"Is my mom okay," she said quickly.

"I don't know," answered Rhea, "I've never met her." Miles seemed to flinch at the coldness of the answer.

"How..." Lillian trailed off.

"We can talk on your break," Rhea said as warmly as she could muster.

Rhea watched as Lillian went back to the bar. Tre and another waitress came over to her. Rhea could tell by the way they were talking and looking their way that Lillian was giving them a quick rundown of what just happened.

Lillian never came back to take their meal order, so she and Miles bided their time and nursed their drinks. Rhea was sure that was a bad sign. Lillian seemed to ignore them with a purpose. Finally, the other waitress came over to their table.

"What do you want," she said to them rudely. Rhea could see that her name was Maia.

"I would like your CJ's burger and another gin tonic," she said. Maia didn't write this down. Instead, she crossed her arms and glowered at Rhea.

"I meant with Lillian," she seethed.

Miles smiled, "I got in touch with her a few weeks ago about a matter of some importance. We just want to talk with her."

"About what," she said to Miles. Rhea looked at him. He still had a kind look on his face.

"I'm pretty sure when she came over from talking with us, she caught you up on what we had to say," Miles picked up his almost empty beer and finished it. "Are you expecting that I'll repeat the information, or are you just trying to be a bully?"

Maia did not like that accusation. She seemed a bit taken aback by Miles's blunt take on the situation.

"It's just," she stammered.

"Just what," Rhea asked, swirling the remaining ice in her glass.

"Just…" Maia huffed. "Nothing. Can I grab you a refill?"

"Yes, please," Miles answered, "and I'd also like the burger."

"She's gonna be a big star," Maia said as she turned to leave. "She doesn't need to be mixed up with family shit that has nothing to do with her."

"I know the feeling," Miles said to her.

Rhea was picking at her remaining fries when Lillian came back to the table.

"We can go back to that room and talk through this," she said as she motioned towards the entryway to the bar's back room. Miles turned towards Rhea, who scooped up a rather large shoulder bag from beside her chair.

Lillian sat down at the first table inside the door while Rhea took the seat opposite her, making sure that Miles was between the two of them. Rhea had already picked up on the fact that Lillian was partial to Miles. He smiled at her.

"Thank you for talking with us," he said. "I'm sure a whole ton of thoughts and ideas are running through your head."

"You can forgive me for being a bit apprehensive," Lillian said. "It's not every day someone claims to be your brother and sister."

Rhea reached into her bag and brought out a folder. She looked Lillian square in the eyes and patted the folder that she had placed right in front of her. Lillian could see that the folder had her name on it.

"I want to tell you a quick story," Rhea began.

Lillian was relatively calm as Rhea and Miles laid out the story of what they knew and what had eventually brought them to her.

"My mother had always been so elusive about her relationship with my father," she said.   "It was the same for me," Rhea told her. "Our biggest fights were about my father."

Lillian nodded and looked at Miles.

"My mom married when I was little," he responded. "My Dad was my Dad, and I didn't need anyone else."

"So why are you going around finding these," Lillian paused, "I mean, us?"

"This is a man who has political aspirations and is pandering to a conservative crowd that's pro-life, yet he paid for our mothers to have abortions," Miles stated. "Who knows how many other people he paid who actually followed through with the abortions? That seems two-faced to me."

Rhea wasn't a fan of that answer. She gave him a look that he knew was urging him to tell her about the danger she could be in! He ignored her.

"I wouldn't say that his two-faced ways are all that secret to the general public," Lillian said, "and they aren't the biggest issues with his burgeoning political career."

Rhea nodded at her while Miles seemed indifferent. They seemed to carry the weight of this differently. Rhea was getting annoyed that Miles wasn't being upfront with Lillian.

"What's your next move?" Lillian asked them.

"Our next move is to see who's willing to do something about this," Miles said. "My biggest fear is that this news will come out, and your mother and a few of the other ladies who are still alive will be in some deep trouble."

"It's not like they're going to kill them," Lillian said flippantly.

Rhea froze for a second, and Miles reacted in a way that put Lillian on her guard. Rhea jumped in.

"Not if we make it public," Rhea said. "If we put this out there in the press and then something happens to any one of us, well, that would look bad."

"What makes you think that something could happen," Lillian asked, an edge of suspicion creeping into her voice.

"It's just a hunch," Rhea answered, glancing at Miles. "The way that Miles found out about us was suspicious. We also don't know exactly how one of the mothers died. And her son is the only one we aren't able to locate. It just points to us needing to be abundantly cautious."

"That has to be a coincidence," Lillian said.

"That's what I thought, too," said Miles. "I've a friend who's looking into it."

"How many of us still have moms that are alive?" she asked.

"Your mom and two others. We're hoping to talk to them, maybe starting with your mom," Rhea said.

"She won't help you," Lillian said, "she's a bit far gone."

"Could we try," Rhea asked.

"I'm done here at 10," Lillian said as she looked back into the bar area. "We can talk more about this when I'm done with my shift." Rhea could sense her anxiousness to move the subject away from her mother. Getting back to work was the way that she was hiding it. Miles stood, catching the hint, and they said their goodbyes and left.

"Should we both come back later this evening," Rhea asked Miles.

"No," he said, to her surprise. "I think maybe talking to only one of us would be better."

"Then why not you? She obviously connected better with you than me."

"I can't put it into words," he said. "I just think she is going to respond better to you."

ଓଞ୍ଚଣ୍ଚ

Rhea had been a bit too anxious to return to the restaurant. She had warned herself that arriving there too early would look desperate. Miles would have arrived at just the right time, waltzed right in, and continued their conversation. Rhea, well, she was Rhea; she was so worried that Lillian would be gone. So, she showed up at 9 and sat in a booth sipping on a ginger ale with lime.

Lillian would check in with her, apologizing and saying that she would try to be finished early, to which Rhea kept telling her not to worry. It was obvious to Rhea that she, not Lillian, was making this more awkward.

When Lillian was finally finished with her shift for the night, she came over to Rhea's table. "Alright," she said, "where are we going to meet Miles?"

"He isn't coming," she told Lillian as she watched her face

fall. Rhea had been right; she had hoped that she had been wrong and that this sister of hers would connect instantly with her. She reminded herself to have realistic expectations.

"Okay, whatever," Lillian sighed. "There's a diner just around the corner from here. We can go and talk there." Without even missing a beat, she turned and headed towards the door. Rhea had to move quickly, not wanting to annoy her.

The diner was only a block away, and by the time Rhea had caught up to Lillian, they were walking in the door. They got a table near the back of the diner and ordered some coffee. Rhea was shocked by Lillian's opening question.

"How many of us survived," she asked.

"Six that we know of," Rhea said.

"Hmm," Lillian sighed. "So, what happened to that kid you're missing, as well as his mother?"

"She's dead," Rhea said. "She died about six years ago."

"And do you think that her death had anything to do with this," Lillian asked.

"We can't rule anything out. We don't have enough information," she responded.

"How did she die," Lillian asked.

"She died in an unfortunate accident at a bar in Iowa, along with about six other coeds."

"Damn," Lillian exclaimed, "where is her son?"

"We have no idea," Rhea said. "Miles is heading to Oklahoma

to find out his whereabouts, that is, if he is still alive."

"What's his name," Lillian was obviously digging up as much information as she could.

"Elliot," Rhea smiled. She enjoyed saying the names of her siblings. Miles, Lillian, Elliot, Dustin, and Esperanza.

"And Miles is working on finding him," Lillian stated, "so what are you doing?"

"I'd like to talk to your mother if that's possible," Rhea responded.

"Possible, yes," Lillian paused, "but profitable, probably not."

"What do you mean," Rhea asked her quickly.

"I mean, her memory isn't what it used to be," she said plainly, "and she is often high."

"Oh," Rhea said with a tinge of resignation.

"What exactly do we want to know about my mom's experience," Lillian asked.

"Our biggest hope," Rhea patted the files next to her, "would be to corroborate the information in the files. We could possibly figure out who sent us this information and what their purpose was for giving it to us."

"Well, my guess, it was to ruin Marcus Brent's political career," Lillian offered freely. Rhea did her best not to roll her eyes at the obviousness of the statement.

"My guess is revenge," Rhea countered. "This doctor had a

bone to pick with Mr. Brent, and he was smart enough to hold on to some collateral in case things didn't work out the way that he had hoped."

"That seems like a possibility, too," Lillian responded.

"Revenge is always a dangerous thing," Rhea said. "It tends to cloud the judgment, so I'm worried that whoever this whistleblower is, is going to be off the grid and hard to find. That's why we need to talk to your mother."

"Fine," Lillian said, "but I can't guarantee that she'll be where she's supposed to be. She tends to wander at will."

"Could you come with me," Rhea asked her.

"Oh, no," Lillian chuckled, "you'll have a better chance of talking to her without me around. I've no clout in that relationship, and to be honest, my making an introduction for you may keep her at bay. You'll have to surprise her."

"I don't want to surprise her," Rhea said, "I want her to know we're coming, and by we, I mean you and me."

"Why not you and Miles," Lillian asked.

"He's heading down to Oklahoma, and then after that, to Mexico," Rhea responded, annoyed to have to remind her of that.

"I can't," Lillian said. "I just got a call back for a role and, not to belabor the point, I don't get along that well with my mother in person. We tend to do a lot better through the written word."

"Do you write to each other often?"

"I write to her once a month," Lillian answered. "I send it to the same address, a friend of hers, and she picks it up and sends me a letter back."

"Where are they postmarked from," Rhea asked, hoping to gain some clues that would help her search.

"Always somewhere in Oregon."

"Where was the last one from?"

"I honestly don't know," Lillian responded, "I didn't look. She was writing about some man who was teaching her how to build decks and expounding on the new edible gummies she just found."

Rhea nodded her head. "I understand you have a lot going on, but this is important, and I think finding your mother would go a lot faster and bring us more answers if you went with me."

Lillian shook her head. "It's complicated. We don't really see eye to eye on anything."

"I'm sure there has to be some common ground."

"No, there isn't." Lillian paused for a second, and Rhea searched for something to say. Before she could get it out of her mouth, Lillian continued. "It's a pretty fucked up situation when your Mom is so paranoid that she's on the run, and your Dad is the type of person who has scared her so shitless that she finds a ghost in every corner."

Rhea had been worried that Lillian hadn't understood the gravity of the situation, but it was obvious to her now that she got what was going on. Perhaps Lillian understood it better than she did.

Lillian asked her a few more questions, all about Marcus Brent, and Rhea answered them the best she could. She had never watched the reality show they were on, but she had heard about it. Rhea had a sense of unease. In the hours since they had broken the news to her, Lillian had seemed to go from shock to morbid curiosity.

"Lillian," Rhea placed her hand on Lillian's, "this man is not going to be your big break."

"Maybe not," she shrugged, "but I'm not sure it will hurt having his connections."

"It may," Rhea exclaimed.

"Listen, I know he is shady af. I just don't want to burn that bridge."

"Please promise me, Lillian, that you won't do anything until we talk with everyone else."

"Sure," Lillian seemed flippant as she said it, and it did not give Rhea any sense of peace.

"I've the information and addresses for your Mom," Rhea said, "is there anything else that will be helpful in finding her?" Lillian screwed up her face. It seemed like she might not have wanted to say much more.

"I mean, what else is there," she shrugged. "Do you want to know about the drug charges? Or the three different end-time cults she was a part of? How else to describe her," Lillian paused, "How much TV do you watch?"

"Some," Rhea answered, wondering where she was going with all this.

"My Mom is part the mother from Weeds and part the mother from Gilmore Girls. A drug-dealing best friend with horrible boundary issues. Once you find her, you'll know what I mean."

Rhea felt that the conversation was dead after that. It seemed that Lillian had other things on her mind, and with addresses and contacts written down, she promised to keep Lillian in the loop. Lillian said that would be 'great.' She got up and left, and Rhea paid for the coffee.

When she returned to the hotel, Miles was reading in a chair.

"How was it," he asked her.

"Miles, I have a bad feeling she's a loose cannon."

"How so," he asked as he put his book down and leaned forward in his chair.

"She seems too interested in what it means to be Marcus Brent's daughter. You know what I mean?"

"Possibly."

"It's as if she wants to know more so she can use it to her advantage," Rhea put down her bag.

Miles sighed and sat back in the chair, "Yeah, I had a bad feeling that could be the case."

"Okay," she was surprised. "Then what do we do?"

"Trust her to stay put," his voice carried a tone that made her highly aware that even Miles didn't think that was going to happen.

"If she doesn't, then we need to get a move on it."

Chapter Seven

Miles could see the gathering storm in the far distance. It seemed like it had formed out of nowhere. The heat outside was visible as it came off of roofs, pavement, and cars he drove by. The town of Jones, Oklahoma, was behind him, and the turn-off for the Sharp Family farm was another ten miles on his left. He wondered if he would arrive there before the storm hit.

The rain would be a welcome relief that evening. Cool down the landscape and water the crops. Miles could imagine sitting on a porch and watching it roll by, enjoying the fruits of a hard day of labor. The Sharps, Jennings and Marcia, had a farm that provided corn and wheat to a major distillery in Kentucky. From his research, they seemed to own a fair share of farmland in different parts of the state, all of which they managed from their home here. Marcia was the one who answered his email. Her tone seemed skeptical but interested in meeting him. This was the day that they had decided to meet. The map on his phone told him that the turn-off was within the next four hundred feet, and he could see it. Out in the field, a tractor was heading towards the house and barn. As he turned onto the driveway, he took in the house. It was a well-kept farmhouse. White with a beautiful garden of flowers in front and a porch right out of a book.

As he drove closer to the house, he saw who he assumed was Marcia coming out of the side of the house onto a small porch. She gave him a small wave as he pulled up to where she was standing. He got out of the car, and he realized how differently he was dressed compared to Marcia. She was wearing jeans and a button-up work shirt, with a bandana tied around her neck. She held her hands together in front of her as he came towards her. He was in a pair of shorts, a polo shirt, aviator sunglasses, and boat shoes with no socks. It was the quintessential city meets country. It made him feel uneasy.

"I'm guessing you're Miles," she said as she came down the steps.

"I am," he replied while extending his hand towards her, "and you must be Marcia."

"It's nice to meet you, Miles."

"Thank you for agreeing to talk to me and allowing me to visit your home."

"If what you say is true, you're family," she said uneasily. She turned to look over her shoulder. Coming towards them was a man wearing a baseball cap, a plain red t-shirt, jeans, and work boots. He was maybe a bit younger than his Dad, but he looked tanned and rugged. Miles could make out the muscles on his arm before he got to them.

"Well," his voice boomed, but not unpleasantly, "you made

it." He extended his arm towards Miles, "Jennings Sharp, I'm happy you could come out, Miles."

"Thank you for agreeing to meet with me," Miles did his best to make his handshake firm.

"So, tell me what a history professor from Pennsylvania wants to know about our Elliot," Jennings asked him.

"It's a long story," Miles said.

"Long stories are always better sitting down," Marcia said, "please come on inside." She motioned for Miles to follow her up the steps and Jennings was right behind him. He saw the rack of shoes at the door and instinctively slid his shoes off as Jennings toed off his work boots.

"Can I grab you something to drink," Jennings asked him as they entered through the door.

"Sure, I would take some water," Miles answered politely.

"I have a feeling that the story you're about to tell us might call for something stronger," Jennings said with a smile as he pulled a bottle of bourbon from the shelf. "I grow for this brand," he said with pride.

"I know," Miles said, "I did some research before coming here."

"Oh, a researcher," Jennings said, looking at Marcia, who was pulling three glasses out of a cabinet. "Neat or on the rocks," he asked.

"On the rocks, please."

"Most definitely from the city," Marcia chuckled.

"This stuff is best neat," Jennings smiled, "but have it your way."

"If you insist, then I'll take it neat as well," and now he was the one letting out a quiet chuckle.

"You won't regret it," he said as he poured up three hefty glasses. "Pre-dinner, drink. You'll be staying for dinner tonight, right?"

"I wouldn't want to impose," Miles said nervously, but he also knew that he was most likely not going to have a choice in this either.

"Nonsense," Marcia said, "I already planned on you staying."

"Now," Jennings jumped right in, "we have our drinks. Let's talk about how you ended up on our doorstep asking about Elliot."

They moved to the porch, which looked out over the garden and to the road in the distance. The wheat in the front field was growing, but it didn't block out the cars that occasionally drove by. Jennings sat next to Miles on the rockers while Marcia took a seat on the porch swing.

Miles began the story in Berlin, hitting on the relevant parts that had brought him to their home. He noticed a sadness passing over them when he mentioned that he knew that Hannah had died in an accident.

"I want to talk with Elliot, but the information trail ended here with you."

"How do we know you're who you say you are," Jennings said.

"Dear God, Jennings, look at him," Marcia said as she got up from the swing and went into the house, mumbling something. She came back out with a picture and thrust it into his hands. Miles saw a young man wearing a button-up shirt, smiling for a senior photo. They looked like each other.

"If he ain't Elliot's brother, we aren't married."

"Fine," Jennings chuckled, "I see your point."

Miles handed the picture back to Marcia. "Thank you, I can see the resemblance. Here's my question, why couldn't I find any information on him?"

"We raised Elliot as our own," Jennings said. "You won't find an Elliot Vaughn. That was how Hannah wanted it."

"Seeing as you're his brother," Marcia chimed in, "it might be good to catch you up on what we know."

"Anything you can share with me would be great," Miles was relieved to hear they were willing to help. He was even more excited that, for the first time in this quest, he had met someone who knew more than he did.

"Before we do that," Jennings cleared his throat. "You mean to tell me that you're his son and that he doesn't know about you?"

"No," Miles replied, "he has no clue about my existence. From what I can tell, my mother took the money, and a doctor helped her fake an abortion."

Jennings hummed before talking, "his name wasn't Abbott, was it?"

"I'm not sure, sir. That's the first time that I've heard a name. Do you know anything more about him?"

"No," Marcia jumped in, "only that Hannah referred to him as Abbott."

"Did she ever give you any way to be in touch with him," Miles asked, sensing that he already knew the answer.

"No, she had only mentioned him once when she and I were spending some time together after she found out she was pregnant," Marcia answered. "We had all decided that the best plan was for us to claim the baby was mine and not Hannah's."

"We lied. We aren't very proud of this, but sometimes you do what you have to do to protect your family," Jennings said.

"So, you knew that Marcus Brent was the father, and that Hannah had made a deal with this Doctor Abbott?"

"Not at first," Marcia said. "Hannah came to us and told us that she was pregnant, and then she started to act funny. She seemed paranoid."

"That wasn't all that unusual," Jennings added.

"She was bipolar," Marcia jumped back in. "One day, the world was the safest place. The next day, everything crashed down, and she started babbling about putting a target on her back. When I finally got her calmed down, she spilled the whole story."

"Except about the money," Jennings jumped in.

"She gave us the money just after Elliot was born. We asked her what it was, and she said it was the reason she was marked and why she needed to be far away from all of us. Elliot knew her as his Aunt, which is what she wanted," Marcia didn't seem to be phased by the lie, not like Jennings did.

"So, you passed him off as your son," Miles asked. "That was smart, especially if you knew who was involved."

"He is our son," Jennings said firmly, "we raised him. Hannah wasn't around more than a week at a time, but when Elliot turned 13, she showed up and threw a wrench into things."

"How so," Miles asked.

"She told him everything," Marcia answered. "Everything!"

"He didn't respond too well to that lie," Jennings said. "He felt betrayed. And he hasn't looked at us the same way since that day. We still cared for him, loved him like our own, but he always kept a piece of his heart from us."

"Elliot knows everything then," Miles asked them both.

"That's what I said," Marcia said as she stood up from the swing. "He definitely seems to know more than you do, which is probably why you want to talk to him so badly. Now," she walked to the door, "you two finish up those drinks, and dinner will be on the table shortly."

Marcia disappeared into the house, leaving Jennings and Miles sitting there. Miles was somewhat in shock. Miles took a swig of his bourbon; it burned on the way down. The Sharp family was the key to unlocking so many things. It was going to be imperative that they find Elliot as soon as they could before Marcus Brent's people started to look into the loose ends of the doctor who had sent him the information.

"Do you think he would be willing to talk with me," Miles asked.

"No," Jennings answered, "but it would be the best damn thing for him. The problem is he's not going to be back in the States for about a year."

"That's not a problem," Miles countered, "I can go to him. Can you help me with that?"

Jennings chuckled. "He'll be pretty surprised! Once you have your ducks in a row, I'll send him a wire to let him know you're on the way. I'm pretty sure it will piss him off."

"Why's that," Miles asked innocently.

"Oh, you'll see," Jennings said as he downed the rest of his whiskey.

Chapter Eight

The dust storm would settle soon, but the dust in the air would cling for days afterward. Elliot tightened the cloth across his mouth and nose, making sure he was breathing in as little dust as possible. He had his glasses on, but the stinging dust hitting his face was uncomfortable. This well project was not going as planned, and he knew there would soon be questions to which he did not have the right answers.

He turned towards the building and began walking that way. Benjamin, his interpreter and village liaison, was coming out of the communications room. Inside was an old radio, which the foreman on the site used like a truck CB. Benjamin was often in the room talking with local tribal officials, missionaries, and humanitarians. He aimed to make this project go smoothly with the locals. He was failing miserably.

Benjamin waved at him as he approached.

"Elliot," he said, wrapping a scarf around his face. "Just got a call on the radio. Two Americans are heading out this way."

"Is this information from your scouts, or are they making an official visit?"

"Does it matter?" Benjamin shrugged and chuckled.

"No," Elliot resigned himself. He could feel the wind calming itself, which meant that the stifling heat would return shortly. "How far out are they," he asked Benjamin.

"Simon says only two hours."

"That should give us enough time to have things looking better," Elliot sighed. If only it could be enough time to actually make it better.

"It's not the only thing," Benjamin said, putting an emphasis on 'thing' that made it sound more like 'ting.'

"What else?"

"These two Americans are being driven by M'boku."

"Fuck," Elliot muttered under his breath. "Now," he continued a little louder, "I've got to entertain two nosy donors and make sure they don't get ripped off. Are you sure we've had no communications about a visit from donors or the organization?"

"None," Benjamin shrugged again. "But this is not a place you normally just show up to, you know."

Elliot nodded. He thought for a few seconds and then rattled off a list of things for him and Benjamin to divide between them and delegate to the workers. This project had already taken too long, and the delays had put them off by another two weeks. He wasn't sure if that could be easily explained to the visitors.

౧౪౦౦౪౧

Two hours passed, and he headed into his small quarters to

tidy up. Most of the investors or donors were not interested in seeing the communications room, the bunk room, or the mess hall. They wanted to see the well construction, and when they came back, they wanted to sit somewhere else to talk about what they saw. That was never the mess hall. It was always his small apartment. He slipped off his boots at the door and brushed the sand from his pants. He always left things tidy, but he now organized some things in the small kitchenette he had so that it was easier to offer the "guests" something when they arrived. When he finished there, he took the books from his table and made sure the chairs didn't have any dirty laundry on them. He peeked in the bathroom and found it not too bad. His aunt had taught him to keep things neat.

Since he was giving a tour, he slid into his flip-flops. He switched out his T-shirt for a light button-up and ran his fingers through his hair. As he exited his room, Benjamin greeted him again.

"Elliot," he called while extending a piece of paper towards him, "dis just came for you. Looks like it was sent a few days ago, but the power outage in Ouagadougou delayed its arrival here."

Elliot took the paper from him. It was a wire from his uncle.

Elliot,

Just had a visitor at the farm. Nice man, named Miles. He may be coming your way. You have the same dad.

Dad/Uncle Jennings (I wish I knew where we stood)

Elliot looked up from the wire. He sighed heavily as he said, "fuck."

"Oh," Benjamin exclaimed with a smirk and raised eyebrows, "dat bad, huh?"

"It's nothing," Elliot said.

"Doesn't sound like nothing," Benjamin said flatly.

"It looks like I'm going to have visitors in a few weeks," he crumpled up the telegram. "When is Scooper due back in," he asked Benjamin.

"An hour, he just radioed," Benjamin cleared his throat. "It seems he knew they were coming; it's not two Americans, but instead it's two French diplomats who want to use the compound for a school."

"Shit," Elliot said, "he's so much better at these things than I am."

"True, *Scott*," Benjamin emphasized Scooper's real name, "is better at this than you." Then he looked at Elliot and said in French, "But your French is better, so that's why he forgets and doesn't come back in time."

"Damn it, Scooper," Elliot said into the air. "Let's deal with this inconvenience, and then we can make plans for this visit," he held up the crumpled telegram, addressing Benjamin as they walked. He hadn't given a thought about Oklahoma, his parents/aunt and uncle, his real father, or his bat-shit crazy birth mother in over a year. Karma's timing was a bitch.

Chapter Nine

Rhea's flight had been delayed a few hours. This trip back to Oregon and from there, a search for Stacey was not high on her list of plans for this summer. As she exited the flight and headed toward the taxi stand, she contemplated how the last few weeks had turned her life upside down.

A week ago, her family was just her and her Uncle Uriah, her mother's older brother, who lived on the other side of the country in New Hampshire. He was only in contact with her at Christmas, trying to distance himself from the reputation of his younger, liberal sister and her illegitimate daughter. Now, there were Miles and Lillian, her half-siblings, with three more possibly located somewhere around the world! It was a lot to process, especially given who their father was. Knowing her mother as she did, she could not wrap her head around how she would have ever fallen for that man. It didn't seem to fit her personality.

Miles had said the same thing about his mother. He wasn't sure how that meeting had ever happened, but neither of them could ask them about it now. Their hopes of figuring out how their mothers met Marcus Brent were gone, but if there were enough similarities in the stories of the women who were still alive, maybe they could understand a motive for what drove them to have an affair with this well-known playboy.

Rhea's cabbie was a quiet one. He asked her for the address, flipped the meter on, and drove out into traffic with ease. The evening hadn't faded completely to darkness yet, and there was a sliver of light on the horizon. "Coming home or here for work," the cabbie finally broke the quiet. "Coming home," she replied, but felt an acute sense of relief as she uttered the word home.

Her curt answer had the effect that she intended, and the cabbie focused his attention solely on taking her home. She was incredibly grateful for his silence as her head was spinning more and more. Left with her own thoughts and ideas about Marcus Brent, Miles, and Lillian, and what it all meant for her life, her head spun into a mix of despair one second and hope the next. Her flight to Portland had been smooth, yet her inner journey home was one of roller coaster peaks and valleys. She needed to focus on the task at hand, and that was finding Stacey Marsden.

଼୪ଞ୦ଞ୯

Rhea's quest to find the elusive, according to Lillian, Stacey started with a few phone calls to some friends in the nomad scene. From the way Lillian had described her mother's lifestyle, she was either living on a communal farm or wandering from one communal farm to another. Either way, Rhea thought, it shouldn't be hard to track down a list of farms nearby where she last sent Lillian a letter.

Things would have been easier if Stacey's address had lined up with what was in the files that Miles had shown her, but when Lillian had seen the address, she was quick to remark that her mother had sold that house years ago and had been living off the profits roaming up and down the Oregon and Washington coastline ever since. Rhea felt the overwhelmingness of the task at hand, but decided to start where Stacey last put down her roots, and that was Tillamook.

What was still very odd for Rhea was the fact that Lillian only ever wrote letters to a P.O. Box in Tillamook. At some point in time, someone was collecting those letters. Rhea was hopeful that it wasn't going to be a complete shot in the dark, but, she knew it could be a seriously long wait-and-see situation.

The next morning, Rhea loaded up her Crosstrek and asked the neighbors to pick up the mail for her again. She wasn't sure how long she would be gone, which made this whole trip difficult. Rhea liked rhythm and certainty. It was unlikely that this mission would provide either. She had Lillian's cell number in case she could help, but Rhea highly doubted that Lillian was going to be of any help. She hadn't seen her mom for over four years, although the letters between the two of them had continued at a surprisingly steady pace.

On the drive to Tillamook, Rhea ran through the order of her search in her mind. If no one knew where Stacey was in Tillamook, her next move was to head south toward Eugene. Her last letter had been postmarked from there. She seemed to be on the move and had met some pretty nice young people. Lillian was sure that she had run into some religious nuts, most likely from the LDS.

Stacey was an only child, and Lillian had grown up without any relatives around her. Lillian's grandmother, Stacey's mother, had had a sister in Utah, but no one had heard anything from her since 1990. They all assumed she had died. Lillian's grandfather had been orphaned when he was seven in a farming accident that took the lives of his father, mother, and younger sister. He continued to work at the family farm—the very one where they had died—up until the mid-90s when he passed away himself. He died of grumpiness, according to Lillian.

Stacey had stayed in Tillamook with Lillian until she was going to 9th grade, which is when she moved them both to Eugene. She worked for a small local business as a receptionist during the day and a bartender in the evening and on the weekends. Between the two home bases, there had to be someone who had seen Stacey within the last month or two who could help point Rhea in the right direction. If she was extremely lucky, and she was praying she would be, Stacey would be there collecting her mail.

Rhea turned onto Route 6 outside of North Plains. The drive was beautiful, the type that captures the essence of what it means to live in the Pacific Northwest. The road remained close to the

Wilson River, and Rhea soaked up the beauty of the drive.

Entering Tillamook, she looked at her phone for directions to the post office. She wasn't exactly sure how she was going to go about this. Her only thought so far was to ask the workers at the post office bluntly, but she wasn't sure what their responses would be.

She pulled into a spot and turned off the car. The post office looked like it was pretty empty, which seemed to play in her favor for a longer conversation. The Post Office sat next to a park that was bordered by the river. It was an idyllic setting.

As she walked into the post office, the air conditioning made its presence known. The smell was unmistakable. It was a mixture of paper and glue. Post office boxes lined the walls, and it occurred to Rhea that she might be able to, as a last resort, send Stacey a letter with her phone number asking her to be in touch. That was an option, but it seemed like the wrong one; it would take too long. Miles was off to Oklahoma and then Mexico, and they were all to meet up in a week in Philadelphia to figure out what they knew and what to do next. Rhea didn't want to be the one who failed.

"Can I help you," the older man standing behind the counter asked her. She was the only customer who wasn't being taken care of. She walked up to the man, still formulating in her mind how she would start this conversation.

"I'm not sure if you can help me or not," she paused.

"That's what they all say," he smirked, "but I'm pretty useful."

Rhea chuckled slightly and thought to herself, *we'll see how useful you can be*. "I'm helping a friend of mine find her mother. She needs to reach her in person."

"Who are you looking for," he asked.

"Her name is Stacey Marsden, and I know that she has a PO box here to which her daughter sends letters."

The man behind the counter, whose name was Marvin, nodded his head, "I know Stacey."

Rhea waited a few seconds to see if he would elaborate on this statement, and when he didn't, she asked him, "Has she been in recently?"

"Why isn't Lillian here asking to see her?"

Damn it, Rhea thought to herself, "I didn't want to lie to anybody, but here it goes.

"We needed to divide and conquer. She is following a lead from the last letter she got from her a week ago."

"Where," Marvin asked, making Rhea feel like he was suddenly investigating things and not her.

"Outside of Eugene."

"Hmm, sounds about right," and Marvin didn't say anything more.

"How so," Rhea decided to pick up the pace and ask the questions.

"Said she was going to be south," Marvin answered.

"So, she has been back here recently," Rhea inquired.

"Can't really say," Marvin retorted.

"You can't say because you don't know, or you can't say because you don't want to?"

"Who are you again," Marvin asked.

"My name is Rhea Baker, I'm a friend of Lillian's from L.A."

"How's that going for her," Marvin asked, and Rhea began to lose her patience.

"Fine," Rhea's exasperation was evident, and Marvin seemed to be happy about it.

"If she's in town, go check The Schooner over in Netart," the postal worker next to Marvin chimed in.

"June," Marvin exclaimed, "we don't know her from anyone."

June addressed her answer to Rhea and not Marvin, "He's an old flame, so he feels it's his job to look out for her."

Rhea's eyebrows shot up as they did when she was surprised by something. Marvin didn't look like he would be anyone's old flame, but Lillian had said her mom wasn't extremely picky about who she went around with.

"Thank you," Rhea said to June.

"You're welcome," June replied kindly, "if she isn't there now, she should be cycling back through these parts some time this week. She's eccentric as hell, but she is a regular at checking for letters from her kid!"

☙❧❦❧❦☙

Rhea got back into her car and searched for the Schooner on her phone. It wasn't much of a ride to Netart, but the Schooner wasn't opening until 4 that day. She had some time to kill, so she headed to the library. She wanted to do some research on Marcus and Harlan Brent and needed to figure out how to access information about the women and children they were seeking.

Those searches netted her nothing, and she was beginning to understand the warnings that Miles gave her often. He said not to get her hopes up, not to become too invested in finding everything out beforehand, and not to be surprised if the people they were working on finding didn't want to be found in the first place.

After lunch and a visit to a few of the places she had heard about from Lillian, just on the off chance that she would find Stacey there, Rhea got in her car and headed out for the Schooner. She found the restaurant quite easily. Her experience at the post office had made her wary of just winging it, so she thought through how she would approach this situation. Lillian expressed more than once that Stacey would spook easily. She always had some sort of quasi-illegal scam running, and often, she would have some amount of marijuana on her person, which she was still under the impression that she could be busted for.

She entered the restaurant and did a cursory scan of the patrons and the workers, but none of them looked remotely like the picture of Stacey that Lillian had given her. She went to the bar and sat down. The bartender was a young man, maybe in his 30s, who probably lived nearby. Rhea rehearsed her lines in her head.

"What would you like to drink," he asked her in a sweet tone.

"I'll take a Jameson and ginger ale, please."

"Coming right up," he said as he turned his back to gather what he needed. "Where are you visiting us from," he asked her. She realized that she was one of the only people at the bar, which meant he was free to make small talk. This could be a big help for her. He didn't seem like some college-aged bartender, so he might have met Stacey at least once.

"I'm visiting from Portland," she said.

"Work or pleasure," he asked as he put ice in the glass and began to pour the Jameson.

"Mostly work," she said. "I'm helping a friend of mine locate her mother."

"Oh," he seemed a bit interested in that, "is she missing?"

"No," Rhea felt his interest fade because of how ridiculous that must have sounded. "She's been living in L.A. for about six years or so, but they haven't kept in great touch. She's afraid that something is up since she hasn't heard from her recently."

"Where's your friend," he asked Rhea innocently as he put the drink in front of her.

"She down in Eugene looking," Rhea answered easily, almost

like she was a pro at lying.

"Would you like to start a tab?" he asked Rhea, and she said she would. She handed him her credit card.

"Have you," she started but trailed off for a second as she rethought how she wanted to phrase the question. "Do you, by chance, know Stacey Marsden?"

The bartender had picked up a tray of glasses and was about to start putting them away. He put them down again and turned his attention back to Rhea.

"Stacey has gone missing," he asked her.

"You know, Stacey," Rhea shot back.

"Yes," he answered, "she picks up a few shifts when she is back up this way."

"When was the last time she was here," Rhea asked him.

"About a month ago," he replied, "is she okay?"

"We aren't sure," was all Rhea replied. "Her daughter hasn't heard from her in a bit, so she is worried."

"Wow," he sighed, "I hope she is fine. Do you have a card or a number for either you or the daughter?"

"Sure," Rhea answered, hoping that he didn't recognize the surprise hidden in her voice that this was working. She handed him her card.

"I'm Dan," he said. "I'll let everyone know that Stacey should get a hold of you when she shows up."

"Thank you so much, Dan," Rhea said.

"It's not a problem; I'm hoping she is fine. She's a real sweet hoot," he said. "My guess is she'll be back within the next few days; she is normally around this time each month."

"That's helpful. I might postpone driving up the coast a few days so that I don't miss her," Rhea said to him. Dan nodded and agreed with her and then went on with his work. A few more bartenders came in during the next two hours, and they heard Rhea's story. They were all pretty sure that Stacey would be there in the next few days.

"It's hard for them to schedule her since she doesn't show up regularly," a young man named Brain was telling her, "but the manager here has a soft spot for her."

Rhea left the Schooner full of hope, but she was surprised by the ease with which she was able to find out information and even glean a vague idea of when Stacey would show up. She texted Lillian when she got back to her hotel in Tillamook. Lillian only texted back a thumbs-up emoji. Rhea reminded herself to dig into what had pushed the two of them apart.

After two days of checking at the post office and again at the Schooner, Rhea decided it was time to move on. Lillian had mentioned a few other towns that Stacey could be hiding out in. She wasn't here, and it didn't seem like she was going to show up soon, no matter what Dan was telling her at the Schooner.

The anticipation that every new day would lead her to something new had caused her not to sleep well, but this evening,

Rhea fell right to sleep. In the morning, she got herself ready, ate her breakfast, and checked out. She had decided to visit a town to the north of Tillamook called Warrenton. It was near the Washington and Oregon border. She was looking forward to the change of scenery and the drive there, which would be beautiful.

She loaded the car and pulled out of the parking lot. It took her a few minutes to realize that she was retracing her daily routines, and instead of heading north out of Tillamook, she was heading west towards Netarts and the Schooner. Rhea shook her head in disbelief, but she also wondered if fate might have pushed her towards the Schooner again.

She pulled into the parking lot and noticed that either Craig or Daniel, the two night managers whom she could never distinguish between, was talking to someone over by the boat launch across from the restaurant. It looked like he took something from the person, and then he turned and walked towards the restaurant. Rhea climbed out of the car as he approached. He saw her and chuckled.

"Well, your luck's paid off, Professor," he said to her. That meant it was Craig since he was the only one who called her that. "That's Stacey," he nodded to the figure standing at the end of the boat launch, finishing what Rhea assumed wasn't a cigarette.

Rhea wasn't sure what she was looking at. As far as she could tell, the woman standing there was tiny and looked as if she hadn't slept in days. Her hair, even from a distance, looked uncombed and greasy. Her clothing hung on her and looked worn out. It surprised Rhea that she would even be allowed to tend a bar at a restaurant.

"Stace," Craig yelled to her, "this lady has been looking for ya!"

Stacey turned towards Craig's voice and squinted towards him and Rhea. The hand that held the joint was raised towards her mouth, while her other hand rested squarely on her opposite hip, hiding her midsection behind her arm.

"Who the fuck are you," she yelled across the road towards Rhea.

Rhea moved towards her as she called back, "My name is Rhea Baker. I'm a friend of your daughter, Lillian." Rhea felt that was a better way to start than saying *your daughter and I are sisters.*

"From L.A.," Stacey seemed confused as she posed the question. "Are you one of her acting friends?"

Rhea had covered some ground and was now standing only a few feet away from Stacey. What looked like a mess from across the street seemed far worse now that she was standing there in front of her. Having met Lillian, Rhea was beginning to understand why the two didn't spend time together and only wrote letters.

"No," Rhea answered the question, "I'm not in the entertainment business."

"Good," Stacey brought the joint to her mouth once more.

"Lillian told me that I might be able to find you here," Rhea began, but it seemed that Stacey wasn't interested. She was staring off into the distance, towards the restaurant. Rhea looked behind her to see if anything was happening, but Craig had already gone back inside with his package. "She said you might be able to help me with some information about…" Rhea paused for a second. She wasn't sure how to proceed.

"About what," Stacey barked at her, startling Rhea out of her thought process.

"About my father."

Stacey looked at her funny. She tipped her head to the side and looked her up and down.

"What the fuck would I know about your father," she spat at Rhea.

Rhea realized that she needed to be a bit bolder than she normally was.

"Lillian and I have the same father," Rhea stated bluntly. "So, I was hoping you could help me out with some of the background information."

The face that Stacey made at the statement that Rhea put out there was one of horror and then quickly morphed into concern.

"What have you done with my daughter, you bitch," the words carried a weight to them as if Stacey were spitting each word at Rhea.

"Nothing," Rhea was frightened by her vulgarity and the force with which she hurled her words at her and loudly protested. "Lillian is fine. She's in L.A."

Stacey walked towards Rhea, but she was only a few feet away. Then she stopped. Abruptly. She looked Rhea up and down, and it was like a light went off in her head. She said nothing more for a beat or two. Suddenly, she grabbed Rhea's hand. Rhea jumped, but couldn't release her hand from Stacey's grip.

"Holy shit," she said to no one in particular, "you're one of his kids too."

"If by him you mean Marcus Brent," Rhea answered while trying to free her hand from Stacey's, "then yes. I'm one of his children!"

"Legitimate?"

"No," Rhea replied, "just like Lillian, I'm illegitimate."

Stacey shook her head. She dropped her joint onto the concrete, not even bothering to put it out, and quickly pulled Rhea into a surprisingly firm hug. Rhea had no choice. She reciprocated lightly. She was equally terrified and curious as to what exactly was going on in Stacey's head.

"Does Lillian know?" Stacey asked Rhea.

"Yes, we talked with her a little under a week ago."

"We?" Stacey asked her as she finally let her out of the vice grip of a hug.

"My brother, I mean my half-brother, and I went to L.A. to

find her."

"Why would you do that?" Stacey asked her. "Don't you know what would happen if somebody found out about you, or Lillian, or your brother?"

"No, what do you think would happen?" Rhea asked her.

"He'll send her after you," Stacey answered. She turned away from Rhea and faced out towards the water.

"I'm sorry," Rhea continued, "you said that he would send *her* after us. What do you mean by that?"

"She's the devil!" Stacey's voice rose as she exclaimed. Rhea was wondering exactly what she had gotten herself into. Stacey couldn't be helpful to them in a public sense. She looked like a strung-out older drug dealer who hated baths and loved to use words that couldn't be heard on national television.

"Who's the devil?" Rhea asked her innocently.

"She works for Marcus Brent."

"What does she do?"

"Do," Stacey yelled, "what does she do?" Rhea expected that an answer would be forthcoming, but no answer came.

"Stacey, could we go somewhere more private to talk?" Rhea's words seemed to slide right through Stacey, who just stood there looking at her.

"You came here alone," she finally asked after a few long seconds of silence.

"Yes, I've been looking for you for a few days now."

"What brought you to the restaurant?"

"A hint from a few people in town. They told me that I could find you here on occasion."

Stacey seemed to be getting irritated as if something was bugging her. She began to roll and unroll the bottom hem of her shirt between her thumb and index finger. She sighed loudly and looked around the area. There was nobody near them. Rhea could only recall hearing one car drive by in the last few minutes. This anxiousness was making Rhea unsettled.

"How many days have you been looking for me?" Stacey asked her.

"About four."

"Have you noticed anyone following you?" she whispered the question to Rhea, who had to lean in to figure out exactly what she was saying.

"No, nobody has been following me," but Rhea wasn't completely sure if that was true or not. She hadn't ever paid much attention to what was going on around her. She had seen the same people over and over during the week, and nothing that happened would have given her the clue that any of them were outsiders like herself.

"Good, you never know."

Rhea ignored that, not sure exactly why anyone would be following her, especially when they didn't even know that she existed.

"Would it be better if we talked in private?" she asked Stacey again.

Stacey's eyes took on a wild look, and she glanced around frantically. Then she suddenly grabbed Rhea's arm and pulled her after her towards the parking lot of the Schooner.

"Which one is yours?" she said. Rhea pointed at her car, and Stacey continued to drag her towards it. "Unlock it and hop in the passenger side," she demanded. Rhea stopped at that moment and dug her heels into the ground.

"No!"

Stacey was jerked towards her at that moment, and Rhea broke free from her grip. She stood there looking at Rhea with a look that was part confusion and part mania. When she started to speak, she spoke slowly and deliberately, as if she were speaking to a child.

"We need to get in the car and drive away from here," Stacey seethed at Rhea.

"No, we don't," Rhea answered. "And if we go anywhere, I'm driving the car."

"YOU DON'T UNDERSTAND!!!" Stacey stood there with her fist balled up and her eyes wide. As she yelled, it seemed that she had gained some amount of strength. Rhea was afraid, but at the same time, she knew that if she wanted to coax any answers out of Stacy anytime soon, she needed to see this through.

"Then you're going to have to explain it to me," Rhea said

calmly and quietly, countering her loudness with calm and quiet words. "I'll take you anywhere you want to go, but you have to get into the car on the passenger's side."

Stacey's eyes darted around the parking lot once more. It didn't seem like she was going to move toward the car, but instead, it felt like she was about to bolt, and her frantic scanning was her way of looking for the easiest escape route. She stood between Rhea and the car, so if Rhea wanted to leave, she would have to squeeze by Stacey to do so. As that was dawning on Rhea, Stacey finally responded.

"Fine," and she turned and walked around to the other side of the car, where she waited for Rhea to unlock the door. As soon as Rhea hit the button twice, Stacey darted into the car. Rhea opened the door and climbed in as well. She closed the door and pressed the ignition button.

"Where would you like to go," she asked, "I know a few nice places where we can grab coffee. Maybe you have a recommendation for me?"

"Head back towards Tillamook," she said, "I'll let you know when to turn."

Rhea put the car in drive and headed out of the parking lot and back toward where she had come from. As they drove in silence, Rhea took furtive glances at her. Stacey had scrunched herself up against the side of the door. She looked like she was asleep at times, but her eyes were fixed on the road ahead of them. Rhea pushed the pedal to the floor as they climbed up to the pastures of Tillamook. It was shortly before they came to town that Stacey had her veer off of the main road and head down an old, worn-down road. There had been a time, Rhea could tell, that this road had at one point in its life been paved. Years of neglect had brought it to a place of disrepair, and it now barely functioned as a road. Rhea was worried about the bottom of her car.

The path wound its way up to a small A-frame log cabin. The cabin was surprisingly well-maintained and sat beautifully on a slight ridge. There seemed to be no one there as they pulled into a spot for parking.

"This is a safe place," Stacey finally said to Rhea.

"Where are we?" Rhea asked her.

"This," she made a grand arc with her hands, "is my mother's cabin."

"Really," Rhea said under her breath, "Lillian hadn't told me about this place."

"Because she's *never* been here," Stacey snapped back at Rhea, "she'd left before I found it."

"What do you mean by found it?" Rhea asked her.

"My mother had stacks of papers in her home, and one day, as I was going through them, I found the deed for this place. I took it to a lawyer, and he said it was legally mine."

"Do you live here?" Rhea's voice betrayed a skepticism about the upkeep of this place, which was based solely on the upkeep of the person saying it was hers.

"No, I only stop in when I'm back from a stint."

"Who keeps up with the house when you're away," Rhea asked, ignoring the urge to ask her what a stint was.

"Michael," Stacey said this as if Rhea had already met Michael.

"Who's Michael?"

"A friend," Stacey opened the door and got out of the car. She began walking toward the porch. Rhea realized that she either had to move or risk the fact that Stacey may just disappear inside the cabin and never return.

Rhea jumped out of the car and closed the door just as Stacey was sliding open the front door to the cabin. She left it open after her, so Rhea took the steps two at a time and followed her inside. As she entered the door, she began to wonder if it was a good idea.

The cabin was immaculate inside. It didn't calculate in Rhea's mind. There was no way that Stacey would keep anything this neat; it must be Michael, whoever that was. Stacey was calling for him, and Rhea heard a deep voice answer back.

"I'll be right out, Stace," he said, "don't touch anything, you slob."

"It's my house," she screamed back at him.

Rhea took in the exchange. Stacey's harshness didn't shock her as much as it had in the parking lot. In fact, it seemed like it was the only way that she would act. Rhea chided herself for not being perceptive enough to realize she was dealing with such a person.

Michael emerged from the back room. He wore a plain black T-shirt and jean shorts. His beard was full and dark, which was in stark contrast to his bald head.

"Shit, Stace," he rumbled, "you didn't tell me you had a guest with you."

"It's my place, Michael. I'll bring people when I want to."

Michael just shrugged at her and turned to Rhea, "I'm Michael."

"I'm Rhea Baker," she responded.

"And how do you know Stacey?" he asked. Rhea looked to Stacey to answer him, but she had wandered off into the kitchen to look in some drawers. Rhea decided that she was just going to put it out there.

"I'm Lillian's sister."

That got Stacey's attention, and she was suddenly present again. Michael looked at her and then back at Stacey. "Your Lillian," he asked Stacey.

"Yes, my Lillian," she shot back at him. "How many other Lillians do you know?"

"You had two kids," he asked her, and Rhea realized that she might have needed to give more context to the statement she made.

"No," Rhea answered, "she didn't. Lillian and I are half-sisters; we have the same father."

Michael kept looking at Stacey. Rhea couldn't read his look well, but she was pretty sure it was wavering between disbelief and the sense of *'ahh, this makes sense.'*

"Look, Michael," Stacey jumped in, "I just found out about this not more than 30 minutes ago, so I'm processing it too. I don't need you to say a damn word about this or *anything*." Rhea felt that there was a very large emphasis put on the 'anything' part and wondered if that had to do with the drugs that Rhea assumed she was running. Or maybe Stacey had told him who Lillian's father was?

"Wait," he said, still looking at Stacey, "you know who Lillian's father is."

"Yes," she answered him, shaking his head, "I know who her father is. I just never thought it was anyone's fucking business."

"But wait," Michael started again, but this time, Stacey cut him off.

"Shut up and take a walk. You can come back when the car is gone. She and I got some things to talk about."

"I'd say you do," Michael said as he obediently went to the door and pulled on some sneakers. He left pretty quickly, and once Stacey saw that he was out of sight, she pulled out the kitchen drawer where she had been standing. It was full of washcloths, which she dumped out on the counter. Rhea stood and watched her as she maneuvered the bottom of the drawer, and it popped out. It was a thin piece of plywood, and under it were four or five pieces of paper. She pulled out two of them, put them on the counter, and then popped in the false bottom again.

"Here's the thing," she said to Rhea, "I'm not sure how I can help you."

"You can help us by being willing to tell your story."

"Why the hell would I do that?"

"Why wouldn't you?" Rhea retorted. "This guy is trying to get himself elected to the highest office of this country, and he is lying about so many things, and this," she motioned to Stacey and herself, "is something that we can point at and say, LOOK, he's a liar!"

"No," Stacey said curtly. "No one is going to care."

"Well, they should!" Rhea shot back at her. When Stacey didn't answer her, she continued, "They should care that he strong-armed women into doing something that they didn't want to do."

"And yet, honey, Lillian, you, your brother, are all proof that he wasn't able to strong-arm all of us into doing what we didn't want to do."

"That's not the same thing," Rhea said, "you live in fear that he is going to find out. My mother never told me, no matter how many times I asked, who my father was. You didn't tell Lillian anything! So don't feed me any bull crap about how you did what you wanted. You lost your ever-loving mind when I told you. You told me that we were in danger, that she was going to get us, that she was the devil. That doesn't sound like someone who made a free choice and then walked away without any worries. That sounds like someone who knew that they were duping a dangerous man and now spends her days running from it."

"And how do you think admitting that is going to take down Marcus Brent?" Stacey asked her skeptically. "What's your plan?"

This was exactly what Miles had been struggling with. She was asking the questions that Miles had laid out as reasons not to pursue this to an end. Rhea didn't have good answers to that. Rhea only held a deep passion for the idea that someone who was grossly misleading people shouldn't be in any way, shape, or form in leadership!

"We're gathering information, making a strong case, trying to figure out a way to break the news."

"The last guy like Marcus Brent said he was going to grab women by their pussies, and no one gave a fuck, so why would this be different?"

"This is different."

"How?"

"None of those people were afraid like you are!"

Stacey didn't look convinced, but she stopped the questions for a second. She picked up the two pieces of paper that she had taken out of the fake bottom. She walked towards Rhea and motioned for her to take a seat at the table. Stacey sat down at the end of the table, and Rhea sat next to her. As she was sitting, Stacey flipped over the two pieces of paper.

"This," she slipped a business card towards Rhea, "was the doctor who helped me."

Rhea picked up the card. Dr. A. Abbott. He was based in Philadelphia, which was what both she and Miles had assumed, according to the postmark.

"Do you know if this doctor was the same doctor that my mother went to?" Rhea asked.

"I assume so," Stacey said. "He seemed completely squirrelly when she came into the room. She was outside; he wouldn't let her in."

"Who was outside?" Rhea asked.

"Satan, keep up."

"Sorry," Rhea replied. Rhea assumed she was referring to the woman that Stacey was sure was after them. The woman who made them travel up to this cabin so they could talk privately. She and Miles needed to figure out who this woman was.

"Anyway, he came into the room. He looked at me and said that he was going to do an ultrasound. I was completely freaked out. This woman had just shown up at my friend's apartment that evening and had forced me to come with her."

"Satan showed up, and you just went with her? Why?"

"Because she worked for him! I recognized her the second I opened the door of that apartment. She had been there that night in the penthouse. We went inside, and she was standing there with his bodyguard, who took me to the elevator to leave. I knew who she was!"

Rhea wondered about her own mother's experience. What was it like for her? She still had a difficult time imagining what her mother, an activist her whole life, would have been doing with Marcus Brent. He stood for everything that her mother was against.

"So, he set up the ultrasound machine, and then he turned on something next to it, which made a lot of static-type noise. He began looking for my baby, Lillian, but it took me a few seconds to realize he was talking to me. He was asking me if I wanted to keep the baby."

"Whoa," Rhea interjected. "Did he know about the money?"

"How do you know about the money?" Stacey asked, and suddenly, the calmness that she had had since entering the cabin disappeared and was replaced with the onset of anxiety that she had shown at the boat docks.

"My mother and Miles's mother both received payments," Rhea answered. "According to the documents that Dr. Abbott sent us, you received a payment as well."

"I did," Stacey said, and a smile crept onto her face. "I had signed a form, and there was a check with it. The devil lady told me it was mine once she confirmed with the good doctor that the abortion had taken place. What surprised me was that the doctor was asking me if I wanted to keep it. I said I did. He told me that he could make that happen, but I needed to do a few things."

"So, he helped you fake an abortion?" Rhea asked.

"Yes, and he helped me steal money from that bastard as well."

Rhea chuckled at that statement. She wasn't the only one. Exactly six women, with the help of Dr. Abbott, stole millions of dollars from Marcus Brent. That wasn't going to sit well when they realized that there were six kids out there that weren't supposed to exist.

"Here is the other thing I wanted to show you."

Rhea looked at the paper that Stacey pushed her way. It was a newspaper clipping, from which publication she couldn't tell. The photo was of a younger Marcus Brent walking into a hotel. He was waving at the camera while surrounded by his entourage.

"This is from the night that I met him," Stacey continued. "I was in Philadelphia working some odd jobs in an effort to stay away from my family. That evening, I was working at the hotel, and he took a liking to me. I got invited up to the penthouse, and you can figure out the rest. He was charming, but he was also a tool. I never thought I'd end up pregnant, but I forgot that I was on antibiotics, and that meant my birth control wasn't working."

"How did they find you? I mean, how did they even know you

were pregnant?"

"I don't know," she replied, "but with a family like that, I wouldn't be surprised if they have people who follow you afterward. I spent most of my life on the move, just in case that was true."

"If that was true, they would have found you already like I did."

"That's a fair point."

Rhea looked at the newspaper clipping and the card. "Could I take a picture of these two things?"

"Fine with me," she said and got up from the table, "would you like some coffee or something? Michael tends to make it strong."

"No, thank you," Rhea responded as she pulled out her phone to take pictures. She realized there was only the picture and the small caption to be seen in the newspaper clipping. She wished it was the whole article.

"Look," Stacey said as she finished pouring her coffee. "I can't believe I'm about to say this, but I want to help you."

Rhea was stunned. "Really!"

"I guess it's not that big of a deal," Stacey shrugged. "I just offloaded some wares, don't ask what, and was just going to shack up here for a few weeks before moving back down the coast. What's your plan?"

"We planned to meet up in Philadelphia," Rhea said. "Miles

is trying to obtain information from a few other sources, and we're supposed to meet up in two days if I find anything."

"So let him know you found something, and I'll go with you to Philadelphia."

"Do you even fly?" Rhea asked her.

"Why would you ask me that?" Stacey shot back at her. "I'm not gonna want to drive across the country with you."

Rhea nodded, "Can we leave later this afternoon? I'm in Portland. We can stay there and purchase our tickets tomorrow and head out."

"No, I need the day here," Stacey said. "I have to organize a few things before I take off again. Damn it," she said out of nowhere, "Michael's gonna be pissed at me!" Stacey shook her head as she began to put the papers back into the fake bottom and load the dish rags back into it.

"I'll come back for you in the morning," Rhea said.

"That sounds good," Stacey answered, "but I need you to take me back to the restaurant first; I left my car down there."

The ride back to the restaurant wasn't as tense, and Stacey elaborated on parts of the story after she visited Dr. Abbott. She had never heard of or seen Marcus Brent again. She was pretty positive that she had at least seen the Devil Lady once, but she couldn't be completely sure because she had just taken some LSD. Rhea dropped her off and drove back to Tillamook. She decided to stay at a different hotel that evening. It was just easier than having to explain to the other hotel why she was back.

She went into the hotel room and tried to call Miles. His phone must have been turned off. She decided not to leave a message but instead texted him.

I found Stacey. She and I are going to head to Portland tomorrow and then fly out to meet you in Philadelphia. I'm attaching a picture of a business card for the doctor that I think sent you the information, and a newspaper clipping from the night that Stacey met him.

She attached the two pictures and hit send. It was hours before she would go to bed, and she hoped that Miles would write back to her soon. She wanted to hear his voice again. To know that the person on the other end of the line was her brother. She needed to feel that connection. She got her computer out and began searching for flights to Philadelphia. She wasn't sure what she was going to do there if Miles wasn't back from Mexico yet, but she would cross that bridge when she came to it.

To pass the time, she headed to the beach. She sat there on the shore on a borrowed towel from the hotel. She looked out into the Pacific Ocean and remembered the years of heading to the beach as a kid. Enjoying the smell of the air and the warmth of the sand, she was always afraid of the ocean itself. It was too wild and unpredictable for her. Yet, she couldn't stay away from it. There was something exhilarating about being that close to something so dangerous.

As an adult, she never ventured to the ocean. Her summers were taken up with research or trying to get another book published. As she sat staring off into the horizon, where she couldn't discern where the sky met the ocean, she realized that she hadn't been to a beach in over twenty years, and now there she sat. Right next to danger. The nostalgia flooded her brain, and so did the parallels to what she was doing. She realized that it was time for her to step into the danger, and coming out here and finding Stacey was doing just that.

Rhea stood up from the towel and kicked off her shoes. The waves crashed onto the beach. She set her mind to it and took off at full force towards the water, immersing herself in the Pacific Ocean and into danger.

Chapter Ten

The taxi ride to Playa del Carmen wasn't that long, but Miles had taken three different flights to arrive in Cancun, and this ride was pushing even his travel-savvy limits. His Dad had gotten him some intel on a surf shop near the beach that he was almost certain belonged to Esme. Adam had also given him some background on her. Her mother was Mexican, and her father, a second-generation Irishman. No amount of sleuthing could help Miles make sense of that.

Her Dad was a surfer and handled real estate transactions for a multi-million-dollar tech firm. Meanwhile, her mother worked as an ESL teacher in a school district just north of San Diego. Esme graduated from UCLA and took a job in Philadelphia. She quit a few years ago and then disappeared in Mexico.

It seemed that she had started the surf shop shortly after arriving, most likely using the money she had taken from Marcus Brent. Now, she was tucked away in a small resort town, thinking she was safe and sound. And who was to say she wasn't? He and Rhea were pretty sure no one knew, but his conversation with Marcia and Jennings gave him some pause. Could it be that Marcus Brent had Hannah killed? Was that why Elliot bolted as soon as he could? Was Marcus Brent as bad as people thought, or was that just a legend?

The sun was setting as he pulled up to the resort. He headed to his room, where he immediately took a shower. He was bone-weary and hungry, making his way to the restaurant in the hotel. A little bit of food helped him to regain his senses. There was no harm in approaching this as if Brent were as dangerous as everyone claimed. On the way out of the restaurant, he stopped at the front desk. He asked about Esme's surf shop, and the desk clerk told him that it wasn't that far from the resort, encouraging him to go by way of the beach so that he wouldn't end up lost in the neighborhood behind the shop.

His mind raced for a bit as he climbed into bed that night. Then the weariness of constant travel caught up to him, and before he knew it, his alarm had woken him up. He climbed out of bed, showered, and headed to grab a coffee at the restaurant. It was early enough that very few people were having breakfast. He was hoping to make it to the shop before it opened just to scope it out.

As he got onto the beach, he felt the morning heat envelop him. He walked barefoot along the water line, carrying his flip-flops in his hands, and headed in the direction of the surf shop. He walked for about ten minutes, and then he began to notice that the resorts were getting smaller. Small developments and houses were popping up between hotels. Palm trees lined the streets, and then there it was, sitting on the edge of one of the developments perched on the beach: the Surf Shop. The shop had a Caribbean vibe to it, and it was obvious that the shop was connected to a house.

He was about to start walking towards the shop when someone came out from that house and stood on the porch, looking over the beach to the water. She was tall with dark hair pulled back into a ponytail. She was wearing a lime green tank top and shorts. When she noticed him, Miles waved.

She cocked her head to the side as he continued to walk towards her.

"Hi," he said as he neared.

"The shop doesn't open for another three hours," she said with her arms crossed while leaning against the porch post.

"I know," Miles smiled, "but I wanted to talk with you. My name is Miles Trent."

"Well," she seemed indifferent, "Miles Trent, is it? What if I don't want to talk to you?"

He stopped about fifteen feet from the porch and looked up at Esme. He could see that she was not amused by his presence. He felt that she was fiercely opposed to him being there. Miles had to think quickly. He pulled his sunglasses up on his head and said, "Are you Esme Connors?"

"Why?" she asked as he took a step closer to the porch. Miles was about to answer when he saw in her green eyes something shift. It was like she recognized him.

"Oh Lord," she said, "you are about to screw up my life royally."

"No," he exclaimed, "no!" She stood there with her arms crossed, staring at him. "It's a long story, but to begin with, Marcus Brent is my father."

"How would you like your coffee?" she asked him.

"Uh," he was speechless. Her reaction was the opposite of what he had expected. She stood there looking down at him, waiting for a reply, but he could barely process the quick shift in her attitude. Finally, he managed, "Black will be fine. Thank you so much."

"Well," she turned, "come on in and see the shop that your father bought me." She opened the door to the surf shop, and Miles moved to follow her inside. At the door, he went to put on his flip-flops.

"It's a surf shop. You can just leave them at the door," she said, walking towards the check-out counter. There was a one-serving coffee machine, and she stuck a pod into it. He wiped the sand from his feet and followed her into the shop.

"I'll give you until you finish this coffee to tell me your long story," Esme crossed her arms and leaned against a wall.

"Well," he began, "I was living in Berlin when I got an anonymous package…"

"Let me guess," she interrupted him, "you never knew?"

"No, I didn't, not until the package arrived."

"What was in the package," she demanded as she took the coffee cup from the machine.

"A list of names, including my mother's and yours," he answered.

"Okay," she handed him the coffee, "let's talk out on the porch."

They sat in two low-slung chairs, looking at the beach and crystal-clear water. "Tell me more about this list."

"There was a total of six names, and attached to it were two sets of medical records," he checked to see if she was tracking with him. "One set recorded an abortion, and the other was information about the birth of the baby that was believed to have been aborted, along with a list of the whereabouts of each of the mothers and their children."

"Abbott," she said.

"It seems that he is the one who sent that information to me; why, I don't know."

"Asshole just broke a shit ton of laws doing it."

"I thought as much, too, which means it makes it hard to use publicly."

"So, you need me to tell my story. Why not your mother?" she asked innocently.

"My mother passed away when I was sixteen," Miles said evenly.

"I guess she didn't tell you who your father was," she seemed to track with him, but then she added with a sad smile, "I wouldn't have either."

Esme's tone surprised Miles. If she noticed, she didn't seem to care. She just looked out into the distance.

"I don't have any desire to put my daughter in harm's way here," she said. "I like my life."

Miles nodded. "When was the last time you saw your parents?"

"There are some downsides," she admitted.

"Wouldn't you like to be able to go back home?" he asked her.

She shook her head back and forth, "It's not gonna happen."

Miles felt crushed. He sipped at his coffee, thinking of what his next step was.

Esme broke the silence, "How many mothers are still alive out of the six?"

"Three."

"Phew," Esme whistled through her teeth. "Only three," she repeated.

"You, a lady in North Carolina and a woman for whom we don't have an address, but we have talked to her daughter who's in Los Angeles."

"Who are we?" she asked.

"My half-sister whom I met in Portland. Her name is Rhea." Miles paused, debating whether to share more, but decided he needed to. "She is currently looking for our other half-sister Lillian's mother in Oregon."

"Where are the children of the other two?" Esme asked him, with what seemed to him to be a great concern.

"As far as we know, there is a brother, Elliot, who's in Africa. Then, the mother who's in North Carolina, Angela, has a son who would be about 18."

"You, your two sisters, these others, my daughter," she chuckled, "it's a network of Marcus Brent's bastard children. Not long ago, children born out of wedlock wouldn't have amounted to much. But look at you, Miles. You look well off. What are the rest of the people like?" She paused for a second, and Miles looked at her with what he imagined was some disbelief. "I can't imagine you're going after his money, are you?"

"I don't want anything from him," Miles told her. "I want to expose him."

"And what exactly are you proposing we do? Are we to walk up to his door and knock?"

"I've a few ideas," he started, "some are more plausible than others," he paused before he continued, "and others are more fantastical. All of them are contingent upon the six of us coming together."

Esme looked past Miles out the front door, over the beach, and out onto the horizon. Miles realized he wasn't a fan of her snarky comments, but he was even less of a fan of the way she went silent and stared off into the distance.

Miles cleared his throat, "Would you like to weigh in on the options we have?"

Esme sighed and shrugged her shoulders, "Not necessarily."

"Why is that?" Miles asked, somewhat puzzled by her sudden lack of interest.

"I swore to myself when I crossed that border four years ago that I would never go back," she said firmly.

"Why not?" Miles responded. "Don't you want to expose him for what he is?"

"No," Esme said resolutely, "I don't. I don't for a lot of reasons, some of which are deeply personal, but most of them have to do with protecting my baby girl." Esme turned away from Miles and looked at the door to her house. "I named her Esperanza, Hope. I had hoped to God this day would never come. I hoped to God that Brent, and that bitch Deavers, would just die, and I could go back."

"Who's Deavers?" Miles couldn't help but ask at this new revelation, "Why does she need to be dead for you to go back?"

"Ms. Deavers," Esme nodded, "she is Marcus's clean-up lady."

"What do you mean by that?" Miles asked her.

"Her job was to make sure that anything the Brent family wanted to be swept under the rug got swept under the rug if you get my drift."

"Had you met her before?" This new information made him feel very uncomfortable.

"Yes, that night in the penthouse," she said. "She was there when I left."

"Do you mind backing up?" he asked. "How did the whole scenario play out?"

Miles noticed Esme hesitate at the question and added, "I don't need details, I just…" but even he didn't know what that "just" actually inferred.

"I need you to understand one thing," she said to Miles, "I wanted to sleep with him."

"Okay," Miles nodded at her.

"He hadn't announced anything about political aspirations. At that point, he was a very rich man running a company so vast in its holdings that it made my head spin. It was this man who was making advances toward me. I don't want to defend myself or make excuses, but I was in a mindless job, on the opposite side of the country from my family. I was lonely, and I felt stuck. He chatted me up for almost ten minutes in that penthouse suite, and I forgot for those ten minutes that my life was less than what I had imagined it would be."

"I understand that," Miles said to her, "and I'm not judging you. My mother had to have felt the same way."

Esme nodded at him and continued with her story.

"I realized I was pregnant about a month later, and I was

actually happy about it. I was hoping to move back to California and live near my parents again. Obviously," Esme motioned to the shop and the beach, "that didn't happen."

"Why?"

"Well," she said, "I was leaving work one day, and this, Ms. Deavers, came up to me in the lobby. She said that she needed to talk with me, and I said okay. She was intimidating, and I wasn't completely comfortable talking with her alone, so I suggested that we grab something to drink at the coffee cart and then talk in the park. The way that she said to me that *it was up to me* should have been a clue to what she was like. It was as if she was saying, 'It's your funeral' and smirking.

"We walked to a spot in the park. She was dressed in a pantsuit that looked very practical, and I wondered exactly what her job was with the Brents. Well, I found out pretty quickly that she was in charge of cleaning up Marcus Brent's messes."

"What happened in the park, exactly?"

"She," Esme paused and took her time before she continued. Miles could tell she was formulating something that seemed hard to explain. "Well, she sat down and reminded me that we had seen each other a little over a month ago at a fundraiser. I said that I did recognize her, and she made it clear that she didn't want to beat around the bush, but she knew that I was pregnant, and she had a proposition for me."

"What was the proposition?" Miles jumped, a little too eager to reach the part he came here for.

"There was no proposition."

"What?"

"There was an ultimatum. I was to meet her outside of my apartment early the next morning, and she would be taking me to a doctor. He would perform an abortion on me, and for that, I would be given a little over 1.5 million dollars."

"Did you ask what would happen if you didn't meet up with her?'

"I did," Esme replied, "and she gave me the weirdest look. She said to me very clearly that I would either go through with it and take the money, or she would take care of it, and there would be no money."

"What did she mean by that?" Miles asked her, and almost immediately regretted it.

"Really," Esme looked shocked at his inability to connect the dots. "I'm pretty sure that she meant she would take care of me, like permanently, Miles."

Miles just stared at her for a few seconds, which felt like minutes. She was waiting for a response from him, and all he could think to say was, "What you did was quite risky."

"You think," Esme replied sarcastically. That seemed to catch him off guard a little bit and snap him back to attention.

"Sorry," his voice wavered slightly, "I didn't mean to trivialize it. I'm just imagining that my mother also had to make that decision."

"I'm guessing since you're here, that would be a correct assumption," she seemed a little less annoyed with him.

"What happened once you got to the doctor?" he asked her.

"He kicked her out of the room and started to give me an ultrasound. He had it turned up so loud that it was annoying. He leaned in towards me and asked me if I believed in choice. I told him yes, and then he said to me, 'You have a choice here, no matter what she has told you, but you need to make the choice now. Do you want to keep the baby?'"

"Wow," Miles sighed.

"I was a bit surprised, too, but of course, I said yes. He went into some detail about what he was about to do to make it look like he aborted the baby. All I had to do was act a certain way and come back for a follow-up a few days later. When I left the back room, I was scared to death. She was waiting for me in the lobby. It was like she had never sat down the whole time I was in there. She looked right past me to him. He nodded grimly, and I remember thinking to myself that he was a great actor. She turned to me and handed me an envelope. She said that everything I needed to access the money was in there; I just needed to sign this document, which said I'd never talk about it or risk losing the money."

"Was it a non-disclosure form?" Miles inquired, using this time to gather as much as he could from Esme. The more Esme spoke, the more thoughts ran wild. His head was spinning stories, and he was picturing his mother in Esme's place.

"Probably, or maybe something a little more sinister." Esme's remarks pushed him back to the present.

"What do you mean?" he asked her.

"What I mean is that I'm pretty sure it was saying that talking about it would cost me more than the money they were giving me."

Miles nodded his head at her. But his mind went back to imagining; this time, he forced himself to stay focused. He couldn't let his emotions take over.

"So, I signed it and then left with the envelope which gave me instructions to access the payoff for my silence. When I returned a few days later, he wasn't there. His receptionist just handed me a folder. In it, he gave me some pointers for keeping everything under wraps. The only valuable advice that he gave, in my opinion, was to get off the grid."

"That's why you chose Mexico."

"It was off the grid."

"Have you ever wondered why they never checked up on you again?" Miles asked her.

"No," Esme responded to him, "I fled to Mexico. I never thought about them following me because, as far as they knew, I had aborted the baby."

"It's been one of the things that has been bugging me recently. It seems like no one ever checked up on any of the women after they had visited the doctor. Why was that? Did they think he did what he was supposed to do, so why ever check up on it again?"

"Possibly."

"If no one was searching, why did you stay here?"

"That's a harder question to answer," she smiled at him, "and not something that I'm ready to share with a man I just met."

Miles chuckled at that. He could only push her so far. The rest would remain a mystery. He put his hands in the air in fake surrender. "No more questions then."

"Good," she said, standing up, "I'm hoping you can understand why I can't help you."

"No," he said honestly as he stood up with her, "I don't fully understand it."

She put her hands on her hips and looked him in his eyes. "I'm not going to put my daughter in danger. Bringing this into the light will only make you all a target, especially me, since I was the last one."

"But that's why you're the most important piece of the puzzle," Miles pleaded with her.

"I'll be the first one they kill too."

Miles didn't have any response.

"Please keep my name out of this," she insisted.

The goodbye was awkward. Miles was leaving with nothing, and she went about it like it was just an ordinary day. Miles walked back to the hotel the way that he came. The sand was warmer, and the waves seemed closer than they were that morning. His mind replayed the conversation with Esme. So many layers and so many new questions arose. Why hadn't anyone ever followed up with these women? That was really nagging at him.

At the hotel, he went to the bar. He was to catch a flight the next day, and he had originally hoped that Esme would join him, but her no was a firm and resounding one. There was definitely no desire to reopen that can of worms. Her fear of this Ms. Deavers unnerved him deeply.

He ordered a tequila, since he was in Mexico, and pulled out his phone. Rhea had sent a text, which he read. It seemed that Lillian's mother, Stacey, would step out and tell her story, or so he hoped. Yet Miles was still wary about what that might mean for her. He put the phone away and took a sip of his tequila. The bar was full of middle-aged people. Not all of them were couples. Yet it was the couples that caught his attention. His mind kept wandering back to his mother. Did she and Marcus Brent have a long affair? Was it a secret affair? Did they jet off to Mexico and dance with each other by moonlight while sipping tequila? Was that even the past that he would want for his mother? Was it easier to just imagine her having a one-night stand with a charismatic man that she knew would go nowhere?

He didn't want to imagine the first scenario because it mirrored his mother's relationship with his Dad. Simon and his mother had jetted off to more exotic places like the Maldives or Capri. He'd travel with them on occasion, and he loved watching them dance with each other, pressed cheek to cheek. He always wondered what they were talking and laughing about while they danced. He could not imagine that his mother would have had anything to talk about with Marcus Brent that would bring her to laughter.

"What brings you down this way?" the bartender asked him.

"It was just a short trip," Miles answered him. He was a tall, middle-aged man. He was muscular and looked like he may have been the bouncer at the bar as well. "I was doing some research," Miles caught himself almost saying that he was doing some investigating, "for a book I hope to write."

"Oh, what type of book?" he asked Miles. He had two choices, and both were lies, so he settled on the lie that would possibly end the conversation.

"It's a book on how the Catholic religion interacts with the sin and excess of the resort culture in these small coastal towns."

The bartender raised his eyebrows.

"Sounds thrilling," he responded while looking at Miles. The way he looked at Miles made him feel funny. Was the guy pitying him for being boring, or was there something else? Either way, his hope of ending the conversation looked to have been successful. Then the bartender looked at him and said, "Anyone ever told you that you look like that asshole running for president?"

Miles hoped that his gasp wasn't audible. He needed to think quickly; this time, he tried on something new, "My roommates in college used to say that, but I told them they were full of it."

"Well, your roommates were right."

"I'll let them know," Miles smiled, and the bartender nodded.

"Enjoy the rest of your stay here," he said as he moved away from Miles to help out a new patron at the end of the bar.

Miles breathed in slowly through his nose. What just happened? Would that have bugged him if he didn't know the truth? Was this going to keep on happening? His processing of these questions in his head couldn't keep up with the speed at which more and more questions arose. He picked up the tequila and shot it down at once. He signed his check and headed to his room. Rhea was going to find that funny.

The next morning, Miles woke up early and headed back out to visit Esme. The walk wasn't so bad as he took in his surroundings. It was early enough that most tourists weren't out and about yet. Young ladies wearing the hotel's polo shirts and the housekeeping crew uniforms were taking a smoke break at the back of the hotel. Miles nodded at them, but they ignored him.

He made his way along the beach, staying closer to the road than the tide. He made his way past a few small stands, working his way toward the more private part of the beach where he had visited with Esme the day before. From a distance, he saw her sitting there on the front porch with a small child playing in the sand in front of the steps. Miles began to wave to catch Esme's attention, but it took a few seconds for her to see him and respond in kind.

As he got closer, the toddler looked up at him and said something in Spanish to him. Unlike Rhea or Lillian, Esperanza looked more like her mother than her father. The dark hair and deep brown eyes were Esme's, which would help keep her hidden in case anyone came looking for her.

"Buenos Dias," Miles said back to her. Esperanza tilted her head to the side and gave him a strange look, and then, in perfect English, she spoke to Miles.

"Surf lessons start soon."

"Sweetheart," Esme interrupted, "Miles is here to talk with me, not take a surfing lesson."

Esperanza looked at her mother and then back at Miles. She seemed to shrug this off and continue working on what looked like small balls of sand.

"Maybe someday your mom will teach me how to surf," he told her. She seemed to ignore what he said.

"Would you like a cup of coffee?" Esme asked him.

"I would, thank you," he replied.

"Come on up," Esme said as she turned and headed into the house. Miles stood on her porch, looking from the ocean to the little girl playing at the foot of the steps. He gathered his thoughts, trying to figure out how to convey to Esme the importance of her joining him and Rhea in bringing this out in the open.

As Esme came through the door, she gave him his coffee. It was black, and his first reaction was to ask for some cream, but he stopped. He took a sip. It was hot, and he winced a little at the scalding liquid as he swallowed it slowly. He looked at her and was about to say something when she started the conversation.

"I know that you're heading out today," she started, "and I know that you came here today to see if you could convince me to change my mind, am I right?"

"Yes," he nodded.

"I don't want to lead you on. I can't do it. I'm not risking it. I've kept all of this from my family," she motioned towards Esperanza. "They have no idea that I came here pregnant. They have no idea they're even grandparents. I don't regret this, but I'm not proud of it either. I won't put them in danger or her, either. If this were only about me, I would be there in a heartbeat. I would take that asshole down on my own, believe me. Yet, I know about that family. I've done my research. I can't prove it, but I'm almost sure they're somehow connected to some international crime syndicate."

That statement made Miles deflate a little. While he felt that the Brents were not good people, he thought that throwing them in with international crime syndicates was dramatic.

"I know that sounds dramatic," Esme said, making Miles feel like she could read his thoughts, "but I stand by it. There are so many stories, rumors, what have you, that point to the fact that people who cross the Brents are hard to find alive."

"How come no one has ever made these accusations before?" Miles asked her.

"Not enough proof," she said. "You work in facts, Miles; I've read about you. You know damn well that you don't go after someone with that amount of power. Marcus Brent has that type of power, the same as his father."

"What type of power?" Miles asked.

"The type of power that can make people disappear. The type of power that causes people to give them a wide berth. And the types of power that they don't possess, they have the money to pay for. And now it looked like they're in a position to wield that power without having to continue to pay for it."

"That's why it's so important for us to talk about what happened," Miles pleaded. "If we can show people the extent of his corruption, we have a shot at stopping him!"

"Everyone already knows he's corrupt," Esme said with a chuckle, "and just when you think you can take the moral high ground, he'll find some asshole preacher to vouch for his spiritual change! You've seen this before; you aren't that gullible, are you, Miles?"

Miles wasn't used to people asking him those types of questions. It jolted him a bit, yet she was right. There was no doubt that would be how they played it.

"Just because they can spin themselves out of this doesn't mean we aren't obligated to present the truth."

"Not if it will get us killed."

"We don't know that. That doesn't seem to be the case. We all seem to have been able to live under the radar. No one knows we exist."

"Obviously, not *no one,* Miles! There was the doctor who sent you the information."

Miles nodded. She was right, and yet he was too. In all of the various situations he had researched concerning the Cold War, he always concluded that those who chose silence caused the most suffering. This ultimately led to situations where death was inevitable.

"We don't know if Marcus Brent will come after us or not," Miles said, "but the more of us that are coming at him, the harder it is to make us all disappear."

She smiled at him and took a sip of her coffee. He braved another scalding sip, but the coffee had cooled enough when he put it to his lips.

"Maybe you have a good point," she said after she brought the mug from her lips and swallowed, "but you know I also have a good point. I've much more to lose in this situation than you do."

He wasn't sure if that was true, but he wasn't a father, so he wasn't about to jump into that debate. He had his father. He had Rhea, toward whom he had developed a brotherly affection. Everyone had something they didn't want to lose.

"Rhea and I'll start this," Miles said, "but at any point, we would love for you to become a part of it."

"Don't hold your breath," she said.

"I'm a little more stubborn than that," he said with a smile. "If we can set this ball in motion and prove it's safe, you could jump in, which would allow you to see your family again." That last sentence landed like a punch, Miles could tell.

"You can't guarantee that type of safety."

"But if I could," Miles asked.

"Miles," she took a long pause, "from what I can tell from our few hours together…" she trailed off.

"What can you tell?" Miles asked.

"It doesn't matter," she sipped her coffee again. "Be careful. The world needs men like you, and it would be a shame for us all to lose you."

ೞ೮౬ೞ

Miles walked away from the beach. His thoughts revolved around all the things he could have or should have said. He was so tempted to walk right back there and say them. She had her points, but she was wrong. They need not fear the Brents. Once they went public, there was nothing they could do to them. They would be safe, but now they just needed to talk with Elliot and Angela. Once they made those connections, it was off to the races.

As he neared the hotel, there was the bartender from the night before talking with one of the ladies who had checked him in when he arrived. They were talking animatedly, and as he approached, the bartender nodded, and then he overheard him telling her, "That guy looks like that Brent dickhead." She looked at him, shrugged a little, and then smiled at Miles.

As he walked towards the front of the hotel, his phone rang. It was Rhea. He thought that he would lead with that instead of the bad news of his meetings with Esme.

Chapter Eleven

Rhea checked out of the new hotel, relieved to know that she would be heading home that afternoon. Her clothes were still pretty damp from her symbolic plunge into the ocean, so she fished out a clean garbage bag from one of the trash cans in her room and put the damp clothing in there. She had packed and was ready to go a good hour before she was supposed to meet up with Stacey.

She headed out to one of her favorite breakfast places in town and enjoyed a cup of coffee. She had rested well and was good to go. Miles had texted her in the night, saying that he was happy to hear of her success, but that Mexico was a bust. He would return to Philadelphia and see her there in a few days.

He texted again a few hours later to tell her that a bartender at the hotel he was staying at had asked if anyone ever told him he looked like Marcus Brent. Rhea sent him a quick surprise emoji while drinking her coffee. It had been a long time since she had any sort of text thread with someone. She wondered if this was what it felt like to have a family.

She had written herself directions to drive back to the cabin deep in the woods. Rhea had thought through how Stacey could have purchased a place like that. It must have been the money she had received from the Brents. Michael, well, that was another unanswered question, but it was one that she planned to figure out in the time that she and Stacey would be spending together heading out to Portland and then Philadelphia.

She wound her way through the outskirts of the town and paid attention to the landmarks that would show her the almost non-existent driveway. She saw the tiny break in the undergrowth and put on the turn signal to head onto the property. She wound her way up to the cabin, taking extra time to traverse the bumps and the holes. As she rounded the bend, she could see smoke rising from the chimney of the cabin. She had half expected to find Stacey waiting for her on the porch, but she was nowhere to be seen.

Rhea waited a few seconds and then turned off the car's engine. She was hesitant to go to the front door, not wanting to look too anxious to be on her way. Stacey was such an enigma to her. One second, skittish and crazy, the next calm and collected. She was worried about which Stacey would show up today, which Stacey she'd have to take on the plane with her, and which Stacey would show up at Miles's door.

When she sensed no movement from behind the glass door, Rhea got out of the car, trying to close the door hard enough that she would be heard. Yet there still seemed to be no one moving inside the cabin. She was worried and also a bit frustrated all at once. She had begun to believe in the dangerousness of the Brent family. She had heard too many things from Miles in his travels and Stacey in her experience that caused her to worry about the people they were dealing with.

As she got closer to the front door, she could see a bit further into the cabin, almost to the back part where the bedroom would be. She knocked and waited. Nothing, no movement whatsoever. Rhea knocked again, hoping that at least Michael would answer the door. Nothing. Rhea walked off the porch and went around the cabin, looking down the path that Michael had disappeared down just yesterday. There didn't seem to be anything that would have suggested that anyone was down that path.

She went around to the front of the cabin and looked inside the car that was parked in the driveway. It wasn't the car that Rhea had dropped Stacey off at last evening. It was a bit too neat inside to have been Stacey's, so Rhea guessed it was Michael's.

Rhea went and sat down on the front porch of the cabin. It was a crisp morning, and she was pretty sure that she had been stood up. It was ridiculous. What was she supposed to do now? She decided to walk down the path a little, just to see what was down there. Maybe there was another cabin, or a lean-to, where Stacey could be staying.

She walked down the path and, after about a minute of walking, decided that there was nothing there. It continued into the woods. As she walked back to the car, she contemplated what she should do. Was it the right move to just leave? Should she have put any stock in Stacey's words, or had something else happened? Did something cause her paranoia to grow, and then she just jetted? Or was somebody really on their tails?

It was too much to process at once. She returned to her car and started it when it dawned on her that she had never tried the door to see if it was unlocked.

"Rhea, you dingbat," she said out loud as she got out of the car and walked up to the cabin door. She knocked hard, wanting to make sure they heard her before she just opened the door, but no one answered. She knocked again and, this time, yelled for Stacey, and when no one came, she yelled for Michael as well. She grabbed the doorknob and went to wiggle it, expecting that it would be locked, but the door knob turned in her hand, and the door unlatched and opened. Based on her extensive crime show viewing, she walked into the house slowly, expecting to find it a mess, with things scattered all over the place. That's what happened in those shows when someone was missing from where they were supposed to be.

The house was exactly how she had left it the day before. Nothing looked out of place. She continued to call out Stacey's name and then Michael's, but there was no answer. The bedroom doors were open, and Rhea could see that the beds were made in both rooms, so it wasn't like they had been taken in the night. It seemed to her now that Stacey must have freaked out and just left town. Maybe Michael was driving her somewhere right at that moment.

She went back out to her car and grabbed her bag from the passenger side, fishing through it to find some paper and a pen to write Stacey a note.

Stacey,

I'll be staying at the Hampton Inn one more night before heading back to Portland. Please get in touch with me there if you are still interested in traveling to Philly with me.

Rhea

She put the note on the kitchen counter, with her business card, and left the house. She closed the door behind her and looked at the woods surrounding the cabin. Nothing seemed out of place at all. No signs of struggle, no skid marks, nothing. The only sounds she heard were the wind on the tops of the trees and the birds conversing with each other as the morning matured into afternoon.

She walked down to the car and restarted it. She backed up and drove slowly down the pitted and rutted driveway. She was so lost in thought that she missed that her phone was ringing. It was Miles calling her to check in, like they had planned.

"Miles," she sighed, "I'm so glad to hear your voice."

"Hey, Rhea," his voice seemed sad. "Are you on your way back to Portland?"

"No," she jumped in, "Stacey was a no-show at her cabin."

"What?" Miles's surprise resonated louder on the speakerphone.

"I went to pick her up, and she wasn't there. Miles," she said, "it looked like no one had even stayed in the cabin last night. The beds were made and everything."

"Wow, which can only mean that she got spooked and left."

"That's what I was thinking as well," she said, "but I was sure she was ready to help us. I mean, she gave me the doctor's name and number, so we aren't leaving empty-handed."

Miles paused for a second, "That's true. Why don't you head back to Portland and return to Philadelphia as soon as possible? Unfortunately, I came up empty-handed here as well."

Rhea was pulling out of the driveway onto the road when something caught her out of the corner of her eye. Before she knew it, the back door of her car was thrown open, never having locked itself on the way down the driveway. A wild-eyed Stacey sprang into the car.

"Drive! We gotta get out of here," she screamed at Rhea.

"Who's that?" Miles asked over the speakerphone, the alarm in his voice apparent.

"Who are you?" screamed Stacey from the back seat.

"Stacey," Rhea said calmly, "that's my brother Miles."

Stacey calmed down for a second and then muttered again that Rhea needed to drive. Rhea pulled out and headed towards Tillamook.

"Are you okay?" Miles asked after a second of silence.

"She's fine for now," Stacey answered from the back seat. "You both are fine for now, but they're coming for us all."

"Why do you think that?" Rhea asked her again, calming her own nerves to help Stacey be more levelheaded. Except this time, it seemed to have the opposite effect. She sat up wide-eyed in the back seat and yelled at Rhea.

"Hang up the fucking phone!"

Rhea was startled by Stacey's screaming, which caused her to swerve. This agitated Stacey even more, and she sprang forward in her seat, trying to grab the phone from the holder. Rhea pushed her back and pulled the car over on the side of the road.

"What is your problem?" she yelled back at Stacey.

"She's gone," Stacey yelled.

"Who's gone?" Rhea shot back at her.

"Angela! Angela is gone!"

"Who's Angela?" Rhea yelled back to her.

"Angela Camp," Miles said over the phone. Rhea froze and looked at Stacey, who just nodded. "Stacey, what do you mean Angela Camp is gone?"

"She is gone," she cried, holding onto the 'gone' for a long time.

"How do you know she is gone?" Miles asked again over the phone.

"How do you even know Angela Camp?" Rhea chimed in

immediately afterward.

Stacey just shook her head, and tears welled up in her eyes.

"Miles," Rhea said, "I'll call you back as soon as possible."

"No…" but she ended the call before he could say anything else.

She turned around, pulled onto the road, headed towards town, and drove straight through it. They were a mile outside of town before Stacey even spoke again.

"Where are we going?" she asked Rhea.

"How did you know Angela Camp?" Rhea asked her, looking into the rearview mirror.

"I don't want to talk about it," Stacey said. Rhea felt the anger burn in her. In her mind, she thought of a million things to spit right back at Stacey.

"You got into my car and scared the shit out of me all because you wanted to tell me Angela was gone!" Rhea was accelerating as her voice rose. "Start talking!"

Stacey muttered something under her breath, which Rhea made out as a vulgar insult.

"I imagine that if I call Miles back, he's already starting to look into what is going on with Angela." Rhea felt bad for getting worked up and circled back to being calm. "We were planning to find her after we met up in Philadelphia."

Stacey sat in the back of the car with her arms crossed tightly against her chest, staring out of the window. Rhea couldn't keep her eyes on her constantly, but when she glanced back at her in the rearview mirror that she had adjusted to see her, she would catch her looking right back at her using the same mirror.

"I don't remember," Stacey finally said. "Are you older, or is Miles older?"

"I am," she replied calmly, betraying the urgent rush she felt inside to get answers to some of the more important questions racing through her head.

"By how many years?" Stacey asked her.

"He is younger than me," she responded.

"What do you think Lillian thought about the two of you?" Stacey asked abruptly, changing the subject very quickly.

"I would assume from our interaction with her that she liked us. I mean, she seemed to believe what we were saying. You know, she sent us your way. She gave us a general idea of where you would be."

"What else did she tell you about me?" Stacey asked again as they began to drive deeper into the surrounding forest.

"She said that the two of you were estranged. Despite not seeing you since she graduated from college, she still keeps in touch with handwritten letters."

"That's all she told you," Stacey said, stopping to look out the window and focusing on Rhea again.

"I asked her to come with me," Rhea said, "but she couldn't. She had a callback for a role, and it wasn't great timing."

"That's what she often says," Stacey answered. "I ask her all the time to come back to visit. I keep that cabin spotless, the opposite of what she grew up with. I beg her over and over again in letters, but she always ignores my invitations and writes on and on and on about her life in LA."

"I'm sorry," Rhea said gently.

"I went out to Philadelphia to find the doctor."

Rhea nodded and went with the change in subject. "Why did you do that?"

"I figured it had been long enough; it was almost 6 years since Lillian was born, and no one had ever shown up at my door and asked me why I had a kid and what I did with the money. It was like they had done their job, and we had done ours, so we moved on with our lives."

"I just couldn't rest until I talked with someone," she continued, "so I flew out to Philadelphia, where I had been staying when I met Marcus Brent. I wanted to ask that doctor some questions that I thought only he could answer. I wanted to know where's and when's and what he was thinking I could expect."

"Did you find him?" Rhea asked her.

Stacey's eyes darted here and there as she spoke. "I did, but I also found something else."

"Angela Camp," Rhea asked.

"Not exactly," Stacey said, "I found Satan."

Rhea knew that meant the fixer, but she wanted to be sure, so she asked her.

"Of course, I mean that bitch! She was there in Philadelphia, walking with a young lady from the car that she had just parked. They went right into the doctor's office, the same one I met her at. I had so many questions. Was she being forced, like I had been, to have an abortion? Were they offering her money as well? What did the devil lady do once she was out of the picture? So, instead of going in and pretending to be a patient, I would just wait. Two hours later, it paid off because she walked right out of the doctor's office, got in a car, and left."

"Who got in the car?" Rhea asked her.

"Satan," Stacey spat.

"Does Satan have a name?" Rhea was tired of not knowing who this woman was that Stacey was so afraid of.

"Yes, it's Ms. Deavers." The name didn't mean anything to Rhea. If she had heard it at all in the course of the work they were doing, she hadn't remembered. "So, you saw her, the same lady who came to you, taking Angela to the doctor's office?"

"Yes, yes, yes, yes," Stacey whined at Rhea, "how much clearer can I say it?"

"Listen, Stacey," Rhea raised her voice, "you might not be aware of this, but you don't make much sense when you're hysterical! You've talked around and around and thrown out paranoid thought after paranoid thought. You don't need to be snippy with me because you can't string a fucking sentence together!"

Stacey was taken aback by the words that Rhea chose. It was obvious that she had gotten her attention. Rhea trudged on, "So to review," she paused to make sure that Stacey was connecting with her, "You saw this. Mrs. Deavers, take Angela to the doctor's office just like she took you years ago."

Stacey nodded her head.

"How did you connect with Angela then?"

Stacey sat quietly in the back seat, and Rhea feared that her stern words had caused her to go mute.

"I waited."

It was only two words, but it was a start in the right direction.

"And, then, what happened?" Rhea felt like she was coaxing the class wallflower along in a public speaking class. If it hadn't been for the vital information that Stacey had, Rhea would have just given up already.

"She was afraid at first. She didn't tell me she had kept the baby until a month later."

"You've stayed connected all these years?"

"Until last night, she had always answered my calls and texts. But nothing. It doesn't even say that she read the text."

"Did you try to contact her kid?" Rhea asked.

"He doesn't know about me, or his father, or any of this! If something happened to him, that would be…" Stacy trailed off.

"I'm sure they're just out of reach; give it some time," Rhea tried to comfort her.

"NO," crazy Stacey was back, Rhea thought as the scream echoed through the car. "YOU AREN'T LISTENING!"

"What do you want me to do, Stacey?" Rhea threw that question at her with some force. "If you give me the number, I'll call her. We can go to the library, get online, and search to see if anyone is missing where she lives. Does any of that seem like a good option?"

"They will know we're searching for her," she whispered in the back seat in stark contrast to the loud yelling seconds before.

"Why would they even care if we're looking for news from there?" she asked Stacey. "If something has happened to her, you don't think that they would have already seen that you've called her?"

That was the wrong thing to say to Stacey. She bolted upright in the car and pulled on the handle, even though the car was still moving. The safety features kept her from opening the door, giving Rhea enough time to pull over in a driveway not far from the center of town.

"If you and Miles know what is good for you, run!" With that, she unlocked the door and jumped out. She took off down the road towards where they had come from. Rhea jumped from the car to follow her, but Stacey ran across the road and into the woods. By the time Rhea crossed, she was gone.

It was over as suddenly as it had begun. She sat in stunned silence for a few minutes before she pulled out of the driveway and headed to the library. She wanted to wait to call Miles, but he was anxious because her phone lit up by the time she hit the next block.

"She's gone," Rhea started.

"We need to move up our trip to North Carolina," was his response. "It seems that Angela Camp and her son were victims of the tropical storm that hit there the other day."

"What?" Rhea was confused. "There was a tropical storm in North Carolina?"

"Yes," Miles responded, "I got onto a local news site, and there were four deaths in the area from the storm. Two from flash floods, and two people who died in their house because they left the car running in the garage."

"What?" Rhea was being reduced to one-word answers. It all seemed unbelievable, but was that because of the things Stacey had said to her? Was she going down that paranoid road as well?

"That was one report; another one made it sound like it was a murder-suicide."

Rhea fought the urge to say what again, "Miles, this is," she paused, but couldn't find the right word to finish the sentence.

"Surreal."

"And then some," Rhea exclaimed into the phone. "Stacey made it sound like this could happen, and I felt like she was such a lunatic for thinking about it."

"We aren't sure that's what happened. It could be a coincidence," Miles didn't sound like he believed what he said either.

"Then let's go find out."

"It's a risk if she's right," was all that Miles said. He was quiet for what felt like a solid minute. She was afraid that he had hung up without any resolution to their conversation.

"Miles?"

"Can you get to Myrtle Beach soon?"

"I can be there tomorrow or the day after at the earliest," she said, not truly thinking through its feasibility.

"I'll meet you there tomorrow. Does that work for you? I'll switch my flight when I arrive in Miami tonight, and if I can't change it, I'll rent a car and meet you at the airport."

"What about Philadelphia?" Rhea asked him, trying not to sound eager in this situation because she wanted to meet Miles' father. Deep in her heart, she already knew the danger of meeting this man. She knew she would be so quick to make him her father figure, and she knew how unhealthy that was. Those wounds couldn't be healed with an ersatz father. It would never be that easy.

"We can fly up there after we're done in North Carolina. My Dad is looking forward to meeting you."

That was music to her ears at a moment when everything they

were doing suddenly felt more dangerous than before.

Chapter Twelve

Miles was getting nowhere with changing his flight. Miami's Airport was bustling with travelers, and it felt like every single one of them had a problem that needed to be dealt with. He had never just not gotten on a flight that he was booked on. He had only traveled to Mexico with a carry-on bag, so there was no reason to wait to cancel. He had seen the boards and estimated that by the time he made it through the line, got his flight changed, and then caught his flight, he could drive to Myrtle Beach.

Going with a rental car was his best option, and he was glad to be out of the airport and on the road. It gave him time to think and process. He wanted to believe that the deaths of Angela and her son could be a completely horrible coincidence. Yet even as he tried to convince himself of this possibility, he knew it wasn't true. Those thoughts kept on playing in his head as he drove through all of Florida toward northern South Carolina.

Rhea was waiting for him at the airport. As he got out of the car, it was pretty clear that she was shaken. He asked himself what the brotherly thing to do would be, and he landed on hugging her. She started sobbing as he did.

"Miles," her voice was muffled in his shoulder, "no matter if this is the work of the Brents or not, we lost a brother."

That hadn't occurred to Miles, but its weight hit him. He had never struggled with his motivation—the *'why'* in his pursuit of information. He felt like it was important to expose a crooked potential politician. It was that sense of justice that pushed him on, but he felt like something had been lacking, and now he had found it. Rhea's words gave him the 'why.' He needed to save his siblings! The urgency of the task at hand was suddenly overwhelming.

As they were driving later in the car, Miles would make a note of that moment. He knew that was the moment that was going to propel him onward. It was the moment he knew he needed to get back to Mexico as soon as he could because he couldn't let anything happen to Esme or Esperanza. It drove the urgency of getting to Burkina Faso and connecting with Elliot, warning him of what could be coming his way, no matter how safe he felt being worlds away from Oklahoma. If someone asked him why he was doing this, now he had an answer.

⚜

Ocean Isle Beach was pretty, but it was also teeming with tourists. The local news had printed the address of the house where they had found the bodies of Angela and Dustin. The local police force had finally landed on a murder-suicide, with the focus being on Angela, who was the town's recluse, according to most people, taking her life as well as that of her son, who was adored by the friends and coworkers that he had.

Rhea and Miles checked into a hotel on the mainland. On the way to Ocean Isle, Rhea looked up information on the memorial service. There was going to be a joint service held at a local funeral home about ten minutes from where they were staying. They had a day before it took place. A day to find out any information that they could, but they had no 'ins' to start conversations. Neither of them was a journalist or a private investigator, but both were very good at discovering and researching events and following leads.

The one concrete piece of information they had was where Dustin had worked, and that was where Rhea wanted to start. Dustin was the only connection to the community because it seemed that Angela managed and cleaned her rental properties but otherwise kept to herself. She didn't belong to a church or a community social club. Dustin worked at a local gas station and had been elected to his high school student government, the irony of which did not escape either Miles or Rhea. He had charisma and was well-liked.

It wasn't surprising that the investigation didn't point toward foul play. Rhea had told Miles over and over that there had to be something that was just a touch off. Something that could point towards this being a double murder. Miles couldn't glean anything from the online articles or the local newspaper. He knew that they wouldn't make it very far with information from the police station. It was pretty much the gas station that offered them the best shot at finding out what had happened. Or at least finding out what Dustin had been like.

Rhea sat in the passenger seat, reviewing possible covers for them to use. Miles had already made the point that just two random people asking questions about Dustin and his mother would come off as weird. Rhea was convinced that Miles should pass himself off as a journalist who was researching murder-suicides. He wouldn't lead with that, but he might as well go with it if it came up.

As they entered the gas station, they saw that someone had set up a little vigil in memory of Dustin. It was only a picture of Dustin, smiling ear to ear. There wasn't a shrine to Angela to be seen. There is nothing more heinous than a mother who kills her children. Not even a father who kills his children is frowned upon as much as a mother who does the same thing.

As he stared at the picture on the shrine, Rhea made her way to the counter and asked if she could speak with a manager. The young lady behind the counter rolled her eyes and turned to a man whose back was to them all.

"Jim," she said, "this lady wants to talk with you."

Jim turned to face them. He was in his mid-forties, looking tired, but seemed to understand that he should at least smile when talking to customers.

"What can I help you with?" he said gently. Miles could tell that he was somewhat emotional.

"We're here," Rhea started, but then she seemed to stall in mid-sentence.

"Hi, I'm Miles Trent," Miles jumped in, "and we're doing some research on the young man, Dustin Camp, who died a few days ago. Would you be willing to tell us about him?"

Miles had read the emotion on his face correctly because a few tears welled up in his eyes at the mention of Dustin's name.

"Are you with the police?" he asked.

"No," Miles answered him, "we're not with the police. I'm doing some research on cases of murder-suicides for a sociology study and wanted to speak with a few people who knew the victims well."

"Victim," Jim corrected his plural use of the word. "There was only one victim."

Miles nodded, "Do you mind if we ask you a few questions?"

"Sure," he answered. "We can talk in my office."

Jim led them past the bathrooms to a small door that opened into a windowless office. There were two seats on one side of the desk and a nice-looking swivel chair on the other. Jim went to that one and, with a wave of the hand, offered the other two to Rhea and Miles.

"What do you want to know?"

"It seems from everything that we have read and seen that Dustin was a well-liked teenager."

"He was," Jim shook his head, "he made us all laugh. He had ambition and was such a hard worker. It's a damn shame what happened to him."

"From what I can gather, it seems like everything points to his mother having a hand in this. What was your experience with her?" Rhea asked.

"Who are you?" Jim asked her politely, "I didn't catch your name."

"I'm Rhea," she answered him, "we're siblings. We do the research together."

"Oh," Jim seemed satisfied with that answer and thought for a few seconds about what exactly the question from Rhea had been. "Angela was his mother. I didn't interact with her much. She would drop him off and pick him up. On occasion, grab a drink from the cooler or a candy bar. She never seemed to have much to say. She was polite enough but never engaged in conversation."

"What type of conversation did you try to engage in with her?" Rhea asked. Miles cringed a little at the question because he knew that the answer was going to be shaded by the news that she had killed her son and herself. Had she asked him this question a month ago, he would have probably answered it differently.

"She was cold and didn't smile much. She'd say to him, 'I'll meet you in the car.' One of the last days that he worked, she forgot to pick him up, and he sat out there waiting for her."

"Was that the day that he died?" Miles asked Jim.

"No, it was a few days before. He'd worked about six days straight and was taking a few days off just to be a kid."

"Was there anything that day, other than Angela being late for him, that stood out as odd?" Rhea asked him.

"No."

Rhea was a little stumped at the finality of his answer. She was willing to let that go.

"Who was working with him that day?" Miles asked. "If you can remember, I know a lot has happened since then."

"Her name is Mindy," Jim said. "She spoke to the police a few times; she's not sold on the mother doing it. She thinks that the mother wasn't capable of such a thing."

"Do you have any way for us to contact her?" Rhea jumped back in.

Jim nodded and wrote something on a sticky note, handing it to Miles, not Rhea. "She's a college student who works here in the summers. She also works at the ABC and the Jamaican restaurant."

"Thank you so much," Miles said as he looked at the note. We're sorry for your loss; it seems that, from what we can tell, he was a really nice young man."

"Sure, as hell was," Jim whispered. Then he spoke a little louder, "He was a brilliant kid. Smart. To be honest, if you don't mind me saying, you remind me of him a little," he nodded at Miles. Miles had worried that it could happen, as it did when he had visited the Sharps in Oklahoma.

"Rhea said the same thing as we were looking at the shrine," Miles shot Rhea a quick side glance, hoping she would affirm that.

"Yeah," she said, "it's a bit spooky." Miles raised his eyes at her choice of words. It wasn't necessarily how he would have steered the conversation.

Jim seemed to agree with her. He stood up and extended a hand towards Miles, "I hope that helps with your research."

"Anything helps," Miles said as he took Jim's hand. "Thank you for your time."

Rhea extended her hand as well, and Jim looked at it for a second and then realized that he should probably shake hers as well. His seemingly dismissive attitude towards Rhea made Miles question his take on any female he would have spoken about.

Rhea and Miles left Jim in his office and made their way out through the aisles of flavored sodas and light beers. As they were walking towards the car, Rhea grabbed Miles's arm and squeezed it. Miles turned to look at her and saw that she was nodding her head to the small group of teenagers placing flowers at the modest shrine set up for Dustin. Rhea let go of his arm and walked over to the teens assembled at the shrine.

"How well did you know him?" she asked, not one person in particular but everyone in general. The crowd gathered around the shrine looked back at her with various levels of confusion or annoyance.

"He was in my AP Composition class last year," a young man answered her, "he was a really smart kid, and he was always so nice to me." A few of the kids nodded.

"Are you planning on attending the memorial service?" a young lady wearing a sundress and dark sunglasses asked them.

"We may," Miles asked as he came closer to the group, "we just arrived in town and couldn't avoid the news about this." Rhea shot him a glance as he said that, knowing full well that they weren't all that far away from where Jim could be standing, who they had just told that they knew about it.

"He was really sweet," the girl said to the two of them. "His mom was crazy, and it's so hard to believe that she would do…" She paused and sniffled, "I mean, I just can't believe that something like this would happen to someone here." Miles was intrigued by that statement. It was not necessarily the shock of the loss of life, but more of a shock that anything like this could happen to someone they knew in a place where they felt comfortable.

Rhea and Miles spent a few minutes talking with the teenagers, but it didn't give them any more information. It confirmed that the town had placed the sole blame for this tragedy on Angela Camp.

ᏨᏌᏍᎩ

Mindy answered the call after a few rings.

"Hello," she sounded tentative, "this is Mindy."

"Hi, Mindy. My name is Miles Trent, and I'm doing some research on Dustin Camp's death."

"I've already spoken to the police," she answered.

"I understand that, but I'm researching murder-suicides, and I would like to talk with you about the last day that you worked with Dustin."

Miles heard only her breathing on the other end.

"I'm pretty busy," was her flat response.

"I understand that, but Jim, your boss at the gas station, said that you have a different perspective than what we've been hearing."

"You've talked with Jim?" she asked him with some skepticism in her voice.

"Yes," Miles answered, "he gave us your contact information."

"Fine," she sighed. "I'm finished at the ABC this evening at 8. We can meet there in the parking lot after that. Do you know where that is?"

"Yes," Miles lied, but he figured they would find it. "I'll see you there."

Rhea raised her eyebrows at him with a questioning look. "So?" she asked him.

"She is done at the ABC at 8. We'll meet her in the parking lot there."

Rhea nodded, and Miles mused out loud, "It's odd that a daycare would close at 8 in the evening, right?"

Rhea giggled, "Miles, the ABC is the state liquor store, not a daycare."

Rhea drove them to the store. It was about five minutes before 8 when they pulled into the parking lot. There were only a few cars in the parking lot, one from Pennsylvania, another from Virginia, but only two cars from North Carolina. They parked their car and watched as two men came out of the store carrying a few bags and went to the Mercedes from Pennsylvania. A few minutes later, a college-aged man came out of the store carrying a bottle of tequila and hopped into the car from Virginia.

Miles saw an older gentleman flip the sign to "closed" in the store window a little before his watch read 8. About five minutes later, a young blonde girl came out of the door, saying goodnight to the man in the store. She looked at the two of them standing there and walked towards them with confidence.

"I'm Mindy," she said while looking at Miles, "you must be Miles." She said it as a statement, not a question.

"Yes, I am. Nice to meet you, Mindy," he answered. He was about to introduce Rhea when Mindy asked.

"Who's this?"

"I'm Rhea Baker," Rhea inserted herself into the conversation.

"She's my sister," Miles added, "and she is helping me with my research. I hope that's okay."

"That's fine," Mindy said. "Was only expecting one of you."

"Sorry, I should have said something."

Mindy looked at them both and shrugged. "So, how can I help you?"

"Jim told us that you were working with Dustin a day or two before he died."

She nodded her head, "we worked together on the last day that he was at the gas station. We were all confused when he didn't show up the day after the storm because he was very responsible."

"We have heard that," Rhea said, "it seems he was well-liked by everyone who knew him."

"He had a brilliant mind and a great sense of humor. I only worked with him this summer, but I feel a sense of loss. He's the first person I know who has ever died."

"I'm sorry about that," Miles said, "if you don't mind me asking, I noticed that you didn't say that he was murdered, only that he died."

"His mother didn't kill him."

"Why do you believe that?" Rhea asked her. "I know people," Mindy answered him. "She isn't that person."

"That may be true, but I can understand if people would need more than 'she isn't that person' before believing you," Rhea added.

"I know that this community sees her as some crazy woman who killed her amazing son. They say that she was a loner and that she wanted nothing to do with the people in this community. That may be true, but I've met her. She's been into the gas station; she's a customer at the Jamaican restaurant and here at the ABC. She is always sweet; she knows who I am and asks how I'm doing. She's a rarity. Most people ignore me."

"Look," Miles said gently, "I understand that. I can relate to having a feel for people. In my line of work, people are often great at hiding their inner demons in public."

Mindy rolled her eyes at Miles, reminding him that she wasn't quite grown up yet. He had hoped she would have more information than she had given them. Rhea must have been thinking the same thing.

"Was there anything at all noteworthy or odd about those last days?" she asked Mindy.

"Nothing, really. When Dustin left work that day, I saw him and his mother drive out toward the island as the storm was getting close. They normally need to board up the properties to minimize the damage."

"Did you see their car come back?" Miles asked her.

"No, but that was a surprisingly strong storm. Two tourists died in a flash flood near the inlet. I got back to my parents' place just in time to hunker down for the night. When I heard that he hadn't called in or shown up the next day, I worried that he had died in the flash flood."

Miles thought through the newspaper reports he had read. He and Rhea had decided not to ask the local authorities for information. Miles asked, "Do you know how they ended up finding Dustin and his mother?"

"Neighbors went to check on them and heard the car running in the garage; at least, that's what Jim told me."

After that, Mindy didn't have much more to add, and they thanked her for talking with them. She said she would let them know if she thought of anything else and asked if they were heading to the memorial.

As they got in the car after she left the ABC parking lot, Rhea said what Miles was thinking, "Let's go talk with the neighbor."

The next morning, Rhea and Miles drove towards Angela and Dustin's house. The destruction from the storm, while minimal, hadn't been completely cleaned up. It seemed that the further away one drove from the tourist areas, the less concern there was for getting things put back together. As they approached the driveway for Angela and Dustin's home, Rhea pointed out that there were a few candles still lit and cards and flowers along the side of the road.

As they passed the house, they saw that the police tape was still draped about halfway up the driveway and over part of the garage door. There didn't seem to be any police cars in the area, but they decided not to risk it. The closest driveway to the Camp house was approximately 300 yards past theirs. As they drove up the driveway to the house, they both glanced to the left to see that the view to the Camps was minimal at best.

You could make out the outline of a house through the trees and the undergrowth, and at night, it was probable that the light from the front porch and the light over the garage shone through, but to be able to see anything that was definite was doubtful.

"I can see why the police weren't all that interested in hearing what they had to say," Rhea said. "If I didn't know to look for a house over there, it wouldn't even register that there was one." Miles agreed with her, but just as he was about to say something, someone came out of the house at the end of the driveway. Miles half expected the person to be brandishing a gun, but instead, he was standing there holding the door open and peering out at them. Miles drove a touch closer to the house and put the car in park.

The man came out of the door a little bit further. The house looked run down, but was not in shambles, which was a good way to describe the man who started to talk to him.

"You Dustin's father?" he yelled from the porch to Miles.

"What did he just ask you?" Rhea whispered to him from inside the car.

Miles stared back at her in disbelief. "He asked if I was Dustin's father."

"Hey," the man on the porch yelled back to him, "did you hear me?"

Miles turned towards him, "I'm sorry. What did you ask?" Miles closed his car door behind him, and Rhea got out as well. They moved towards the man while Miles thought through how he was going to answer.

"I asked you if you were Dustin's father," he said, looking over at Rhea.

"No," Miles answered him, "I'm not his father."

"You look just like him." Rhea looked at Miles and raised her eyebrows at him, giving him a look that expressed a lot at once.

"That would make sense," Miles said, "I'm his half-brother."

"Huh?" he responded. "You all have the same dad?"

"Yes," Miles said, "and this is his half-sister."

"You just get here? He's been dead for days, said that they couldn't reach no kin of his."

Miles could sense that Rhea had tensed up at this line of conversation. Miles could completely understand why because he had just realized what he had done. As Miles stood there contemplating what he had just revealed to a complete stranger, the silence stretched further.

"Sir, we're sorry to bug you," Rhea started with an apologetic tone, "we were just asking a few people who knew him some questions. We've never met him. We only just recently learned that our father had fathered," it was Miles's turn to raise his eyes at that poor turn of phrase, "another kid. Do you mind us asking you what he and his mother were like?"

"Nah," he said, "come on up to the porch."

Rhea led the way as Miles fell into place. He seemed to be more taken with Rhea, so Miles felt that she was the key to this conversation going well. The porch was tidy and had a swing and a few lawn chairs on it. In between the lawn chairs were small little tables, all of which were empty but bore rings from where various bottles or glasses had sat too long in the muggy afternoon heat.

"Go 'head and grab a seat," he motioned to the lawn chairs. "Can I get y'all something to drink?"

"No, thank you," Rhea said, "we're on a tight schedule…"

"I guess you would be, with the memorial and all," he interrupted.

Miles just nodded, thinking that it wasn't exactly a lie, "I'm sorry," he said, "but I don't recall catching your name."

"'Cause I didn't throw it at ya, just like you didn't throw yours my way either," he smiled at Miles, who was unimpressed with his attempt at humor. "It's Jack, Jack Millward."

"My name is Miles Trent," he stood and extended his hand towards Jack Millward, who took it and shook it very firmly.

"I'm Rhea Baker," Rhea chimed in. She offered him her hand as well, and he took it gently and shook it.

"So, what can I help you with?" he asked them as he sat down on the porch swing.

"Do you think that Angela killed them both?" Rhea shot right to the chase.

"Hell no," Jack exclaimed, "not at all. But I'll tell you that Angela wasn't always the most together, and it doesn't surprise me at all that she left the car running."

"Wow," Miles responded, "why would you say that?"

Jack shrugged and looked at the two of them, "She was a bit, not to speak ill of the dead, ditzy."

"How so?" Rhea asked in a way that made Miles feel like she was getting defensive.

Jack must have sensed her annoyance, so he continued on with a bit of caution, "She called me a few times because she'd run out of gas. She forgot to change the oil in her car once, and it stranded her on the side of the road. I had to go grab Dustin from school. It was things like that, built up over time, that make you not surprised when something like that happens."

"So, she wasn't great with cars," Miles asked.

"No, she'd leave the lights on in parking lots, and I had to go give her a jump at least twice a year." Miles could see Rhea's face, and he was guessing that she was realizing that Jack was making a good point.

"What was Dustin like?" Miles asked Jack.

"Dustin," he paused for a second, and it was obvious that he felt some attachment to the young man, "he was special," he perked up a bit, "not like that type of special with extra classes and stuff, but special in that he was nice, and he was smarter than all get out. When my wife passed a few years back, he spent the whole summer checkin' in on me, making sure I was doing okay and stuff." Jack started to tear up and took a brief moment to gather himself. "It's a damn shame to lose such a fine young man."

"Do you mind if I ask you a question about the night that they died? " Rhea asked, breaking the solemn moment.

"No," Jack snapped back to the present, "but I might save you the breath. I didn't see them leave or come back. I just saw that the next day, it looked like the car was running in the garage, and I went to knock. When no one answered, I first called Angela, then Dustin, and then the police."

"How did you see the car running in the garage?" Rhea asked him.

"I was on my morning walk, and when I went by, I could hear it. I saw that the garage door was down. It just didn't sit right with me, so I thought I'd check. The coroner said they'd been dead for about 8 hours by the time I got there. Died in the middle of the storm."

Jack stared at the floor a little, lost in thought again. Miles felt that their time with Jack was over and that they should try to leave as soon as they could. He stood up to signal this to Rhea.

"Thank you so much," he said to Jack. "It really means a lot to us to hear you talk about him. It's all new to us, and it's hard to process it all right now."

Jack gave Miles his hand, and when Miles took his hand, he clasped the other hand around Miles's. "It's a damn shame that you two never met him, just a real damn shame. He would have been so happy to have an older brother and sister. I know he would have been."

Miles and Rhea thanked Jack again for his time and headed down to the car. Miles glanced as much as he could through the trees and brush, and yet he still couldn't make out any part of the house all that clearly. If someone had messed with Angela and Dustin, there weren't going to be any witnesses to it. Marcus Brent would make sure of it.

☙❦❧

That afternoon was the memorial service. Rhea and Miles met up in the hotel lobby. Miles hadn't brought any clothing for a memorial service with him, so they had to make a quick visit to a local men's shop to pick out an outfit. Rhea had helped him choose something that looked somber. Halfway through the shopping trip she realized he was letting her help but didn't actually need her guidance. She had chuckled to herself, but she was far from feeling joyful this morning. This was going to be tough, not because it was just a memorial service, but because they had spun two different stories out into the public, and they were going to need to tread lightly as they interacted with the other attendees. They had decided to arrive as late as they possibly could so that they wouldn't need to talk with anyone they had already met, yet wouldn't be coming in after the service started and making a scene. The parking lot was nearly full when they arrived.

As they entered the church, Rhea spotted Jack Millward right away. He was seated on the right-hand side in the front row. The seats next to him were filled by an elderly couple and a few other adults who looked to be a part of the memorial service. Rhea saw Miles scanning the room as well. His eyes seemed to focus more on the front of the sanctuary. She'd been so busy looking for the people that they needed to manage that she had missed the sight of the coffins at the front of the room. One coffin was smaller, and it was a dark wood color. On it lay one wreath, nothing else. The picture beside it was of Angela Camp, smiling, not looking like a mother who would have killed herself and her son.

The coffin next to it was the same color but longer. There was an array of flowers and wreaths laid around it. Dustin's school picture was next to it, and Rhea felt a little unsettled by the similarities between Dustin and Miles. She was sure that others would see Miles and make this connection as well.

"Mindy is about three rows back on the far left," Miles whispered to her, "and Jim, the manager, is about five rows back on the right side in the middle."

Rhea nodded and looked at the room. She thought that she recognized at least one of the students from the shrine, but she couldn't be all that sure. As she scanned the room once more, Mindy caught her eye and nodded at her. Rhea nodded back at her. The room was full of students and their families. Rhea wondered how many of the students in attendance knew Dustin that well. People love a tragedy and often show up en masse to observe one. As the service began, it was clear to see it would revolve around Dustin.

A few times, Rhea could see that Jack was looking around from his seat in the front. It was logical to assume that he was looking for the two of them, but they had placed themselves in a spot where it would be very difficult for him to see them. She seemed to be able to match most of the adults with the teenagers sitting next to them. Only a few older people were on their own, and Rhea wondered if they were teachers or folks who knew one or the other from work.

As people shared, Rhea's mind wandered. This trip to North Carolina had been a failure. Why hadn't they chosen to come here first? There were so many questions. What if Stacey had been more upfront with her? Could they have changed their plans? She felt angry at the time she had wasted trying to connect with that lunatic! Now, here they sat at the funeral of one of their siblings, and while she felt so much anger towards Stacey, it paled in comparison to what she felt towards her father, Marcus Brent. However, he had pulled this off, she would make him pay for it. Her impression was that Miles didn't need convincing anymore, either. It was time to make a move. She wasn't sure what that move was, but they would figure it out once they got to Philadelphia.

As she was lost in thought, the memorial service came to an end, and people began to file out, starting with the front row. Jack noticed them there and gave them an enthusiastic wave, causing the people behind him to look at them too. At least one of the people behind Jack glanced at Miles in a way that indicated a level of recognition. It was clear that his presence brought a level of confusion for some, which would only be compounded by Jack Millward informing those around them who they both were.

Once the first few rows were empty, most people began to file out of the side of the rows and head outside to their cars. Rhea stood to leave with the rest of the row they were sitting in, but Miles stayed seated, looking towards the front where the two coffins were. There were a few people who were silently standing there paying their last respects, mostly teenagers, except an older-looking lady dressed in a dark pantsuit. She stood by Angela's coffin and leaned over to look at the wreath. She could see that Miles had also seen her. The look on his face scared her; it was like he had seen a ghost. Miles grabbed her arm tightly and stood up, "We need to move," he whispered to her. "I'll tell you why once we're outside."

The two of them exited as quickly as possible and walked through the door into the parking lot. As their eyes were adjusting to the light, Rhea noticed that Mindy was making her way towards them. She was dressed in a very plain and modest black dress, with flat black shoes and a golden necklace. Her eyes betrayed the fact that she had been crying.

"Hey, you two," she said to them as she got nearer. "Do you have a second?"

"Sure," Rhea said, looking at Miles. He had turned to glance black at the door. He was worried and knew that Rhea was picking up on that.

"I know this might not be anything," she said, "but there was someone here today that I remember seeing a few days before Dustin died."

"I'm sorry, what do you mean?" Rhea asked her, and Miles directed his attention towards her.

"So, about two days before he died, this woman rolled into the gas station. She was definitely from out of town, dressed in a business suit, totally out of season for this area." At this piece of news, Miles glanced back at the door. "I wouldn't have thought anything of it, but she came in the next day again, but Dustin had already clocked out and was waiting for his mom to pick him up. I only remember her because of how out of place she looked and the fact that she asked me where my sidekick was."

"You saw that same lady here today?" Miles asked her with a sound of seriousness in his voice.

"Yes, she was here; she was at the end of the row, about two behind me. I saw her as I was leaving. I think she was trying to get to the front to pay her respects."

Miles's hand tightened around Rhea's arm. "Thank you," she said to Mindy, "that's really helpful."

"You're welcome," said Mindy, "it's so sad. I still can't believe that he is gone."

"I know," Rhea said as she tried to shake her arm free of Miles's grip. "Dustin sounded like such an awesome kid. You won't be alone in missing him."

Mindy nodded, then stopped mid-nod, looking past both Rhea and Miles. "Right there, her."

Mindy was pointing at the woman they had seen at the front of the church, who was looking at the wreath on Angela's coffin. She was pulling her sunglasses down onto her face. There was a fierce look about her, and she carried herself with a confidence that didn't seem to fit her age. She scanned the parking lot and looked right past the three of them. It seemed to Rhea that she had found who she wanted and started walking towards that person. It didn't take Rhea more than a second to realize that she was walking towards Jack Millward. Rhea glanced back at the woman, and suddenly her thoughts were filled with Stacey's description of the woman she called Satan. Was she just reading into it? Could this older lady be the 'fixer' that Stacey went on and on about? Miles grabbed her by the wrist again.

"We need to go now," he said politely, "or we're going to miss our flight." Rhea knew there was no flight, but she began to realize that Miles was not comfortable with where this woman was heading. Jack Millward knew who they were, and if that lady was who Rhea thought she was, that could be real trouble for them.

"Sorry again for your loss, Mindy," Rhea said as they began to walk towards their car. They hurried as quickly as they could without looking like they were running to escape. Miles unlocked the car from a distance, and they got in. They drove away as quickly as they could, but Rhea saw that the lady was talking with Jack, who was looking around the parking lot to locate someone.

As they pulled out of the parking lot, Rhea saw Jack and the lady approaching Mindy. If she had been uncertain before, she was sure of it now; that lady was Ms. Deavers, aka Satan.

Chapter Thirteen

Until an hour ago, Elizabeth had firmly believed that Dr. Abbott had only ever helped Angela Camp cheat and run away. Now, every case that man had been involved in was in question. Who else had he helped, and how in the name of God did she not have any clue that he did this right under her nose? This was the type of colossal screw-up that Harlan would have had her ass for. But Marcus was different. He wouldn't just have her ass; he would use another one of his people to "fix" her in the same way she had fixed so many other problems.

As she entered her hotel room, she ran through scenarios of what to do next. Between the girl, whatever her name was, and the old man, Jack, who was the neighbor, she was pretty sure that she was dealing with something deeper than just Angela Camp taking the money and the baby and running. If there were others, what were they going to say or do? What was the timeframe she had to operate in before this shit all hit the fan?

By the time Jack had pointed out who he claimed were the dead kid's brother and sister, it was too late. They had torn out of the parking lot. She didn't get a good look at them or at their license plate. When she talked with the young lady that Jack had said they had been talking with before they left, she said they were researching murder/suicides. Who should she believe? If she had learned anything from her inescapable mistake, then it was that it was always worth looking into something, even if it led to a dead end. If they were just researchers lying to some old guy, so be it. But if they were truly siblings to the kid and children of Marcus, then it was what she feared the most: that she had missed something. And that was a mistake that would cost her her life.

Fortunately, the young lady had remembered their names, but only the first names: Miles and Rhea. She seemed suspicious of Elizabeth, but after she showed her a phony badge she had with her, she became compliant. Now, she had a number.

Elizabeth picked up the hotel phone, not wanting to use her phone, and called the number. It rang and rang, and then the voicemail came on.

"Hi, this is Rhea. Leave a message."

"Damn it," Elizabeth whispered to herself as she hung up the phone. "Guess I'll be doing this the hard way." She dug out her computer and opened it up. It took only a few seconds to find the information she needed. She typed in the number and, with a few checked boxes, got the information she was looking for. She drew in air through her nose and sighed it out. Her worst fear had been realized, the name Rhea Baker.

She was, without a doubt, the daughter of that writer and activist, Ellis Baker. The first one. It took only a few more keystrokes to find that information as well. She was about the right age, but the information didn't give her an exact date of birth. She pressed on. Ellis Baker's obituary referred to a daughter who survived her but did not mention how old she was. Rhea was a professor at Portland State and seemed to be pretty successful as a writer as well, but there wasn't much else available about her, specifically her exact age, which is what Elizabeth needed to know.

Elizabeth remembered Ellis well. It was during that weird phase that Marcus Brent went through when he thought he could be a tree-hugging socialist. Marcus Brent knew there were a few things in this world that would drive his father to an early grave. One of them was if his son became an activist or a "red"; Marcus knew this and was pretty hell-bent on giving Harlan a coronary. That motivation, coupled with feeling like the women associated with these movements were wilder and more open to experimentation, was pretty much the only thing that had attracted him to that group in the first place, and led him to encounter Ellis Baker.

He met her at a crazy party on the beach. He had been scheduled to attend a financial meeting set up by his father. Instead, he stumbled upon a group of college-aged environmentalists smoking pot and summoning the spirits of the beach, and Ellis Baker was their leader. It was Marcus Brent himself who had told Elizabeth that Ellis was pregnant. Thus,

Elizabeth was called into action for the first time. Thankfully, she already had a plan in place.

Ellis had looked down her nose at Elizabeth when she showed up at her door. She had moved out east in the month after her fling with Marcus Brent and had gotten in touch with him via a letter. Marcus was scared, but he hadn't been privy to the same information that Elizabeth had been. He didn't know, at that point, that her job was to clean up these types of messes. Elizabeth had shown up with three plans to enact. Plan one was the only plan she had to present because Ellis had no desire to have a future capitalistic despot— her words exactly.

And yet, Elizabeth found herself looking at the picture on the website for Portland State, and she was pretty damn certain that those features could have only come from one person. Rhea Baker was Marcus Brent's daughter. It took her one glance to see through the hole in her bulletproof plan from years ago, which meant that Ellis must have bailed on the procedure, and Dr. Abbott had lied to her.

"Damn it," she said out loud, "he lied to me from the get-go." Her voice fell flat in the hotel room. There was no one there to hear the confusion and the fear that mixed with those words as she spoke them into reality.

She sat there silently, running scenarios through her head from situations close to forty years ago. She couldn't recall anything that would have made her suspicious of Abbott. Nothing that made her think he wasn't doing what they were paying him to do. Angela and Ellis both seemed to have gone along with the plan quite easily. What had Abbott said to them when she wasn't present in there? She had never questioned, not even once, his insistence that she was not permitted inside the office when he performed the abortions. She had assumed it had to do with medical sterilization policies. Now, she was wondering if there was a different reason for that altogether.

She picked up her cell phone. The voice on the other end of the line sounded like his father, Saul. "Barton," she barked, "I need you to do some research for me."

"You got it, boss," he replied, as usual.

"I'm going to send you a list of people. I need to know everything about them," she spoke firmly.

"Everything," Barton repeated. "Okay, I'll look into those names. In the meantime, something just came up out in LA."

"What do you mean by *came up*?" she asked.

"Yesterday, a woman came into the offices asking to speak with Marcus," he paused. "Claiming she was his daughter."

Elizabeth felt that gnawing feeling in her stomach. "Why am I just now hearing about this?"

"She said she had proof," Barton continued, "but just not on her. We were waiting for her to bring it to us."

"What's her name?" Elizabeth interrogated further.

Strings of transparent beads lined up on her confident face. She could feel her heart accelerating.

Barton's voice forced itself into her ears. First as a whisper, and then as clear as day.

"Lillian Marsden," Barton seemed to be reading it from a piece of paper. That last name rang a bell, and uneasiness washed all over her body.

"Damn it," she said to him, "I'm coming back. I'll send you the names and then get your ass on the company plane with the information and come pick me up. I'm not fucking driving out to LA."

"You got it, boss," he repeated. Elizabeth had never wanted a protégé, but Saul had insisted on it, given her imminent retirement. She was a bit annoyed, and in the end, it was his son that he had hired.

She hung up and opened her secure email and sent him Rhea Baker's name and, on a whim, Betsy McDonal, the second person she had taken to Dr. Abbott.

Elizabeth sat down on the edge of the bed and, for the first time in decades, felt a wave of anxiety. Hopefully, Barton could use his connections to obtain more information. She was slipping, and Saul Traeger was the one person who knew whose fault it had to be if a child had made it into the world.

Elizabeth stood. Her fear was not going to get the best of her. She was capable of taking care of this mess, and damn it, she was going to do what it took. She closed up her computer, slid it into its travel case, and finished packing her room.

Dustin and Angela Camp.

Rhea Baker.

Miles. She wasn't sure of his last name, but her list was short.

Now a young actress in L.A.

It was abundantly clear that she had missed something all those years ago, and now it was up to her to right the wrongs of the past. One last time, she was going to be getting her hands dirty, and then, hopefully, she would be away from the Brents for good.

She sat down and stared out of the window. She needed someone to blame. She needed to pin this on Abbott, but that was going to be impossible without him, or at least his dead body. She could paint the picture that he lied and hid these things from her. That would take some of the heat off of her. Yet she could already hear the ghost of Harlan reminding her that she had an important job to do, and that was to clean up one specific type of mess. What was she thinking, not ever checking up on these ladies afterward? Was she honestly that delusional to believe that these women would just go along with anything she told them to do?

The short answer was yes. While she would be reluctant to say that she was delusional, her own opinions on that matter may have clouded her judgment. Having met Marcus Brent, she couldn't understand why anyone would want to sleep with him, let alone have his child. He was a teenage dirtbag in a middle-aged man's body. His treatment of women was horrible, and he couldn't be charming for more than an hour before he inevitably started acting like a misogynistic asshole.

❦

He handed her a folder and motioned for her to board the plane. As she settled into her seat, she opened it. Inside was a picture of Lillian. Elizabeth looked at it dismissively. *She came across like every aspiring actress in Hollywood—a generic, pretty American girl.* The only physical attribute that set her apart from just another face in the crowd was the distinct resemblance she had to Marcus' daughters.

According to the information in the folder, Lillian was demanding an arc on Marcus' reality show. She had pitched how to introduce herself and everything. Elizabeth rolled her eyes and looked up at Barton.

"Is this the first time you've experienced something like this?"

"No," he responded, "people are always showing up, claiming that they're his illegitimate children."

"Why, then, is this one any different?"

"Like I said on the phone, she claims to have actual evidence," he pointed to the folder clasped in her hand, "medical records that say that her mother was paid to have an abortion."

Elizabeth rubbed her temple with her fingers. She could feign absurdity, but she was too tired to pretend. "Would you be surprised if it turned out to be true?"

"No," he said calmly. "I would not be surprised."

"Why is that?" she asked him.

"They wouldn't bring you and me in if there wasn't a possibility of it being true."

Elizabeth closed the file. Her scan of it revealed that Lillian was only claiming to know about her own case. She mentioned nothing about anyone else.

"I don't see any of the records in this file. Did she not bring them with her?"

"No," he sighed as he said it, meaning he had probably already told her this. "She claims to have access to them, but she wanted assurances that she would be cast in the reality show before she brought them."

"And what did they tell her?"

"They wanted her to come back with the proof before they would promise her anything."

"Let me guess. She said no."

"That's correct. But they convinced her to come back tomorrow for a meeting with you."

"They told her I was the casting agent, didn't they?"

"Yes, that's the angle we're presenting."

"And you, are you, my assistant?"

"No," he smiled, "I work in the legal department. I'm there to make it seem like we're willing to work with her."

"Got it," Elizabeth said, looking out of the plane window. During that brief conversation, they had already taken off and were ascending to their cruising altitude. The more information she was able to cull from her files, the more insight she would have. At this point, Lillian hadn't revealed that there were more kids. It was a move that didn't surprise Elizabeth. She was angling for her own 15 minutes of fame, and she was willing to share that with anyone else.

Barton cleared his throat, and Elizabeth looked up at him. "Yes?"

"I'm going to go out on a limb here," he said to her, "but I am wondering if this has anything to do with Dr. Abbott in Philadelphia?"

"Why would you think that?"

"Well, he was just passed over as the candidate for Surgeon General when Mr. Brent gets elected. He has a motive to release information like this."

"Motive," she paused, "that he does have. But this young lady would have been born when Mr. Brent was nowhere near considering a political run. I'm curious, did she happen to mention the name of the doctor that her mother went to?"

"No, but as you can see, she said she was fairly certain that her mother was in Philadelphia at the time she got pregnant."

Elizabeth nodded, "That would point to Dr. Abbott." She knew damn well that it was Dr. Abbott. She had taken Lillian's mother, Stacey, there. *Marsden,* that was why the name was so familiar. It was all coming back to her, which was saying something, given that it was more than 20 years ago.

"Did you know Dr. Abbott?" Barton asked her, a question that immediately put her on alert. Barton may well be training to take over for her later, but he could also have instructions to deal with her as if she was a mess to clean up as well.

"Yes, I did." She replied, her voice steady but monotonous.

"Do you think he could be behind this?" he asked her as if trying to dig into something.

"Yes, I do," she decided not to be coy. Instead, she was going to throw him off a bit. "He always seemed a bit too compliant. Then he began working directly with the family, and that seemed odd."

"What do you mean directly?" he asked, narrowing his eyes.

"That's above your pay grade," she smiled at him. "Nevertheless, I think the sneaky little doctor is a good place to start looking. As for Ms. Lillian Marsden, well, let's see how much she's willing to budge when we dangle what she wants right in front of her nose."

"My guess is she will be quite willing to talk. She's been out here for almost 3 years and has only had small background roles. This would open doors for her."

"Hope always motivates," she said. So does fear, she thought. For her personally, fear was always the greatest motivator. And she feared it was becoming apparent that she was to blame for this.

"It does," Barton agreed. "But this only ends one way."

"Yes, it ends only one way, but we'll need to cover our asses," her tone was now colder.

She opened the file he had given her. "This is everything," she asked him.

"Yes," he confirmed. "Not much on Betsy, and only a little bit more on Rhea Baker."

"When we get back to LA, can you check Rhea Baker's travel history?" she asked Barton.

"I can," he said, "how far back?"

"Only a few weeks," she said. "Also, check to see if anyone named 'Miles' was booked on a flight with her?"

"Sure," he said, confusion written over his face. "Why are these people of interest to you?"

"Possible connections to Dr. Abbott," the half-truth coming off her lips so easily. "They may be able to help us figure out where Lillian got her information from."

"Got it," he said. He leaned back in his seat and looked at his phone.

"Are you having trouble connecting to the Wi-Fi?"

Barton glanced up from his phone, "I haven't tried to connect to it. Flights are my only time to not be connected," he held up his phone to show her the video game he was playing.

Elizabeth leaned back in her seat and let her mind run through the details for each of the eight women she had escorted to Dr. Abbott, but the details were foggy. She needed data in front of her to jog her memory. It was going to take everything in her to remember back to the days of Ellis Baker when she was a lot younger. A lot younger and, if she was honest, a lot more exasperated with the fact that Marcus Brent's dalliances were keeping her busy instead of the more interesting political aspects of clean-up work.

Then, as she racked her brain for the details of the past, it dawned on her. A simple truth before her eyes. She never followed up. Never. Not once. Her job ended as soon as Dr. Abbott told her the procedure was done. She deposited money in their banks within the week, and then she was on to the next thing. Never once did she ever think to question the loyalty of Dr. Abbott. She just went on with her job. Marcus made a mess, she cleaned it up, and Harlan stayed happy. Most important, Harlan kept the damning evidence of her negligence locked away.

Boredom crept in, and she picked up the folder containing the information about Lillian Marsden. They had already completed thorough research on her. It looked like she had recently auditioned but hadn't gotten a role. That might have been what pushed her to play this angle. Elizabeth sat there running through all of the scenarios for this interrogation. Her main goal was to gain a few more names from Lillian, ones that lined up with what she had learned in North Carolina. Then she could nail Abbott, but not before. She didn't want to rouse any suspicion from Saul or Marcus or now Barton.

The next steps were completely dependent upon this young, ambitious lady. The quicker she talked, the quicker Elizabeth could move on to the next cleanup. If Barton was right and Abbott was behind it all, she could use that to her advantage to keep the heat off of her.

As she began to regret her negligence, it hit her. Fate had given her a chance to make things right. Fate had allowed her to run into Marcus Brent's younger double at a gas station in North Carolina. Had she not had that miraculous encounter, she would have come into this situation completely blind. Now, she seemed to be one step ahead of the game.

Chapter Fourteen

Simon had been sitting in the living room for hours in his deep leather chair, his left leg crossed over his right, his argyle socks bouncing up and down. Rhea hadn't come up for air since coming through the door. Rhea's experience with Stacey, combined with their experience in North Carolina, had made her more anxious than ever. Every sentence was filled with a heightened sense of urgency, and every action item was couched in an amount of intrigue. How should they proceed? What were they going to do *if she* came after them — or, as Rhea put it, *when she came after them*?

"We should never have told any of them our real names," she sighed, looking at Miles. "If she is who we think she is, then she'll be able to connect the dots."

"We don't know that, Rhea," Simon said calmly, "and even if she finds out your names, it will be very difficult for her to do something to two higher-profile figures like you and Miles."

"Dad, that doesn't make sense," Miles countered. "She made Angela and Dustin's murder look like an accident. There is no reason to believe she couldn't do the same to us."

"In theory, yes, but in reality, she doesn't know about me. And if she does, she isn't going to attempt to take care of me before she takes care of you."

"Oh, that's comforting," Miles said sarcastically.

"You two have a few options. First, you could take the information that you have and give it to the press. Let them publish what you have and put Brent's people on notice. If your names are out there, and something happens to you, then people will be suspicious for sure."

"I don't want to do that, Dad," Miles jumped into the conversation while standing up from his seat. "We need to talk with Elliot and see if we can find Abbott. Until then, we don't have anything. I don't want to put more people in danger without them knowing what's happening."

"But it looks like we've already done that," Rhea added.

"There's no way that we had anything to do with what happened to Angela and Dustin," Miles sighed, feeling like he was a broken record as he and Rhea had had this same conversation more times than he could count. Now, she was saying it just to have Simon weigh in on her theory.

"Rhea," Simon said with some semblance of composure, "I understand why you would feel that way, but there is no way anyone knew you were looking for them. And while we're on it, Ms. Deavers might have just been there because she was checking in. It wouldn't surprise me if she attended the funerals of the other ladies that died, including your mother's."

"To see what," Miles asked plaintively.

"I don't remember her being at my mother's funeral," Rhea said.

"Nor do I recall anyone at my wife's funeral," Simon replied calmly, "but why would I have? I didn't know any of this, so I would have never thought that the people at the funeral whom I didn't know could have been someone like Deavers tying up loose ends."

"That could be the case for you, too, Rhea," Miles added. "The issue at hand isn't so much what could have happened in the past, but what we need to do right now."

"Go to the press," Simon repeated his suggestion.

"Maybe, but not until we talk with Elliot," Miles answered him. "We need to see how many of us are willing to tackle this thing, head-on."

"That's fine," Simon said, "but right now, it's just the two of you. Lillian and Stacey are out, right?"

Rhea and Miles nodded simultaneously. Simon couldn't help but smile at this rhythm.

"Stacey," Simon continued, "seems unlikely to come around. And if she does, she would most likely hurt your case more than help it."

"No kidding," Rhea whispered.

"As for Esme," Simon turned to Miles, "she seems to be happy staying put and off the radar."

"She said no," Miles confirmed, "but I don't think it was a solid no."

"Why not?" Rhea asked.

Miles thought about it for a few seconds, but wasn't sure how he would explain it. He felt like he'd made a connection with Esme. A connection that he could in some way use to help her change her mind.

"Just a gut feeling," is what he landed on.

Rhea and Simon both looked at him quizzically. Miles wasn't going back there again, especially not after what happened with Angela and Dustin. He couldn't risk someone finding out where Esme and Esperanza were.

"For what it's worth, you two," Simon sounded official, "you need to have a plan of action. If I were you, this is what I would do. First, prepare something that could be sent to the press. Include your names and all the information, and explain the situation. You're both writers, so this shouldn't be that hard. Second, get on that plane and talk to Elliot. See if he's on board with going public with this information. Best-case scenario, he comes with you. Finally, find the doctor. Which is exactly where I can help you."

"No," they both said in unison, but Miles responded the loudest. "You're not getting involved in this, Dad."

"I'm already involved in this, Miles. I've been involved since the day you showed me that USB in your kitchen in Berlin. I'll admit I pushed you to do this. Now, I need to step up and play my part."

"You can't blame yourself for this either," Rhea retorted.

"I'm not," Simon smiled, "I'm saying that this got kicked off because I pushed Miles to dig deeper. What hasn't registered with you two yet is this: I've connections throughout Philadelphia. Heck, I've got connections *everywhere* that I can put to use. I've a better shot at finding this, Dr. Abbott, than you do. He's going to run from you, but not necessarily from me."

"He knows who you are," Miles said, "your name was on the list in the file."

"Miles," Simon continued, "it doesn't matter if he knows my name. I've been a lawyer longer than you've been alive, and I can find out his whereabouts."

"Then so can they, Dad!"

"Not before I do," Simon said confidently. "You two need to head to Africa, talk with Elliot, and then come back here and start getting this story out there before something else happens."

"I understand," Miles hoped his voice didn't betray his skepticism. "Our flights are this coming Friday. Until then, we'll work on our story for the media, and maybe we can get in touch with Lillian and see how she's doing or if she's heard from her mother yet."

"I doubt Stacy's checked in with anyone," Rhea said, tucking her leg under her. "I tried to call Lillian since we landed in North Carolina, but she hasn't returned any of my messages."

"I'll try to be in touch with Esme again before we head out to Burkina Faso. It would be great to contact both of them before we leave."

"I would agree," Simon nodded, "make sure they're on board with you all proceeding with or without them."

"It will be without them," Rhea replied. "Though I wouldn't be surprised if Lillian uses this to further her career."

Miles tensed at that comment. He felt like Rhea was right. Lillian came across as an opportunist. Esme, on the other hand, wasn't anything like that. His thoughts led him back to his visit with her. Esme had a quick wit and knew what she wanted. It was a wit that challenged Miles in a way that no one had challenged him before. He felt drawn to her. The only issue was her relationship with his biological father. He wasn't sure if he would be able to get over that in the end.

⋈⋈⋈⋈

The next day was a flurry of activity as they prepared to leave the country for a week. Miles needed to stop by Penn and catch up with colleagues and see what his fall semester would look like. His lengthy sojourn in Berlin had left him feeling disconnected from Penn, but his colleagues and friends had already been in contact with him since his return and expressed their excitement to have him back lecturing and teaching. It was hard for him to reconcile these feelings, one of disconnect and another of acceptance.

Rhea's inability to get in touch with Lillian gnawed at him. He was almost certain by now that she was in trouble— a dread he didn't want to carry with him to Burkina Faso. Yet, he couldn't shake the feeling that Lillian had tried to use this situation to get her foot in the door in Hollywood and that she might have had a run-in with Ms. Deavers. He wondered what Ms. Deavers would do to Lillian if that really was the case.

Miles walked out of his room into the hallway at his place. It was quiet here. The tenants who had rented the house while he was abroad had treated it well, but Miles noticed the wear and tear of the last few years, and it bugged him. They were only little things, but they were his belongings. A new wobble in the banister, a nick in the lower cabinet under the kitchen sink, and a faint fishy smell in the refrigerator, that nothing could completely get rid of.

Being back in the house was putting a damper on the task at hand. He would rather stay here than jet off to Africa and who knows where else, chasing down leads and avoiding what seemed to be a nefarious hitwoman. It wasn't what he wanted, and it felt like this was the last safe place he had. Sooner or later, his lineage and whereabouts would be out there, and then what? Was he to run? Was there a way to avoid being hunted? Was he just overreacting about this whole thing? Was it such a big deal that Marcus Brent sired kids out of wedlock?

Miles had acknowledged that the answers to those questions were only beginning to scratch the surface of what was truly going on. Marcus Brent had paid them to abort babies. They had lied and run off with his money, and the Brents didn't take well to being deceived. But was killing their solution? What ideology was even behind such a course of action?

Esme had a straightforward explanation for all of it: the Brent family was evil. *Spawns of Satan* might have been her direct quote. Miles had never imagined that anyone could be that evil, but the facts pointing towards the strange death of Angela and Dustin seemed to say something else. Miles began to wonder if his mother's death, as well as Rhea's mother's death, had kept them from the same fate that befell the Camps.

Last night, he spoke with Jennings. It sounded like they were about to meet the son of Marcus Brent, who most resembled him in action and attitude. Miles could tell that most of what Jennings said was tinged with a deep hurt due to the ways things had played out after his sister-in-law's death. Marcia, who did her best to stay positive about Elliot, even gave the impression that Miles was about to meet a young man as amoral as they came.

Miles sighed. Esme was a hard loss for them in this battle. Elliot may be a loose cannon, and that could hurt them more than help them. Miles hadn't shared any of this with Rhea. Having gotten to know her over the last few weeks, he realized it was better for him to keep things to himself.

Last evening during dinner, Rhea had teared up while talking about their time in Ocean Isle Beach. Over and over again, she'd said how she just couldn't believe all that had happened. Miles knew that she was processing this all in a way that would either propel her to quit or strengthen her resolve to take Marcus Brent down. This is why he had decided it would be better for him to muster the positivity she often had. After their experience in Ocean Isle Beach, it wasn't a given that Rhea would be the positive one anymore.

That evening, as Miles welcomed Rhea and his Dad into his house, he could see in her eyes that she was nowhere near ready to quit. She was all charged up to fight.

She hugged him tightly and asked about his time at Penn that day. Then, he forcedly gave in to the moment.

"It was nice to be back," he told them. "My fall looks interesting."

"How so?" his Dad asked him. It was the first conversation between the father and son, apart from everything that had been happening since Marcus Brent and their mission came up.

"I'll be sitting in on two different dissertations and teaching two new courses," he answered. "They were pretty interested in my trip to Burkina Faso next week, but I played that off as information gathering."

"Well, that's not really a lie," his Dad replied as he slipped off his shoes.

They went into the kitchen where Miles poured a glass of wine for each of them.

"How was your day?" he asked them. Simon and Rhea looked at each other.

"You go first," his Dad nodded toward Rhea.

Miles mindlessly held out a glass, lost in his own thoughts, as Rhea reached for her wine. The information that they had found snapped him back to the present quickly.

"Lillian called off her last two shifts at the bar," she said worriedly.

"Okay, did he say that something felt off to him?" Miles asked, a bad feeling brewing in his gut.

"He said he couldn't say concretely, but he felt something wasn't quite right with her when she called. Then, she didn't enter her availability for this week, so he thought something might be up. I asked him if anyone had been in to see her since we were there?"

"He remembered us," Miles asked her.

"He did," Rhea answered, "but there's more. He said that just a few days ago, he wasn't sure if it was Monday or Tuesday, a lady came into the bar looking for Lillian. He said she was frantic and looked strung out."

"Stacey!"

"That's my guess. He didn't get her name; he just said that she was super agitated and was going on and on about her being in danger. He said at first that it didn't bug him; it's normal for people like that to wander into the bar, and apparently, Lillian is known for giving them food and water, but after Lillian didn't put in her availability for work, he got nervous."

"Has he done anything about his hunch?" Miles wondered.

"He's tried calling her, just like I have, but nothing so far."

"Best case scenario is that Stacey found her and whisked her away," Miles said.

"No way Lillian goes with her," Rhea responded. "No way in the world."

"Should we go out there and see what's going on?"

"You can't," Simon interrupted their exchange. "It's more imperative for you to talk with Elliot. And before you say you should split up, Rhea, I'm going to make my feelings clear. You both need to go and meet Elliot. We don't know how he's going to react to Miles, and maybe he'll take better to you."

Miles nodded, mostly because he couldn't think of what else to do. He knew he didn't want to meet Elliot alone, but he was also worried that something had happened to Lillian, and someone needed to look into it.

"We can't just leave Lillian in limbo," Rhea said, rather calmly considering the situation.

"We won't," Simon responded.

"No way in hell you're going out to LA, Dad!"

"That wasn't my plan, Miles."

"Thank God! Then what was your plan, Dad?"

"I've a friend out there who can look into it for me," Simon said.

"Adam," Miles asked him.

"Yes," Simon answered him. "Since you visited him out in L.A. he's checked in with me, he's willing to help however he can."

Miles didn't spend a lot of time in his younger years thinking about Simon's job, but as he got older, he realized that his Dad had abundant connections. Mostly, they investigated large corporations. Some of them were good at finding things out very discreetly. Miles was grateful that his Dad was willing to leverage these connections to help them out now.

Over dinner, the mood was much less solemn than they'd all expected. Simon laid out his plan to figure out where Dr. Abbott was and how he could be in touch with him. Miles gave them information on what to expect in Burkina Faso, but left out what he knew about Jennings's assessment of Elliot. Miles wanted Rhea to think the best of Elliot. He was their last shot at winning over one of their newfound siblings before they would have to decide to take on Marcus Brent alone.

Chapter Fifteen

Elliot hung up the phone. His brother and sister had made it to the ride he had arranged for them. Matt was a bit of a wheeler and dealer and would try to fleece them when they arrived, but he was safer than most of the alternatives. They'd be arriving in the next five hours. He had been grateful that Jennings had sent another telegraph the day before announcing that Miles, the name of his brother, would have another person with him, his sister. No name, just "your sister."

He played over and over the words on the wire from a week ago. It didn't matter how often he told his Dad that he didn't pay per word, he still kept it short. This was one time when longer would have been better. You have the same dad…the line kept rolling over and over again in his head. If his Dad thought the man was nice, then this couldn't be something bad, right? Why the urgency, though? Why come to find him in the middle of nowhere? That didn't make sense.

ભ⁸જ⁸⁸ભ

Elliot thought back to that day. It was the middle of his summer break, and he remembered his Mom being a little tense and on edge about something. As he came in from the field with his Dad, he saw a car that he didn't recognize and, as always, realized it was his Aunt Hannah, who couldn't keep the same car longer than a year. His Aunt seemed frantic and somewhat perturbed at everyone, even him. His Mom was holding her arm and keeping her from moving towards them. She was yelling something, but Elliot couldn't really make out what it was until they were closer. His Dad told him to stay put on the tractor until he came to get him.

Elliot stayed in place for exactly three seconds and snuck off the tractor towards the front porch where his Mom and Dad had gone with his Aunt Hannah. He could hear them, his Dad using his commanding voice with her and his Mom reminding her over and over that this was not the plan. His Aunt Hannah kept telling his Dad it was beyond important for him to know. He couldn't go on living his life in ignorance. He was an heir to a kingdom! His Mom's voice petered out, and before he could begin to shuffle back to the tractor, his Dad rounded the corner.

As they climbed onto the porch, Elliot remembered having heard how he was an heir to a kingdom at vacation Bible school and Sunday school. That made sense to him, but for some reason, his 13 years on this earth made him pretty damn sure that wasn't what Hannah was talking about. His Dad's hand never let go of his shoulder, but he pushed Elliot towards his Aunt, who looked disheveled and had a crazed look on her face.

"Fine," his Dad grunted, "tell him. Tell him and then leave like you always do. He's not going to fucking believe you anyway."

Elliot was taken aback by his Dad swearing, especially in front of him. What was his Aunt going to tell him…and why wouldn't he believe it when she did? His Aunt grabbed his arm and pulled him to the front porch, which overlooked the entrance to the farm from the county road. He sat himself down on a chair as his aunt leaned against the railing of the porch, leaving her somewhat backlit from the Oklahoma sun.

"I don't have any easy way to say this," she began. "I know I'm not around and that I don't hold any amount of sway with you, but what I'm about to tell you is true." She paused for a minute. "Elliot, I need you to believe me. Tell me you will believe ME," she raised her voice to yell. "Tell me you will believe me!"

Elliot remembered pausing and then uttering that he would believe her, knowing deep down that anything that was being stated hysterically could only be a delusion or part of her "problems," as his Dad called them.

"It's about your father," she said in a calmer manner. Elliot pitied her at that moment. He was sad for his aunt, who was so easily calmed by a 13-year-old's lie. A lie that had to seem obvious. Yet she continued as if he had given her the utmost of honor by believing her hysterical rantings. He would never see her again after that afternoon. While that was sad, he had barely ever seen her before that either. She was a mystery to him, and her arrivals and departures were never whimsical or sweet. They were always hectic and frantic.

"What about my Dad?" Elliot turned his face back to see his Dad standing at the edge of the porch, his Mom burying her face in his chest. The panic in him rose quickly. What was wrong? What couldn't they tell him that they had to bring Aunt Hannah to tell him?

Elliot looked back at his Aunt, and something came over her face. He wasn't sure what exactly, but it was like she realized something. She lifted her hand and pointed at his Dad, "That's my sister and her husband," she started, but Elliot wasn't sure why she was stating the obvious. He'd known this his whole life.

"Aunt Hannah," he said tentatively, "I know that. You're my mom's sister." Elliot was so afraid that she was having a breakdown on the porch, but he couldn't figure out why his parents were letting it happen.

"I'm not your aunt, Elliot!" she had screamed at him. Her voice carried across the porch, "I'm your mother!"

Elliot sat in stunned silence. The volume of her voice rang in his ears. The force of her statement, even from three feet away, stung his body. He looked at her sideways and turned his face towards his parents.

"Elliot, stop looking at them! Look at me!" She reached for his hand with hers and clamped down on it, which made him turn back to her. "I'm your mother."

Those words splashed onto him like the lye they used to paint the fence. They stung and burned. Of all the people in the world that he didn't want as a mother at that moment, his Aunt Hannah was one of them. He said nothing, and again, he looked toward his parents. It was their faces that told Elliot that what he was hearing wasn't the ravings of some lunatic woman but was instead the truth.

It was that day that Elliot had felt the most alone in his whole life. It was the day that shattered his family picture forever.

ⳓⴲⴳⳍ

Elliot shook himself from that memory. He was sixteen when it all finally made sense, but by that point, it didn't matter. Hannah, his mother, was dead, and his Dad and Mom were still his Dad and Mom, but he also knew that they were biologically his Uncle and Aunt, and that had eroded every ounce of trust between them. It was what had propelled him to sign on with the civil engineering corporation digging wells in Africa. Trust was hard to break when there were no lines of communication. He had always hoped it would stay that way.

The sound of trucks arriving always preceded their actual arrival. There were a few gates to drive through, but most days, they were left open, so it wouldn't be long before they would be there. He was about to meet his brother. His mother had always said that she didn't think he was the only one. Guess she was right about that.

As the truck came into view, Benjamin walked up behind him.

"Everyone is ready, Elliot," he said to him. "Scott is to be back by dinner. Did you tell him?"

"No," Elliot shook his head. "I didn't want to talk about it."

"Dat is no surprise," Benjamin laughed.

"Can you make sure the driver doesn't cheat them?" he asked Benjamin.

Benjamin nodded his head, and as the truck came to a stop at the end of the compound, he moved towards its window. Elliot could see that the driver was talking with his brother, and his brother was shaking his head. Benjamin rapped on the window to get the driver's attention. When he put down his window, Benjamin launched into a long speech. Matt, the driver, had a long history of driving people to the compound, and that history always meant dealing with Benjamin.

Elliot understood only a few words of the tribal language. He knew he was telling Matt he did not need US Dollars. As the two spoke, Elliot stood back and observed the two people in the back. Miles, who had contacted him, seemed a little anxious. The woman, whom he had figured was his sister, seemed panicked. They looked like siblings, and while he wouldn't say that looking at Miles was like looking in a mirror, he had to admit he thought they looked like brothers.

Benjamin switched to English, "You can give him what you were planning."

Matt seemed to disagree with this statement, but Benjamin hushed him with a look.

Miles handed over the money, and they opened their doors. As they were doing that, a few of the other men, mostly the kitchen workers, were grabbing their luggage from the back of the truck. Dust seemed to pour off their suitcases as they did. His sister seemed disconcerted by it.

"My name is Benjamin. Welcome to Burkina Faso."

Elliot moved towards the three of them. They were thanking Benjamin, who was looking back at Elliot.

"Elliot," he said to them, "you have visitors."

Miles moved towards Elliot with his hand extended while his sister stood behind, not moving as quickly. Her eyes were searching his face, and it made Elliot uncomfortable.

"Elliot," Miles said to him, "I'm glad to meet you!"

Elliot took Miles's hand in his, "I'm not sure if I'm glad to meet you." He looked past Miles to the woman behind him. "And who are you?"

She walked forward and put her hand out, "I'm Rhea Baker," she smiled at him, "I'm your sister."

"Welcome," Elliot said, "now how the hell did you find me?"

"Your Uncle told me where you were," Miles began, "I would have contacted you myself, but he was pretty sure you would have ghosted me."

"Damn right," Elliot responded to them. "Benjamin," Elliot turned towards him, "can you take their luggage and get it cleaned up? Then can you bring it to my room?"

Benjamin nodded, but it was clear that he found this meeting of long-lost siblings intriguing and would have rather stayed.

"You don't have to give up your room," Rhea said to him.

"It's the nicest one," Elliot shot back, a little annoyed at her attempt to act like she didn't want to impose.

"It will also be safer for you to stay with your brother," Benjamin said to her, "and Elliot's room is the only one with two beds."

"It's a futon," Elliot added. "Let's head to my quarters to talk about this," he said to the two of them as he turned to walk past them.

Elliot led Miles and Rhea to the end of the block building. He opened the door for them to enter his living quarters. He noticed that Miles was only focused on him, but Rhea took in the room. Her eyes glanced over the door to the bathroom, the single bed in the corner, the small kitchenette and dining table, and the couch and chair.

"Have a seat," Elliot said, motioning to the couch. "If you need to use the bathroom, it's through that door right there," he pointed to the door directly across from the entrance to the room.

"Thank you," Rhea answered, "I'll take you up on that."

"Can I get you something to drink?" Elliot asked as Rhea headed for the door to the bathroom. No answer came from either of them. Rhea had the door closed before he could finish the sentence, and Miles was immersed in the map on the wall.

"What's this?" he asked Elliot.

"It's a map of the area surrounding the well. It's to give us an idea of which villages it will be able to functionally serve."

"Interesting," Miles answered. "What drew you to this line of work?"

"Getting out of fucking Oklahoma," Elliot answered.

Miles chuckled. "I can understand that, having visited your family farm." Miles moved towards the couch to take a seat. "How long have you been at this site?"

Elliot sighed, "About five months."

"How much longer will you be here, in your estimation?" Miles asked him.

"God only knows," Elliot sighed and pulled out a seat from the table to sit on. "We've had some issues with locals sabotaging our equipment. It seems at least one tribe is not happy that we're going to be building a well in the area."

"Why's that?" Miles asked.

"Because they have the only functioning well in the area, and they charge a pretty penny to draw from it. It's why we chose to build here."

"It offers these smaller, most likely poorer, villages a basic necessity without fleecing them," Miles concurred while slightly intoning a question.

"That's correct," Elliot answered as he turned the chair from his table to face the couch. He looked at Miles thoroughly, and he could see it. They were built similarly. Miles had dark hair, while Elliot's was closer to blonde. Their eyes were the same shape, which Elliot's research had shown him was also true of their biological father.

The door to the bathroom opened, and Rhea came out. "Thank you so much," she said. "Those roads were rough, and I've been trying to stay hydrated."

Elliot glanced at Rhea as she sat down next to Miles. There they were. Three bastard children of America's biggest asshole.

"How was your flight?" Elliot asked.

"It was fine," Rhea answered, "thank you for arranging a ride for us."

"Well, as far as rides go," Elliot began, "I found you the one least likely to rob you blind."

"I caught that he had a different idea of what we owed him," said Miles.

"Let's just say it could have been way worse," Elliot countered.

"Why's that?" asked Rhea, looking less relaxed than before.

"He could have had his men hijack you," answered Elliot. "Would either of you like that drink now?"

Elliot could see that Miles realized he was trying to warn them. They were out of their depth coming here. And truly, he hoped that they were reading between the lines. Elliot didn't want them wasting his time.

"I'll have some water if that's alright," Rhea answered.

"How about you?" Elliot asked Miles.

"Do you have anything stronger than water?" he answered, making it clear to Elliot that the realization of what he'd shared had sunk in.

"I got a bottle of Jack," Elliot answered, "but no ice. Neat, okay?"

"Guess it'll have to be," he responded. Elliot chuckled and went into the kitchen to grab the water and the whiskey.

"The electricity here is a bit spotty, so I need to keep the fridge stocked with things that won't go bad in case it shuts off." He pulled out a bottle of water from the fridge. "You become used to it after a bit," he said as he pulled out his bottle of Jack from behind a bowl on the shelf. "The generator has enough power to run the office and the shared kitchen, but not all our individual rooms. Because of the kitchen, I don't need to keep much in the way of food here. Mostly just water," he poured some whiskey for Miles and then himself as well. He observed the two of them, wondering when they were going to break from this shallow small talk and get down to business. They just sat there nodding their heads, saying nothing. He handed Rhea her water and Miles his whiskey. They thanked him. "It's a different world than Oklahoma, that's for damn sure," he added.

"It's a different world from anywhere I've ever been," Rhea added.

Miles seemed overwhelmed. He took a silent sip of the whiskey, looked into it, and then looked up. Elliot could sense he didn't know where to start.

"Well, I'm guessing you didn't fly halfway around the world to hear me prattle on about wells and semi-functional refrigerators. So, what's the urgent request that had to be told to me in person?" Elliot asked.

"It may have been too dangerous to send electronic correspondence," Miles began.

"Why?" Elliot threw back the remaining whiskey. "If they can track email and wired messages, they can sure as hell track you flying here."

"We can't take any chances," Miles said. "We just came from the funeral of Dustin and Angela, and now Lillian is missing."

"You say those names like I should know who the hell they are," Elliot shot back at Miles. "You're going to need to assume I've no clue what you're talking about."

"Dustin was our brother," Rhea said, making a gesture that included all of them. "He was only 18. Lillian is your sister; she's about two years older than you."

Elliot noticed that Miles was still reeling from his last sentence. His brashness towards him seemed to disarm him slightly.

"And how do we know that has anything to do with us?"

Miles stared at him, and Elliot realized that he was being an ass, but if these two had something to say, then they had better spit it out! Especially if his biological father had figured out that he existed.

"Fine," Elliot shrugged, "here's what I know. I'm Marcus Brent's son. My mom was Hannah Vaughn; she's dead. Died in a fire, which I assume my Uncle already told you. I was raised as their son to hide me from Brent, but as far as I know, he's never had any idea who I was. I found out when I was 13 that he was my father and that everything in my life up to that point had been a lie. I freaked out, acted out, and then got the fuck out. I thought I was fine until my Dad, I mean my Uncle, sent me a damn wire about you," he pointed at Miles, "and that you're to be trusted."

"I can be trusted," Miles said to him.

"Fine," Elliot said flatly, "then prove it. I've shown you my cards; you show me yours!"

"Well, I was working in Berlin," Miles started, "and just before I returned to the States, I received a USB stick in the mail. On that stick were the names of six women, including notes on what was to have been done and what did happen."

"My mother was to have an abortion," Elliot said very casually. "I know this part."

"Really," exclaimed Rhea, "how?"

Elliot crossed his legs at his ankles. His arms were crossed high on his chest. He sighed and then looked at Rhea. "As I said before, my mother told me!" He knew now he was being an asshole, but he didn't have time for this. The dig was a mess, and Scooper was going to be back soon, and he needed to talk to him about his trip. This was one more annoyance he didn't need or care about. He could tell that Rhea was a little hurt by his tone, so he continued while trying to soften his delivery.

"I thought it was bullshit because mostly she talked about this type of bullshit all the time. She was crazy. Until the day she told me, I thought she was my crazy Aunt Hannah. My Dad, who's really my uncle, was pissed at her for telling me, and that's what made me realize she was actually telling me the truth. If it had been more of her normal bullshit, then my Dad would have waited for her to finish, swooped in, and comforted me. That time was different."

"What exactly did your mother tell you?" Miles asked him.

"She had met my father at a fundraiser she was working at. She had checked people in for the event, and he chatted with her on the way in. Later, one of his bodyguards came by to invite her to join them. She partied, they fucked, and she got pregnant. Pretty basic."

Miles nodded while Rhea sat there looking at him, her pain replaced with pity. Elliot hated pity. If his sister knew what he was really like, she would not pity him; she would pity Marcia and Jennings.

"She realized about three months later that she was pregnant. She didn't call anyone and said nothing to the father. But about a week after finding out she was pregnant, a random woman showed up at work and asked to speak with her. I don't remember the lady's real name; I was thirteen and reeling from what she had just told me. Whoever this lady was, she was authorized to take my mother to a doctor in Philadelphia, and there she would have a procedure done, and then she would sign some papers, and they would deposit money in an account for her to withdraw."

"So, what happened in Philadelphia?" Miles asked.

"Her version," Elliot smiled, "she fucked over Marcus Brent for knocking her up and forcing her to have an abortion."

Rhea raised her eyebrows. "That's what she told you?"

"She was crazy," Elliot said, "she said a lot of things and used a lot of colorful words. The reason I can't remember the lady's name who showed up to take her to the doctor is because my mother referred to her the whole conversation as *that bitch*."

"So how did she end up screwing him over?" Miles asked in a placating manner that annoyed Elliot a bit.

"Well," Elliot looked at Miles and deliberately and somewhat mockingly continued, "she screwed him over by taking the money and keeping the baby."

"Do you know how she pulled this off?" Rhea jumped in.

"With the help of the doctor would be my guess. She never told me anything about that part."

"Did your Aunt or Uncle ever elaborate on it?" Miles asked, "I mean, did they know the whole story?"

"Yes, but not at first would be my guess," Elliot answered with a shrug. "What they knew was that my mother got pregnant and that she was very scared about what would happen to the baby." Elliot paused for a second and noticed that his big toe was moving quickly, and it was causing his leg to shake a bit. "It's complicated and hard to explain, but whatever she said to them scared them too, and they agreed to be my parents. She would only visit once in a while, just in case someone was following her."

"How did they pull it off?" Rhea jumped in with a question Miles already knew the answer to. Jennings and Marcia had told him all about it. How they had spirited Hannah and Marcia off to relatives in Iowa, and when they came back, Marcia was a mother, and Hannah wasn't on the radar. With the healthcare system in Oklahoma not being the greatest, most people applauded Jennings for sending her to relatives to be cared for.

"If Miles has talked with my par…," Elliot stopped short. It was the first time he had slipped up during their conversation, "My uncle and aunt, then he knows the story."

Rhea looked at Miles, and he nodded, "I'll explain that later."

"Listen, Elliot," Rhea said to him in a way that he imagined big sisters generally spoke to younger brothers. "This has become serious. That lady, we believe her name is Deavers, and from what we can tell, she does clean up for the Brents."

"And?" Elliot asked.

"And," Rhea's inflection gave away the fact that she expected him to connect the dots on his own.

"We're all going to end up in the crosshairs if we don't come together and expose what has gone down," Miles said to him with a stern tone.

"And what exactly is there to expose?" Elliot smirked. "Have you ever thought that our mothers didn't want that information out there? My mother was scared shitless of what Marcus Brent could do. What about your mothers?"

"They're dead," Rhea said. "Both a long time ago."

Elliot again realized that his tone had been hurtful, and he was slightly mad at himself for not controlling his words. "I'm sorry," he said to her. "Listen, you two, I understand what you're saying.

I understand that this kid and his mom dying, this other lady missing, that all seems to point to Brent cleaning up his messes, but my understanding is he had no idea we existed."

"He didn't," Miles said, "he still might not, but it seems the woman who was responsible for taking care of the messes seems to know that we exist and have lived a life longer than we were supposed to."

"She knows about you two," Elliot asked him.

"We can't know for sure," Rhea interrupted, "but we saw her at Dustin's funeral, and she saw us, and unfortunately, we let it slip to a neighbor," she glanced at Miles, "that Dustin was our brother."

"Okay, so what," Elliot interrupted, "did the neighbor talk to her?"

He could tell by the look on their faces that she had.

"Fuck," he sighed.

"Here's the thing," Miles started again, "she may still believe that you're Marcia and Jennings's son, so you may be safe."

"And you want me to put myself in danger to take him on? To what end," Elliot was heating up again, "from what I read here, he could murder puppies in front of a crowd, and those whack jobs would still vote for him."

"Not if they knew the truth," Miles said.

"You're naïve," Elliot shot back at him.

The rest of the conversation was a back-and-forth. It was clear what they wanted, but he was positive that it wouldn't help at all. The idea exhausted him and felt like a waste of his time. Yet, as he talked more with them, he felt a bond between them that could only be explained by their connection—a familial connection. For him, having a brother and a sister didn't change much. He wasn't going to go back to the States with them, but on the other hand, their sincerity made him feel less alone in this world. It was hard to put into words; these were complicated feelings to work through.

As the day wound down, it was apparent that Miles and Rhea were growing tired. Elliot knew that they would need to eat and go to bed soon, as the flights to Ouagadougou were long and tiring.

"I'll let the two of you freshen up for dinner and settle in here," Elliot interjected into the conversation. He was hoping they would get his point that he was done talking…for now.

"Where are you going to stay?" Rhea asked.

"I'll bunk tonight with Scooper."

"Scooper?" Miles asked.

"Scott Cooper," Elliot began, "is the other American working on this site. We met at Oklahoma State, and we signed up for this job together."

"When do we meet this Scooper?" Rhea asked.

"He's due back for dinner." Elliot couldn't recall if he had let the mess hall know two more people would be joining them, but then remembered the kitchen guys helped unload the bags. "I'll go grab your bags and have them brought here," he said as he headed to the door. "Dinner is in about forty minutes."

Elliot didn't wait for a response; he simply headed out the door. As he stepped out onto the covered breezeway, he saw Benjamin at the end and walked toward him.

"Everything alright?" he asked Elliot.

"It's fine," Elliot lied, "is Scooper back?"

Benjamin raised his eyebrows, "he just got back from the western villages."

"I'll go talk to him. If you don't mind taking their things to my room," Elliot said, "I would be so grateful."

"No problem," Benjamin replied.

"Don't let them tip you," Elliot said, "it will feed into their savior complexes. God knows you make more than I do at this job, they should be fucking tipping me."

Benjamin laughed at him, "Elliot, Elliot, Elliot," he muttered.

"What," he glared at Benjamin.

"Always hiding his feelings behind da nasty words," he walked towards the two suitcases that were sitting near the office.

"Take them their things and make sure they have anything that they need…if we have it."

Elliot walked out from under the breezeway and headed across the compound to where the trucks were parked. He could hear Scooper before he saw him.

"Scooper," Elliot called to him as he walked up. "How was the visit?"

"Fine, but it sounds like I should be asking you how your visit was," he smiled. He was a short, muscular man with tanned skin and the bluest eyes. His hair was light brown, and the mustache he wore made him look older, even though he was only 23. He came over and hugged Elliot. "Everything okay?" he asked, concerned.

"No, is the right answer, but it's also an overreaction," Elliot answered. "We have guests tonight, so I'll be staying with you."

Scooper nodded his head as he raised his eyebrows. "Sounds okay to me," he said.

Elliot's room had a single bed and a couch, but Scooper had a double bed. It was a room that Elliot was no stranger to. He and Scooper had shared it a few times in the months that they had been there because of investors visiting the site. Elliot always gave up his room and stayed on Scooper's couch. Those nights were the nights that Elliot felt the least alone out here. And tonight was one of those nights when he didn't want to be alone in his room or even alone with his thoughts.

"They'll be joining us for dinner tonight," Elliot said, "which I'm sure is going to bring up more questions than answers." Elliot put his hand on Scooper's shoulder and looked him in the eyes. "I promise I'll explain it, but it may take a while."

"That's the Elliot I know," Scooper giggled, "bottling up all these emotions and waiting until later to deal with them."

Elliot took his hand off Scooper's shoulder and smiled. "That's the cowboy way."

Elliot made sure that Miles and Rhea were set and then grabbed his few things and went down to Scooper's room. He opened the door and saw that Scooper was pouring some whiskey in the kitchenette. He stood there in his khaki shorts and nothing else.

"I poured you one, too," he said.

"You're the best," Elliot said as he set his stuff on the end of the couch, slipped off his flip-flops, and unbuttoned his shirt. Scooper moved out of the kitchenette and over to the couch where Elliot was sitting. Scooper could walk so quietly that he often ended up scaring the shit out of people. It was one of his favorite things to do in college with the new kids on the floor.

"Do you want to tell me about it," he asked Elliot, "or are we still doing this the cowboy way?"

"Yes," Elliot answered as he took a sip of whiskey, "but I need a minute."

"I get that. I'm going to jump into the shower," he nodded, turning his head to the bathroom. "Once I'm done there, we can talk."

"Thanks," Elliot answered. Of all the people that Elliot knew, Scooper was the only one who had ever seen him with his rough-hewn facade down. This year of digging wells had broken him often, and Scooper helped him put the pieces back together. Elliot heard the shower go on and took a sip of whiskey. He took off his shirt and laid it over the back of the couch. He was going to need something stronger than whiskey.

He got up from the couch and began to walk through the apartment. He knew that Scooper had so many different hiding places for his contraband, but Elliot was only looking for one thing: his weed. Weed and whiskey, he kept thinking, just like good old Willie Nelson. He moved through all of the usual places but didn't find any. Scooper had some chocolate in the compartment in his fridge, and Elliot grabbed it and lay down on the bed.

Scooper emerged from the bathroom just as Elliot's eyes were beginning to close.

"So, do we want to talk about this now?" Scooper asked Elliot. "Or should we wait until after dinner? What were their names again?"

"Miles and Rhea," Elliot rolled on his side to face him, "They're my half-brother and half-sister."

"No flipping way," Scooper whispered. "Miles and Rhea?"

"Yes," Elliot answered, "and it gets more complicated."

"That's impossible," he said as he patted himself dry and stood there naked under the fan.

"There are more than just us three," he said plainly.

"Sperm donor," Scooper asked.

Elliot rolled his eyes. "One way to look at it." Elliot propped himself up on his elbow and looked over at Scooper. "What I'm about to tell you needs to stay a secret. You understand?"

"What, you suddenly don't trust me?" Scooper feigned hurt.

"You know what the fuck I mean," Elliot said. "Unless I say so, it goes to the grave."

"Hundred percent," Scooper said, sensing the seriousness of Elliot's tone. He grabbed his boxers from the dresser and started to put them on.

"My biological father doesn't know I exist because he paid my mother to abort me so it wouldn't stand in the way of his political career."

At that moment, Scooper's face was a mystery to Elliot. He stood there staring at Elliot with confusion and shock, all rolled into one look.

"Did they tell you that?" Scooper asked as he moved Elliot's feet so that he could sit on the end of the bed.

"No," Elliot answered, "I've known that part. My mother told me that when I was thirteen."

"So, Jennings isn't your dad?" Scooper asked Elliot in disbelief.

"No, and Marcia isn't my mother; they're my Aunt and Uncle."

"Then, who's your biological father?" Scooper's face was awash with intrigue and anticipation.

For the first time since he was thirteen, Elliot said the name out loud. He'd said it in his head a million times since that fateful day. He'd said it every time he'd Google searched the asshole, but always with an undertone of disbelief. He'd been horrible to his Dad and Mom for years, but there had never been a doubt that, although it was hurtful, they loved him as their own and had only wanted to protect him.

Scooper looked at him in sheer disbelief, "damn it, Elliot, your daddy is going to be president!"

"God, I hope not," was all he could say as Scooper jumped off the bed and finished getting ready for dinner.

☙❧☙❧

Elliot slipped out of the room later in the evening. The desert air was still warm, and it encompassed him as he walked out the door to smoke a cigarette. He stood at the edge of the concrete that was laid in front of the row of rooms and leaned, fully naked, against the post. Benjamin had said that the local tribespeople had seen him doing this once or twice and had taken to calling him the white devil.

"Why the white devil?" he had asked.

"Because you're white," Benjamin said bluntly. Elliot shrugged at that, and Benjamin continued, "You exhale smoke into the night, and your hair is all crazy and looks like horns."

It was a fair assessment. Being the devil hadn't helped them any with this project. It seemed no one was willing to do anything without them greasing a few palms along the way. He took a drag on the cigarette, held it, and spewed it out. As he did, he heard the door open from his room, which gave him a start. It hadn't dawned on him that there was now a woman on the premises and that she might happen upon his nightly cigarette in the buff.

"Oh, sorry," he heard Miles say, and he heard him begin to shuffle and turn away.

"No worries," Elliot said, "luckily it isn't our sister."

Miles paused, and Elliot sensed that he was turning around; Elliot hadn't bothered to turn and look at Miles, thinking that it would probably make things a lot more awkward if he did.

"Listen, Miles," Elliot spoke out into the darkness hanging in front of him. "I can't figure out what possessed you all to come out here and talk with me. There are other ways to get hold of me."

"I know," Miles answered, "but we just felt that this would be the best way for us to be off the grid."

"You keep saying that," Elliot said as he turned to face him. Miles still had his back to him, "but it seems to me that you're in danger, and I'm not."

"I feel like you aren't getting this, Elliot. We had a younger brother," Miles said with a deep sadness in his voice. "He's dead now, and we're sure that Brent had something to do with it."

"Sorry," Elliot said as he exhaled. "That sucks."

"It does, he was only 18."

"Fuck," Elliot felt a twinge of loss and sadness, "his poor mom."

"She's dead too," Miles said, "like we said earlier."

"So, they're hunting us," Elliot said. "Sounds like I made the right choice in coming here."

"Is that why you're here?" Miles gestured to the compound, but Elliot knew what he meant by here.

"I've known since I was 13 years old, Miles. You just learned this, when? A few weeks ago? A few months ago?"

"A month and a half ago."

"Doesn't matter; it still isn't that long of a time to know. You and I, well, we're brothers, biologically, but how has that changed your life, knowing that a bastard like Brent's your father? Has it improved things? Because from where I stand, it looks like it's made things worse."

"It has," Miles assented, "but…" he paused as he looked Elliot in the eyes.

"Did you grow up thinking your Dad was really your dad?"

"No, I knew that my Dad wasn't my biological father," Miles answered him.

"You know my story, Miles. You know that my whole life got flipped upside down the day I found out. I suddenly had absolutely no one I could trust! Not a single one of them!" Elliot felt the emotions of what he was saying, and his voice was trembling. He had to get it together before he woke the others. "Miles, you saw where I grew up. Marcus Brent was never going to find me there, even if he did have my mother killed. They had no reason not to believe that I wasn't a Sharp."

"I know, but Elliot," Miles started, but Elliot held up his hand to stop him.

"Miles, I didn't leave Oklahoma to get away from a man who didn't even know that I existed. I left because I couldn't be around people I couldn't trust."

"You can trust me, Elliot," Miles said to him. He knew that Miles was being sincere, but it was easy for someone like Miles to say that. Miles had never had his trust so seriously broken. Yet, a deep part inside of him longed to trust somebody again. He spent so much time avoiding trust, even with Scooper, that the mere mention of it scared him shitless.

Elliot looked at Miles, who had locked eyes with him. "Can you trust me, Miles? Do you even want to trust me?"

"I do," he said calmly, "you're my brother."

"I'll only disappoint you, Miles, brother or not. Elliot Sharp only looks out for himself; I've got no room to look out for anyone else."

"That's a lonely way to live your life, Elliot."

"Don't I fucking know it," Elliot broke eye contact with Miles and walked to his room.

Once he was inside, he searched for his boxer shorts, pulled them on quietly, and sat on the couch staring into the dark of Scooper's room. He could hear Scooper breathing softly on the bed. Scooper would definitely want to see him step up and take on this monster, his father.

Well, he thought to himself, Scooper's going to be disappointed.

ເຊຍ∞ເຊ

The next morning, after breakfast, Elliot gave Miles and Rhea a tour of the compound. Rhea shocked him with her understanding and her questions. She was wiser than half of the idiots they sent out to the sites to check on their progress. Miles nodded a lot, but Elliot knew that he was giving him some space. He was dealing with the disappointment of their conversation. He knew that Elliot showing him and Rhea the work that kept him here in Burkina was his way of saying, no, you're on your own.

While they got ready to head back to Ouagadougou, Elliot spent some time making sure they were checked into the right hotels and that the people there would make sure they got to the right places for dinner and then, ultimately, to the airport. He had just hung up the phone with a young lady at the hotel when he realized that Miles was in the office with him. He swiveled in his chair to face him. Miles sat across from him, not more than four feet away, and yet between them stood not just diagrams, work orders, legal papers, and a full ashtray but the space of emotional distance.

"Will you come back and help us?" Miles asked him straight out.

"No," Elliot answered him as he leaned forward, placing his elbows on the desk. "You don't need me."

"That couldn't be further from the truth," he said, and Elliot felt that Miles truly believed that.

"Here's the thing, Miles," he paused for a second to make sure that he was going to say it right, "I believe you. I believe that Marcus Brent, our biological father, forced women to have abortions. I believe that you're right and that the doctor helped our mothers keep us. Yay!" he said somewhat sarcastically, "and my google search of you says, that we should thank that doctor because you and Rhea have been successful."

"That's not what this is about," Miles jumped in.

"Let me finish," Elliot said, "there is more."

"By all means," Miles leaned back into his chair, "don't let me stop you."

"I believe that my Aunt and Uncle meant well, and I do think one day I can forgive them for the way I found out. I believe, with my whole heart, that they were all looking out for my best interest and that they loved me like their own. Hell, they still love me like

I'm their own. I look at what you're telling me about this poor kid, Dustin, and his mom. I believe that shit happened, just like you think it did, and that makes it even more possible that my mom was killed for similar reasons. I believe all of this stuff. You'll leave here with Rhea, and I'll talk about how my brother and my sister were here on a trip to visit me. I'll eventually come around to grieving for a brother I didn't know, as much as you can grieve in that situation. That all being said, I don't have anything else to offer you other than the fact that I believe it all."

Miles looked at him and waited a few seconds to see if he was done. Elliot looked at him and said, "You can say something now if you want."

Miles shook his head, which, if he was being honest with himself, hurt Elliot a little. He wanted some words tossed back at him. Some amount of retort or pithy wordplay to try and put him in his place, and all Miles did was shake his head. This must be what it was like to have a brother, he thought to himself.

"You believe me," Miles shook his head. "I guess that's all I could ask for, and yet somehow, coming from you, I feel like that's the biggest cop-out. You believe me." Miles stood up from his chair and turned to leave. Elliot prepared himself for a verbal barrage, but Miles didn't even turn around to address him; he just asked him, "When does our ride get here?" and left without ever hearing the answer.

ଔୠଏୠ

Rhea hugged him and kissed him on the cheek. "I'm sorry you can't come with us," she said to him. "Please keep in touch."

"If I don't, I've got a feeling you will," he told her as she let him go. He looked at Miles, who had made sure that the luggage was loaded and had just tossed two bottles of water into the back seat of the truck.

Scooper was talking with him, but Elliot couldn't quite hear what they were saying to each other. He was sure that it wasn't anything of consequence. Yet, it bugged him that Miles and Scooper were talking with each other so naturally and without any constraints. He didn't feel like that was possible for him and Miles, at least for right now, and it was odd to him that he'd feel bothered by it.

Rhea had walked over to Scooper and enveloped him in a hug, which he ate up. Scooper had acted more like their brother than he had. Scooper had been so gracious to them, listening to their stories and asking questions while he'd sat about, resenting the disruption to his life. As he watched Miles walk towards him, he noted that it was Miles who was taking the steps to say goodbye to him, and that he was standing still, not moving. He wasn't even going to meet him halfway. It was so typical of him. Push anybody away the second they seem like they're in a place to penetrate his walls, his layers of protection. It was unfathomable to him that in the 48 hours they had been together, Miles could have had that effect on him.

Elliot reached out his hand to Miles, but Miles pushed it aside and hugged him. Tight. Squeezed in a brotherly embrace. Elliot, at that moment, felt held. Felt protected.

It was a hug that only a brother could give you. That would be how he'd describe it later to Scooper when he asked, because Scooper would ask. It disarmed him as he stood there, and then Miles said to him, "We're family. You can't change that, but you can help protect it. Please reconsider."

Elliot hugged him back, wishing that he could change his mind. Unfortunately for him, it was too late; he was too far gone down that path of self-preservation. He was for himself, and that was it.

As they drove away, Scooper waved until they were out of sight. Then he turned to Elliot and looked him in the eyes. Scooper's cheeks were tear-stained, and his eyes were still watery. Elliot could see the disappointment. He could see the sadness. He knew that Scooper was going to hound him for the next few days.

"What," he said to Scooper with a shrug.

Scooper shook his head, similarly to Miles, and walked away. Suddenly, Elliot wasn't such a fan of being on his own.

Chapter Sixteen

Elizabeth looked at the notes she had written for herself on the flight. L.A. was her least favorite place to work. The traffic was hell, the people were fake, and without fail, always mistook her for some sort of talent scout. The number of times she had to look at a waitress or barista and tell them she wasn't an agent was ridiculous. That wasn't the worst part of it; it was just the annoying part.

This young lady, Lillian Marsden, had shown up, and now things were looking worse than they had been before. Up to this point, Angela and Dustin, hell, even Hannah in Nebraska, had stayed off the radar of Saul and Marcus Brent. A young lady showing up, claiming to be the daughter of Marcus Brent and saying she had proof, made its way to the higher-ups. At this point, she felt there was no need to mention two more possible children. She wasn't sure of that herself. At least, that was the lie she was telling herself.

What she knew for sure, she had written down on a note. She looked it over.

-Hannah Vaughn had died in a fire. (Which was an unhinged story, which involved one of Marcus's former bodyguards, Mike Davidson. He lived, she died.)

-Ellis Baker had died of cancer.

-Angela and Dustin had died of carbon monoxide poisoning.

-Melanie Chinook, a lady with five children who had passed away in a car accident, along with two of her kids. (Which was NOT Elizabeth's doing.)

-Sophia Bonarzo, a Brazilian journalist, who she'd seen at least two other times at events, but she had always steered clear of all of them and had no children.

-Esme Conners, the Hispanic one, who took the money and ran, where to, she didn't know.

That left two more. The nut job drug addict and the quiet, reserved one, whom Marcus Brent may have had feelings for, at least for a few seconds. She would have been only a year after Rhea Baker's mother. She looked at her files. The old man and the college girl both said that his name was Miles, but they both had two different stories about who they were. The old man thought they were Dustin's siblings, and the college girl thought they were investigative reporters. Either way, problems, but the gut punch was knowing that, most likely, the old man was right.

Stacey Marsden would be Lillian's mother, the girl she'd be meeting at an office in L.A. If her hunch was right, that made the young man with Rhea, the son of Betsy McDonal. She entered the name Miles McDonal into the search bar. There were no entries for him. If he was Betsy's son, he might have a different last name. She googled obituaries for Betsy McDonal, and all the variants, but nothing specific came up. She may not have included her maiden name in the obituary. In her analysis, Miles may be the least of her worries.

She was getting closer to cracking this open, but what exactly could she do once she had succeeded? Without Dr. Abbott, she had no one but herself to blame this on. She was scheduled to meet Lillian in the morning, so she needed to figure it all out tonight.

In the morning, Barton picked her up. He was wide awake and seemed ready to take on the world.

"She's scheduled to arrive in about an hour, which should give us some time to make sure we have our ducks in a row," he said to her as he pulled away from her hotel.

"We don't need to hash it out, Barton," she said. "She'll either give us the information freely, or we'll get it out of her. After that, she's just another mess that needs to be cleaned up."

Barton nodded and then cleared his throat, "I'm guessing you want me to do that."

"If you don't mind," she smiled.

"You said you wanted to dangle some hope in front of her," he said to her. "What are you thinking?"

"I'm going to offer her a role on the show," she said, looking out the window as they drove. "Have her tie up loose ends here so that no one comes looking for her anytime soon, and then," she paused.

"Clean up," Barton finished.

"Exactly."

"In other news," he said, "I just got a text from Greg, and he said that the DNA test confirms it."

Elizabeth panicked a little bit inside but knew it was important not to show it when she asked, "Did he let your dad know?"

"I don't think so," Barton said casually. "Not how Greg usually works."

"Okay," Elizabeth said, "I'll read him in on these new developments the first chance I get unless you want to?" Elizabeth knew that was the last thing that Barton wanted. Saul Traeger was not exactly the proud papa and constantly bad-mouthed Barton behind his back, and to his face.

"No, you can do it," he chuckled, "I'm not scheduled to see him until Thanksgiving dinner, and I'd like to keep it that way."

They drove on in silence. At the Brent headquarters, they traveled to the fifth floor and took on their roles. They were the only two who would be dealing with Lillian. Someone would meet her at the front desk and hand her off. That was when Elizabeth would take over and hopefully get to the bottom of everything quickly.

About an hour later, the elevator door opened, and out stepped Lillian Marsden. She looked like she was one of Marcus Brent's own daughters. She was slender and tall with beautiful features. She must have been a shitty actor if she hadn't been cast with those looks.

"You must be Lillian," Elizabeth said as she walked towards her.

"Yes," she smiled, "Lillian Marsden."

"You can call me Lizzy," she sneered, "I'm in charge of casting for the show."

"Hi, Lizzy," she smiled back, not knowing what was going on inside the head of the lady in front of her. Elizabeth could see the confidence in her building. She had taken the bait, and now they just needed to land the fish. Barton was sitting in the conference room. He had his feet up on the table and was leaning back in his chair, talking on the phone.

"Well, you tell her that litigation is a bitch," Barton was pretending, "and we'll squeeze every penny out of her by the end of it." He pretended not to notice them entering the room. He nodded his head, "Make it happen," he said loudly, and then pretended to hang up. Elizabeth noticed that Lillian had tensed up.

"Bart," she said with a smile, "you remember Lillian, right?"

Barton stood up and walked around the table. "Sorry you had to hear that," he extended his hand towards Lillian, "Bart Thomas, legal. We talked the first time you came in."

"Yes," Lillian cleared her throat, "I remember."

"Well," Elizabeth said, "grab a seat here, and let's get to the matter at hand."

Lillian slowly lowered herself into a chair, hanging her small purse on the back of it. Other than that, she didn't have anything with her.

"Thank you for meeting with us," Elizabeth said, taking a seat across the table from Lillian. "Bart here has caught me up on your claim of parentage. From the looks of it, you've not brought any documents as evidence with you?"

"I haven't been able to get them yet," she responded, stumbling slightly over her words.

"Why not?" she asked Lillian calmly.

"I…" Lillian paused for a long time, and Elizabeth imagined that she was trying to figure out a way to not talk about how she found out.

"We were pretty clear that it was a part of this deal. Bring us the evidence that you, Ms. Marsden, claim to have. Are you asking us to simply believe you?" Bart conveyed a slight annoyance in his voice.

Lillian looked at Elizabeth, who leaned back in her chair. Elizabeth looked back at this young lady. She could remember her mother well, which only caused Elizabeth to be more perturbed with Lillian.

"It's not as easy as that. I need more time."

"How much time?" Elizabeth's voice took on an urgency.

"A couple of days," she said. Elizabeth could see that Lillian knew that wasn't the right answer the second she blurted it out.

"In a couple of days, you could forge documents that say that you're his daughter. What made you think that claiming to have documents you don't have will get you any further than every other money-hungry twat that walks into this office, claiming to be his kid?" As Barton said this he stood up and walked to the door. He made to open it and leave, "either you have something, or you don't."

Lillian sat there stunned. The wheels in her head were turning, and Elizabeth saw the exact moment when she had decided on her course of action. "They did not tell me who they worked for. They just showed me a paper that said I was Marcus Brent's daughter. It was pretty cut and dried. They weren't necessarily looking to talk with me. They wanted to know where my mother was."

"So, you're telling me," Barton said, "that you had a conversation with two people you didn't know about a birth father you didn't know about?"

"When you put it that way, it sounds worse than it really was," she pleaded with him and looked towards Elizabeth for sympathy. "They were both very reputable. Like I said, they only really wanted to talk to my mother. They could not find her because she was very transient. I told him where I thought she could be, and then they left me alone. Unfortunately, they also left with the information because it was not mine. It was my mother's." Lillian was getting very flustered, and Elizabeth could tell she was beginning to see how stupid she sounded.

Silence fell over the room. Elizabeth drummed her fingers on the table and pretended to think.

"We've talked with each other about your story," Elizabeth started. "It's interesting on a few levels and could be exactly what we need to spice up the show and possibly help his political run."

Lillian nodded and looked over at Barton to assess his reaction to the situation. Barton showed no emotion, and Elizabeth continued, unpacking the levels of the story, which she found interesting. All of these were Lillian's pitches the first time she walked into the building to request this meeting. Elizabeth wasn't saying anything that Lillian hadn't already said. When she finished, she looked at Lillian, "Does that sound familiar to you?"

"Yes," she said with some annoyance, "it's exactly what I said the first time I was here."

"Listen, Lillian," she continued, "you have a choice in front of you. You have brought this whole idea to us, but without any proof whatsoever to back your story. Of course, you tell us that some investigative reporters showed you some documents saying you're Marcus Brent's child, but you don't have those documents." Lillian wanted to interrupt, but Elizabeth held up her hand to stop her.

"Instead, you sit here with nothing," Elizabeth motioned to the empty table in front of them. "I've done my job for a long time, and normally, there are a few reasons for that. Let me tell you what I think may be going on here." She stopped talking for a second, and Lillian went to jump into the conversation, but Elizabeth held up her hand again, "You can say something when I'm finished," and Lillian leaned back.

"You have always wondered who your father was, and this was the first time someone presented you with tangible information. My guess is your mother ignored your requests completely, never giving you any insight into who your real father was, and that drove you away from her all the way to Los Angeles, where you found you aren't alone in that story. Now, two random people show up at your doorstep and put a piece of paper in front of you. It makes sense. Why would someone make this up? I imagine you might have thought that you resemble his daughters. Maybe, if you look close enough, you think to yourself. So, you, the struggling actress that you are, make a decision. You show up here with no representation, with no proof, and expect us to jump at your ideas. I imagine you thought we might have already known about you. Possibly, maybe, in your dream of how this would go, we'd been tracking you all these years. Am I close?"

Lillian was suddenly speechless. She just nodded.

"It would be nice for the record if you gave me a verbal 'yes' or 'no,'" Barton said to her.

"Yes," Lillian said.

"Now here you are. In the room where you wanted to be, well, maybe not this room. I'm sure you'd rather be in a casting room where you could land major scripted roles; at least, that's what I would have wanted, but here you are, angling for a spot on a reality television show. You're doing your best to keep ahead of the story that these reporters have, coming to us with the information to use to your benefit. Not caring one bit about the nice reporters who gave you answers to the one big question you have asked yourself for years. It's that shrewdness that makes me think you may just be Marcus Brent's daughter."

Lillian's eyes looked hopeful again, which meant that Elizabeth was on the right track.

"Where is your mother?" Barton asked her.

"I don't know," she answered, "we've had a very complex relationship, and she lives like a nomad. I couldn't possibly tell you where she is."

"You have no contact with her," Elizabeth asked her.

"I write to her on paper and mail her a letter about twice a month," she answered. "I send it to our neighbor's house, and they collect them and give them to her when she travels through."

"Do the reporters know what you're up to here?" Barton asked her.

"No, I figured that for this to work on the show, there needed to be an element of surprise. Look," she paused dramatically, "if you want proof, you could always run a DNA test."

"That's something we thought about," Barton answered, "but as far as the idea for our story that we have, we'd rather save that for later."

"What story?" Lillian asked, with a touch of hope in her voice.

"We plan to sequester you," Elizabeth answered, "so you'll need to cancel your appointments, work schedule, and any dates that you might have." Elizabeth raised her eyebrows at the last part, almost like she was asking a question.

"That won't be difficult," she answered, "how long should I call off work?" she asked.

"Indefinitely," Bart answered, "we'll most likely find you a different job once we reveal you to the audience."

"I like my job," she objected.

"I don't care," Elizabeth shot at her. "If you want to do the show, you do it our way."

"Fine," she said, "I'll call off. I have a question," she said.

"You can ask any question you want after I finish," Elizabeth smiled at her to put her at ease. "We plan to have you come in almost exactly like you did a few days ago. We'll film that meeting, and then from there, we'll begin to map out how you're going to meet the family. It will all play out on national TV. Are you, or are you not, Marcus Brent's daughter from a long-lost love affair?"

"I would hardly call what they had a love affair," Lillian shot off.

"Really," Barton broke in, "how would you know?"

"My mother told me that he was a one-night stand and that she had nothing to do with him since."

"One-night stands can be very romantic," Elizabeth said, "at least on TV."

"That's not the case," Lillian mumbled.

"Again, I've a story to tell, so I don't care," Elizabeth continued with her facade. "We're going to let the world decide what they want, and it isn't going to matter what you want."

Lillian suddenly looked confused.

"As this drama plays out on TV, and before you ever meet Mr. Brent, we'll be watching social media and the like, and the public will decide if you'll be his daughter or not. It doesn't matter what the genetics say. If people like you, you're in; if they don't, your career is ruined."

"What do you think about that twist?" Barton asked her. "That wasn't in your original pitch, was it?"

"But I can prove I'm his daughter," she protested.

"And yet you haven't," Elizabeth calmly retorted.

"Listen to me, Lillian," Barton started, "once you're out there, your presence will open up the doors for more people to come forward. It's a headache I don't think anyone at Brent Industries wants. We'll use your story to discourage anyone from making false claims. It's a win-win."

"For all of you, it is," Lillian suddenly seemed less timid, "but not for me."

"Again, I don't care." Elizabeth stood up. "You want this break or not?"

"God, I should have listened to them," she said out loud.

"Who should you have listened to?" Elizabeth asked her. "The reporters?"

"It doesn't matter," she answered them and then said as an afterthought, "friends of mine from work."

"Oh," Barton asked, "and they know about this?"

"No," she shook her head, "they don't know about this."

It was clear to Elizabeth that she was lying to cover for Rhea and Miles, who she was almost certain were the 'reporters.'

"Then what advice of theirs are you upset you didn't listen to?" Elizabeth asked.

"Not to go into fucking show business," she retorted.

"It's a bit too late for that now," Elizabeth answered. "You always have a choice, but as far as I can see it, you either walk away from this right now and sign a massively binding non-disclosure agreement, which would be so restrictive that it could cost you your life, or you go along with our plan, and maybe, just maybe, become famous. In my opinion, both will cost you your life as you know it."

"Well, what will it be," Barton asked her.

"I'll do it," she sounded resigned to the fact.

"Then," Lizzy said, "follow me this way, and we'll get you started."

ଓଝଠଞ୍ଚଠ

The L.A. sun was shining as Elizabeth walked out of the office building to her car. Lillian had been at a cabin in northern California for the last two days. In those two days, she had briefed Saul on what they knew, keeping her cards close to her chest. As far as he knew, Lillian was an anomaly, and he was firmly of the opinion that Dr. Abbott had pulled a fast one on them.

She had then dug up all that she could on Miles and Rhea. Esme Connor was still in the wind, but she seemed to be the least of her worries. As far as Elizabeth could tell, only four kids were born who should have been aborted. She placed all of her research in her bag and got into her car. Barton had his orders, and he was ready to finish what she should have taken care of long ago. Barton didn't seem any wiser.

The drive out to the cabin was hectic for the most part. Between the traffic and her mind working in overdrive, she couldn't relax. She wanted to be relaxed when she interrogated Lillian. She drove up the driveway and passed the guys at the gate, who waved her through.

She turned the key in the lock and walked in.

"Can't you idiots knock?" she heard Lillian yell.

"The house doesn't belong to you, so there's no need for me to knock," she said as she put the keys back into her pocket and walked towards Lillian's voice. She saw her sitting at the dining table next to the sliding glass door. The house was still rather tidy, which she hadn't expected. Most of the people who they had kept up here treated it as a hotel and left the place a mess. Lillian had kept it neat.

"Sorry," she said, "I thought it was one of the assholes you have guarding the premises," she said.

"No, it's me," she said. "And those assholes, if I'm correct, are bringing you your groceries, and I told them they could just let themselves in."

Lillian rolled her eyes at Elizabeth and then glanced out the sliding glass door. "When are we going to get to my story?"

"Your story," Elizabeth asked.

"Yes, my fucking story, Lizzy," she spat back at her. The two days had emboldened her, and Barton, who had been there the day before, had warned her.

"Lillian," Elizabeth spoke calmly, "do I look like a Lizzy to you?"

"I don't care," she said, irritated.

"Ah," Elizabeth said, "but you should care. You see, Lillian, my name is Elizabeth Deavers; most people call me Ms. Deavers."

"And…"

"I'm not a talent scout," she said, looking directly at Lillian, who was still looking out the sliding glass door. As the realization of what she said dawned on Lillian, she slowly turned her head and looked at her.

"Then what do you do?" she asked.

"I'm a fixer. I clean up messes."

"What?"

"Let's say, for example, Marcus Brent would find himself in some trouble. Maybe, like getting some random woman pregnant." Lillian nodded. "I would then step in to make sure that the best interests of Marcus Brent and Brent Industries were represented."

"Like paying them to have an abortion," Lillian whispered.

"Exactly," Elizabeth smiled. "Stacey, your mom," Elizabeth watched as Lillian's eyes grew in terror, "was a bit wacky, so I should have guessed that she might have found a way to get around the deal, but I am somewhat surprised to learn that Ellis Baker, Rhea's mother, did the same thing."

Lillian looked like she was going to throw up. "I wouldn't know anything about that," she said hastily. "You knew my mom," Lillian circled back to that, either to change the subject or because she was searching to see if Elizabeth truly had met her mother or just googled her.

"I met your mother the night that she slept with Marcus. I didn't see her again until she showed up at his hotel in Philadelphia, saying she needed to talk with him."

"So, you forced her to see the doctor," she said disgustingly.

"I offered her a deal, and she seemingly took it," Elizabeth answered, "but obviously she reneged on her deal because, well, here you sit."

"You don't know that for sure," she spat back at her.

"Lillian, I'm good at my job, and if I weren't, you wouldn't be sitting here thinking you were going to be on a TV show."

"Fuck you," she said as tears formed in her eyes. "You kidnapped me!"

"No, you got into the car on your own recognizance."

"You lied to me," she screamed.

"Did I?" Elizabeth said to her, "I don't remember if I did, or if that was Barton."

"You aren't going to get away with this," she said with flowing tears.

"Well, if that isn't the most cliche thing I've ever heard," Elizabeth mocked her. "Now, if you're finished with your little breakdown, I can give you the real offer."

"You've known the whole time, haven't you?"

"Tell me who exactly this Miles is. I've figured out Rhea, but I need you to confirm information about Miles for me. Then you tell me exactly what they showed you."

"And then what?" she asked.

"Then I won't kill you." That last sentence hung in the air, reverberating with shocking effects. Lillian seemed to go listless and white. Then she seemed to want to form words with her mouth, but couldn't do it. "My deal has an expiration time, not a date. You have approximately until I finish telling you what I know to make up your mind. Ready?"

Lillian just stared at her, shaking her head as tears welled up in her eyes.

"Ellis Baker was the first, then came a young woman by the name of Betsy McDonal, that's who I assume is the mother of Miles. It was quiet for a while, and then there was a young lady by the name of Hannah Vaughn. She was pretty volatile, just like your mother, who was the fourth instance, followed by two more women, both in the same year, neither of which have children the right age, one of whom is dead. Finally, in the home stretch, there was a lady named Angela Camp and another named Esme Conners. Angela is dead, as is her son, Dustin. That surprise tropical storm caused some havoc and cost them their lives. Esme is nowhere to be found, and I doubt that she's going to pop up on my radar like you did."

"Why are you telling me this?" she asked Elizabeth.

"To show you I know what you know, but I think you can fill in some blanks for me. For example, does Miles work for a newspaper?"

"No," she said, shaking her head, "He's a professor, just like Rhea."

"Where?" she asked.

"I don't remember, but Rhea had mentioned something to him about Pennsylvania once," the tears continued trickling down her face. Elizabeth recognized in Lillian's face a deep regret. The regret of not listening to those who meant no harm to her. The regret of walking right into the arms of the enemy, leaving her crying in a place that no one knew about. At this point, Elizabeth was sure of one thing: Lillian had wished she had never thought to leverage this information.

"Do you know his last name?" she asked slowly and methodically.

"Trent," she said through a sob.

"Miles Trent." It rang a bell. He had written a few books on Eastern bloc countries that she had found fascinating. He *was* going to be a pain to deal with. He was very good at what he did.

"What else should I know?" she asked Lillian.

"I only remember a few things about the other mothers and kids," Lillian said. "All of them were paid to have an abortion, but it seemed that some doctor helped them lie about it."

"I'm aware of that part," Elizabeth stated monotonously.

"You know about Rhea and Miles," she sobbed, "and me. I know there is a kid who grew up in Oklahoma, but they don't know where he is now." Elizabeth felt very uneasy. Was it possible that Hannah had a kid?

"Anything else?"

"You found the kid in North Carolina, I guess, but there is one in Mexico, too."

"Mexico?"

"They thought that she was in Mexico."

"Why would they think that?"

"I don't know," Lillian whimpered.

"You do know," Elizabeth yelled back at her, "so think!"

"Apparently, the doctor knew where everyone was."

"Do you know the doctor's name?" Elizabeth asked unnecessarily, as she already knew who the doctor was.

"No, they never said what his name was, only that he was from Philadelphia."

"Finally, Lillian, where is your mother?" she asked her.

"I don't know," she said. "Rhea scared her off."

"Rhea found her," Elizabeth said more than asked.

"Yes, she found her and talked with her. She texted me the whole time."

"Are the messages on your phone?" Elizabeth asked.

"Yes, as well as both of their contact information," Elizabeth was amazed at how quickly this girl gave up the information. Brents are normally harder to crack.

"Where is your phone?" she asked, and Lillian pointed towards the kitchen, where it was plugged into the wall. The battery would have drained pretty quickly, looking for cell reception. She handed it to Lillian. "Open it."

She did as she was told, and Elizabeth found what she needed. She took a few pictures with her phone so that she didn't need to send the information from Lillian's phone to her own. She handed the phone back.

"What were they planning to do with this information?" Elizabeth asked her.

"I'm not sure," Lillian answered between sobs. "He wanted to find everyone. That was all he talked about."

"And what about Rhea?" Elizabeth asked. "Did she have an end game?"

"I hope to God she does, and it better be to take you and your fucking boss down!" Lillian yelled and then put her head in her arms on the table, sobbing.

"Thank you," Elizabeth said as she stood up.

Lillian sat, shaking her head, crying. Elizabeth recognized that look. It was the look of mourning that came with the death of hope. It was the look of selling people out.

As she left herself out, she could hear the loud sobs coming from the table. She had everything that she needed. She got into her car and drove off down the road. An hour from the cabin, she pulled into a diner and slid into a booth across from Barton.

"And?" he asked her.

"She's told me everything she knows," and some things I didn't, Elizabeth thought, but didn't say. The boy in Oklahoma and Esme's location in Mexico were information she was keeping close to her chest.

"I'll confirm when it's done," he said to her as the waitress came over.

"Coffee, please," Elizabeth said to her. As the waitress walked away. "I'm heading to Oklahoma to check on some problematic donors," she lied, "use the secure lines."

"You got it," he said. "Have a good trip." He got up and left the restaurant. His hamburger was half eaten, and his bill was unpaid.

"This one's on me," she whispered to herself.

Her coffee came, and she scrolled through her phone. She found Mike's number and called it. He didn't answer, nor should he, she thought. He got away from this whole circus quite clean. She put her phone down, and immediately, it lit back up.

"Mike," she said, "sorry to bug you."

"I can't imagine why you would be calling," came the gravelly voice on the other end.

"Quick question," she began, "on our little trip to Oklahoma, how old would you say that Sharp boy was?"

"Thirteen," he said with certainty, "that's what one of the ladies from their church told me. Why?"

"It means I'm taking a trip to Oklahoma."

Chapter Seventeen

The two days since Miles and Rhea left had been miserable. Elliot couldn't get Scooper to talk to him for more than a few minutes, and when he did speak with him, he ended every conversation with the statement, *"I wish you would reconsider."* Even though Elliot wanted to talk to Scooper, he didn't want to deal with the guilt trip, which forced him to avoid Scooper as much as possible, which was part of the reason he felt so miserable.

The other part that was making him feel out of sorts was knowing that he let Miles and Rhea just leave, without really giving them anything but a nod, and sending them off to what he imagined was imminent danger. Marcus Brent was going to find out, and when he did, that asshole was going to do something. He hated that man, and yet he knew he, himself, was partially to blame for his terrible rise to prominence. Silence kills people. It kills people in this country all the time. People just looked the other way when injustice occurred. So, why was it that he didn't give a damn about anything happening back home? He cursed the moment that he'd received that wire from his Dad/Uncle, the moment his siblings arrived on the compound, and the request from Miles. If they had never come, he would have been able to go on in ignorance. He would have lived thinking he was the only bastard child of the dickhead next president of the U.S.

He looked out across the desert to the area where they were working on the well. It was going to be finished in the next few days, and from there, they would move on to another location about 200 miles from where they were now. It would be more remote, and that was his only hope of escaping this dread. It was there that he might have a shot at getting Scooper to drop the whole thing. It was there that he knew he had a better shot of being hidden from anything that Miles and Rhea might stir up.

He walked down towards the office. He figured it was time to write back to Jennings. If there was anything that he could thank Miles for, it was that he had helped him see something he had been avoiding. Jennings would always be his uncle, but it was Miles talking about his father that made Elliot realize that Jennings was the only father he knew, and it was what Jennings wanted. He wanted to be Elliot's father. It was what Marcia wanted, and maybe it was time for him to stop hurting them. Maybe it was time to mend that fence. It was the only thing he could fix, and in all honesty, it was the only thing that he wanted to fix.

Elliot walked into the office. It was spartan in its furnishings. The CB radio was next to the window, looking out on the breezeway and towards the well site. There was a table along the wall that held the plans for this well and the beginning stages of the next one. The desk with the computer ran perpendicular to that, and behind the swivel chair, there was a door to the bathroom. Its location at the end of the compound meant that there was a second set of windows, providing the best possible lighting for the work done there.

He walked behind the desk and sat down in his seat. He tapped a few keys, and the computer started. As the computer connected to the internet through the DSL, he tapped out a cigarette from the pack sitting on the desk. They were his, he thought, and if they weren't, they were Benjamin's, and he owed Elliot a few. Elliot appreciated the ability to smoke wherever he wanted in Africa. Scooper wouldn't let him smoke in either of their rooms, but in the office, it was another story. He lit his cigarette and leaned back in the chair, stretching his legs as far as he could under the desk.

He opened up his email and clicked on the compose button. He drummed his fingers on the desk for a bit, and then he just went for it.

Dear Mom and Dad,

Thanks for sending Miles and Rhea my way. I'm grateful to have met them, and even more so to know that in some ways I'm not alone. The reality is I've never been alone, you've always been there. I'm sorry for how I've acted. We're almost finished here, and our next dig is located about 200 miles from here in a small village called Tasya. It's close to the border of Niger. I wanted to let you know since it will be more remote, and I won't be able to communicate as much. I know that Scott's Aunt keeps you up to date, but I wanted to as well. I may be home in the new year, but I don't know.

Love,

Elliot

He reread it. It was sappy, yet it did his heavy heart good to have written it. He was well aware that it was only the beginning of mending that fence, but it was the only fence he was willing to mend. This was the best he could do right now. He let out a puff of smoke and looked at the mail that had come in. He knew it wouldn't be anything of interest. He pushed away from the desk and rolled over to the stack of papers sitting on the small table next to the bathroom door. This was where the wires from different places were kept. It was such an antiquated system, and yet so many of the places where they were working still used them. He thumbed through them and stopped at the third one down. It was from Miles, time-stamped from earlier that morning. It wasn't addressed to him, and that was the part that upset him. It was addressed to Scooper.

"What the fuck," he said to no one, "why is he writing to him." He scanned the correspondence, feeling a touch nosey, and yet feeling justified. It was, after all, from his brother, not Scooper's. It was thanking Scott, not Scooper, for the small gifts that he had given them. What small gifts? What was Scooper up to? Miles went on to say that he was also (*ALSO*, Elliot thought) upset about Elliot's unwillingness to help them out, but that Elliot had his own reasons for not doing so (no kidding, Elliot said out loud) and that Elliot would need to come around in his own time (that would be never, Elliot again responded to the empty room).

"For fucks sake," he said as he took another drag of his cigarette.

"Elliot," he heard the voice from behind him, "what are you up to?" Benjamin looked at him with consternation.

"Sorry, Benjamin, I thought they were mine," he motioned to the packet of cigarettes on the desk.

"Not the cigarettes," Benjamin nodded at the paper in his hand.

"Why didn't you tell me Miles wrote to Scooper?" he asked him, waving the page at him.

"Because he wrote to Scott, not you," he said as he moved towards the desk. "It doesn't matter that he's your brother."

"It does matter," he shot back at him. Benjamin sighed at his outburst and shrugged his shoulders.

Elliot rolled the cigarette between his fingers and then took another drag on it. "Scooper doesn't get what's going on," he said to Benjamin without looking at him.

"I tink he does," Benjamin responded. "Look, Elliot, I'm not surprised dat you didn't go wit dem. I could tell you were fine seeing dem go. Scott, he's worried about you, just like I'm worried about you. They're your brother and sister, and you didn't care dat they asked you for help."

"It's way more complex than that, Benjamin."

"Oh, I understand dat it's complex. I understand complex. I work with two very broken, complex Americans."

"Broken," Elliot raised his eyebrows as he said.

"Yes, you are both broken men," Benjamin continued, "but broken in different ways."

"Really, how are we broken?" Elliot asked him as he took one last drag from his cigarette.

"Scott is okay, broken. He has no family. You're his family. He loves you in ways dat you don't love him, even if you pretend to for your own selfish reasons."

Elliot's heart jumped to his throat because he knew that Scooper saw him as family. He didn't see Scooper as a family— just as a friend he was glad to have around out here in the middle of Africa.

"Scott is lonely, but he's lonely because he's an orphan. He has no one, and you became his someone, which is what makes him so broken but different than you."

"Fine, tell me how my broken is different from his," Elliot taunted Benjamin.

"Elliot, you are broken in a bad way. You are broken in a way dat people can't fix. How do I know this?" he tapped his forefinger against his temple, "because you don't like yourself!

You do tings all the time to hurt you. You push people far away. You block the love from your Dad in America. Even your naked smoking is just a sign of how much you hate yourself. Dat's messed up broken."

Benjamin paused and looked at Elliot. Elliot stared back at him, wondering what was coming next. It was true, and in some sense, it hurt to think that Scooper had no family, and yet all he did was talk shit about his own.

"Two white boys," Benjamin shook his head, "running from da world around them. Helping build wells. Tinking dat making a difference here will make a difference here," Benjamin pointed towards his own heart. "The world found you Elliot, and you should tank God dat it still was looking for you."

"What do you know about running from anything, Benjamin?" Elliot sighed as he moved towards the desk to grab another cigarette.

"What do I know? Do you tink you're the only person here running from family? You aren't! I grew up in Mali, my given name was Moosa Kolabali. My family is Muslim, but when I was studying in Bamako, I met an American, and he told me about Jesus." Benjamin slowed down, "who you have probably heard of," Elliot nodded at him. He had spent a lot of time in the church until his teenage years. He knew where this story was heading. "I became a Christian, and my family disowned me. My brother put a price on my head for bringing shame to the family, so I fled. I took a job dat keeps me moving. I changed my name, Elliot. I know a few tings about running, but you're lucky, Elliot Sharp, you're lucky," Benjamin wagged a finger at him, "because your family came for you, my family, Scott's family, they won't ever come for us. What makes you more broken is dat you reject dat love and then turn around and hate yourself for it."

"Shit, Benjamin," Elliot stared at him as he spoke, holding the unlit cigarette in his hands, "you've been holding that in for a while."

"No, I haven't. It has only just become plain to me why you're here. Now, put down Scott's note from your brother. It won't make you feel any better."

Elliot turned and put the paper back on the pile. "Since you have such strong opinions, what do you think I should do?"

"I've already given you my opinion. You need to figure it out from there." Benjamin grabbed a walkie-talkie off of the table. He turned to leave and called back to Elliot, "Those are your cigarettes. I stopped smoking last month," and left the room.

Elliot sat there flabbergasted. He struggled internally with feeling entitled to run, entitled to be pissed off at people, and entitled to say no to putting his ass on the line to stop some asshole from getting more power. It wasn't really his problem. In the end, he was here, and they were there. There, he had problems. Here, he had a job to do.

Chapter Eighteen

Elizabeth hadn't set foot on the continent of Africa for over thirty years. It was insane to think of that time. The last time she had been there, she was with the Brent family, Harlan included. The Brents visited Kenya on a safari and hunting expedition. Her job was a hundred times easier here because Marcus was scared to death of catching a disease. When he did find a woman to spend some quality time with, he had used double protection. A fact that he complained bitterly to his friends about the whole flight home. It was enough to make her sick.

The air in Ouagadougou was hot, and it greeted you instantly. She hastily walked across the tarmac to the main building, where she budged and nudged her way to the front of the line. The questions in French didn't throw her like they did the first time she landed in Africa during the late 60s. She wasn't fluent yet, but it had become one of three languages she could operate in with ease.

She walked out into the sun and pulled her sunglasses out of her bag. She covered her head with a scarf as well to make it seem like she was more compliant than she was. She scanned the crowd of drivers waiting and saw who she was looking for. She headed to the one woman who was standing there next to a car.

"Fatima," Elizabeth said, "thank you for picking me up."

"You're very welcome," she said. She had aged a lot since Elizabeth had seen her last in Spain. Fatima had three kids, all studying somewhere far from here. She was the third wife of a tribal chief, which allowed her much more freedom. It may have helped that the tribal chief was a mercenary of sorts and that Fatima was skilled in helping people in that line of work. Fatima would tell her in the car that theirs was a marriage of convenience. He gave her three kids, and she gave him access to her underground network of illegal arms, illegal drugs, and illegal people.

"Everything you requested is at the hotel where I'm taking you. I've done some research on the compound, and from what my sources say, it should be very easy to just drive right up to it and then drive out of there quickly. They're limited in their vehicle use."

"Anything about the American working there?"

"Not much," she said. "Most of the tribes in that area are happy that the well is being built, so they aren't saying much about the men they're dealing with. They talk more about the Malian who works with them and the disgusting French donors who show up to their villages and take pictures with all of the sick children."

"Are you sure this is the site with the American boy?" she asked her again.

"That I'm sure of," Fatima replied, "but you asked me what I had heard about him, which isn't much of anything other than he's white."

Elizabeth raised her eyebrows at that last sentence. "Are there any foreseeable problems that I need to be aware of?"

"Not right now," Fatima answered, "if you were here a few months ago, there was some fundamentalist activity here in the city, but it has been calm since then."

"And this Malian, he's made an impression?"

"Apparently, he has, but he won't be a problem for you. He's a Christian who, from what my research tells me, was disowned by his family and fled when a relative put a price on his head."

"Sounds manageable."

"It should be," Fatima said, "the nearest hospital is about an hour away by truck, which should allow you to be halfway back here before they can get to it."

"How about my driver? Can he be trusted?" She made sure to cross-check everything from her years of experience.

"He's a friend of my brother-in-law, who's always glad to have one less American in the country helping."

As an American, Elizabeth wasn't sure that made her feel all that comfortable.

The hotel was fine. It wasn't what she had become accustomed to working all these years for the Brent family. That level of comfort was hard to find here. She settled herself in and looked through the briefcase that Fatima had left in her room. It had the gun and the information about the compound where the well was being dug. It showed her where she was going and gave her information about her pick-up time and how to dispose of the gun after the job was done.

Oklahoma had been easier than expected. She had driven to that god-forsaken farming town, talked to exactly one waitress at a diner, and didn't even need to find where Jennings and Marcia lived. That was a stroke of luck since messes like these were very difficult to clean up in a small town. She left knowing all about Elliot Sharp, his success at Oklahoma State, and how he was making the whole county proud by working to dig wells in Africa. A few little follow-up questions, and she knew all about his crazy aunt who died in a fire.

Elizabeth had made the connection pretty quickly. Her search of Miles's recent travel had allowed her to see that he and Rhea were heading to Ouagadougou, Burkina Faso. A place that Elizabeth herself had visited at least twice in the early 70s before starting her work at Brent Industries. He and Rhea had been very busy. It looked like Rhea had headed back to Portland and was there for a few weeks before jetting to Myrtle Beach, where their timelines connected.

Miles, on the other, had been to Oklahoma, flown to Cancun, where he seemed to be for a few days, before landing in Miami, and from there, his trail went cold, but it was only a few days before she had seen him, or who she thought was Miles, at the funeral for Angela Camp. After that, nothing came until they made a reservation to fly to Burkina Faso. By the time she had all that information, they were back in Philadelphia, but she was getting on a flight to take care of the loose ends here. If she did this right, she wouldn't need to clean anything up in Oklahoma, and the Sharps could mourn the son that was never theirs.

She wasn't enjoying chasing Miles and Rhea, but they were leading her straight to the problems that she needed to deal with. Barton had reported back that he hadn't yet run into Stacey Marsden, but he would continue looking for her. Miles and Rhea would be the last ones she dealt with, and it would take some planning. And planning always took some time. In a sense, they were the easiest of the living children to deal with. They were predictable and were leading her to each of the other children. Once she finished here, she would head back to Chicago before booking a flight to Mexico.

With all of her plans finalized, Elizabeth laid back on her bed. Tomorrow, she could check a third of the six children off of her list.

ᘕᘐᘔ

"These men," her driver was saying to her, "they're mercenaries. They fight for these companies to build their wells, they're people who don't have a home, and they don't have a fuck."

Elizabeth cocked her head to the side. She wondered if he knew that wasn't how you said it, "you mean they don't give a fuck?"

"Oh no, ma'am, they don't even have a fuck to give, they're that hard."

"Why would such hard men take up well drilling? Isn't that something that helps out the local villages?"

"Oh, it does, but that means that the tribes, who have gotten rich off of existing wells, won't be as rich. So, they need to have men who are scary to keep the tribes who already own the wells from attacking the independent well sites."

The setup didn't matter to Elizabeth, she wasn't even sure that the driver was right. It was hot, the car was uncomfortable, and they still had about 40 minutes to drive. Her driver, who said his name was Hank, kept on babbling. Meanwhile, old twangy country music played from his car radio. It was most likely the source of his Anglo name. She could ask him about that, but she really had no capacity to care if that was the reason or not.

"Have you been to Burkina Faso before?" he asked her.

"I have, but it was a long time ago," she said as she pushed her sunglasses up her nose.

"Anywhere else on the continent?"

"Angola, South Africa, Mali, and Kenya, to name a few."

"I've never been anywhere but here."

She nodded, not surprised. "Have you ever been out to this site where we're going?"

"No, but I've been to the villages near it. There is a white man who works with them. They say he's the white devil because he is still pale after working in the sun for days. His hair is spiked up, which they call his horns, you know," she nodded. Fatima had put that in her report, but it didn't necessarily make it a fact.

"He's not the only one," he continued, "there is another white man there, but he doesn't have a nickname that I've heard, and no one really talks about him. He may have already left for the next site that they're going to build."

Elizabeth nodded. Fatima had said that it was possible that the other man, Scott Cooper, was already en route to the next place and that reports were that Elliot was the only one at the compound, wrapping things up.

As time slowly moved on, Elizabeth reviewed her plan for the day. She had a headscarf that she would wrap around her on the way up. Hank had one as well. He would drive onto the compound, and they would surprise the people there. Once she had Elliot in her sights, she would take aim and then get out of there. It would be reported as a hit, which made sense with the tribes getting up in arms about lost business. She would be on a plane in the morning. This was going to be easier than Angela and Dustin. If it hadn't been for that storm, she wasn't sure how she would have pulled that one off.

The small village that was closest to the compound began to take shape as they drove up. There was a small gas station and a few dirt roads leading to the main one. There was a market along the side of the road to the left, and to the right, there were a few small trucks parked next to a long building. From her experience, it was a place to pick up supplies, such as grain or rations, for villages further away from the main road.

It was only a 20-minute drive to the compound now, so she began to prepare herself. It was an easy in-and-out job. Her driver knew the ropes. He had told her early on that he had done a few of these before. He had a second license plate in the car that they could change once they got back to this village. They turned off the main road and onto a very rutted path, which was barely distinguishable from the rest of the landscape except for a sign that told drivers where to head.

The road got better as they kept moving forward, but she was unnerved by the height at which the dust was flying as they drove.

"Slow down," she hissed, "I don't want to alert them to our arrival."

"Don't matter," he said, "if we drive slow or fast, the dust will fly high. They probably already know we're coming."

"Shit," she said under her breath and got her gun ready. She pulled her face covering into place and watched as Hank wrapped his while he was driving. Soon, she could see the outline of the compound, as well as the equipment. If they were heading to a new site, why was their equipment still here? It dawned on her that she was going to have to deal with a lot more people than she'd expected. She saw someone moving towards the long compound. They had come from the truck, and as they got closer, she noticed that they were talking to someone standing just inside the compound door.

The man outside was African, but she couldn't tell who was inside the building. As they pulled up, the African turned towards them, and as he did, a white man in a baseball cap and beard stepped out. Her eyes locked in on his as she readied her gun. Hank stopped about 100 feet from them. Elizabeth jumped out of the vehicle, took aim, and fired. The eyes that she had locked in on closed as his body was flung backward.

Hank began yelling, but she knew that she didn't have time to see if she had finished the job. She jumped back into the car, and he peeled out of there. She looked in the sideview mirror as they drove off, but all she could see was a mass of commotion through the rising dust. She felt relief that the only people she saw moving were black.

She turned forward and began to take off her face covering. It was too hot to keep it on, and she hated that it had impeded her ability to have the best shot possible.

"Do you even know if you hit him?" Hank was yelling at her.

"I don't miss," she yelled back.

"In my experience, people do miss," he said, "and how do you know that was the guy?"

"Our intel said he would be the only white guy there," she yelled back, but the doubts began to flood. She was sure she had hit Elliot, those eyes closing as he flew backward. She had seen it, she replayed it in her head, but now she was worried it might not have been Elliot.

"Our intel," was all Hank said back to her, and he stepped on the gas. The dust behind them made it hard to see if anyone was in pursuit of them, but they could assume that was the case. The trucks wouldn't be able to catch up to them as quickly as a Range Rover or Jeep, yet they needed to make it to the village quickly. The idea of a new license plate was okay since the majority of the automobiles she saw on the road looked like theirs. It just wasn't a permanent fix, and changing the plate was going to cost them precious time.

Chapter Nineteen

Elliot turned onto the main road. He had been successful in securing the permits that he needed to wrap things up at the current site. He was eager to send the rest of the team on to the next one. Scooper and Benjamin often joked about his knack with government officials, unaware that the knack was simply a matter of US dollars—never setting him back as much as he let on.

The market was in full swing, and Elliot decided to stop by. There were a few things at the back side of the market that he could pick up that would hopefully allow him to continue to rebuild his relationship with Scooper and Benjamin. He found his contact easily, or his contact found him easily, he thought to himself, and he paid him for the whiskey, beer, French wine, and cigarettes. He boxed them up and carried them back to the beat-up Land Rover. He was going to need to stop at the Petrol station before heading back, but just as he was loading into the car, he saw that the medical clinic, run by an American mission group, was open. The couple that worked there would always check in on his team when they were in the area. He figured he'd preemptively pay them a visit.

The long, white-washed building reminded him very much of the compound at the well. That compound was to be repurposed as a school by the end of next month. It was partly one of the reasons he was staying behind. He wanted to hand over the keys personally to the group coming in to run the school and the well. He didn't trust leaving the building and the well under the guards' supervision. As he pulled up to the clinic, he saw that both Keith and Penny were in. Keith had taken early retirement as a surgeon and invested their retirement to join the mission. He performed important surgeries back in the capital, but he could do minor work here. Penny was about his mother's age, well, Marcia's age, not Hannah's. At first glance, she seemed stern and angry all the time, but she was far from it. Her French was amazing. That, combined with her perceived sternness, gave her the ability to run staff and volunteers in a way that most American women could have never managed.

Keith was the opposite. Slight in build, he always wore a smile on his face. He was the more caustic of the two, often making backhanded comments about Elliot's health and Scott's (he refused to call him Scooper) disregard for sunblock. The comments weren't meant to alienate them from Keith, but they were warnings that he took his job very seriously, even when it came to the privileged American boys on some sort of "find yourself" expedition. Keith's skepticism of Elliot was understandable. He once had to treat him for an STD he had picked up when he had been a bit indiscreet with a female Spanish tourist while visiting the coast of Dakar. He was pretty sure *that* didn't endear him to Keith or Penny, yet they were always welcoming.

"Elliot," Keith said as he saw him jump out of the car, "I thought you would have already moved on to the next site."

"Not yet, sir," Elliot responded, falling easily back into his Mid-west politeness. "We hit some hiccups with handing the building over to the school, but I took care of that this morning."

"Nothing ever goes as planned here, does it?"

"No, sir, it doesn't." Penny came around the corner as he was saying that; her hardened face broke into a small but heartfelt smile.

"Elliot," she moved in to hug him, "you look haggard and tired. Are you still smoking?"

Elliot nodded at her, "and drinking."

"No wonder," she sighed. "Did you ever think digging wells in an African nation would be so stressful?" It was a rhetorical question because they all knew how hard it was to administer medical care in an African nation.

"Well, how much longer will you be on site?" Keith asked him.

"At least another two weeks, but Scooper, I mean Scott and Benjamin are taking the crew on to the next site."

"How is Scott?" Penny inquired.

"He's fine," Elliot replied, "he and I are a bit out of sorts with each other right now." This seemed to always be what happened when he spent time with these two. It was their nature, they would ask you one question, and you found yourself opening up in ways you never imagined. He wanted to tell them he needed an adult view of what was happening.

"Anything we can help with?" Keith asked.

Elliot shook his head and heard himself start, "About a week ago, we had visitors from the US, but not investors. They were my half-siblings."

Keith and Penny registered some surprise. "They needed my help with something, and while I like them, I don't have a desire to help them."

"And Scott feels like you should," Penny took a guess.

He went on to explain everything. Marcus Brent, his Mom and Dad, being his Aunt and Uncle, Rhea and Miles, and Benjamin, telling him that he was a broken boy. It all came out in a matter of minutes. The look on both of their faces went from surprise to disbelief.

"Wow," Keith said when he finally took a breath. "I guess I won't be voting for him." This made Elliot chuckle. "Can you put a finger on why you think you don't care enough to help?" he asked.

"No," Elliot answered him. "I just know that I don't."

"Do you truly know that," Penny asked him, "or is that just how you feel right now?"

Elliot smiled at her, "Probably the latter, but I don't really have any capacity to deal with this. If I leave now to help them break this news, that will take me away from here."

"And put you right back in the middle of all the things you've run away from," Keith said as he picked up a clipboard. "I don't want to cut this short, Elliot. I know you're processing this, and you have us here for the next week, so come back one evening for dinner when things settle down. I know a thing or two about running from the past."

Elliot nodded. He knew that they were busy when they were in the village, and he could already see the line of patients forming under the porch. The Malian and Burkina nurses were doing their best to assess the severity of the needs, but soon, it would be time to see the doctor, and Elliot was holding them up.

"I'll give you a call on the CB tonight," Keith said, "and we can pick a night or even just talk a bit more." He patted Elliot on the back, and Penny took his hand. Then, she was off to rattling some instructions in French while Keith went to the wash basin to get ready for his first patient.

Elliot walked to the Land Rover and started it up. He drove slowly past the village kids as they played in and around the streets. He came to the crossroads where the petrol station was and hopped out of the vehicle to tank up. He talked with the attendant for a little while. His French was better than the attendants', but they said their normal greetings and asked about the well-being of one another's family.

As he stood by the car waiting for the attendant to finish, he thought about the last thing that Keith said to him. Was that the core of what it was? He didn't want to go back. He'd said that a million times, but it was always a flippant answer to tick off Scooper, who didn't have anyone to go back to except for an elderly aunt who often didn't remember he was her nephew. Engaging with the task at hand would make it tough not to end up back in Jones. It wasn't that difficult to visit and see Jennings and Marcia, but it was those hard conversations that he didn't want to have at any cost. That email had been an apology enough, and he didn't need to process through that with them again.

The attendant finished up and told him the price. He pulled out the cash to pay for it and asked him for a receipt, which he returned to the stand to get. He looked out over the village. The petrol station was almost on the edge. He could see the road heading towards the turn-off for the well. In the other direction, he could see the village proper, and past that, the road disappeared in the direction of the capital. He smirked as the attendant walked to him and thought to himself, *I really have disappeared into the middle of nowhere.* And yet that thought also reminded him that disappearing hadn't kept his past from finding him. It was always lodged in his mind, and not more than a week ago, it had shown up on his doorstep. The middle of nowhere hadn't proven to be the best hiding place.

He jumped into the Rover and began heading towards the site. About a mile from the turnoff, he saw another Rover heading towards him, driving at the automobile's limit. He could see that the driver was African, but next to him sat a woman who was a bit older and seemingly looking nervous and agitated. They flew by him without even looking at him. He turned his head to watch them drive by and continued speeding toward the village. He hoped they would slow down when they got there; he didn't want any of those kids getting hit.

He continued on, but something suddenly came over him. A weird sense of dread. He looked at the CB radio on the dashboard and realized that he had turned it off. He flipped the switch and began to hear a voice yelling.

"Elliot, Elliot, come in! Elliot, are you there?" It was Matthew, the younger brother of the bulldozer operator. His English was second only to Benjamin's.

"Matthew, what's wrong?" Elliot said back into the handset.

"Scott is shot," he said.

"Come again," he yelled into the CB.

Elliot sank into silence. It didn't make sense to him. How could Scott have been shot? What on earth happened? His mind went numb; he could hear the handset reverberating with Matthew's voice.

"Scott, they shoot him. Are you listening, Elliot?" he yelled back at Elliot once again.

"Is he dead?" was all Eliot could ask.

"No," but then he heard Benjamin break into the conversation and, in French, tell Matthew to get off the line.

"Elliot," Benjamin inserted his voice into the scene. From the background noise, it sounded like he was in a truck. "He's not dead, but he is bad. He won't make it to the hospital."

"The doctor is at the medical center. Take him there," he yelled into the handset. His heart started to pound.

"We'll meet you there," Matthew was back on the CB, and just as he was about to turn around, he saw the truck coming down the road. Benjamin was driving, and wedged between him and Henri was Scooper. Henri was holding a compress against his chest, or at least it looked like it. Scooper looked unconscious. Elliot spun the car around and caught up to them. He grabbed the CB and turned the knob to the channel that the medical center was on.

"Keith, come in," he shouted. No response.

"Keith, we're on our way in! Scott's been shot," he heard his voice pleading for someone to answer.

"Elliot," it was Penny who returned the call. "I didn't catch that. What happened to Scott?"

"He's been shot," Elliot said almost hysterically.

"How far are you all?" Penny asked.

"Ten minutes tops," he said back.

"We'll be ready," Penny assured him.

ഗ8ഇ8ാ

Benjamin may have given up smoking last month, but the events of the day caused him to pick it up again. Elliot watched as he lit his third cigarette in the last two hours. He was in no place to judge; he had already had half a pack of the newly purchased cigarettes from earlier that day. They sat out under the awning, alternatively pacing and sitting with their heads in their hands.

Benjamin had replayed what had happened a million times. Elliot felt like he had every detail that he could use and was now positive that the white lady with the African driver was responsible for the shooting. Benjamin knew it wasn't an attack from the local tribe; they couldn't afford to hire someone else.

"How did you know she was white?" Elliot had asked him.

"It doesn't matter if you have on a face covering or not; if your eyes aren't brown, you're white."

"White people have brown eyes, too," he tried to correct Benjamin.

"Elliot, shut up," he kept screaming. "This was someone else, and I don't think they wanted to shoot Scott. They probably wanted to shoot you."

Elliot was sure that Benjamin was anxious for Scott, but what he had just spat out didn't sit right with him. Did Benjamin say this out of frustration, or was he really right about it? Could it have been that he was their target?

"Why do you say that," he tossed the question at Benjamin.

"I don't know, but it was something else. They didn't get close to us, yell at us, or shout to let us know that we were under attack. She jumped out of the car, took aim, and left! That isn't how the tribes doing it."

"Why do you think it was me they were after?"

"I don't, Elliot, I just need you to shut up!"

"Fine," Elliot sulked.

"Why is it the good ones always get hurt?" Benjamin sighed.

"Oh, fuck me," Elliot said with his head in his hands, "do you have something else to say to me?"

"No," Benjamin replied flatly. "No, I don't."

"It sounds like you do," he shot back as he looked up.

"Elliot, I'm not one of your wishy-washy American friends. I say what I mean."

Elliot exhaled and went to take a new cigarette out of the packet. He wanted to go out and grab the bottle of whiskey out of the Land Rover, too, but he didn't want to let on that he had some.

"Scooper is going to be okay," he said for the first time out loud. "He has to be okay."

"Elliot, shut up. Scott has been shot. IN. THE. CHEST." Benjamin drew out the last three words with emphasis. His eyes widened so much that Elliot thought they might pop out of his head.

"Keith was a surgeon in the U.S., Scooper is in good hands!"

"Scooper, Scooper, Scooper," Benjamin sounded so frustrated. "It's a stupid name for him, you know that, right? He can't even use the backhoe to scoop things!"

Elliot wanted to laugh at that, but had the sense to realize how Benjamin was enveloped in the gravity of his emotions. It was clear that he was mad at Elliot for what happened, and he was going to pick him apart. It was best to just shut up, and yet he couldn't. He was so nervous, and Benjamin was the closest person to him at that moment.

"He chose that name," Elliot yelled back at him.

"I know, but you encouraged him, you let him think it was cute," he was screaming now.

"His nickname isn't why he got shot, Benjamin!"

"I know, but I need to blame you for something, you asshole!"

It felt good to Elliot to see the professional facade fall from Benjamin. He always thought that Benjamin found him repulsive. Again, he wanted to laugh at Benjamin calling him an asshole, but his heart was too grieved. He chose not to respond and stood to light his cigarette. They hadn't had an update from the nurses in a while, but Elliot was of the opinion that no news was good news. He was just worried that if they didn't finish soon, the power could go out.

He and Benjamin sat in silence for the next hour. He watched as one of the nurses turned away patients, telling them to come back tomorrow. The village seemed to move normally, their world remained unaffected at all by what happened to Scooper. He sat there and kept envisioning the lady sitting in that car over and over. He could still see her plain as day, and something about her made his stomach turn. He couldn't shake the feeling that he had seen her before, but he often felt that way when white people showed up in the remotest parts of Burkina Faso.

After he had sat long enough, he got up and radioed the compound. Matthew took the update and exchanged his side of the story. Everyone clamored to hear how Scooper was, and Elliot had to tell them over and over that he didn't know anything, but he was alive when he got to the clinic. When everyone had said their piece, he came back to the porch where Benjamin had finally sat down again.

"What were you up to?" Benjamin asked him.

"Keeping the compound updated," he said, avoiding the true reason behind his call.

"We don't know anything," he said.

"I know, but I thought they might like to know that."

Benjamin didn't respond. He just sat there staring off into the distance. He was looking past the world around him. He was contemplating saying something else when Penny came out from the far end of the building and slowly approached them. They stood and walked toward her; her face looked like it always did, which meant that they couldn't tell how things had gone.

"We were able to stabilize him, and he is breathing on his own now. It looks like he may pull through this." Penny sounded like a true medic at that point to Elliot.

"Can we see him?" Elliot asked.

"Oh, no," Penny replied, "he's still critical. The bullet went right through his chest, but it didn't hit anything vital. He lost a lot of blood, but we were able to give him some from our storage. What are your blood types?" she asked them both.

"I'm O negative," Elliot announced. It meant that he was a universal donor. "I can give some blood."

"Thank you, Elliot. I'll have Leticia come and get you started."

"What are the chances he'll survive?" Benjamin took his turn.

"Good, but he needs to stabilize before we move him to the capital, and then most likely from there to a hospital in Germany."

"Why not the US?" Benjamin asked.

"We could, but Germany is closer. We have some contacts there that can help." She paused for a beat and then looked at them, "I'm gathering that you both don't really know what happened."

"We do, but it isn't easy to explain," Benjamin answered.

"We know what happened. We just don't know who it was or why," Elliot added.

"Once he's stable, we can move him," she said. "Keith will come to talk to you as soon as he can. God was looking out for Scott," she added while pulling off her gloves.

"Amen," Benjamin agreed.

"If this happened last week, he most likely would have died from that gunshot."

"Or it could have been me," Elliot added.

"Well, it wasn't," Benjamin shot at him. "Thank you so much, Penny."

"You're welcome. Just sit tight, and Keith will be with you."

"I need to use the radio to let everyone know," Elliot said as if requesting information.

"You know the way," Penny said as she turned to walk back to the OR.

Elliot made his way back to the office and picked up the CB.

"Matthew, over," he said.

"How is Elliot?" he heard Matthew's voice.

"He's alive," Elliot answered. When Matthew came back on, he could hear the relief in his voice and the excitement and relief of the others nearby.

Elliot gave them the update.

"Thank you, Elliot," Matthew said.

"Keep praying," Elliot informed him, wondering where that came from.

"Oh, now you're spiritual," Benjamin said to him.

Elliot shook his head and walked away. "Shut up, Benjamin."

He heard Benjamin chuckle, "Elliot," he called after him.

"What?" he was fighting back tears, and didn't want Benjamin to see him crying again.

"You need to go home; I'll go with Scott," he said firmly, and he knew that Benjamin was right, he just didn't want him to be.

"I should be with him," he shot back at Benjamin.

"No, Elliot, you should be going after the one who meant to do dis to you; for him!"

"I don't think you understand what you're asking me to do." The tears began to roll down from his eyes to his cheeks. "I've burned that bridge."

"Maybe you have, but dat doesn't mean dey have," Benjamin said, taking Elliot by the shoulders. "You need Miles, and you need to get out of here as soon as you can. Whoever she was, she will find out soon enough she didn't shoot the right American, and she will come back for you."

"You do make a good point, Benjamin," Elliot said, looking at him.

"I know," he smiled big, "and thanks for finally realizing it."

"Do you have anything else you want to say?" Elliot allowed a half-suppressed smile to spread across his face.

"Tons!" Benjamin was serious.

Chapter Twenty

It had been nearly three weeks since Miles had returned from Burkina Faso. Jennings had called him at least three times ever since his return, wanting to know every detail about the visit. Miles humored him because he could only imagine how Simon would have reacted if he had gone off the radar for so many years. Marcia seemed to be relieved to hear that Elliot was somewhat nice to them, and seemed to have accepted that they were family.

He had continued to correspond with Scott, but in the last two days, he hadn't heard anything from him. That made him a bit nervous. He knew that they were most likely delaying the transition to the next site, but he was surprised that he hadn't heard anything. Scott had been hoping to convince Elliot to change his mind.

Simon's contacts out in L.A. hadn't turned up anything new about Stacey, or Lillian for that matter. She hadn't been seen or heard from since before they went to Africa, and they were starting to be very worried. Adam, the private investigator, had met with a few people. All of them said that she had a callback for a role, but she didn't get it, or it could be that she had been cast on a reality show, like one of the survival ones, where you are sequestered to keep it secret.

Rhea was gearing up to head back to Portland and see what she could find out about Stacey. She was prolonging her goodbye, having said more times than he could count, how good it was to have a family again. Simon hadn't helped any; he had taken her in, just like he would have if she were his own daughter. Miles hated the fact that he felt that all of this was an intrusion in his life when, instead, it should be exciting and important. If things were happening the way they appeared to be, Marcus Brent already had his clean-up lady take out a mother and her son, and now made a young actress disappear. Miles was beginning to think Simon was right, they needed to involve the press. They needed their names in print so that if something happened to them, people would notice.

His cell phone buzzed, but he didn't recognize the number. He decided to take it anyway.

"This is Miles," he answered. The voice he heard on the other end made him stand up.

"Miles, it's Elliot."

"Elliot," he said, holding back his surprise. "How are you?"

"I'm not good," something in his voice had changed. It was as if he was seeking some solace, Miles thought. "Scott's been shot."

"What," Miles gasped. "When?"

"Two days ago, he is recovering in Ouagadougou, but tomorrow they're sending him to Frankfurt, Germany."

"Who's sending him?" his mind started to crank out questions.

"The company we work for," Elliot answered. "I…" he trailed off.

"Elliot, what's wrong? Are you safe?" Miles asked him.

"I'm leaving tomorrow for Philadelphia; can you pick me up?"

"I'll be there, send me the information," Miles kept his voice steady, but inside his feelings were all over the place.

"I gotta go, this call costs a shitload," Elliot said. "Miles, thank you for coming to get me."

Miles didn't know what to say. Elliot expressing gratitude like that was very unexpected. It was a completely different Elliot. Whatever had happened, it had accomplished what he and Rhea couldn't. It had gotten Elliot to change his mind. A smile crept across his face as he said, "You're welcome, Elliot. I'll see you tomorrow."

"Yeah, see you tomorrow. I'll tell you everything then," and Elliot hung up.

ೞ౪ಬ౪ೞ

Rhea could hardly contain herself. "What the hell, Miles, why didn't you find out more?"

"We can all find out tomorrow," he said with as much patience as he could. "You know all that I know. Scott was shot, he's fine, heading to Frankfurt."

"Why isn't Elliot going with him?" she asked.

"I don't know," Miles said.

"Why didn't you ask him?" she pestered him once more. Simon seemed to sense that Rhea wasn't getting the answers she was looking for, but she wanted more than Miles could offer at that moment.

"Rhea," Simon chimed in, "it was obvious that Elliot wasn't saying much. He'll be here in less than 24 hours, and you can pepper him with all of your questions."

Rhea shook her head. Why was it that men never asked good questions? If she had been on the phone, they would have had a much longer conversation. Simon was opening his computer. "Let's see what we can find on the internet," he said.

Simon typed on the keyboard for a few seconds and then started to scroll. He kept shaking his head, it became obvious that he wasn't finding anything on the internet.

"I don't see anything about shootings in Burkina Faso," he spoke to no one in particular, "but that doesn't mean anything."

"So many questions," she said again, but noticed that Miles had already disconnected from their conversation.

He moved towards the kitchen, where he opened up the liquor cabinet and took out a bottle of bourbon. He grabbed a glass from the cupboard next to it and put some ice in it. He poured himself a double and took a long swig of it. Simon watched him over his glasses, while Rhea tried not to stare. She was a touch surprised at his behavior.

"Um," Simon started, "what was that about?"

"I'm about to admit that I was wrong," he said. Rhea smiled, but Simon didn't seem amused.

"About what?" he took the bait.

"We probably should have gone to the newspapers first."

Simon crossed his arms in front of him, looking at his son with compassion instead of annoyance. "You did what you thought was right, and it was a good idea to get in touch with everyone first."

"But," Miles asked, taking another swig of the bourbon, leaving only ice in the glass.

"But, what?" Simon asked him back. "Regret is a luxury for the incapacitated. You still have moves left, so lose the regrets, and let's start doing what you're able to do."

Rhea spoke up, not wanting to interrupt the two of them. "Guys," she said, "we need a game plan. My guess is that if we go to a larger paper, they will check the source and tip off Brent Industries that we're about to say something."

Miles and Simon turned towards her.

"That's probably true, but what should we do?" Miles asked her.

"Hamish," Simon suddenly said.

"Oh, Dad," Miles answered him with a look on his face that Rhea had never seen before.

"He has contacts that we could use," Simon said to Rhea, ignoring Miles.

"Who's this Hamish?" she asked in her typical investigative style.

"Hamish Yoder," Simon said, "he's worked with me in the past."

"Hamish," Miles said with disdain in his voice, and that same weird look, "we were at Yale together, but never ran in the same circles. He was a very indiscreet coed in the day, flaunting his British accent and attracting a following of the most unprincipled guys and young ladies, who were often behind the mischief that happened on campus. Hamish headed back to London when he graduated, and that was when he fell off my radar. That was until we ran into each other in Berlin two years ago."

"You were at Yale with him," Simon said, "I forgot about that."

"He didn't tell me he was working for you when I saw him in Berlin," Miles responded. Rhea was observing how the two of them handled conflict. It was obvious that Miles and Simon were on two different pages with this Hamish guy.

"He may not have been at that time, but you know that he has connections that he can use to get this information to someone who can funnel it into hands that will matter."

"I'm aware of his connections," Miles said, annoyed. "He used me to make one while he was in Berlin."

"Can he really help us?" Rhea wanted to know.

"Absolutely," Simon responded with certainty. "He knows people in the exact media outlets that can disperse this information without alerting the Brents."

"I don't want to see him," Miles chimed in.

"I'll meet with him," Rhea said. "I don't have a history with him, but I have you two as a connection."

"Great," Simon said, "I'll head home and start the process of contacting him. I wanted to try contacting Adam in L.A. as well. I'll be back for supper," he paused and looked at them both. "It's good that Elliot is coming. I'm looking forward to meeting him."

Miles nodded. He seemed defeated by the involvement of Hamish, and Rhea now saw a different side of him.

An hour later, Miles had Elliot's flight information and was busy arranging the pick-up. As he made up the second room in his house. Rhea went out to the grocery store to pick up some provisions. She wasn't sure what brand Elliot smoked, but she grabbed him a pack of cigarettes anyway. She figured someday she would try to convince him to stop, but this wasn't the right time. When she returned to the apartment to drop the supplies off, Miles was on the phone. He looked frustrated.

"What's wrong?" she came closer and whispered to him.

"My Dad's contact in L.A. has stumbled onto something," he filled her in. He held up a finger and nodded. "Thank you for looping us in on that. What do you suggest we do?" Miles nodded his head again, adding a few "mmhmms" and a couple of "okays" to the mix. "Please let us know as soon as you can," and he hung up.

"What was that?" she asked him.

"Dad's investigator, Adam, got hold of some closed-circuit footage near the building where Brent Industries is located. They have video of Lillian going in, but none of her coming out."

"Oh, no," she said. "Could it be possible that she is still in there? Like in a cell or something?"

Miles shook his head in a way that said he wasn't sure. "He's going to send us some freeze frames from the camera, the few days leading up to it, to see if we recognize anyone, other than Lillian, of course."

Rhea nodded at him. Her gut feeling was that they would see Elizabeth Deavers in that video. If they did, then they would have to accelerate their plans.

"Rhea," Miles asked her, "do you think that Brent had anything to do with Scott getting shot?"

"No, why would you think that?"

"My gut tells me that could be the case."

"Why would they go after Scott?" she asked him.

"I don't think Scott was the intended target. I think they were going after Elliot."

"Oh, God! No," she exclaimed. "How would she know that he was there?"

"I keep asking myself that as well," Miles uttered. "I need to make a phone call," and he stood up and left the room.

She put the groceries away and stood looking out the window in the kitchen. She was worried across the board. If it was true that Elliot was a target, that meant that she and Miles could well be the next targets.

Miles came out of the room, and he looked relieved. "Jennings and Marcia are safe."

"Oh, that's good," she exhaled a long breath, and continued. "Have they had any unwanted visitors?"

"No," he answered her.

"Did you let them know Elliot was coming back to the states?" she asked him.

"I didn't, that's his story to tell. Not mine."

"I understand that," she said, "but if I were his parents, I'd want to know." He looked at her and shrugged. "I know, we shouldn't meddle, but have you stopped to think that we're already involved?"

"I need to check in with Esme as well," he said, ignoring her question.

"There are only five of us left," she reminded him. "I hope you can convince her to come back."

"I doubt that," he shrugged. "Right now, I hope that we can harness the storm Elliot brings with him."

Chapter Twenty-One

Elliot exited the arrivals terminal looking like a college student returning from spring break. He had heavy bags under his bloodshot eyes. He hadn't shaved in days. He had on a dark blue T-shirt and khaki shorts. He was wearing flip-flops, a baseball cap, and carrying just a backpack. Yet, Miles thought that every girl he walked by took a second glance. When Elliot spotted them, he nodded. He was too cool to wave.

"Elliot," Rhea said as she moved towards him. She threw her arms around him and hugged him. He hugged her back, and when he let go, he moved to Miles. Miles wrapped his arms around his brother, who embraced him tightly in return.

"I smell," he whispered to Miles.

"Yes, you do, let's take you back to the house and clean you up."

Miles watched Elliot doze in and out of sleep as he sat in the back seat. It must have been the first time in a few days that he felt safe enough to sleep. They kept the sunroof open to keep the smell from being too much. When they arrived at the house, Simon was there to welcome them.

"Elliot," Miles said to him, "this is my Dad, Simon."

Elliot eyed him up a bit and extended a hand. "Elliot."

"Yes, nice to meet you."

"Same," Elliot put his bag on the floor and slipped off his flip-flops. "Can someone point me to the bathroom? I need to shower."

"Of course," Miles said. "Let me grab you some water as well. You'll find a towel in there for you and anything you need in the shower."

"Thanks," Elliot responded as he followed behind him. "Do you have some clothes I can borrow until I get mine washed?'

"I do," Miles responded as he realized that he and Elliot were about the same size, but they weren't even remotely the same style. "I'll bring you some clean things." Rhea was standing at the door with a glass of water, which he took from her. "Would you like me to start your laundry?"

"Sure, just don't be too shocked about what you find in my bag," Elliot said as he took off his t-shirt, which must have been the cue for Rhea to leave because she was no longer behind him.

"Why? What am I going to find?" he asked Elliot.

"I was just fucking with you, you can't get weed past those dogs in customs," Elliot said as he took off his shorts and his underwear and headed towards the bathroom. "You can just bring in the clothes, thank you so much."

"Sure thing," Miles replied as he left the room feeling slightly bewildered.

Rhea was sitting on the couch when he came from the bedroom. "I can't tell, is he hungover or trashed?"

"Is it possible to be both?" he answered.

Simon just shook his head, "Either way, I've got something to help sober him up a bit."

"He's seen a lot," Miles reminded them, "or at least we think he's seen a lot."

"Scott is his closest friend out there," Rhea said, "I'm sure his head is still spinning."

Miles agreed with her and continued into his bedroom. He was completely at a loss for what to pick out for Elliot. He grabbed some underwear and one of the many Penn polo shirts that he typically wore, which was gray and embroidered with blue. For shorts, he grabbed a pair of navy cargo shorts and a belt. He carried them into the bedroom, where he could hear the shower running and what he thought was Elliot crying.

"Everything alright?" he called into the bathroom. The sound of crying stopped.

"I'm," Elliot paused for a second, "fine. I'll be out in a few minutes."

"No rushing, just checking on you," Miles walked away from the door. "I put some clothes on the bed."

Elliot didn't answer him, so he picked up Elliot's clothing on the floor and left the room. Simon was getting an early dinner ready for them, and Rhea was on her laptop typing away. Miles went to the kitchen, took down a few plates, and began setting the table. Rhea turned and looked at him.

"Is he okay?" she asked him.

"I don't know," Miles replied. "He definitely seems different. The Elliot we met in Burkina Faso would have never asked for help."

Simon raised his eyebrows, and Rhea nodded her head, "I agree. I told you he'd come around. I felt like he looked up to you."

"I don't need him to look up to me, Rhea," he replied. He figured that it wouldn't be long before Elliot came out of the bathroom, and that meant he could hear what they were talking about. The last thing that he wanted was for Elliot to hear them talking about him.

Miles grabbed Elliot's bag and took it into the laundry room. He opened it up and was confronted with the stale smell of cigarettes and body odor. He removed the clothing from the bag and unrolled it. He couldn't throw it into the washing machine fast enough. Along the way, he found a few half-empty mini-bottles of Jim Beam, a few unused condoms, a journal, and some folded-up pieces of paper, which Miles recognized as the paper at the compound that they used to print out wires that they received. The only shoes he had brought with him were generic boat shoes, which didn't seem to have been worn much.

There was enough for a full load, and what wasn't laundry, he stuck back into the bag. Once Elliot went through the bag, he could wash it as well. He put in the detergent and started the machine. As he came out of the laundry room, he saw that Elliot was coming out of his room. He had on the shorts but hadn't yet put on the polo shirt. Miles remembered seeing him at the compound smoking in the nude. He had a pronounced farmer's tan, and it hadn't improved since they'd last seen each other. He padded barefoot through the hallway as he pulled the polo shirt over his head. He cleaned up pretty well, and the polo shirt gave him a grown-up look. He had only towel-dried his hair, so it was dark.

"Did you start my laundry?" he asked Miles.

"I did," Miles answered him.

"Did you happen to find any cigarettes in the bag?" he asked.

Miles was about to tell him he didn't when Rhea piped up.

"I took the liberty to buy you some," she said, "just to hold you over until you can go to the store and buy yourself some."

He looked at her and then at Miles.

"Is there somewhere I can smoke?" he asked.

"Sure," Miles answered, "there is a small balcony off the living room here." Miles pointed to the sliding glass door that was out of his line of sight. Rhea stood up and grabbed the pack of cigarettes she'd purchased and handed them to him. Miles took out a cigar lighter from a drawer and gave it to him as well.

"I've made you something to help you with that hangover," Simon said to him.

Elliot looked a little startled at that statement, but thanked him and took the concoction that Simon gave him. Miles noticed how both Simon and Rhea watched him as he moved through the living room to the balcony. The poor guy wasn't sure what he should do. It was like he had inherited an audience that he hadn't asked for but was stuck with. Miles followed him out to the balcony.

"Welcome to Philly," he said and held out the lighter. Rhea must have been thinking ahead because she had placed a small ashtray on the table on the balcony.

"Thanks," he said as he inhaled. "I bet you never thought you'd see me again,' he said with a sad smile.

"No, but I hoped I would," Miles answered him. "What happened?"

"I'm not sure," he began. "I was in the village getting permits and paperwork filed. I had stopped by the market, visited with the missionary doctors," Miles was surprised by that, "and then got petrol. The next thing I knew, a Land Rover was flying towards me with an African man at the wheel and an older white woman in the passenger seat. The look on her face made me ill. At that point, I turned on the radio to check in at the compound and found out that Scooper had been shot."

"Wow," Miles responded, "is he okay?"

"It just missed vital organs, he almost died from loss of blood, but the mission medical clinic was opened that day, and the doctor who was there was able to stabilize him. We moved him to the capital a day later, and they were able to finish up work on the wound. Our company is shipping him to Germany to recover in a hospital there."

"Why didn't you go with him?" Miles asked.

"He told me not to," Elliot responded. "He said he didn't want me there. We hadn't been on the best of terms since you left. He was mad that I didn't go with you."

"Did you tell him why you didn't come with us?" Miles asked him.

"I did, but he felt that it was a pathetic excuse. Scooper doesn't have a family; he's an orphan who grew up with his elderly Aunt. I was the closest thing he had to family."

"And still he didn't want you to travel with him to Germany," Miles said.

Elliot picked up the cocktail that Simon had mixed for him. He put it to his lips and winced, "I remember drinking shit like this back in college, it does the trick." He downed the drink with a few gulps.

"Why did you decide to help us?" Miles asked him more pointedly.

"He told me to."

"Scott did," he asked Elliot.

"No, Benjamin did," Elliot responded. That was a bit of a shock to Miles. His time at the compound had shown him that Benjamin was important to the two boys, but Miles hadn't expected that he would hold such sway in their lives. "He told me," and Elliot mimicked his voice, "Scott is going to be fine, but you aren't going to be fine if you go back to dat compound and just sit on your sorry white ass. Go to Miles, go and do something bigger dan yourself," Elliot paused for a second. "That's when I booked my flight and called you."

"I'm glad you did," Miles said to him as Elliot was putting out his cigarette. "I'm sorry about what you've been through, and I'm sorry that you're going to have to relive it and retell it again," Miles nodded to Simon and Rhea inside.

"Miles, when you left, there was that part of me that was relieved. I felt like I was still outrunning everything I wanted to avoid. You were the closest to ever catching up to me, and when you got in that car with Rhea, it was a victory for me. Except that my victory came with a price. Scooper and Benjamin were both disappointed in me. Scooper, deeply. Benjamin, more on a fatherly level. Scooper froze me out, but Benjamin talked at me for a few days. I ignored him, and then once he wore me down, I listened. That was a few days before Scooper was shot. I was trying to make amends, and I almost didn't get to."

"That had to be hard," Miles tried to sound comforting.

"It was hell," Elliot said. "I'm not a damn softy, but I broke that day at the clinic. I realized that no matter what, my past was going to catch me. I can't prove that I was the target, but I damn sure feel like I was supposed to be, and now I'm pissed off, and I'm ready to make her pay."

"Revenge is a dangerous motive, Elliot," Miles said, looking at him. Elliot nodded his head and took a drag on his cigarette.

"Nobody fucks with my family," he said as tears welled up in his eyes. "Scooper was my family, just like you're my family. Just like Rhea is my family. This ends now."

"This ends now," Miles repeated back, and Elliot broke down into sobs. Miles stood up and hugged him. They stood that way for what felt like a long time. He held him tight and just let Elliot cry. Miles wasn't sure what he was witnessing, but he was pretty sure it was exactly how the prodigal son had felt when he finally got home and his Dad ran towards him.

⋐⋛⋧⋐⋨

By the time dinner was served, Elliot didn't look like he had been crying anymore. His language was as peppery as usual, but he engaged with Simon and Rhea and indulged them with the story again. He answered minute details the best he could. He would get choked up when he talked about Scott and get misty-eyed when he told them about the way Benjamin had shown him the right path.

"What was it about that woman that made you quiver?" Rhea asked him.

"I don't know, but as I sat at the clinic, I couldn't help but shake the feeling that I had seen her before."

"If so, where do you think you'd have seen her?" Simon took over the questioning.

"That's the kicker, I don't know. It could have been in the capital; it could have been when I was on vacation in Senegal, it could be from my childhood," he said somewhat flippantly and then paused. Miles felt a lightbulb go off in his head. He stood up and went into his office, and came back with a picture.

"Was this her?" he asked Elliot.

Elliot looked at the grainy picture of Elizabeth Deavers. His eyes widened. "I can't be sure if that was her in the car—it was flying—but I can tell you with certainty that this woman was at my mother's funeral."

Miles felt a sensation he hadn't had for a long time, it was that of utter dread. He could tell by the look on Rhea's face that she was starting to panic.

"We've got a lot to catch you up on," Miles told Elliot, "but I'm almost certain that you were her target, and we'll be next."

"Whoever was driving her has kept her off the radar," Elliot said.

"What do you mean?" Rhea asked him.

"None of my people are hearing any chatter about an older white woman," he said. "If her target was me, she must not know she got the wrong guy."

"Or she does, but needs to lay low," Miles added. "You should probably check on Scott."

Chapter Twenty-Two

Elizabeth walked out of her hotel. It was blazing outside, and she had spent the last two nights lying low. Fatima was waiting for her under the carport, and when she saw Elizabeth, she unlocked a car—the same one she had picked Elizabeth up in—and they both got in. "Your driver took his time getting me back here. Was it necessary for me to lay low in that shit hole of a village you found?"

"Yes, unfortunately," she said with a hint of tension in her voice.

"What do you mean, unfortunately?" Elizabeth asked.

"You didn't kill the white devil kid," Fatima sounded annoyed as she answered.

"What do you mean?" Elizabeth's voice betrayed her panic.

"You shot the other white man at the compound; Elliot was in the village," Fatima said. "I told the driver to tell you, but he refused to; said you were the closest thing to a demon he had ever met."

"Oh, well," Elizabeth paused. "What was the name of the guy I killed?" Elizabeth asked.

"You didn't kill anyone," she said. "Scott Cooper is

recovering somewhere in Europe, and Elliot Sharp is no longer in the country. Most likely, he left with Scott."

Something sickening churned inside of Elizabeth's stomach. More mistakes. She had kept this escapade to herself because she was sure it was an easy in and out. It would have been a straightforward job in her heyday, but she had relied on others instead of herself.

"Where did they send the kid?" she asked Fatima, tamping down the panic and taking back control of her emotions.

"No way to find out for sure. The company they work for went into protective mode, and I don't have anyone on the inside there."

"You can't track their flight information," she probed Fatima further.

"Elizabeth, you need to let this go," Fatima spoke firmly. "You're lucky that this hasn't shown up on any international radar. You shot an American citizen in Africa, a place known for Islamic terrorists, and it hasn't landed in any news source."

"That may change once Scott or Elliot start talking," she said, gazing outside the car's window.

"They've been out of Burkina for almost 24 hours, and nothing has shown up on any of the news sources, so you're safe for now."

"Twenty-four hours," Elizabeth whispered.

They might as well have had a five-day head start. She needed to figure out where those two boys were, because she couldn't afford to leave any trace behind.

"You may make it out of this pretty much unscathed," Fatima said as she turned her face towards Elizabeth for the first time since they started talking.

"How so?" Elizabeth asked.

"They have no idea who your employer is," she uttered. "Up to now, no one knows that you've been here."

"That's okay and all, but if my intended target pops up on any radars, that could be a problem," she sighed. "I need to find where they took the boy I shot."

"I'm on that," Fatima winked, "but that information won't come cheap."

"Damn it," she abruptly shifted her focus to Fatima. "Even you're on the take."

"Hardly," she laughed, "but the guy I need to get the information from is."

She continued explaining the possible contact to Elizabeth, but Elizabeth's mind was concentrated on something completely different. Elliot Sharp was still alive. Elliot Sharp could give her some massive headaches. Miles and Rhea would have to wait their turn, but she would need to get to Elliot first.

☙❧☙❧

The drive to Lagos was horrible, but it was the only way to get out of Burkina Faso and to Frankfurt. Nigeria was the only

West African country she liked, but her time there was short and full of negotiations with incompetent airline workers. Unfortunately, the information that Fatima paid for only provided her with the names of four possible hospitals; two were in Frankfurt, one in Kaiserslautern, and the other in Hamburg. She decided on Frankfurt first and was on the way to the second hospital to find Scott Cooper.

The taxi dropped her off at the entrance, and she went inside to the front desk. She didn't even wait for the lady at the desk to initiate the conversation. "Do you speak English?" she asked.

"Yes," the woman replied, "what can I help you with?"

"I'm looking to visit with an American patient who just came in. His name is Scott Cooper," she stated.

"One second," she replied and typed some things into her computer, which Elizabeth could see on the screen in the mirrored glass behind the reception desk. The name popped up on the screen, but she could tell that he wasn't having any visitors by the way that the receptionist looked at the name. What she could make out was that he was in a 300-level room.

"Sorry, he is not allowed visitors," she communicated.

"Oh," Elizabeth feigned surprise, "I'm a friend of his family, who haven't arrived yet, and they wanted me to check in on him."

"Sorry, he isn't to have any visitors, which is all I can tell you."

"Sorry to bother you, but is your cafeteria open," she changed their discourse. Elizabeth had to find another way through this.

"Yes, it's down that hall to the right," she pointed to Elizabeth's left.

"Thank you," she said and headed that way. As she rounded the corner, she saw the elevator sign and pressed the button. Once she was in, she pressed the button numbered 3 and waited. The door closed, and she went up. She thought of just walking by the nurses, pretending not to understand them. Most of these European countries would be frustrated with you if you talked loudly, complained, and pretended to play dumb. She had used that tactic often in Paris, and she would see how it worked with the Germans.

The door opened, and she saw a sign. One pointed to the neonatal unit, and the other to the intensive care ward. The doors were closed; she approached them, and they swung open. They led her to a small waiting room with a window where no one was currently sitting. There were doors next to the window, but when she tried them, they were locked.

"Frau," a voice came from inside the window now. She was talking animatedly, telling Elizabeth that she needed to check in. She understood her, but instead, she feigned ignorance.

"Oh, my God," she said, "thank God someone is here. My nephew is in there, and he's an American."

The lady behind the window looked at her strangely and then said to her in English, "he cannot have visitors. How did you get up here?"

Elizabeth was a touch surprised that her frantic nature wasn't phasing this nurse. "Do you have an ID?" the woman asked her. Elizabeth was about to say something, but just as she was to open her mouth, the lady told her to hold on for a minute and disappeared. She heard a rustling behind her and turned to see a young Black man taking a seat. He looked up at her and nodded. He was on the phone with someone but had his earphones in. "Hold on," he said in accented English, "let me put you on speaker phone."

God, Elizabeth thought, *why the hell would you do that?* She turned to face him completely. "Could you not do that?"

He smiled, "I could, but then my friend wouldn't be able to speak to you."

"Why would your friend want to speak to me?" she asked.

"Elliot," he said into the phone, "is she the one in the picture?"

Elizabeth realized that he was on a video call and that whoever he was talking to could see her. At that moment, she felt her heart take on a new cadence.

"That's her," the voice on the other side said, "hang up with me and call security."

Elizabeth didn't wait around for that to happen. She went through the doors as quickly as she could and took the steps down three flights. She ran out of the hospital as fast as she could and jumped into the taxi waiting at the taxi stand. As they pulled away, she saw two armed police officers appear from the entryway of the hospital. She had far more problems than Scott Cooper being a loose end to tie up. Elliot Sharp knew who she was. What was worse was that she wasn't exactly sure who he was and, even worse, where he was.

She gave the driver the address of the hotel where she had made a reservation. As the car drove through the city, she contemplated her next moves. Scott was off-limits. The company they worked for had hired security. Elliot had figured out who she was by photos, most likely.

When she got to the hotel, she opened up her laptop and logged into her command center. She had an urgent message from Saul, but it was too early to call him, and she needed to have some ducks in a row first. Elliot Sharp, she'd seen his driver's license photo, but that was her only reference to him. She did a travel search, looking for his passport to have been scanned. He had landed in Philadelphia close to 40 hours ago. Why Philadelphia? He was from Oklahoma, and she barely finished that thought when it hit her that Miles Trent, too, lived in Philadelphia. If Elliot knew who Elizabeth was, that meant Miles did, too, and her guess was that Rhea did as well. The element of surprise was gone. This was now a full-on hunting expedition, and the prey knew they were being hunted.

She waited an hour and called Saul. He picked up at once.

"Where the hell are you?" he barked from the other side of the world. Elizabeth could sense his panic.

"I was in Africa, and now I'm in Frankfurt," she answered truthfully since he most definitely already knew.

"Why?"

"I was following up on some information I got from Lillian. She mentioned two names, and I wanted to see if they knew anything."

"You couldn't call them," he asked.

"No," she responded, "this demanded a face-to-face type of meeting."

"We have a problem," he said sternly.

"What now?" she asked in a raised pitch.

"Don't what now me, Elizabeth," he yelled this time. "Someone is snooping around about Lillian."

Elizabeth's spirit sank. It was all catching up to her now. "Are they going to find anything?"

"I. Don't. Know," Saul said, emphasizing every syllable, "that's why I'm asking you."

"Were efforts made to shut this down?" Elizabeth demanded.

"Of course, but you know as well as I do that someone sneaking around could lead to someone talking to the press, which could lead to something being published, etc..."

"So, they won't be able to publish it," she said while steadying her voice.

"It's the goddam internet age, Elizabeth!" Saul was getting

irritated, "They don't need a paper to publish it. They can put it online!"

"Nobody believes what they read online," she said jokingly.

"The constituency we're counting on for votes sure do," he shot back at her. Elizabeth thought that through. People who read the legitimate press wouldn't be shocked by such news. Most of them wouldn't care, but the generations that gather their news from the "truer-than-the-Bible" internet would. "I don't need to remind you how important it is that something like this doesn't come out. If you remember correctly, you were hired to ensure that something like this never happened. So now my question to you is, where did you fuck up, Elizabeth?"

"It's under control," she hissed back. "No one will find out anything about Lillian."

"I don't want to know," he said, "just get the results or a certain unsealed document will be sent to a few of my friends in the FBI, and I'm pretty sure the first charge they will be leveling at you has the word treason in it."

He hung up on her. She sat stunned. That *file* had not been mentioned since the day she signed her contract with Brent Industries. Keeping that file shut was the reason that she did what she did. Without its existence, she would have lived an entirely different life. She closed the computer and sat at the desk for a few minutes. It was time to change her plans. It was one thing to have someone snooping around about Lillian, but it would be another thing altogether if Saul and the press, and God forbid Marcus, found out about the rest of the "heirs."

Chapter Twenty-Three

Elliot stood in the middle of the living room, staring at Miles in the kitchen. He hung up the phone. "She's in Frankfurt."

"Is Scott safe?" Miles inquired.

"Benjamin is with him, so he's safe. She took off when he mentioned security."

"My guess is we've got about a day before she shows up here," Miles said. "I'll have my Dad reach out to his contacts in immigration. Once her passport hits customs, he'll receive an alert, and we can go from there."

"Time to catch the spider in her own web," Elliot said, eagerly rubbing his hands together.

"A little over-dramatic, but that works," Miles said back while smiling.

෴

"Adam has some information for us," his Dad said to him as he came through the door. "He's going to try to call in about an hour."

Miles sat at the counter in the kitchen, looking through some notes in preparation for the fall semester. He had made the decision that morning that he needed something else to occupy his time in between the waiting. Elizabeth's passport hadn't popped up on anyone's radar yet. This call with Adam would be the first new piece of information they had had in almost a week.

"Elliot's still asleep," he told Simon.

"Well, wake him up," he demanded.

Miles shot him a squinted, annoyed look. Rhea had convinced Elliot to quit smoking, and it had been anything but an enjoyable experience. Miles would have preferred Elliot smoking to having to deal with him as he went through withdrawal. Miles had started wondering if he'd need to go to rehab himself since his drinking had increased to put up with Elliot's mood swings.

"It's better for all of us if he just wakes up on his own," Miles said to his Dad and went back to finishing up his work. Miles looked at his syllabus and began to imagine what it would be like to be back in the classroom again. Teaching in Germany was a different experience. The students were interested in discourse, here, they were interested in grades and getting a degree.

"If you aren't going to wake him," he countered. "I'll do it."

"Good luck," he said.

Miles heard him walk back to the room and knock. He heard a grunt from behind the door, "Elliot," he said, "it's Simon. Adam is calling us with an update in about an hour."

He heard a small grumble from the bedroom but couldn't make out what Elliot had said to his Dad. He heard his Dad open the door and then an exclamation of discomfort from Elliot. Miles guessed he had flipped the light switch on. He could tell they were talking but couldn't get a pulse on the tone of the conversation.

Simon came from the hallway into the living room area and didn't look any worse for the wear. Miles's nerves had been on edge for the last few days as Elliot tried to clean up his act, which was a phrase he repeated often when talking with Miles. Miles bounced between love and aggravation with him. Today, he'd just started out being annoyed. Rhea never wanted to be an only child, while he, on the other hand, never thought about being anything but an only child. It felt like suddenly he had a lot of people relying on him, and that was something he'd never asked for, nor wanted.

Slowly, the house came alive as Elliot stumbled out of the bedroom and made a beeline for the coffee. He looked at Miles but didn't say anything. He slept in ill-fitting boxer shorts, which had caused some awkward moments for Miles, but Elliot seemed unaffected. He didn't seem to care who saw what, and what they saw. Miles wasn't sure if he was ever going to be used to having a brother, especially one like Elliot.

"Rhea will be here in about 15 minutes," Simon addressed Elliot. Miles chuckled. He knew what Simon meant, even if he hadn't said it. He also knew that the chances of Elliot getting the hint were pretty slim.

"He's trying to tell you to go get dressed," Miles said to him as he got up and closed his computer. Elliot nodded at him and sat down on the couch anyway. Simon rolled his eyes at Miles, and Miles just shrugged his shoulders. It was how things worked with Elliot. He did what he wanted, when he wanted. It was still a shock to him that Rhea had been able to convince him to quit smoking, and he was hoping that this nasty withdrawal period would end soon.

"I heard from Hamish this morning," Simon began.

"People still call their kids Hamish," Elliot interrupted as he stood and headed back to the bedroom.

"It's a traditional name in Scotland," Simon corrected him. "How are you feeling today?"

"Ugh," was all Elliot said, "but not as bad as yesterday."

Miles took note that he didn't use his normal profanity to explain his condition, which he acknowledged as a good sign. Deep down he enjoyed the exchange between his father and his half-brother.

"Is Hamish good to go?" Miles asked Simon, who was taking a sip of coffee, and responded with a thumbs up.

Miles took his computer back to his office. He paused a beat, enjoying the quiet. Elliot normally wouldn't cross the threshold of the office, so it was the one place he had privacy. At night, sometimes, Elliot would come into his room and sit on the edge of his bed, talking to him about his time in Africa, or the girls who had broken his heart in college. But for some reason, the office was not a place that Elliot ventured into. He'd knock and then stand at the door, but he never entered.

Miles sat at his desk and looked at the books on the shelf and the plaques that denoted achievements. He looked at the items around him that cataloged his achievements. He wondered what his life would have been like if Marcus Brent had been a part of it. He suspected it wouldn't have been a pleasant life, even if a certain amount of privilege had come with it. Yet, if he was honest with himself, he *had* grown up in privilege and comfort, especially when compared to the childhoods Rhea, Elliot, and Lillian had experienced. They had lived differently from him. Maybe being a part of the Brent family would have been preferable to them.

His thoughts were interrupted when he heard Rhea arrive. She'd taken to hugging them all when she got there, and they had become somewhat used to it. He was okay with hugging on occasion, but the consistent hugs were something new to him. They meant everything to Rhea, so Miles put aside any amount of discomfort he may have felt. Elliot also seemed to be a bit taken aback by it and had remained shirtless when he knew she was expected, thinking that would stop her from hugging him. He had underestimated her. The power of a woman who had always wanted to be a sister to someone was not going to be overcome or extinguished by the awkwardness of her newly found younger brothers.

Miles came out of the office, and Rhea swooped towards him

and hugged him. "How's he doing?" she whispered as she wrapped her arms around him.

"He's not as grouchy today," he said to her above a whisper.

"Stop talking 'bout me," Elliot's voice broke in. "I'm going to be just fine. I feel better every day. It was more of a nervous habit for me."

"Hmm," Rhea said, "habit is a great word." Elliot rolled his eyes and gave her the middle finger, but Rhea just laughed it off and kissed him on the forehead.

Simon, who seemed to have disappeared from the room for a while, spoke up, "Miles I just sent a file to your printer, can you grab it?"

"Sure," Miles said, and headed back into his office. He watched the papers sliding out of the printer, and he waited to hear the chime that would tell him that it was finished. He picked them up and realized that they were documents, including a few pictures from Adam. It was the fourth picture that made him stop dead in his tracks.

A picture of Elizabeth and about three other men walking in or near her as they surrounded Marcus Brent. The man on the left-hand side of Marcus Brent looked very familiar to him. He could see him standing behind the bar. He rushed out to the living room holding the picture out to his father.

"I've seen this guy," he said passing the picture out to Simon and pointed at the dark-haired muscular man.

"What, where?" Rhea asked.

Simon snatched the picture and looked at it as Elliot came over to the two of them.

"Do you remember when I told you there was a bartender in Mexico who told me I looked like Marcus Brent?"

"Yes," she responded confusedly, "why?"

"It was him," Miles said.

"Are you sure?" Simon asked him more like a lawyer than a father.

"I'm positive," he said. "This was the guy, and that means that Esme is in trouble."

"You don't know that," Simon said to him. "It's possible that he doesn't even know she's there."

"Or he does know and has been tasked with keeping his eye on her," Miles tried to make a point, "or worse yet, he was assigned to find her, and I just led him to her."

Elliot had taken the picture from Simon and was staring at it. "I'm almost positive that I've seen him before. At my mother's funeral."

"What are you talking about, Elliot?" Simon asked as he switched to his lawyer side.

"She was there," he pointed at Elizabeth, "and he was with her as well."

"You were young," Simon said, "are you sure?"

"I *am*," Elliot said with his signature stubbornness that Miles had become accustomed to.

"It does confirm what Marcia and Jennings told me about that day. They said that an unfamiliar man and woman attended the funeral."

"After we are off of the phone with Adam, we'll send them this picture to confirm," Simon was in his full boss mode now.

Miles scanned through the other photographs as they waited for Adam to connect with them. One picture was of Barton Traeger getting into a black sports car. The next was of a gated entrance to a driveway. There was a guardhouse, but that was about it

When Adam finally called, he was greeted by a dozen questions in turn.

"Whoa," he said in his somewhat gruff style, "how about a hello first?"

"Hi, Adam," Simon said. "As you can tell, we're anxious to connect with you."

"I can hear that," Adam uttered, "what's everyone on about?"

Miles, feeling like Esme's life was in trouble, jumped in first, "one of the bodyguards in the picture with Elizabeth is in Mexico. I'm not sure why he's there, but I fear that it isn't a good thing."

"Which one?" Adam asked.

Miles described him to Adam, and Adam looked at a sheet in front of him. "I just got most of this information back from my search, so I'll send it to you, Simon, but that guy, I know him."

"Really," Miles asked, surprised, "who is he?"

"His name is Michael Davidson; he'd be in his mid-50s now and used to be one of Marcus Brent's bodyguards. He stopped working for Brent about 3 ½ years ago, and said, he was done dealing with that "loathsome dick", his words, not mine, although I would agree. He disappeared about 2 years ago, which normally means that Brent had something to do with it."

"So, he left Brent Industries," Simon said as his eyes drifted upwards.

"Yes," Adam answered, "he and I weren't close, but I knew him, and he knew that Brent was enough of an asshole that he couldn't keep working for him. Almost everyone I know who has worked for Brent has iron-clad non-disclosures when they leave. If they don't break them, they live out their lives happily."

"And if they break them?" Rhea cut in.

"They disappear."

That hung out there in the air. Miles was wondering what Michael was doing in Mexico. Was he hiding too? If he wasn't hiding, then he would have been sent there; either way, it wasn't good in Miles's opinion. He needed to get back to Mexico as quickly as possible.

"What about the other pictures that you sent us?" Rhea asked him while sensing the need to change the subject.

"I tracked Barton Traeger," Adam informed. "I found out two things, neither of which is good."

"Well, let's have it," Simon coaxed him on.

"He stopped at a random diner where he met up with Elizabeth Deavers. After that, she took off towards LA, and he headed up north. It was hard to follow him at night on deserted roads, but by the time I figured out where he was heading, all I got was a picture of that gate and a guard."

"Did he come back out?" Miles was the first to lead the follow-up questions.

"No one has been in or out of that compound for about three days now. I set up a camera, and it's like the place has been abandoned."

The group stood there silently and exchanged glances from one to another and then to the screen in front of them.

A sense of dread burrowed its way into Miles's gut, and he knew that this story wouldn't end well.

"Is there a back entrance?" Elliot piped up.

"Probably, but I can't find it," Adam flipped some papers over, "at any rate … if Lillian was there, she isn't anymore."

The way they stared at the screen was captured in the tiny box at the top left corner. Miles saw the horror on Rhea's face, the mental processing on his Dad's, the flash of anger on Elliot's, and the shock on his own. They all forgot to form words as this probability struck their ears and processed inside their brains.

"That's all I got," Adam resumed, sensing the gravity of the news he had delivered, "but I'm working a few leads on my end to see what's going on. I've a few favors left to call in, but after that, Simon, I might need to get out of L.A."

"We can make that happen," Simn responded. "Keep us updated."

☙❧

After the call with Adam ended, they spent about an hour running through ideas and thoughts about what to do next. Miles was ready to fly down to Esme right away. Rhea and Elliot wanted to head to L.A. and bring the fight to Brent's front door. *None of them seems to be thinking straight*, Miles thought. He knew his thoughts were equally blurred.

"Listen," Simon finally said, "those are all legitimate things, but that doesn't mean they're the most pressing things. If we can put this in the hands of the press, we have enough picture evidence to make it look like Marcus Brent is trying to make Lillian disappear."

"Then we need to meet with Hamish as soon as we can," Miles said, annoyed by this prospect.

"Yes," replied Simon. "Here's how I think this can play out. Rhea," he turned away from Miles to address her, "You and Miles meet with Hamish, and see what he can do in the media realm. He has one or two connections who owe him, and I'm sure he'll be ready and willing to use them. Then," he turned back to Miles, "you can run down to see Esme. Talk to her and let her know what you've found out."

"Can't Rhea just meet up with Hamish?" Miles questioned Simon, at the same time realizing that his Dad wasn't exactly in charge of the investigation. He was just offering ideas. "It would be more advantageous for me to head down there now."

Simon just shrugged, "You have time to do both. You need to get in touch with her before you head down there, and while you're waiting for a response, you can meet with Hamish."

"What am I going to be doing?" Elliot asked.

"You're going to Oklahoma," he said firmly, "Enough of this bullshit with your family."

೮೮೦೮೦೮೩

Hamish was waiting for them as they arrived at the restaurant. Miles checked his watch to confirm they weren't late, but Hamish seemed to be early. He stood to walk towards them, and Miles pointed him out to Rhea.

"That's Hamish Yoder coming towards us," he said to her. She locked eyes on him, and he could tell that, like most women he knew, she had immediately noticed his handsome features. If she hadn't fallen for his looks, the second he opened his mouth, she would be melting over his accent. Simon had always encouraged him to pick up an accent when they lived in Germany and Belgium, but he had stuck with the American accent of his mother and father.

"Miles Trent," Hamish stood before them with his hand outstretched, "you're looking good." Rhea stood next to him, just staring, as Miles took Hamish's outstretched hand, but instead of a handshake, he was pulled into a very tight embrace. It wouldn't have dawned on Hamish that this meeting was awkward because Miles in no way let on that it would have been. Their short time together in Berlin was over two years ago, and Miles was the only one who felt less than stellar about that time together.

Miles let go of the embrace a little too quickly, and he was sure that Hamish felt that. "This is my sister, Rhea," he said to Hamish, who turned to greet her.

"I would have known from a mile away you were his sister," Hamish said as he took her hand into both of his. "The only difference is that you're way more beautiful than he is."

Rhea chuckled at that, and Miles felt a stab of regret for not giving her any background on Hamish. It wasn't why they were here anyway.

"Thank you for meeting us, Hamish," Miles said to him.

"Anytime," Hamish smiled at him, "I've gotten us a table over here, let's head that way, and you can catch me up on what your father deemed a 'very important matter.'"

Miles and Rhea followed Hamish to the table that he had been at when they arrived. The waiter came over shortly after they had seated themselves to take their orders, and as he left, Miles wasted no time getting to the point.

"We need you to help us break a news story."

"What type of news story?" Hamish asked.

"One that could destroy a politician's career," Rhea chimed in.

"Is it credible?" Hamish fired off the question like an investigator.

"Yes," Miles's flat voice responded.

"Which politician are we gunning for?" Hamish dug deeper and tried to contain his excitement.

Rhea leaned in a whispered, "Marcus Brent."

"Hell no," Hamish exclaimed instantaneously. "Nobody wants to touch that man!"

"Why not?" Miles asked in shock.

Their raised voices had caused a few of the neighboring tables to look their way. Hamish smiled at the people looking at them, and they seemed to go back to their own business. Miles looked back at Hamish, raised his eyebrows, and motioned with his hand for Hamish to answer.

"Because he fights back," Hamish muttered. "He learned that from his old man. You don't just throw out a story to discredit him without him discrediting you or, worse, making it all disappear completely. Story. Storyteller. Poof," he made a gesture with his hand at his mouth as he said poof, "gone."

"We're aware of the dangers," Miles stated.

"Are you, Miles?" he gazed into his eyes. "That hasn't always been my experience with you."

Rhea looked at him, and Miles's face flushed with

embarrassment and anger all at once.

"I didn't have all the information that time," Miles stammered. He was having a difficult time keeping his emotions in check. "I have it all now."

"You better hope you do," Hamish whispered as the waitress brought them their coffees.

"Before we go any further," Rhea jumped in, "are you willing to help us?"

"Depends," Hamish said as his gaze landed on her. "What do you have on him?"

"Us," she said bluntly.

Hamish shook his head. He wasn't exactly sure what she meant by "us". "You're going to have to elaborate on that one."

"Well," she paused for a second, and Miles debated jumping in to help her, but she picked up strongly. "To be exact, Miles, myself, Lillian, Elliot, Esperanza, and Dustin, who just recently died. We are his children."

"Yeah, right," he said, somewhat shocked, but then looked at them both. "Bloody hell, I've never thought about it, but Miles you do look like that twat."

"I know," Miles hissed at him.

"So, these other names, I assume, are also your siblings?" Hamish asked, returning to his investigative work.

"Yes," Rhea agreed.

"Miles, I know your mom has passed," he leaned forward,

"but what about the mothers of these kids? Are they still around? Can they corroborate the story?"

"My mother is dead, so is Elliot's mother, and Dustin's mother died with him," Rhea answered.

"I'm sorry for your loss, Rhea," Hamish said and halted for a second before shooting the next question, "That would leave the mothers of Lillian, and what was the name of the last one?"

"Esperanza," Miles spoke quietly, worried that if someone were spying or eavesdropping, they would learn her name, preventing him from helping both her and Esme.

"Can they help give validity to this story?" Hamish started again.

Miles closed his eyes in resignation. He knew the answer, but that didn't mean they shouldn't reveal the story.

"Well," Hamish was prodding, and Rhea was looking at him, waiting for his move. He paused too long because she jumped right in.

"Lillian's mother is in the wind. I talked with her about a month ago, and now she's gone. Esme, the mother of Esperanza, won't work with us."

"Well, if you want this to work, you'll need her," Hamish advised.

"Won't our DNA tests work?" Rhea asked as she fiddled with the dangling charms of her bracelet.

"Do you have them for all of you?" Hamish responded, his

eyes briefly catching the motion of Rhea's bracelet.

"No, just for Miles, Elliot, and me," she answered him.

"That won't get you very far. Let's back up. How did you find out about all of this?" Hamish straightened his posture, his interest in the matter growing again.

Miles narrated the story again as he calmed his emotions. Hamish asked questions along the way but never interrupted him. When Miles had finished, Hamish threw out a question that Miles knew was coming, "Where is this Dr. Abbott?"

"We don't know," Miles sighed, seeing how the information was stacking up.

"You know what," Hamish shrugged, "it doesn't matter. He will have a non-disclosure agreement, not to mention an ethical code that prevents him from discussing anything about his patients."

"Probably true," Miles acquiesced.

"Definitely true," Hamish responded, "you can count on that having been in place from the first day he started working for Brent Industries. If someone breaks that silence, we aren't talking about a lengthy and expensive court case with this family; we're talking about people disappearing, never to be heard from again."

"We know," Miles said, lowering his gaze and staring into the coffee, "and we also know who's doing the dirty work for him. Her name is Elizabeth Deavers."

"What do you mean, you know," Hamish asked, lifting his

brows.

"Dustin and his mother Angela were most likely killed because of this."

"Explain what you mean by *most likely*," Hamish said, taking a sip from his coffee.

Rhea did her best to piece together the story from the moment Stacey popped up in her back seat to the second they saw Elizabeth Deavers in the parking lot at the funeral. Hamish was paying attention, and when she finished, he fell back in his chair, rubbing his chin.

"You may have something," he finally spoke. "That makes sense, but only if you know what to look for in the Brent family."

"It's not the only incident we're looking into," Miles said while fixing his eyes on Hamish. "Lillian has gone missing."

"That doesn't sound good," Hamish said, leaning forward.

"Also," Miles said.

"There's an *also*," Hamish raised his eyebrows quizzically again.

"Yes, there seemed to have been an attempt made on Elliot's life in Africa," Miles added.

"An attempt? But he survived?" Hamish posed the question, knowing the answer.

"He did, but only because they shot the wrong white guy," Miles answered.

"Shit," Hamish said as something registered in his eyes, "did that kid live?"

"Yes," Rhea was the one to speak this time, "he's in a hospital in Germany, most likely coming back to the US in a few days."

"Do we know who put the hit on him?" Hamish asked.

The rapid fire from Hamish was getting under Rhea's skin, and Miles had noticed it. He had come to know that look of Rhea very well, and he nudged her underneath the table, ensuring Hamish didn't see it. She gave him the side eye and took the first sip from the cup that had already cooled down. Miles carried on to give Hamish his take on the situation.

"It's not hard to make the jump, considering Elizabeth Deavers was in Burkina Faso then and made a follow-up appearance in Frankfurt to clean up the mess."

Hamish looked at them both. He smiled, "That's your story," he exclaimed as he pointed an index finger at them.

"No, it isn't," Miles objected.

"Trust me, the only way to get to Marcus Brent is to go at his people," Hamish said as he lowered his voice. "His people are dear to him, not because he loves them, but because they're all expendable."

"That makes no sense," Rhea shot back at him.

"Listen," Hamish smiled at her, "the most precious commodity that you can have in his position is people who will take the fall for you without implicating you. They know he can replace them, so they'll do whatever it takes to stay in his good graces."

"So, what are you thinking?" Miles interjected, breaking the tension that seemed to be building between Rhea and Hamish.

"You leak a tiny story about the shooting, tying it to a white woman of her build and age. Then you start building on that by pinpointing that this Deavers lady was there and also in North Carolina."

"And we have her in L.A. at the time that Lillian goes missing," Rhea interrupted as she put the cup down.

"Exactly, we don't leak what you want to at first," he said with a smile, "we let that information be slowly uncovered."

"What if no one takes the lead on it?" Miles asked skeptically as he leaned in towards Hamish.

"Trust me, I'll make sure that every part of this ends up in the press," Hamish sounded amused. "My guess is Simon has already contacted his people at immigration so that you'll be notified when Deavers crosses back into the US."

"He has, but there hasn't been any movement yet," Miles answered.

Hamish sank into the chair and held his coffee mug in his hands. It was clear that he was satisfied with his game plan. Miles had learned the hard way in Berlin that you don't mess with a plan that the great Hamish Yoder has crafted. He would follow Hamish's lead on this one. Better yet, he was going to let Rhea follow up with Hamish. He wanted to be on a plane to Mexico to make sure Esme was alright.

Chapter Twenty-Four

Elliot was bored. It had only been a few days since Miles and Rhea had left for their assignments, but it seemed like much longer. Simon would soon pick him up for dinner and had explicitly warned Elliot to listen to him this time.

"You *will* dress decently," he told Elliot.

"What if I don't have anything," he retorted.

"I'll bring you something," he replied flippantly. "Just be showered and ready to go."

Simon arrived about forty minutes before they were to leave. He handed a bag to Elliot, and he opened it up and peeked in. There were very nice-looking button-up shirts, a few pairs of dress pants, and a tie.

"Here are some shoes for you as well," Simon smiled. "If you're going to be on TV soon, you better look good."

Elliot just nodded as he pulled out some of the clothing and spread it on Miles's dining room table. He stared at it. He didn't even have them on yet, but he already felt constricted.

"That shirt, with those pants, and then you can wear these shoes," Simon drew out a pair of brown loafers from a second bag, "without socks. Kind of ease you into it."

"Okay," Elliot said, and he began to strip off his shorts.

"Good lord, kid," Simon said and shook his head.

Elliot ignored his discomfort, "have you heard anything from Miles and Rhea?"

"When that boy gets something in his head, there's no deterring him," Simon commented.

"Why are you so worried about him heading back down there," Elliot said to him as he pulled on the pants. They fit perfectly.

"Isn't that obvious?" Simon said plainly, almost without any emotion.

"He'll be killed," Elliot ventured to guess.

"That's part of it," Simon sighed, "but really, I fear losing him."

"You won't lose him," Elliot said, trying to reassure Simon. Simon headed to the kitchen, his sights set on a bottle of Miles's scotch.

"Those sorts of platitudes don't help people, Elliot. Just ask Jennings and Marcia," Simon took down a glass and poured himself a drink.

Elliot stood there stunned. Simon was always cordial and patient with him. He had been way more caring to Elliot than he had needed to be as he stopped smoking. That last sentence had stung, but Elliot knew well enough that it was meant to sting. It was a rebuff and a reminder. Elliot had a journey to go on that had nothing to do with this current chapter. Elliot had always stood firmly in the camp that he had been the victim of this whole thing. He had never stopped to think that his actions had caused his family so much pain that others would see them as the victims of his selfishness.

"Would you like a drink, too?" Simon asked him.

"Bourbon, on the rocks," Elliot was sliding into the shirt that Simon had picked. "Double."

Simon nodded sideways. "That wasn't very kind of me."

"It wasn't a lie either," Elliot said as Simon pushed the drink across the counter to him. He picked it up and took a long swig of it.

"Elliot," Simon said, "you're a great kid. I can see it. You put up this facade, making it look like you were running from everything. Where did you land? Africa, digging wells and helping build schools? I love that about you. Yet," he paused and stared outside before continuing, "you break my heart. I mourn for your parents." Elliot went to interrupt his sentence, but Simon put up a hand, "I know, but they were the ones who chose to raise you. They've remained invested in you even after you began to chip away at them. They're your parents and the only family you had until recently."

"It's so complicated, Simon," Elliot whispered as he took a small second sip.

"I don't care. Family is complicated," Simon's voice cracked slightly. "Call them."

"I," Elliot stammered a little. He wasn't sure how to continue protesting, so Simon carried on.

"Just call them and stop being a baby about it," and with that, Simon sat down and finished his drink.

Elliot just stared at him. "Well shit, I guess I'll give them a call."

"Good," Simon said, standing back up, "your flight is booked for tomorrow. Maybe try to call them before we head to dinner."

"Let's wait until after dinner. I need a few minutes to think it through," he said.

"Fine," Simon smiled. "Pack up your things because you're staying at my place tonight. I want to make sure you make it to the airport."

☾☽

Dinner went well, and Elliot felt he should have paid Simon for a therapy session. They drove to Simon's place. It was a brownstone-type house in the Old City section of Philadelphia. Simon parked his car in the back of the house off the alleyway. The two of them were walking up the pathway when suddenly Simon's arm sprang out and stopped him.

"Whose there?" he yelled to the dark.

"It's been a long time, Simon," they saw a thin, muscular man emerge from the shadows. He was older yet still fit. His silver head of hair and beard made him look distinguished, but something about him made Elliot very uneasy.

"Dr. Abbott," Simon sounded more like he was asking a question than confirming the man's identity.

"The fuck," Elliot said out loud.

"Elliot," the man said, "just as crass as your mother."

Elliot tensed at the comment, but Simon grabbed him before he could move.

"You're right; it has been a very long time," Simon said. "Why are you here?"

Elliot looked confused, "wait, Simon, you know this asshole?" Elliot quickly shook himself free of Simon's hold.

"We don't know each other," Dr. Abbott was the one to answer, "we've crossed paths here in Philadelphia. We've been introduced."

"That's putting it generously," Simon responded. "What do you want?"

"Can I come in?" Dr. Abbott requested and stepped out under a streetlight, giving Elliot his first full view of the doctor. "I want to talk with you."

"Miles isn't here," Simon relayed.

"I would have been surprised if he was."

"Okay," Simon said, walking past him to the door. "Let's hear what you have to say."

Elliot tried to protest, but Simon gave him a look as he moved to unlock the door.

They entered through the back door into the kitchen. Elliot motioned for Dr. Abbott to follow Simon. Simon slipped out of his loafers and turned to Dr. Abbott, "You can leave your shoes here."

"Really, Simon," he asked.

"Really, Abbott," Elliot answered as he toed his loafers off. "You're making a house call here, not at your place. House rules."

Elliot was surprised at how taking off his shoes seemed to bug Dr. Abbott. Simon motioned them into his living room. "Elliot, can you make us some drinks?" Simon said in a restrained yet measured tone.

Elliot was about to object vehemently when he noticed the seriousness in Simon's eyes. "Sure thing. What are you drinking, Doc?"

"Whatever red you have," he smirked.

"Simon," Elliot addressed him.

"Scotch, rocks, please," and he disappeared into the living room with Dr. Abbott.

Elliot needed to cool down, *so Simon had him make their drinks. Nice*! He began to work at lightning speed, not wanting to miss anything. As he came out of the room, he saw Simon and Dr. Abbott sitting in chairs opposite each other.

He couldn't make out exactly what they were saying, but he knew that Simon would catch him up with the information later. He cleared his throat as he entered. The men turned to look at him, and Simon smiled while Dr. Abbott just nodded. He handed them their drinks and stood off to the side with his.

"What's up?"

"I was filling Simon in on the work I did for Marcus Brent," Dr. Abbott said.

"I bet that's a decision you regret," Elliot quipped without thinking as he sat down on a lounge chair facing the two of them.

"You're alive because of that decision," Simon said, trying to deflect Elliot's perceived rudeness.

"That's a bit of an exaggeration if you ask me," Elliot said as he sipped his drink.

"Our relationship started in boarding school," Dr. Abbott told Elliot.

Elliot noticed a flash of something he couldn't name in Dr. Abbot's eyes. It was somewhere between regret and sadness, but it was only there for a fleeting instance.

Elliot just nodded and gulped down another sip. "I'm not so interested in that."

"What exactly are you interested in, Elliot?" Dr. Abbott sounded tired.

"I'm interested in knowing what your endgame is here, doctor?"

"My endgame? Isn't that clear to you?"

"Oh, so you want us all killed?"

"Dear God," Dr. Abbott perked up, "how in the world could

you believe that was my endgame?"

"Well, currently, one of the kids and his mother are dead. Lillian is missing. Someone tried to kill me but shot my friend instead. You tell me, does that look like the endgame you had in mind?"

"Listen, Elliot," Dr. Abbott said and leaned forward, "you can be pissed all you want, but you've got to understand that I had no idea that by giving you the names, this could happen."

"Bullshit," Elliot turned and looked at Simon, who had been the one to say what he was thinking. "You knew damn well what could happen, and you sent that information so that it wouldn't happen to you. I guess that you know how this Deavers operated well enough and that she would do the cleanup of the kids and moms first, and then come for you. By that time, you could be completely off the grid."

"You two do not know who you're messing with," Dr. Abbott responded. "I do."

"Which is exactly my point," Simon called out. "You knew who you were messing with, yet you sent my son, Rhea, and Elliot into it blind. Were you hoping they would just luck out and fly under the radar?"

"They would have flown under the radar if it weren't for Lillian," Dr. Abbot said matter-of-factly.

"That's not true," Simon said, "Dustin and Angela were killed before Lillian was seen going into Brent Industries, so they knew something before that."

"Ms. Deavers took my files days before Miles got the flash drive. Maybe she was doing some research about it."

"Then why didn't she find me before I went to Burkina Faso," Elliot shot at him.

"Because you don't exist as Hannah Vaughn's son," Dr. Abbott said aloud. "Your parents are Jennings and Marcia Sharp. You have been afforded a cover that has given you the freedom that none of the other kids have had. Your parents saved your life and have kept you off the radar until now."

Elliot wasn't sure how to process that. He wanted to simply shrug his shoulders and say, 'so what,' but, in the time since Miles and Rhea had shown up in Burkina Faso, he hadn't stopped thinking about his parents' role in his life.

"Are you saying that they didn't know about me?"

"No, they didn't, and to answer your next question, I'm not sure how they found out about you. It was a secret that, from what I can tell, only your parents, your birth mother, and I knew about."

"None of this makes sense," Elliot complained. "Dustin and Angela don't make sense because they were murdered before Lillian went to the Brents. Before you jump back to your 'maybe she's doing her own research' idea, I don't buy that. She didn't need to research if she thought they all did what they were paid to do."

"I agree with Elliot," Simon chimed in. "I keep asking myself if it was possible that Ms. Deavers accidentally ran across Dustin and his mother. I've seen pictures of him, and he looks exactly like Marcus Brent did as a teenager."

"That would make sense," Dr. Abbott said as he put his drink down. "Angela's looks were very similar to Marcus's mother."

"That's fucked up," Elliot said, becoming vexed with each passing second.

"Elliot," Simon chided him and then turned toward Dr. Abbott, "I've never seen pictures of his mother."

"She was a complete background character," Dr. Abbott paused and then emerged from his contemplation to respond. "I saw her at the boarding school about five different times. She was never there by herself. Harlan was always with her, imposing and sucking the air out of every room he entered. We feared him and pitied her. Other mothers, including mine, doted on their boys. Not her; she sat back and let Harlan talk to Marcus, not with him. It was hard to watch, and most of our parents would do their damndest to make sure that they were nowhere in the vicinity of the Brents."

"What was her name?" Elliot asked the men.

"Beatrice," Dr. Abbott answered, and Simon's face visibly changed. "I know, Simon, that was your wife's name."

"What the actual f…," Elliot said, and both men turned to face him and shot a look that made him stop halfway through the sentence.

"Dr. Abbott," Simon began again after a few moments of silence, "did all of the women who came to you have similarities to Marcus's mother?"

"No," Dr. Abbott shook his head, "Elliot, your mother was feisty, which was what he was into then. Stacey, Lillian's mom, had drugs, and if I'm honest, that was the only reason they hooked up. Esme Connors doesn't make much sense to me; she seemed to be his type, but he was suffering from some major issues then. I was surprised that she showed up pregnant since I'm not positive he could have managed."

"He was having problems getting it up?" Elliot asked.

"That would be a crass way to describe what I'm saying."

"So, Angela looked like his mother, and Simon's wife had the same name?"

"Betsy was different," Dr. Abbott said with a pause that set the tone for what he was about to say.

"How so?" Simon asked, trying his best to brace himself for whatever Abbott was about to say.

"Well, this might be hard for you," Dr. Abbott said, "but she was probably the only one of the women that Marcus liked, possibly even loved."

Simon stared at his drink, and Elliot noticed that this newfound discovery had affected him.

"Did he know that Betsy was pregnant?" Simon picked his head up and faced Dr. Abbot. Elliot sensed that his tone carried sadness, and he was trying hard not to lose his temper.

Dr. Abbott gazed out the window, and Elliot wasn't sure why he turned still and did not answer. Instead of a definitive reply, Dr. Abbott asked, "Would it change things if he did?"

Elliot's eyes widened with shock. It sure as hell changed things, and Dr. Abbott knew it. Simon didn't answer, but Elliot wanted to. He was utterly shocked by the fact that Marcus Brent may have known that she was pregnant.

Simon cleared his throat and took a sip of his drink. "Did he know she didn't go through with it?"

Dr. Abbott arched an eyebrow and shrugged. "If he didn't, he may know now."

"Damn it," Elliot sighed, "stop talking in riddles. You know this guy; you know what's up. Stop pretending like you don't have a clue. Did you choose Miles to do your dirty work because he would be safe?"

Simon peered at Dr. Abbott with expectation. He wanted an answer, too. But he held back his anger as best as he could.

"I can't know for certain," Dr. Abbott said, but Elliot jumped right in.

"Cut the shit, Abbott!"

Dr. Abbot leaned forward and fixed his eyes on Elliot. He was visibly broiling with anger but maintained his control and said, "If I say I can't know for sure, that's what I mean, you little brat. You two have theories," he pointed towards Simon and Elliot,

"I've heard them all, and they're equal parts probable and crazy. This whole plan is a gamble! At the end of the day, who gives a shit if Marcus Brent knows about Miles? But I'm banking on it. He didn't want to let Betsy go, so I'm sure that under his father's nose, without his father's knowledge, he found out what happened to her. Does that make him safer or put him in more danger? I don't know. I took a chance to allow him to do what he needed to do. We have to show the world who Marcus Brent truly is!"

Elliot was surprised at what bitterness could do to a man. Dr. Abbott was bitter, and he was sure that if they dug deep enough, the root of bitterness would date back to boarding school. But it had reached its full fruition when he was told to shove off instead of being placed in a prized political role.

It was Simon who broke the quietness, and he was seething, "You put this in motion, and none of these kids wanted that. They were all perfectly happy living their lives and doing their work. Now, one of them is dead, one is missing, and Elliot was targeted, nearly killed. These kids owe you nothing, yet out of their sense of making things right, they're putting their lives on the line, which is something you weren't willing to do. I can't figure out if you truly believe he must be stopped or if you're simply a pathetic piece of shit hellbent on revenge."

"They didn't need to act on it," Dr. Abbott roared.

"Like hell they didn't," Simon roared back. "You gave them

a choice – they could be complicit or they could put their necks on the line."

Dr. Abbott shrugged off Simon's comment. "I gave him everything that I could. Your son made his choice, Simon, and he didn't need to involve everyone else, but he did. Which is what I assumed he would do. But if you hear anything I say tonight, it should be this: this information needs to be public before you all meet similar fates as Dustin."

Elliot snapped as he rose from the chair. "Why, so you can enact your revenge?" The volume at which he yelled this caused his own ears to ring, and he felt the strain on his throat. He had never imagined he could be this angry.

"No," Dr. Abbott stood up as well, "so that you have a better chance of surviving this shit storm!"

"You created this shit storm, Abbott," an unexpectedly enraged voice cut through the air. Elliot was shocked by the way words were uttered, but was more worried that Simon, at this point, might start punching Dr. Abbott.

"I've overstayed my welcome," he said as he walked back into the kitchen, shrugging past Simon. He picked up his shoes and didn't bother to put them on. Before he went out the door, he turned his head slightly and spoke calmly, "She will clean up her messes if you don't do something soon," and walked out the door, leaving it open.

Elliot knew that Simon had been the one who had pushed

Miles to act upon Dr. Abbott's information. He was sure that was why Simon had just let Dr. Abbott leave.

"Well, look who discovered his potty mouth," he said to Simon, lost for a way to break the silence.

Simon's stern-looking face softened into a smile and he managed only to say, "Don't tell Miles."

"Miles needs to lighten up a bit," Elliot said as he returned the gesture.

"Yep," Simon continued to smile, "I think I'll call him and let him know you said so."

Simon drew his phone out from his pocket, "I've a text from Miles. He's safely landed in Cancun."

"Good," Elliot said, grabbing his phone from the counter where the liquor bottles stood. He didn't have any texts. He glanced at Simon, whose fingers were hovering over the screen, about to text something. "You know the upside to Miles being so cautious is that he won't do anything stupid."

Simon looked up and stared at Elliot, "I know. Thank God we didn't send you to meet Esme."

Elliot responded as he poured more bourbon, "I was thinking the same thing." He went into the living room, sat down on the couch, and sighed.

"I'm heading to bed," Simon said. "When you are drunk enough, it might be a good time to call your parents. You're in the room at the top of the stairs. I'll leave the door open and the light on."

Elliot chuckled, "Good night, Simon."

"Don't be a baby," he yelled back to Elliot, "call them." He went up the steps to his room, and Elliot glued his eyes on the lit-up screen. No notifications. He searched his contact list and chuckled. There wasn't really a need for a contact list; he just dialed the number he knew he'd never forget. He could never truly erase it. How could he forget the digits he'd committed to memory the day he got lost in the mall? Back then, he'd wept uncontrollably until his mom appeared from the crowd and scooped him up. That day, once they were home, he memorized his parents' phone numbers, vowing never to be separated from them again.

It rang twice, and he heard the voice that he knew so well.

"Hello," Jennings's voice held a sense of longing and hope.

Elliot had to stifle his tears. "Dad, how are you doing?" He stretched his legs out on the couch.

Jennings didn't utter a word; he just sighed, and Elliot could hear him weeping. *I'm such a dick,* Elliot thought to himself.

"I'm good, Elliot," he said to the sniffles on the other end of the phone. "I'm in Philadelphia helping Miles figure out what's going on." Elliot moved the phone from his ear. Simon had told Jennings he would call, but Jennings may not have been ready to actually hear Elliot's voice.

Jennings was trying to form words, and Elliot's heart

shattered. Jennings was the epitome of a tough man, and he and Elliot butted heads all the time. Jennings never budged, never showed any emotion. But tonight, he dropped his guard, and that broke Elliot. He felt the tears well up in his eyes. He hadn't communicated with either of them since he had sent that telegraph a month ago. His lack of communication had to have been pure torture for them.

"I've always wanted to visit Philadelphia," Jennings finally said.

"Don't lie, you'd hate it here," Elliot said as a few tears ran down his face. "I'm okay, Dad. Tell Mom to stop worrying, I'm okay."

"We love you. You'll always be our son, please don't forget that," Jennings whispered in a hoarse voice.

"I realize that now," Elliot said, his voice trembling. "I've been struggling to understand so much of what has happened."

"I know, son," Jennings's voice was evening out, "it's a lot to process. We all wanted to protect you."

"You did," Elliot said as the tears kept rolling down his face. "I realize that now."

"We tried," Jennings's voice gathered some strength, "but I'm starting to realize that what happened to Scott may have been our fault."

"What do you mean?" Elliot asked as he adjusted his posture.

"I was in town yesterday," Jennings began, "and I ran into Gia

Leslie, who works at Grottons.”

“Yeah, I know who that is,” Elliot said, “what’s up with her?”

“She and I got to talking, and she asked me about you, and before I could answer, she told me that someone had been in at the restaurant a while back. The lady said that she had been here years ago for a funeral.”

Elliot’s heart sank. “Mom may have been right,” Elliot questioned. “Someone was checking up on Aunt Hannah.”

“It seemed so,” Jennings’ voice came out rather slow, “she said it was a funeral for a young lady that died in a tragic fire at a bar that her company owned.”

“How did I come up?” Elliot asked.

“She asked how the family was doing,” Jennings continued, “and Gia told them that we were fine, that you had gone on to college and were working for a company that built wells and schools in Africa. Gia’s memory is solid, so she knew exactly what the company was called, and told the lady, who she said seemed delighted to hear that we had all moved on as best that we could.”

“When did she say she spoke with her?” Elliot's tears subsided, and his brain kicked into investigative mode.

“Not more than a week before the shooting,” Jennings said. “She must be that lady. I believe it with my whole heart!”

“As far as I know, she’s still in Europe,” Elliot reassured him.

“Just,” Jennings paused, “please, be safe. I’ll be at the airport to fetch you tomorrow."

"I'll try," he said. "I can't guarantee anything."

"We love you."

"I love you guys too," Elliot said as he rose. "I'm guessing you've been in touch with Miles's Dad, Simon."

"I have," he chuckled. "He's a real cool chap. He sent me your flight information."

"Figures," Elliot was regaining his composure as he paced the room, "I'll see you tomorrow."

"Promise," he heard Jennings say.

"Promise," and then they said their goodbyes.

He stopped pacing, dashed to the couch, and collapsed onto it. He felt happy to have talked to his Dad like that after such a long time. He knew he'd soon need to have a good talk with his mom, too, but that was always easier in his mind. He had taken the step he'd dreaded, and now he felt a sense of freedom. His focus was now sharper than ever on the task at hand: removing Marcus Brent from the presidential race.

He stood up and grabbed his bag from the kitchen where he'd left it. He went up the stairs and found his bedroom. He took off his clothing, draped it over the chair in the corner, and climbed into his bed. He rolled onto his stomach and felt sleep slowly overtake his tired body. The emotions of the evening had taken a toll on him, and his mind wound in and out of consciousness. He was in the presence of Scooper one second, warm and real, his bearded face talking to him about the well depth; and then he saw the Spanish woman he'd met at the hotel in Senegal, her dark flowing hair framing her face as she opened her mouth to tell him to keep looking; Benjamin smiling and pointing in the distance to something that he couldn't make out, followed by Miles standing there at the airport, motioning him to hurry because there were things to do. He wasn't sure how long he had been asleep, but into the carousel of faces, he thought that he heard a knocking sound.

"We need to get going, Elliot," Simon's voice rang in his ears. "You're not missing this flight on my watch." He mumbled something back to Simon and swung his feet out of the bed and onto the floor. His dreams had left him with a sense of urgency.

Chapter Twenty-Five

Elizabeth sat in the cafe, looking out at the group of Japanese tourists as they streamed by on their way to see the Manneken Pis. She wondered how disappointed they would be when they would see the tiny statue with its tiny penis pissing into a small pool. It was a letdown, as far as she was concerned. It seemed that the only ones who found it funny were Americans or school-aged boys.

She had been lying low in Brussels since getting out of Frankfurt. Saul had asked her why she had been in Burkina Faso in the first place. She lied to him like she almost always did regarding this aspect of her job. She had told him that she had gotten wind of the news that Hannah Vaughn's nephew was talking about what happened to his aunt and that she needed to take care of that loose end.

Saul never asked her any follow-up questions when she used phrases like "taking care of loose ends." He would just ask what she needed; this time, she said she would have to lie low. A week in Brussels wasn't all that exciting, but at least she ate well and blended in with the people there. She was about to order another coffee when her phone buzzed. A text alert that she knew well.

She needed to check in with Saul as soon as possible.

She walked through the streets toward the apartment that Brent Industries kept under a different name here in Brussels. It was small but private, located on the upper floor of a stand-alone structure. When she got to the apartment, she bolted the door behind her and turned on the noise-canceling device that would keep others from hearing what she was talking about.

Saul picked up on the first ring. "How's Europe?" he asked hurriedly.

"Boring," she said as she sat down.

"Are you able to move?" he asked.

"I think so," she said. "Why?"

"Bart," Saul sighed, "has taken care of the Lillian problem."

"Any more rumblings on the PI snooping around?" Elizabeth asked, fearing the answer.

"No," he said bluntly, "but if I were to guess, these reporters that brought Lillian into the loop were the ones who approached the investigator."

"Maybe so," Elizabeth quipped, "but sooner or later, they will start digging into where Lillian disappeared." On one side, she was relieved that Saul hadn't figured out that she knew who Miles and Rhea were and why they were a part of this. On the other hand, it would be a real problem when people began digging for information on Lillian's location. She was almost certain that, if they hadn't done so yet, Miles and Rhea would soon.

"Listen," Saul had the grit to his voice that meant he was at the end of his patience. "This is all shit we can talk about it when you're back here. I'll send you your flight information when it's ready."

"Thank you," she said, "tell Bart I need him to meet me at the airport."

"You think you're hot shit, don't you, Elizabeth. Here's the thing. Under great duress, Bart told me that the last time he saw you, you told him you needed to go to Africa. That was shortly before you went missing from my radar. My son seems to be more loyal to you than he is to me."

"I told *you* what I was doing," she sighed. "Hannah Vaughn's nephew was running his mouth, so I needed to deal with it."

"We're all perfect liars, Elizabeth, and I'm starting to suspect that you're hiding something. Something crucial. Bart thinks you know a shit ton more than you're telling us, and he's pretty sure you went off to cover up some of your mistakes."

"Well," she said coyly, "what can I say?" She was angry with Bart for saying anything. She should have known he would look for an opening to move past her.

"You can tell me that you had nothing to do with the shooting that took place at a well site in Burkina Faso."

"You'll send me that flight info soon, right, Saul?" she said sweetly, avoiding the question. "I've got to run; I want to have my last waffles before heading back to the States." She hung up on him. It felt like the walls were closing in on her. She had sat on this for decades, and now, she was paying for the fact that she'd never followed up on these women. Would this have even been a big deal if Marcus Brent weren't running for the presidential nomination? Would Abbott have betrayed him if Marcus was going about his own business buying and selling, trading, and smuggling? She should have known that as soon as Marcus threw his hat in the ring, all the shit would hit the fan.

She pulled the files out of her lock box and looked at them. She knew who each one was now. It was only Esme Connor for whom she had no concrete evidence. Lillian had spilled the beans that at least one of them, Miles or Rhea, was heading to Mexico, but she couldn't say where. Esme remained the last one and was off the grid. At least for the moment. She made a note on the file to check the flight records for Miles and Rhea when she got back. She'd already seen that Elliot had landed in Philadelphia, but she had no idea where he had gone from there. Her best guess was that he was staying with Miles.

Her only consolation was that none of this had leaked to the press yet. They didn't know about it, which meant that Marcus didn't know about it either. It was all becoming a reality to her now. Harlan had set this whole thing up so that no matter what happened, Marcus would never have his name on anything. It would always be her. She was the one who made the payments to the women and Dr. Abbott. She was the one who cleaned up the messes. And why? All so that an asshole with horrible daddy issues could run for the highest elected position in the free world. It wasn't fair, but it was what she had to do. If she failed, and Marcus found out about what she was doing and how she had fumbled at the finish line, he would only need to do one thing. He would just open the folder containing all the information that would put her away for the rest of her life. She was stuck, and the only way out was to make sure no one was left to talk about it.

Chapter Twenty-Six

Hamish Yoder was undeniably good-looking; Rhea couldn't shake this thought. He was the kind of guy that you sure wouldn't mind sitting next to in public. Her only concern, her whole life, whenever she was with men like him, had always been that others would wonder, *Why is he with her*? Yet at this moment, she was ready to throw her drink in his face.

"It's not that big of a deal, Rhea," he said condescendingly. "The doctor showed up at their door. What's the big fuss?"

"Hamish," she pleaded, her voice was tight with frustration, "he was there. They had eyes on him."

"And, then he was gone—poof," Hamish said while mimicking a disappearing motion with his hands. He thought he was being cute, but it only annoyed her further. "He didn't tell them anything you didn't already know."

"But he knew my mother," her voice tinged with sadness. "I would have loved to talk to him, too."

For a moment, Hamish's demeanor softened. He seemed to understand her position.

"I'm sorry," his hard-edged tone faded. "I understand now why it's a big deal to you. How did Miles react?"

"Simon didn't say much, but Elliot made it sound like Miles didn't care. That upset him a little."

Her thoughts drifted. Elliot had painted the doctor as arrogant, not the hero everyone believed him to be. He was out for revenge, but didn't have the guts to do it himself. Of course, Elliot had used much more colorful language to express this, which made her smile slightly. However, after talking with Elliot, her mind continued spiraling.

Hamish had been talking, but her mind had wandered down its usual rabbit hole. She quickly refocused; there was no time for distractions. In just a few minutes, a journalist from a well-known newspaper would be meeting with them. Hamish was running some ideas by her.

"Do you see why this is important?" Hamish asked, but she was too distracted to follow the conversation. She wasn't even sure what they were talking about.

"Hamish," she said smiling, "there is a lot on my mind right now. If I'm being honest, my thoughts were somewhere else just now."

"That's fine," he said, unaffected, "I was just explaining why we are switching tactics."

"Why?" she asked, knowing that they had already been over this.

"It needs to look like we're protecting all of you as our source. That way, we can avoid using your names for as long as possible," he explained.

"I get it," she replied. "It buys us a few extra days to see what will happen with Esme."

"Correct," he said.

"Are you still sure we don't want to put something in there about Dustin or Lillian?" she asked him as frustration crept in. This had been their biggest point of contention. Since their first meeting, Hamish had backtracked on using that angle to target Brent.

"Not yet," he answered just as she knew he would.

The journalist, Hector *something*, she couldn't remember, was due to meet them in about an hour, so they had some time to kill at the restaurant. Hamish had worked for Simon on and off, always freelance, for the last four years. She had started to piece together a picture of Simon as someone who didn't reveal all his cards. Hamish explained that Simon had hired him for various insurance cases, often to dig into people involved in fraudulent claims. Occasionally, Simon would bring him in to leak information to the press. That's why Hamish's involvement was important now.

"What was Miles like in college?" she inquired.

"What's Miles like now?" Hamish countered, but didn't wait for her to reply, "because that was exactly what he was like in college. He was serious, worked hard, and hardly wasted his time on anything that didn't involve being serious or working hard."

She chuckled at that. "So, he wasn't much of a risk-taker." She smiled as she recalled her own experiences with him. His sudden decision to head off to Mexico was out of character; she sensed it in how Simon talked about it with him and even in the way Hamish raised his eyebrows when they'd first met. He said he would leave it up to them to handle this as he was off to Mexico.

"He," Hamish tilted his head before he spoke again. "He isn't always risk-averse. The time that I spent with him in Berlin a few years ago showed me a side of him I didn't expect."

"Really?" she asked, leaning forward with a spark of curiosity. He smiled. Rhea felt the cloud of distraction lift, and her change in mood seemed to light up Hamish's face. She'd noticed in the way he responded to her questions that he'd grown to appreciate how her curiosity surfaced so naturally.

"Yeah," Hamish said and paused to drink in the moment. "That's a story for another time. One where I come across as an arrogant asshole who didn't read the situation right."

Her curiosity piqued. "Now I'm intrigued. What happened?"

"Let's just put it this way," he smirked, "I might have either saved him from making the worst mistake of his life or ruined any chance he had at love."

"You can't drop a bomb like that and not elaborate," she squealed at him as she grabbed his arm.

"Oh, I can," he tried to suppress his laugh. "You're welcome to pull it out of me, but I've been questioned by people with much more dastardly tactics than yours, and I've never talked. So, trust me, your tactics won't work. Besides, part of why I was there involves confidential information." He winked and added, "Can't share it."

He was toying with her, and she realized it. He liked to wrap himself in an air of mystery. She'd already pegged him—a trust-fund playboy dabbling around in the world of private investigation and black-market espionage. He wasn't that hard to read, despite what he wanted her to think.

The meal went on, and she learned more about Hamish than her own brother Miles. Hamish's favorite topic was, by and far, Hamish himself. His exploits, those that he deemed fit to share, were scandalous and wild. Even in stories where he claimed to only be a drop man or courier for someone, he spun it like a life-or-death adventure. He sounded more like a hero on the edge of danger. As his stories continued, Rhea found they were also becoming similar, and her interest began to wane. Sure, he was handsome, she thought, but there was no need to tell him. It seemed that he already knew it.

When Hector showed up early, Rhea had had her fill of Hamish stories. "I've got it all set," Hector said as he sat down. He was a good-looking middle-aged man. Rhea guessed that he was about her age. He looked confident and wasn't at all impressed by Hamish's charms. To Rhea, he appeared a bit rude;

above all, he didn't bother introducing himself to her.

"Hamish," he gestured towards him, "will bring the article to Bree Gray at TMZ. They will break it. Breaking news, blah, blah, blah! Someone—God knows who—will run with it and start digging. With any luck, it'll blow up within a day and spread like wildfire. Any news from the others involved?"

"No," Hamish replied. His cocky side had slipped into the background, and Rhea was once again engrossed in watching Hamish do his job.

"So," Hector collapsed back on his seat with a sigh, "we still have no mothers willing to talk, and we haven't tracked down the doctor." Hector paused, "All we have are three siblings claiming to be Marcus Brent's bastards. That's a hard sell."

"No, it isn't," Hamish jumped in. "That's exactly the problem with so-called legitimate journalists like you."

Rhea felt like she was watching a high-speed verbal tennis match. She wanted to interrupt and at least introduce herself as one of the so-called bastards, as he had put it, but she didn't want to disrupt the rhythm. Their back-and-forth, while serious, was oddly fascinating.

"I'm glad you think I'm legitimate," Hector replied dryly, sarcasm dripping in his tone. "But the problem with journalism these days is people like you, who think they can toss out whatever the hell they want. Sooner or later, it'll either be proven or disproven, but it won't matter. The damage will already be done.”

“Well,” Hamish shrugged, “that’s exactly what I am paid to do.”

Hector shook his head in exasperation and then turned his attention towards Rhea, who was not enjoying their tense exchange. It was as if he had noticed her for the first time.

“And you are?” His sharp gaze locked on her as he asked bluntly.

“I’m one of the bastards,” Rhea said in a steady tone. “Rhea Baker.”

Hector nodded, his expression unreadable, and then turned to Hamish. “You didn’t tell me one of them would be here.”

“You didn’t ask,” Hamish smirked and kept on. “Rhea, this is Hector,” he turned towards Hector with a smug expression, “what was your last name again?”

Hector exhaled aloud while shaking his head. “Fine. We’ll proceed with the less savory options. I have people discreetly working on following up with Brent’s whereabouts around the time of his relationships with each of the mothers. The information you gave me is solid,” he looked at Rhea, “I assume we have you to thank for that.”

“And my brother Miles,” her words landed with very little impact in comparison to the way that Hector and Hamish had spoken to each other. Hector looked at her, then at Hamish, and she sensed an annoyance in his voice as he continued.

"Good," Hector's voice sounded perturbed, "Now, with what we already have, and what some of my sources have found, we can cross-reference his movements and meetings and prove that he had met some of these mothers. I've a call scheduled this evening with my two researchers. We should know more after that."

"How trustworthy are they?" Rhea asked.

"Who?" Hector seemed surprised that Rhea had spoken. "The researchers," he questioned her, but then continued, not waiting for a response. "Very! They know how to stay off the radar and how to avoid any red flags being raised, which is important when dealing with Brent Industries."

"How are you justifying using them to your bosses?" asked Hamish, leaning back with crossed arms.

"I've been in journalism for over a decade. Claims like this used to come across our desks all the time, illegitimate children, affairs, anytime someone grows in popularity. It would shock you. It was tabloid gold. They don't happen as much nowadays because assault and sexual misconduct grab all the headlines. Most are dismissed before they go anywhere. And without fail, all of them fade away after a few news cycles."

"So, all that to say, you didn't set off any alarms by putting researchers on it?" Hamish pressed.

Hector narrowed his eyes. "No, why? Do you know something I don't?"

"I don't," Hamish said gruffly. "But what I'm worried about are the people we're dealing with. Brent Industries isn't just real estate, fossil fuels, and the future of AI. Their money runs deep and comes from places and operations they don't want to have exposed. Any crack in the surface, like say, illegitimate children, invites deeper scrutiny. That deeper scrutiny means cleanup; by clean up, I mean what happened to Angela and Dustin." He paused to catch his breath. "I'm talking about why we can't find Lillian. Soon, they'll connect the dots if they haven't already, and what will make them pay even closer attention is some legitimate journalist looking into some salacious gossip."

"A legitimate journalist can break this story legitimately," Hector snapped.

"Is that before or after he's killed?" Hamish shot back instantaneously.

Hector leaned forward and hissed at Hamish, "Are you implying I made a mistake?"

"No," Rhea jumped in, trying to defuse the situation. Though she didn't know if Hamish was insinuating that or not.

"Oh, I'm saying that," Hamish cut through Rhea's calm demeanor. "Hector, I said be discreet. Not to cause waves, yet you have not one, but two researchers looking into this."

"No one knows what they're working on. Give me a chance to break this as it should," he was not asking Hamish, but he was putting his foot down.

"Thanks," Hamish said coldly. "But I can handle it from here."

"Like hell you can," Hector lashed out. He was pretty heated, and his tone confused Rhea. One moment, it appeared he didn't want to break the story; the next, he was ready to fight for it. Perhaps Hamish was right to take matters into his own hands.

"That's the best you've got? Like hell, you can," Hamish mimicked with a smirk. "Listen, Hector, you can walk away without getting yourself dirty and keep those impeccable journalist credentials intact."

"It's your story," Hector said, pointing at Rhea. "Do you want it handled by this hack?"

"Hack," Hamish chuckled and relaxed against the back of his seat. "You've got to be kidding me. You fumbled the handoff, Hector. I recovered it, and now I'm taking over."

"You don't have to do this," Hector said to Rhea without looking at Hamish. His voice carried an edge of desperation that nearly broke into a plea.

Rhea took a deep breath and stared at Hector. Something about the way Rhea looked at him made him visibly perturbed. Despite his growing unease, Hector's eyes never left her.

"You're not serious," he complained.

"You called me a bastard. He's never done that," she said quietly.

"I can land your story in the legitimate press," Hector

insisted. "He'll dig up some hot gossip internet rag."

"And then you can swoop in once it gains traction," Hamish interrupted.

"What?" Hector blinked as he asked.

"God, you're slow," Hamish muttered while sipping his coffee.

"What," Hector repeated. Rhea sensed his frustration mounting.

"You aren't out of the picture," Hamish sighed as he stretched his neck. "You're just outside of the first frame. You and all your covert research come in later."

Hector stared at them—Rhea and then Hamish; Hamish and then Rhea—his mouth half open as if forming another question. Before he had the chance, Hamish cut him off. "Please don't say *what* again."

Hector closed his mouth and clenched his jaws. Hamish continued, "Listen closely because I don't like repeating myself."

Rhea sat back and listened to the plan. Hamish was indeed a genius. Hector was somewhat in awe, his frustrated expression vanishing. The longer Hamish talked, the more he seemed convinced, although he played down how impressed he was. After about 20 minutes Hector stood to leave. He looked at Rhea, "You okay with this?"

"Very much," she said without hesitation.

Hector nodded and left the restaurant without saying

anything. She saw him turn left outside the door and put his phone to his ear.

"Was there a reason you didn't just lead with that plan?" she asked Hamish.

"I needed to know what he's done so far. Simon tasked me with finding the safest and best way to get your names out there," he signaled to the waiter. "Hector wasn't a part of that plan, but he has his uses, as you can see."

"Are you sure he's the right person for this?" she asked, wanting his reassurance.

"Absolutely," he sighed, "you'll see later. Now," he paused, "I've another request."

"How can I help?" she asked with a chuckle.

"I need you to be my date tonight," he smiled as the waiter placed the check on the table. He reached into this pocket and took out a credit card.

"Where are we going?" she asked as she leaned forward.

"I'm taking that as a yes," he said, "you'll want to put on your dancing shoes. We're going to a club in NYC."

Rhea raised her eyebrows. A club? "I'm more of a dinner and movie sort of girl."

"I'll remember that for when I actually ask you out," Hamish said nonchalantly. Rhea was hoping he couldn't see her blush.

⁂

Rhea's skirt felt extremely short, and her top looked like it was cut too low. She literally sat in the cab, wondering why the hell she'd agreed to this. Hamish sat next to her in the back of the cab, looking out the window, talking on his phone. His handsomeness had faded in her mind, as he more and more showed the side of himself that was solely focused on himself.

Rhea hadn't been to a club in a big city in her whole life. It wasn't what she was into in college, and even as a young adult, she was so focused on getting her master's and Ph.D. that by the time she finished, she felt that window had passed her by. Now here she sat in her early 40s, heading to a club with one of the most self-absorbed men she'd ever met, pulling at the hem of her skirt and wishing she hadn't let the lady at the department store talk her into this outfit.

"How's this going to work out again?" she said to him once he'd finished his call.

"Molly Grant is a gatekeeper of sorts," he replied, "and as far as being a gatekeeper goes, she's pretty awful."

"So, why are we trying to talk with her?" she continued.

"She's our "in" to getting your story published," Hamish smiled at her, "she seems to be a bleeding heart when it comes to human interest stories that will fuck over anyone in the establishment."

"And you know for sure that Molly Grant is going to be at this club?"

"No," he said, "but if she isn't there, someone will know

where she is."

"Do you mean we might have to go to more than one club?" she said with shock in her voice.

"Possibly," he said, giving her a suspicious look. "Have you ever been to a club?"

Rhea laughed nervously and hoped that would be enough for him. He nodded and she felt like he was being dismissive and that pissed her off. Screw it, she thought I'm a grown-up, I can admit that I've not been to a club. "It's not my scene," she said.

"Really, could have fooled me," he smiled. "Just follow my lead; do what I do."

"I can't talk about myself that much," she heard the words slide right off her lips.

Hamish chuckled, "You aren't the first person to tell me that, but you're sure as hell the quickest of my friends to say so."

"Sorry, this dress is too tight for me to be polite," she said as she tugged at a corner of her dress.

"You look good in it, though," he smiled. "I brought you some earplugs for when we are in the club."

She shot him a glance that she hoped conveyed the fact that he should shut up. They rode the rest of the way in silence. She saw a queue for the club but was surprised when the taxi driver drove them past the club and into a side alley.

"Why is he leaving us off here?" she asked Hamish.

"I never go in the front at this club," he explained. He thanked the cab driver and handed him three twenty-dollar bills. He was out of the cab in one swoop, while she carefully and deliberately adjusted herself to exit the cab in heels and a tight skirt. Hamish opened the door and extended his hand just before she was about to open it.

"Rhea," he said.

"Thank you, Hamish."

He walked with her to a door that opened just before they got to it. The man who opened it was tall and muscular. He wore a suit and shirt with no tie. He had an earpiece in and nodded at Hamish. "Mr. Yoder, Ms. Baker," he sounded welcoming as he put his hand out to allow them to pass.

"How does he know my name?" she whispered to Hamish, who ignored her and shook the hand of the doorman. They walked past him, and Rhea could feel the pulsing of the music coming from behind a large steel door at the end of a hall. She looked over her shoulder as they went down the hall and saw that the doorman had a list which he was checking off. He hung it up under a TV monitor displaying a closed-circuit video of the alley they had just driven into.

As Hamish pushed the door open, the sound intensified, and she kind of wished that Hamish hadn't been joking about those earplugs. It was an assault on the senses; all of them. The darkness that hugged them was pierced by flashes of bright, colorful lights. The bass shot through her body. The dance floor was teeming with people, and there was no room at the bar. They walked right past the dance floor and the bar and then went up a flight of stairs to a balcony of sorts that contained more tables. Hamish walked past a few open tables, and she followed closely behind him.

He stopped at a curtain, and before he swept it aside, he turned to Rhea. "No matter who's sitting on the other side of this curtain, act like you've never seen them before in your life."

"Wait, what do you mean?" she said as she grabbed his elbow. "Who might be behind there?"

He slid the curtain and walked through the space he made. He held it open for her to follow, but he had already focused his attention on the people sitting in the room. She heard a few people say his name, and he began to greet them. As her eyes focused on the people in the room, she suppressed an audible gasp and froze as Hamish moved into the room. She recognized at least two famous pop singers, one actress, and an athlete. Hamish was leaning and extending his hand to the athlete. She could see that he was introducing Hamish to the woman sitting next to him. It was quieter in this part of the club, but she still couldn't hear much.

She walked up behind him as he was telling them to enjoy their evening. As she came up to him, he smiled, "we're in luck, he said to her."

"Why's that?" she asked.

"Molly is over there in the corner," he said and as she turned to look at the corner, a tall sultry brunette in a shiny red dress that barely covered her was standing up and heading towards them. "She'll need a few more drinks before we drop this on her, but I think we've got a shot." He smiled at her and then turned to walk towards Molly. He grabbed her hand this time, making sure she was right behind him.

Molly had the type of voice that you could hear over the noise. "Hamish, you hot fucking devil," she said as she hugged him, kissing him on both cheeks. "You owe me a phone call or two?" A chuckle escaped Rhea's mouth, not knowing what she found funny, and it caught Molly's attention.

"Who's this?" she said, stretching a hand towards Rhea. Just as Rhea was about to grab it, Molly withdrew it. Her eyes widened as she looked at Rhea. Rhea and Hamish exchanged looks, and just then Molly exclaimed, "I know you!"

"Really," Hamish said while facing Rhea.

"Yes, you're Rhea Baker! Your mother was Ellis Baker, I love her books," she said. "I've read everything she ever wrote, and even some of your writings!"

"Wow, I don't meet many fans anymore," Rhea said to her.

"Please tell me you aren't involved with Hamish," she said, her hand still caught in a lingering handshake with Rhea. "He's an absolute asshole."

Rhea was taken aback, and Molly could see that her words had confused her, "I mean I love him, but you're so far out of his league!" Molly seemed to over punctuate every sentence.

"So, now that we're done eviscerating me, I need to talk with you, Molly," Hamish's voice rang out and interrupted the ladies. "Can I buy you a drink?"

"I never say no to a free drink!"

"Oh, I know," Hamish responded as her turned towards Rhea and winked. Rhea could see Molly roll her eyes at him. "Rhea, what can I get you?"

"A simple red wine would be great," she said, and heard Molly clicking her tongue.

"Sweetie, this is not a place for red wine," Molly jumped in. "Grab us two paper planes, love."

Molly grabbed her arm and led her to the booth in the direction she had come from. "So, Rhea, what are you doing out here on the East Coast? Are you selling a new book? Tell me all about it!"

"Not much to tell," she lied, as she cursed Hamish for disappearing and leaving her alone. "I wrote a book about my mother, but no one wants to publish it." The only thing Rhea wanted more than that drink right now was not to have to talk about her mother.

"Fucking fools," Molly said to her as they settled into the booth. "I've connections. Do you want me to help?"

"That's sweet of you," Rhea faked a smile, "but I'm not sure it's ready. Or maybe I'm not ready for it to be published yet."

"If you change your mind, there is a copy editor at Doubleday who owes me a massive favor!"

Hamish returned to the table but without drinks.

"Our drinks will be here in a few minutes," he said as he slid down next to Molly. The way in which they interacted with each other made it quite clear that they had a history. Rhea didn't want that to bother her, but deep down it felt wrong.

"Hamish, how in the world do you cross paths with someone as amazing and sophisticated as Rhea Baker?"

"What do you mean?" Hamish said coyly. "Are you saying my dates aren't usually as classy as Rhea here?" He gave Rhea a sly nod.

"HA!" Molly laughed somewhat impulsively. "You're a riot. So, what do you want to talk about, Hamish?"

The drinks arrived just as Molly asked about the matter. They thanked the waiter.

"To Hamish, may he pay for all of our drinks all night long!"

Rhea gave Hamish a glance and a smirk. He rolled his eyes, which made him look younger, and lifted his glass. Molly, to Rhea's utter shock, downed her drink in one giant gulp.

"So, back to the reason for your visit!"

"Well," Hamish said as he put his drink down, "we have a story for you."

Chapter Twenty-Seven

The steamy Cancun air stung his face as he walked out to his car. He threw his hastily packed bag into the back seat and set off for the hotel closest to Esme's home. It was the last place that he had seen the bodyguard. He had planned precisely how this would go, but was beginning to doubt himself. If Simon had made him promise one more time not to engage with the bodyguard, he would stop taking his calls. He ran through the plan, then ran through his change of plans. His what-ifs and his what-nows. Normally, he would have thought through all of these for weeks, but now he was working with plans birthed on two flights and a layover. It was pretty much as unprepared as it got.

Since seeing that picture, his thoughts were consumed by getting back to Esme. She invaded his mind and haunted his dreams. He felt responsible for her and her daughter, praying that his presence hadn't stirred any trouble for them. But he wouldn't know for sure until he was standing in front of her, talking to her face to face. He had to see her, and only then would his mind feel a sense of peace.

He drove with purpose, knowing what awaited him. Getting Esme to be a part of what they were doing was integral, but it was going to be next to impossible. She did not want to be involved because she seemed to have been the only one to get off the grid. Maybe knowing she wasn't completely off the grid might help him win her over and reverse her decision. He tried to imagine what he could say to help convince her, but he was clueless.

He checked into the hotel, completely ignoring the beauty that surrounded him. He dropped his bag in the hotel room, shoved the key into his pocket, and headed to the bar. Simon wasn't there to check up on him, and he needed to know if the guy was still around. He hustled out to the bar, hoping he would be there where he had last seen him, but he wasn't. He took a quick look around, wanting to ask someone on staff about him, but he wasn't sure if he wanted to do that. He had only ever referred to him as the bodyguard despite knowing his name was Michael Davidson. He was confident that he wasn't using that name down here. He walked up to the bar, and a young woman asked him what he wanted to have.

"Um," he said, "a tequila on the rocks."

She nodded and then turned her back on him to pour his drink. He turned to scan the bar and the pool area, but the bodyguard was nowhere to be seen. Doubt began to creep in. What if he had run down here based on a mistake? What if the guy wasn't Michael Davidson?

The waitress came back with his drink, and he just stared at it for a second. If the bodyguard wasn't at the hotel working that day, he could move on to what was next on the list, Esme. He lifted his drink and swirled it. He drank it in one gulp and asked for the check.

⊗⊗⊗⊗⊗

Miles noticed that there was no breeze coming off of the sea. The walk along the beach was hot, and the air felt close to him, causing him to sweat underneath his shirt. He held his shoes in one hand and kept his focus on moving forward. Esme was standing outside the shop, saying goodbye to three teenage boys, who he assumed had been her pupils for the day.

"Damn, you're persistent," she called out to him as he walked towards her.

"I tried to let you know I was coming," he replied, as he neared her.

"Yeah, I know," she said. "Sorry that I didn't get back to your voicemails, plural," she chuckled, then bent forward to hug him. Her sudden warmth took him off guard.

"I'm so relieved that you're okay," he said to her.

"Why wouldn't I be okay?" she responded as she let him go and looked at him.

"I need to tell you something important," he said as Esperanza toddled up to Esme from behind.

"You remember Mr. Miles," she said in Spanish, and Esperanza gave a subtle nod. "He's come back to say hello."

"We need to talk," he said as they headed towards the porch.

He knew his voice betrayed his annoyance.

"I'm sorry, really, that I haven't been in touch," she replied. Miles could read that there was something more.

"I was worried," he picked up again as they sat down on the porch. "Some days ago, we got some information that I'm afraid might mean you're in danger."

"Danger," she said with a smirk, "trust me, I'm not in any danger. Would you like a glass of wine or a beer," she changed the subject.

"Esme," he pressed. "You need to listen to me."

"I will," she smiled and tilted her head as if willing to listen to him, "but not unless we both have drinks in our hands."

Miles tried to interject, but she raised a finger, "Drink first! Death and doom second."

"I'll take some wine," he knew that was supposed to be amusing, but his reply came off as if he was annoyed.

"I'll be right out," she said and disappeared into the kitchen. Esperanza was playing near the steps that led to the beach. Miles remained on the porch and stared at the child. He forced a smile, but the weight he was carrying made it feel hollow, as if it didn't quite belong.

He looked up at her as she came back out of the door. She held a glass of wine in one hand and a bottle of beer in the other. "Here you go," she said, "Salud." She extended her glass towards his, and he obliged.

"What's up, Miles?" she asked as she plopped down.

"You might not be as out of reach as you think you're," he said with urgency. "I think it would be safer for you to come back to Philadelphia with me."

"Oh, Miles," she turned her gaze away and said, "what are you talking about?"

"It's just," he paused and looked down, "do you trust me?"

Esme moved to the edge of where she was seated and focused her attention on him. "Miles, I don't trust many people, so don't be offended. If it helps in any way, I sort of trust you." She smiled subtly at him.

"I need you to trust that I've your best interest at heart."

"That I do, but Miles, but I can't come back to the US with you and take on Marcus Brent."

She gazed out at the beautiful blue sea, her eyes fixed on the horizon for what felt like minutes to Miles. Then she looked at Esperanza and shifted in her seat.

"Miles," she paused and began again. "You ask me to trust you. I understand that. And, like I said, I kind of trust you. The fact is, you shouldn't trust me."

"What do you mean?" It didn't sit right with him the way the conversation was heading, "I don't have a reason to not trust you."

"I've not been honest with you," she delivered the words in a way that made him feel like she pitied him for not knowing she hadn't been honest with him.

"I'm sorry, what do you mean?" he stared at her in disbelief. His mind raced, trying to process all the lies she could have told. After all, he was dealing with someone who had lied about aborting a baby and then made off with over a million dollars.

"Esperanza isn't Marcus Brent's daughter." That possibility had never crossed Miles's mind, but there it was. The sentence felt surreal.

"No, wait … I mean, how," he stumbled over his words, finally picking up the pace. "Can you explain it to me?"

"I can," she said as she slumped back against the seat. "It's embarrassing. I was in a different head space back then."

"I'm the last one to judge," he told her.

"I was going to sleep with Marcus Brent," she went on. "I was at a conference where he was a keynote speaker. We were introduced, and he seemed charming." She paused and let out a quiet breath before continuing. "He got whisked away to talk to some people with money, I assume, and I thought that was the end of it. I just met one of the richest men in the world."

"Where was the conference?" Miles wanted to know.

"In Philadelphia." A smile spread across her face as she faced him. "I used to work in a law firm, and we represented some of his holdings in the area."

"So, what happened?" he probed.

"Suddenly, one of the waiters brought me a drink, saying it

was from Marcus Brent. In the course of the night, he bought me three more drinks. Then, about two hours into the event, one of his bodyguards approached me and said that Mr. Brent would like to invite me to his suite for a cocktail. I was curious to see how the other half lived, and I wasn't dumb. I knew what he wanted, and I wondered what it would be like to sleep with someone of that status."

"I went to the suite with the bodyguard, who escorted me into the room where Marcus Brent met me. We talked, and he said he was familiar with the work I did for my firm. He turned on his charm, but you know what?" She took a moment to catch her breath and began again. "He was plastered. Wobbly from the get-go. When we went back to his room in the midst of getting undressed, he passed out. I thought he may have died, so I called in the bodyguard, who checked on him and said he was just passed out."

"I'm following you," Miles said to her, "but if you didn't sleep with him, why did they think it was his baby?"

"Well," she said as she shrugged her shoulders, "I'm pretty sure when he woke up, he thought he had slept with me. At least that was what the bodyguard was going to tell him."

"Okay," Miles was trying to think about a delicate way to ask his next question.

"You probably want to know who her father is," she said, somewhat teasing the story out.

"If you don't mind telling me," Miles said. But deep down, he knew it would kill him not to know.

"The bodyguard was very attentive and very handsome. Rugged, well built," she stopped and smiled at Miles, "everything that Marcus Brent wasn't. I'm not proud of it, but I sort of put the moves on him, and then," she pointed at Esperanza, who was playing, "the rest is history."

Miles pulled out a picture of Michael Davidson and showed it to Esme. "Was this the bodyguard?"

"Miles," she said without looking at the photo. "Please, don't be upset at me," she looked down at the picture. The shock came over her face. "Yes," she said with a gasp, "that's him."

"Esperanza is Michael Davidson's daughter?"

"Who's Michael Davidson?" Esme asked, as confusion washed over her now.

Miles realized that he was now the one surprising Esme. "Michael Davidson is the name of the bodyguard," he said while stretching out the photo to Esme.

"Then, yes," Esme said, "Look, I said I'm not proud of it, but it is what it is." She pushed the photograph away, and Miles put it down and continued.

"Then why did they force you into an abortion?"

"Because the bodyguard never told anyone we were together that night."

"Would he have been aware of what was happening with the

ladies that did end up pregnant," Miles delved deeper.

"I don't know," she said with a shrug, "maybe."

"Esme, look at me," he said. "You have never heard the name Michael Davidson?'

"No," she sighed, "I never asked him his name. I didn't want to."

"That doesn't matter," Miles took her hand. "What does matter is that he is here," his words came out with an urgency that snapped Esme back to attention.

"Here," she was shocked at what he had just said. "In Mexico?"

"Here in Playa del Carmen, at the hotel where I'm staying."

"No way," she sprang forward in her seat. "Are you sure?"

"Yes, I mean. I'm almost certain it's him."

"Oh my god," Esme's voice took on a frantic tone. "How did you find this out?"

"When I was here before, I went to the bar after we met. He was the bartender. He told me I looked like Marcus Brent."

"You knew he was there and didn't come back and tell me!"

"No, I had no idea who he was until a few weeks later. My Dad's PI in L.A. sent us some pictures of former associates of Marcus Brent. The second I saw the picture, I knew where I had seen him."

"How long do you think he's been here?" she asked, turning fully towards Miles.

"I don't know," Miles said. "He wasn't at the hotel today when I checked in."

Esme sat there stunned. Miles could only imagine how Esme felt. All these years living under a false sense of security, hiding here, while Marcus's goon had been lurking only a few miles away the whole time.

"Hola," Esperanza's voice broke the tension, and Esme and Miles looked down at the person Esperanza greeted. Standing only a few feet away was Michael Davidson.

ႣჂႬჂჄჂႣჄ

There he sat. Larger than life. Michael Davidson stretched his legs and bare feet out in front of him. His button-up shirt was half unbuttoned. His hair was salt and pepper, and Miles could see the rugged handsomeness that Esme had described. As Esperanza stood there staring at her father, it was finally evident to Miles that she wasn't Marcus Brent's child, his half-sister, as he'd believed.

Michael Davidson, or Mikey as he wanted to be called, had come in peace, so he said after Esperanza had made them aware of his presence. Miles looked at Esme, and he could sense a fear and shock in her that betrayed her ordinarily calm and confident demeanor. Mikey's choice of attire only seemed to strengthen his case, but Miles couldn't shake the unsettling thought that Mikey had likely followed him to the bungalow.

Yet, there they all sat, and Miles didn't sense even a touch of any malevolence from Mikey. He smiled and sipped his beer. It was clear that Mikey knew he needed to explain himself.

"First off," he commenced. "I don't work for Brent or Deavers anymore."

"Okay," Esme said, "but why are you here?"

"To protect you," he said, like it was the most sensible fact ever.

"Protect me," Esme scoffed.

"Let's not pretend that you're unaware of how dangerous the people you took that money from are," he said with a smile.

"How did you know about any of this?" she asked, almost rising from her seat.

Mikey sighed and began the story. Miles listened to it intently while Esme peppered him with questions, one after another. He would just hold up a hand, and Esme would quiet herself.

He happened to walk in at the end of a phone call between Deavers, which was how he referred to Elizabeth Deavers, and Dr. Abbott. She had been going at him about not moving up Marcus Brent's vasectomy, and how she now needed another appointment. He overheard her say something about some Hispanic girl, and he knew right away it was Esme.

"I followed her," he continued, "and I saw you go into that doctor's office."

"You were there?" Esme was taken aback.

"I was, but there was no way you could have seen me. Deavers didn't see me, and she normally sees everything. After that, I followed you and immediately knew that you didn't go through with it."

"How?" she asked. Miles noticed that she wasn't very comfortable with what she was hearing.

"You weren't paying that much attention," he said calmly. "I did."

"How long have you been here, in Playa del Carmen?" The question from Miles turned his attention away from Esme. Miles could see she needed a second to process what she just learned.

"About five months," he answered. "I've known, though, for years you were here. An old employee of mine works at the hotel. He kept an eye out for you. Six months ago, he told me he was getting worried for you since Marcus Brent was eyeing the White House. I knew what he meant, and I headed down here shortly after that call. He gave me a job managing the bar."

"When was the first time…" Esme trailed off with her words. It seemed to Miles that Mikey knew what she wanted to ask, so he answered her unspoken question.

"I got here, and a day later, I took a walk on the beach past here and saw you both from a distance. She's beautiful," he paused and glanced over at Esperanza. "I'm not here to interfere in your life and your plans. I'm only here to protect you two. I know things are going to get hard."

"Why would you think that?" Miles threw the question at him.

"You know why," he said, looking directly at Miles. Mikey's voice carried a tone that reminded Miles of being reprimanded by Simon.

"They know about us," Miles said with a nod.

"No, not exactly," Mikey replied. "I'm sure they don't know about you, Rhea, or Esme here, but from what I'm hearing, one of the others turned up at Brent Industries the other day."

"Lillian," Miles said out loud.

"That's the name I've heard as well," he said. "Look, I've people on the inside who keep me updated, mainly because this whole ordeal looks bad for Deavers, who I hate."

"I'm catching that," Esme jumped in.

"But you worked closely with her for years. What makes you want to turn on her now?" Miles asked as he arched his eyebrow.

"Now?" Mikey answered with a grunt of disgust. "I've been against that bitch for well over a decade. She was sloppy, and when she'd fuck things up, she'd just off people, make it look very much like an accident. I drew the line there."

"What about Elliot's mother?" Miles asked. "It didn't seem like you drew the line there."

"Who the fuck is Elliot," Mikey said to him. "I was a bodyguard, not a hitman."

"Hannah Vaugh's son," he said to Mikey. Mikey's eyes widened as he heard this name.

"So, you're telling me that the little guy at her funeral wasn't her nephew," his voice trailed off.

"No, it was her son."

"That makes so much sense now. And just to set the record straight, I didn't kill her."

"Why were you at the funeral?" Miles fired back at him.

"Deavers made me go with her," he said. "Hannah was crazy, you know that, right?"

"We shouldn't speak ill of the dead," Esme chimed in.

"I'm not speaking ill of her," Mikey protested, "she was crazy. Certifiable. If her sister took that kid away from her, it was the right move."

"What happened that night?" Miles probed.

"She stabbed me in the leg and started a fire," Mikey said. "She had seen me the night before and knew I was Marcus Brent's bodyguard. That made her go batshit crazy," he turned to Esme, "May she rest in peace," he said as he feigned the sign of the cross. "She planned to burn the whole place down with me stuck to a bar stool."

"What the hell," Esme exclaimed. "Is that where you got your scar from on your arm?"

Mikey chuckled and then blushed slightly, "I forgot you saw those."

"I asked you about them," she said bluntly.

"Whatever I told you was probably a lie."

"Figures," Esme huffed as she looked out at the sea.

"Listen," he said calmly while looking both at her and Miles, "There is so much I can tell you, but I won't right now. What I want you to know is that I know who you're dealing with. If Deavers has picked up on the fact that our asshole friend, doctor Abbott, has pulled a fast one on her with the hopes of smearing Brent's name in the mud, she is going to clean up after herself. You're both in a shitload of trouble."

"She's already tried to kill Elliot," Miles said. "And she already succeeded in killing Dustin and Angela, too."

"I remember Angela," Mikey said. "She was the last one before you, Esme. I truly thought that he'd stopped dicking around. Then you showed up at the event, and he sent you his signature drink the second he got a shot."

"Whatever," Esme responded tersely, "it didn't end that badly for you that evening, now did it?"

Mikey laughed and shook his head. "No, it didn't," and he motioned to Esperanza.

"What are your intentions there?" Miles asked him, nodding towards Esperanza. Esme glared at him, seemingly upset that he asked that question but curious to know the answer.

"I'll leave you two alone as soon as I know that you're safe."

"I'm safe," she shot back at him.

"You're anything but safe," he retorted. "She'll find you. You will die. She doesn't give a fuck if it isn't his kid, you took his money and pretended it was!"

"Shit," Esme's voice dissolved into the air but picked up again. "What do you propose?"

"Hide," he said.

"I've been hiding for four years!"

"Hide in plain sight," he corrected. "Deavers is great at turning over rocks, but not great at looking at the rock she is turning over. She's sloppy, and she won't be taking her time."

"Do you have an idea?" Miles asked him. "I mean, how can we throw her off our trail?"

"She's not on your trail yet," he said. "She must have something else keeping her occupied, which is probably something to do with Lillian and Saul's satanic spawn, Bart."

"Barton Traeger?" Miles asked.

"Yes," Mikey responded, "do you know him?"

"Of him," Miles said. "He may be involved in Lillian's disappearance. But he isn't the real threat; Deavers is."

"First off, if Lillian is missing, she's dead. She would be dangerous to keep around because she will talk. Secondly, anyone she has talked to is in just as much danger."

"She wouldn't give us up," Miles said calmly.

"You underestimate your opponent," Mikey said to him with a tone of condescension.

"So, there's nothing to do, just stay out of their way and hope not to die," Miles lashed out with a sense of defeat in his voice.

"No," Mikey responded coolly, "You and your siblings are

too important to let that happen to. If you can make an impact in the media, you'll keep him from being nominated, and that should stall him for a few years. You need to piss off the conservatives, make them understand he stands for nothing he says he does."

"That's what Rhea has said," Miles interrupted him. "I don't think they care. He ticks the boxes that allow them to continue voting the party line."

"He ticks none of those boxes," Esme jumped in. "He forces women to have abortions."

"Which you didn't go through with, despite acting as if you did!" Mikey raised his voice a little to attract Esme's attention.

"That makes Dr. Abbott a damn hero then!" Esme was getting heated.

"You obviously haven't spent much time with Dr. Abbott, or you wouldn't be calling him a hero," Mikey said. "He's pompous and arrogant and always thinks he's four steps ahead of everyone else. So, let's calm it down," Mikey spoke with a voice that commanded attention, and the two of them backed off. "It doesn't matter that you didn't go through with it. What matters is that you were forced into the situation."

Esperanza was walking towards the porch, and they all looked at her. "I'm not asking you for anything," Mikey said quietly, "but that's my daughter, not his. I won't allow her to be slaughtered to help Marcus Brent land a nomination for president. Does that register with the two of you?"

"Yes," they answered him.

"What do you suggest?" Esme seemed defeated.

Miles knew that Mikey's use of the word slaughtered hit home with her as it had with him. "Do you have a plan?"

"I do," he said, "but it may be better if you don't know what it is."

"I don't want to be in the dark," Miles said, partly out of bravado and partly because he wanted to know exactly what was up this guy's sleeves.

"Fine with me," he said, "but you need to trust me because I know how these criminals work. Let's talk back at the hotel. I need to know what you have planned as well." He stood up from his chair and addressed Esme, "Now go pack, and we can talk about details later. We leave in the morning."

Chapter Twenty-Eight

Dr. Abbott's visit weighed heavily on Elliot's mind as he boarded his flight to Oklahoma City. Elliot would have been consumed with dreams of seeing his family again two days ago, but now his thoughts were elsewhere. He wasn't exactly ready for this trip; it was sort of thrust upon him by Simon. As he had learned, when Simon suggested something, it wasn't a suggestion at all—it was an order and non-negotiable.

In a few hours, he would land at the Oklahoma City airport, where he would come face-to-face with Marcia and Jennings for the first time in over three years. It should have been a reunion of tears and happiness, but before it could be, Elliot had to apologize, this time in person, something he wasn't good at. He knew he'd been wrong, but every time he tried to put it into words, he could only think of reasons why he was justified in doing what he did and acting how he acted.

Simon had told him not to show up in Philadelphia again until he or Miles phoned him. Until then, he was to spend time with his family. Visit Scooper in OKC. Lay low. Elizabeth Deavers was not going to be looking for him exactly where she had already been, or so Simon thought. He disagreed with him, but he was sure that no matter what happened, there was no shortage of weapons at his house.

His flight was mostly empty. Oklahoma City wasn't really a tourist destination at the end of summer. He slept on and off, as he often did on flights, but he was afraid to fall into that place of dreaming. His dreams had been haunted by so many ghosts lately. He saw the truck racing past him. Scooper would be talking to him, and a bullet wound would appear out of nowhere, and then Scooper would turn into Miles and then into Simon. The whole time, they would be talking to him without realizing that they had a bullet hole in their chest. He would wake up abruptly, drenched in sweat.

As he collected his bag from the carousel and moved towards the arrivals, he could already see Jennings towering over most of the people in the waiting line. He didn't have on his normal ball cap. His hair showed no signs of graying and was dusty blonde, just like Elliot remembered. He caught Elliot's gaze, and Elliot saw his green eyes light up, and tears started to form. His hand went up in a wave. Elliot waved back as he walked out towards him. He looked to see where Marcia was, but he didn't see her standing there.

Jennings had moved his way over towards the exit and walked towards Elliot. A smile crossed his tear-streaked face. His arms open wide to welcome him. Elliot felt deep in his gut the feeling of being loved. He gasped as he fought back heavy sobs and found himself enveloped in the arms that had picked him up as a child, carried him to bed, and hugged him when he got home from school. An embrace that Elliot had pushed away from him at the time when he needed it the most. Now, he was lost in it. He whispered over and over, "I'm sorry. I'm sorry." Jennings just held him.

∞∞∞∞∞

The car ride to Jones wouldn't be all that long. It always felt like it was in the middle of nowhere, but it was only about an hour outside of OKC. Elliot asked where his Mom was, and Jennings began to tear up, causing him to panic that something had happened to her in the few hours between their last call.

"No, she is fine," he assured, "she stayed home to ready things. Didn't you have a voicemail from Simon?"

It turned out that Simon had tried to call Elliot before he got on the flight, but unfortunately, Elliot was horrible at keeping his phone charged, and it was dead. Jennings didn't have a charger in his truck, so Elliot would just wait until they returned to the house to charge it.

As they drove east out of the city, Elliot asked him what Simon wanted.

"How was your flight?" was his response.

"Fine, what did Simon want?" he asked again.

"He needed us to help him with something, and he wanted to make sure you contacted him when you got here."

"That's it," Elliot said.

"It's better if he explains it," said Jennings.

Elliot could tell that Jennings was struggling with how to proceed. He hated lying, and Elliot sensed that he wouldn't budge. He let it go and figured he'd call Simon back when they got to the house.

"Have you heard anything from Scott's family?" Elliot had to fight back using his nickname.

"Mom visited him yesterday; they're happy to hear you're okay and said you should visit soon."

"I don't think he wants me to visit," Elliot said as he looked at Oklahoma City disappearing.

"Why would you say that?" Jennings asked, turning slightly to face him.

"He's not answered my texts," Elliot sighed.

"You should have called him," Jennings replied, "but that wouldn't have mattered either. His phone got smashed in the shooting. I thought you knew that."

"I didn't," Elliot said. "Maybe I'll go see him tomorrow. Is he doing well?"

"He's up and moving, according to your mother."

"I'm glad to hear that."

"I don't want to pry here, but I'm guessing you two had a falling out before this whole thing happened."

"Yeah, he drew a line in the sand, and I told him to mind his own business."

"Was he right?" Jennings asked.

"He was."

"Miles told me about their trip to visit you, you know," Jennings was looking at him again, wanting to see his reaction.

Elliot raised his eyebrows and shrugged. "Miles," he shook his head, "the older brother I never wanted, and now I can't live without."

Elliot paused momentarily, thinking about how he wanted to tell the rest of the story. He was at a distinct disadvantage since Miles had already reported back to Jennings. Lying to make things look better would not be the best thing.

"He and Scooper, Scott, hit it off. He was so happy for me, finding this new family. Then he started asking me questions and realized that I didn't intend to do anything about it. His orphan heart broke, and I ignored the fact that he felt that if Miles was my brother and Rhea, my sister, they could be like brother and sister to him. It was ridiculous to me; we had known them for two days, and I just blew him off and told him it wasn't his family, and it wasn't what I wanted to do. He stopped talking to me, and that was horrible. It's lonely out there, and losing the one person who made me feel like I wasn't alone was probably what made me rethink what I did to *our* family."

Jennings nodded, "You're here now. That's a start."

"I hope so," he said. "Miles has been great to talk with. Rhea, god, I can't believe that I suddenly have siblings, and they're all up in my business. Rhea got me to stop smoking."

"Hallelujah," Jennings looked excited. "I can't wait to meet her and thank her properly."

"You've not met her," Elliot said.

"No, only Miles came. She was in Oregon or Washington, I forget which one, looking for one of the mothers."

"Lillian's mom, Stacy," Elliot said matter-of-factly.

"About Lillian," Jennings started and then stopped.

"We don't know where she is," Elliot's voice broke as he spoke. Jennings shook his head as he listened. "So that leaves only Esme's daughter Esperanza, and that's where Miles is right now."

"Where's that exactly?" Jennings was turning off the highway and onto the road that led to town.

"Somewhere in Mexico. Rhea is in New York trying to land some low-level news websites to break the story. She's with a man named Hamish, who Simon and Miles knew."

"Simon has filled me in on that," Jennings said.

"When," Elliot ventured casually, but he didn't expect Jennings's answer.

"This morning," he said as he stared at the road ahead of him.

"It must have been after he dropped me off at the airport," Elliot said.

"It was. You were probably on the plane," he paused again.

"Some things have come up, and…" he trailed off.

"What things?" Elliot felt panic welling up.

"Everyone is heading our way."

"What the fuck, why?" Elliot knew his voice betrayed his panic.

"They think you'll all be the safest here," Jennings replied. "They found Lillian, she's dead."

⋙⋘

Simon had explained, between Elliot's constant questions, that Adam, his private investigator, had gotten a tip about a Jane Doe found in the area where he had thought that Lillian could have been taken. He got there quickly. He said the body was in terrible shape, but it was most definitely Lillian.

Miles had news, too, Simon told him, and he was on his way back to the States. Within the few hours that he was on the plane, things had kicked into gear. Rhea was driving down with Simon, and they would use his parents' place as a base of operation as the last details were made to make their announcement to the world.

Simon asked to speak to Jennings at the end of the conversation, and Elliot listened to his Dad respond. He hung up the phone and looked at Elliot.

"You okay?" he asked him gently.

"I'm not great," Elliot shrugged.

"Well, I figured as much."

"I'm struggling with guilt, like maybe there was something I could have done to save her, but I'm also glad that it wasn't Miles or Rhea."

"Or you," Jennings said somberly.

"Or me," Elliot looked out the window. Everything looked the same. Nothing had changed. The houses looked run down, the fields were green, and everything had stayed stuck exactly like he'd left it.

"God, I didn't miss Oklahoma," he said under his breath.

"It didn't miss you either," Jennings responded, and they both laughed.

They were only a few minutes from their house, and as the distance grew smaller, Elliot became more and more excited to see his mom. As they pulled into the driveway, he could see the side door that led to the kitchen swinging open, and there she was, Marcia Sharp. Waving.

He barely got out of the truck before he was wrapped up in her arms. He was home.

Soon, his home would be fuller than it ever had been. Simon, Rhea, and Miles were on their way. Simon's PI, Adam, was due to arrive later that evening to provide some protection for the group. For now, it was just like it used to be. He was with his Dad and his Mom. He felt whole again.

Chapter Twenty-Nine

"Nice of you to pick me up," Elizabeth seethed through her teeth as she got into the car with Saul.

He mumbled something in response as he got in behind her. Their driver was separated from them by a thick sheet of glass. "Can I offer you a drink?"

"I'll take a water," she said absent-mindedly. Saul grabbed a bottle out of the mini fridge. "Why are you picking me up?"

"Lillian's body was found," he spoke without pretense.

"Can it be tied to us?" Elizabeth asked.

"Probably not," Saul responded.

"Why am I here then?" she asked him. "You don't need me for this."

"The private dick that was snooping around discovered her," Saul proclaimed.

"And what did he do?" she asked.

"IDed her," Saul said, facing away from her, looking out his window. "The medical examiner is one of ours and said that he was looking for a missing person, so his people let him in to see her."

"So, as far as we know, he identified her, and that was it," she said flatly as if unbothered.

"Yes," he looked irritated. "I don't like this, Elizabeth. This feels sloppy."

"Then talk to Barton," she suggested. "It was his gig."

"I did," he said. "He told me to fuck off."

"He's not your biggest fan," she said. "Do you want me to talk with him?"

"No," Saul said, turning towards her. "He's off on a lead to find Dr. Abbott."

"You know where Abbott is," she asked and sprang forward.

Saul paused for a minute. He looked at her long and hard. When he resumed, it was not to answer her question but to ask his own, "Who were the other doctors?" he asked.

"Stop playing coy, Saul, you know damn well who the doctors were," she sighed. "Abbott is the only one who would ever double-cross Marcus."

Saul went quiet again. Elizabeth had learned not to lead conversations with Saul. It was always better to follow his train of thought, it kept you from showing your cards.

"Why are you so tense? No one is going to trace Lillian back to us," Elizabeth said, "unless there's something you aren't telling me. Did that PI talk to any of our people?"

"No," he said. "Is Lillian the only one?" he asked with a sudden sternness

Elizabeth hoped that her face didn't betray the lie she was

about to utter, "yes."

Saul shook his head. "Then we can move on."

Elizabeth felt her phone start to vibrate. She drew it out of her bag and looked at the number. She hadn't talked to him since the diner.

"I didn't expect to hear from you today," she said to him, as she motioned to Saul that it wasn't any of his business.

"The last one is in Mexico," he said to her.

"Is he with her right now?" she asked, knowing exactly who he meant. Saul had started scrolling through his phone and didn't seem to be listening.

"Well," he started to answer, but stopped mid-way, "he was. He just left her this afternoon. It's his second visit; he looks just like his dad."

"Where in Mexico?" she asked him.

"Playa del Carmen," he said, "I'll text you the details later. You've got some cleanup to do, and from what I hear, that makes four you somehow missed."

"What have you heard?" she hissed.

"I'll send you the text," he said. "Let me know when you arrive, I'll have some recon for you."

"I'll see you tomorrow," she said and hung up.

Elizabeth looked over at Saul, who was reading something on his phone. "What was that all about?" he asked without entirely looking at her.

"The people who talked with Lillian," she answered. "I've a lead on them. I'm heading to Mexico, so you can handle this on your own."

"Mexico," he seethed. "I need you here. You're not going anywhere."

"No, you need me there," she pressed. "If they're there, and I can get to them, I'll be able to see what they have."

"Mexico, Africa, who the hell are these two talking with?" he asked her flippantly.

"That's what I'm trying to find out," she stated.

"Elizabeth," he turned to look at her intently, "there aren't more surprises out there, are there?"

Her heart skipped a beat. Saul had asked her the same question twice. Did he already know that she had slipped up with North Carolina? She shook her head again, "No," she lied once more. They sat in silence as they made their way to the hotel where she was supposed to stay. She got out of the car and looked back. Saul looked dead calm, steely even. The fear rose in her as she said to him, "I'm leaving, you know how to get hold of me."

Chapter Thirty

The time Elliot managed to spend alone with Jennings and Marcia passed in the blink of an eye. The next day, Adam, Simon's PI from LA, arrived. Three hours later, Simon and Rhea rolled in from Philadelphia. The rest of the day was full of information, questions that couldn't be answered, and waiting for Miles. It bugged Elliot that Miles hadn't been in touch with him like he had with Rhea. His sister had texted him constantly throughout their different side quests, but Miles had gone completely MIA. Elliot tried to convince himself not to take it personally, but it was hard not to.

The only thing that had become clearer to Elliot was that with Lillian's body being found, there was no turning back from breaking the news to the world. Their story was about to go public, but he didn't feel ready yet. He had some unfinished business to take care of. Walking in from the barn, he sensed that most of the house was still asleep. Just three of them were up and moving: Marica, Jennings, and himself.

He climbed the stairs to the porch off the kitchen. The familiar aroma of coffee hung in the air, welcoming him even before he opened the door. It was quiet as he entered the kitchen and took his boots off. He hoped this stillness would remain for a few minutes. He found his coffee mug, filled it, put some milk in it, and sat down at the table. As he took a slow, long sip, he took in the room that he knew so well.

The first sip was like stepping back in time—it was home in a cup that stirred memories he hadn't thought about in a long time. His mother's coffee was more than a drink. It had tasted exactly like this in the mornings and evenings spent with his family. Elliot suddenly felt nostalgia hit him hard.

He leaned back in his chair and continued sipping his coffee as the burden he felt crept back into his mind. Scooper—there was unfinished business. Visiting him had been on the list of things he wanted to accomplish, but it just hadn't happened yet. Scooper was supposed to be discharged at the end of the week. Jennings had given him Scooper's new number, but the courage to write him hadn't come yet. He opened up a message box and typed Scooper's name in the bubble. The cursor just blinked at him. And he blinked back at the cursor.

For a couple of seconds, the staring game went on. Elliot breathed deeply and let his lungs fill before exhaling slowly. He began typing.

"Back in OK, heard you were getting better."

Elliott erased it and started again.

"I'm so sorry. How are you?"

Elliot stared at it again. His finger hovered over the delete button.

"You look worried," a booming voice startled him, and he almost jumped out of his seat. Adam came into the kitchen wearing a T-shirt and jeans. He had switched out his Pierre Cardin suit he was wearing the day before for Carhartt and North Face. With a baseball cap on his head and white athletic socks on his feet, he blended in better than Elliot. He and Jennings had hit it off, and Adam was taking pride in being able to help around the farm.

"It's nothing," he said and turned the phone off.

"If that's your 'it's nothing' face, I wouldn't want to see your 'it's something' face," he said as he walked over to the counter. "Your dad is still out in the field," he asked Elliot.

"Yes," Elliot answered and nodded his head towards the door.

"Sweet," he murmured. "I'm going to head out to see if I can give a hand. Did I tell you that I spent three summers working on my uncle's farm outside of Sacramento?"

"I spent my summers, falls, winters, and springs working on my family's farm right here," Elliot responded sarcastically.

"Touche," Adam said as he turned and leaned against the counter. He was a tall man and large without being fat. His hands were so large that they covered the coffee mug he held in them.

"How did you end up in your line of work?" The question popped into Elliot's mind and instantly came out of his mouth.

"Which line of work?" he rebutted.

"The private investigation line," Elliot said with a shrug.

"That's a long story," Adam savored his coffee and looked out the window to his left.

"Aren't they all?" Elliot put his mug down. "Can I ask you something?"

"If I say no, you will anyway, so fire away."

"Did you know Miles's mother?" Elliot had wondered about that since they met.

"I did, but not for long. She was diagnosed maybe a month after I met her, and she was gone within the year."

"What was she like?" Elliot asked.

"She was a woman who had secrets," Adam responded. "You could tell."

"How?" Elliot shifted uncomfortably in his seat, trying to mask any behavior that might reveal his own secrets.

"It's a gift of mine," Adam responded casually. Elliot chuckled nervously at that response. Adam looked at him with a smirk. "You don't believe me?"

"Maybe a little, but not completely," Elliot shrugged and shifted slightly back in his seat.

"You're a man of secrets, Mr. Elliot Sharp. For example, there's that text you couldn't finish. The way you were looking at it, fretting over it, tells me something." Adam focused his eyes on Elliot.

"What does that tell you?" Elliot fixed his eyes back on Adam.

"That you're texting someone who cares more about you than you do about them." Adam shrugged and raised his coffee mug to his mouth before pausing to add, "Maybe because the relationship doesn't feel necessary to you anymore."

Elliot looked at Adam as he felt the tears well up in his eyes. Benjamin had been right. His family had come for him, and Scooper's had not—nor would they ever. The guilt he felt for just leaving Scooper on his own to recover from a gunshot was eating away at him. He hadn't even told his Dad how he felt.

"Am I pretty accurate, Elliot Sharp?" Adam shot him a wink.

"It's possible," Elliot replied as the burden he was carrying took on a new weight.

"Just text him and tell him you hope he's recovering well," Adam said. Then, he drank the last bit of his coffee and put the cup in the dishwasher. Elliot sat there with his mouth open.

"How did you know it was a 'him,'" Elliot probed as Adam headed to the door where the boots he had just bought in town stood.

"In my short time of knowing you, Elliot, I would say, and forgive me for being indelicate about this, that if this were a lady, you would have no problem moving on, so it had to be a friend whom you didn't want to hurt. A friend who possibly had been hurt because of you."

He wasn't ready to buy that Adam simply used his skills to build this whole story about him at a mere glance. "What did my

Dad tell you?"

"Does Jennings know about the guilt you are carrying for Scott?" Adam shot Elliot a look that confirmed that Jennings hadn't said anything to him.

"No," said Elliot, "nobody does. It was just a…what you said, a relationship of necessity."

"Elliot, you need to buck up, realize that your actions have consequences, and mend those fences. He did take a bullet that was meant for you," Adam said gravely.

With that, Adam picked up his boots, walked out the door, and sat down on the top step to put them on. Elliot just stared at the door, not knowing what to think. Had he truly screwed things up with Scooper because of his selfishness? Reasons and justifications for his behavior ran through his head, all pushing him farther away from taking any responsibility. His phone stared back at him, and it became quite clear. His inability to write one damn text should have been a clue that at least he knew it had meant something to Scooper. But what?

Elliot shook his head back and forth. His eyes welled up. The first tear slipped down his cheek before he could even stop it. All those years of building walls around his heart, of hardening himself against anticipated hurt, had only led to a deeper ache. What was meant to protect him had only isolated him further, and worse still, damaged the innocent souls who had only ever wanted the best for him. The realization hit him like a bullet. He wasn't immune to pain, he had just numbed himself. He needed to change. He needed to accept that pain sometimes wasn't the enemy. It was what drove you away from greater harm and saved you from an even deeper loss.

He mustered the courage and unlocked his phone; the abandoned text was still there. He deleted it.

"I'm so sorry, Scott. How are you feeling? I want to visit, I'm back in OK with my siblings."

He hit send, put the phone down, and let the tears flow. He lost track of how long he sat there, but soon, his mom came into the kitchen.

"Would you like to come with me to the grocery store?" she asked him.

He looked up at her with his red eyes, and she returned a smile.

"How about you come with me and get your mind off whatever it is that's bugging you."

He agreed and got up. Time with his mom would refocus him, and it would help pass the time until Miles was back. It would keep him from having a deeper conversation with Rhea, who always wanted to talk about how he was feeling.

As they drove off the farm, Elliot knew that every second from here on out would move him light years away from any sort of normal. It was time for him to reshape how he approached his scars so that when he struck out against Marcus Brent, it would do the most damage without hurting himself or those he loved.

◌◌◌◌◌

It had been a crazy few days, but now, as Miles stood in the Sharps' living room, surrounded by his Dad, his sister, his brother, his brother's parents, and his Dad's PI, Miles sighed and took them all in.

"So," Simon interrupted his thoughts. "What did you find out in Mexico?"

Miles took a sip of the beer Jennings had served him. What he was about to drop on them would be a mild shock, but it was also the green light for them to make their move.

"Esme and Esperanza are both okay." He put the beer down and inhaled before starting again. "They're on their way back to her parents in southern California."

"What? Why?" Rhea shot the question out abruptly.

"That doesn't sound like a good idea," Simon added.

"Please let me finish," Miles interjected. "It's a longer story, but I'll make it short."

"I'm a fan of the longer stories," Jennings said to him with a smile. "Take your time and give us all the information that we need."

"When I got there, I went straight to Esme's house. She was there, so was Esperanza, and they were safe. I pleaded with her to come with me, back to the US, where we could keep her safe, but then she told me something. It turns out that Esperanza isn't

Marcus Brent's child."

The shock settled in quickly. Rhea, Simon, and Elliot fired their questions at the same time, while also simultaneously talking to each other.

"Let him answer and finish the story," Adam spoke up this time, his voice booming over the others. When the room quieted Adam nodded at Miles.

"Marcus Brent couldn't perform that evening and passed out drunk. His bodyguard, who was outside of the room, well, she found him quite attractive," he paused. It was the toughest part of all the pieces of this story. He knew he had felt a real connection with her, but this part ached. He knew it shouldn't. It wasn't like he didn't have a past. He continued. "It's his baby."

Again, the room erupted into questions and statements.

"It's Michael Davidson's kid?" Adam asked, more for clarification than out of shock.

"Yes, that's why he was in Mexico," Miles answered, holding up a hand to stop everyone from jumping into their questions again. "Mikey knew about the plan with the women. When he overheard a conversation about Esme, he knew the drill. Sure enough, a few days later, he watched as Deavers hauled Esme into Dr. Abbott's office. He knew it had been his kid; at first, he was happy that she wouldn't be saddled with that burden. Then he realized something was off, and he kept tabs on her. He's known for years that she kept the baby. Last year, a friend of his, who had also worked security for Marcus Brent, began keeping track of Esme in Playa del Carmen. Six months ago, Mikey felt it would be better for him to be the one keeping eyes on her, and he moved from Miami to Playa."

"I have a hard time trusting his intentions," Elliot said as he crossed his arms.

"I think that it dawned on him that she would be in trouble if this ever leaked. From my time with the guy," Miles paused to find the right words, "he's a control-the-narrative type. He isn't leaving his kid or his own life up to chance, so he moved."

"How can we trust what he's saying?" Elliot asked from the couch where he was sitting next to Rhea. "He could be a plant from Brent."

Miles pointed at Adam. "Adam had already told us, in the written report, that Mikey had left on his own terms, and he was off the map completely."

Adam nodded, "he cut all ties. If he hadn't, I would have found something."

"So, you've met him?" Elliot asked, "Since you keep calling him Mikey."

"I have, and he's legitimate."

Adam kept nodding his head subtly. Simon looked at him with questions in his eyes, "How can you be sure?" his Dad was the one to ask him this time.

"Because he's been there for six months, tending bar, keeping an eye on her, and until a few days ago, she had no idea he was there. He was really there to protect her. When I was down for the first time, he realized that something was up. He'd even commented on the fact that I looked like Marcus Brent. He did his research, guessed that I was somehow related, if not a son of Marcus Brent, and got worried. When I popped up the second time, he was not at the hotel, but his coworker told him I'd shown up. He wasn't that far behind me, and he said he stood and watched us for a few minutes. He timed it perfectly. She told me Esperanza was Mikey's daughter and bam, there he stood. It was surreal and scary."

"So, what's his angle?" Elliot questioned as he got up and began to pace the room.

"He's on our side," Miles answered.

"How do you know that?" The doubt in Rhea's voice was palpable.

"Because he's going to help take care of our two biggest problems," Miles said, emphasizing his point by holding up two fingers.

"What are our two biggest problems?" Elliot asked him.

"Ms. Deavers," Rhea piped up, "is one. Marcus Brent, the second."

"No," Miles shook his head. "It's Ms. Deavers' protégé, Barton Traeger, who is the second one. He's the son of Saul Traeger, the man pulling a lot of the strings for Brent Industries.

Barton's the guy who Adam followed to figure out where Lillian was."

"And most likely the one responsible for her death," Adam added.

"What is this Mikey guy planning to do?" Jennings asked Miles.

He laid out the plan that he, Mikey, and Esme had worked on together. As far as he knew, Ms. Deavers was on her way to Playa del Carmen as he unfolded the plan. A second phone call to Saul Traeger would send Barton on his way after her. Mikey would have them both in his sights as the news here broke. Once they were both there, Mikey would spring his trap.

Miles left out some of the details, including that shortly before he arrived at the house, Mikey had gotten word that Barton had found Dr. Abbott, and now no one else knew where Abbott was. Mikey was sure that Barton now had everything he required to piece together the complete puzzle and, being the opportunist he was, go after Elizabeth Deavers to clean it up. The rest of the plan was tricky and not his idea, but he figured he would explain to them when and if he needed to.

ভ৪৩৪৩৪৩

The evening air felt electrified with their discourse. Everyone had ideas, and each idea had its detractors. The conversations bled into one another evening flew by. Rhea saw that she had missed a call from Hamish and excused herself to call him back. It rang, but it went to voicemail. She couldn't explain why she was a little sad that he didn't pick up.

She felt the phone vibrate, and his text message brightened the screen.

"On a call, call you back asap."

She decided not to go back into the living room and instead headed out to the kitchen to make her way outside. She walked around the corner of the house to the front porch and sank into one of the chairs. The stars shone brightly in the sky, giving her enough time to reflect and revisit the last few weeks. She had gone from a spinsterish orphan to an older sister in half a second, or at least that was how it felt. Now she sat by as Miles planned and arranged and she felt helpless. She felt like she should have been thinking through these things. Rhea tucked her legs under herself, and then her phone rang; it was Hamish.

"Hey, you," she exclaimed.

"How are you holding up with all the new developments?" he asked.

"As good as I can," she said, and then it hit, "how do you know about them?"

"Miles," he answered casually. "He put me in touch with the old bodyguard, Mikey. That's who I was on the phone with."

"Is he willing to talk to the press about what he knew?" she asked him, something that she had wanted to ask Miles, but he had been adamant that Mikey had a plan, and that was what they were going with.

"Oh, no," Hamish said with a chuckle. "Mikey does not want that heat. In fact, he doesn't want any heat. He knows what he's doing, and I think Adam has signed off on it being a good plan."

"When did Adam talk to him?" Rhea was amazed.

"I don't know," Hamish responded. "Possibly today, just like me. Miles called me yesterday and caught me up on things. I've been working some angles here."

"I know I've heard," she said. "It looks like it's a go tomorrow."

"It is," Hamish's voice took on a softer, caring tone. "Are you ready?"

"I guess … I'll be," she said feebly.

The next morning at the house carried an atmosphere of anticipation. Everyone was waiting for the text telling them the article had dropped. Hamish had worked his magic, and his contact, Hector, was set to go in the legitimate press area, passing the story from the gossip rags to his people.

The three of them would then head out tomorrow to Dallas for a press briefing. That was the plan for now but the debate raged about where they should do it. Rhea had suggested that they target a larger market, but she was overruled by Simon and Adam, saying that staying small initially was safer. They could control the area better.

Adam was heading out that afternoon on a mission that only

he and Simon had discussed. He was usually one of the first ones up in the morning. Rhea sat in the kitchen with Jennings, reading an actual newspaper. Marcia sat to his left, writing a list. Someone dropped something upstairs, and Jennings's eyes followed the sound.

"It's nice to have a full house," he smiled at her as she scrolled through the news.

Adam wandered into the kitchen. Today, he dressed like he did for his PI work. He had on his button-up shirt and his dark trousers. He was as kind as ever, moving through the room and asking everyone how they slept. He was thanking the Sharps again for their hospitality when Simon entered the room.

"I'm off to Dallas," Adam said to them. "If this all goes well tonight, it looks like we'll be heading there to meet the press."

"Wow," Marcia seemed excited. "Do you think this will be that big of a deal?"

Rhea was surprised at Marcia's comment. It had to be a big deal; this was what they had put their lives on the line for. If Marcia thought it might not be a big deal, what hope did they have that the rest of the U.S. would think it was a big deal?

"Not at first, but we'll know within the next 48 hours. Either this will blow up huge, or it will fizzle out. Either way, the three of them should be safer with their names out there. Hopefully, Mikey can keep Barton and Elizabeth in Mexico long enough for us to get their faces out there. Once they're recognized out there,

Brent's crew won't be able to touch them in the same way as when they were unknown." Adam paused and then added, "at least not without raising suspicions."

Miles had snuck in as Adam was speaking. Everyone greeted him, and Jennings got up to pour him some coffee and put on a new pot. He rested against the counter as he took a sip. Rhea wondered what was going through Jennings' mind.

It couldn't have been more than a few weeks ago that Miles had shown up here asking questions. And now, here he was, standing again in their kitchen. Jennings and Marcia had expressed how happy they were that Elliot was finally home. Marcia would often just shake her head and sigh, "how did you ever pull it off Miles?"

Miles had responded, "I didn't," he chuckled, "you have Simon to thank for that."

Jennings headed out with Adam. Miles grabbed his coffee and went to the front porch. Simon stood at the kitchen sink, scrolling through his phone. Marcia completed her list and patted Rhea on the hand.

"It's going to be okay," she assured. "Once it's spread, you're safer."

"I hope to God you're right," Rhea said.

Marcia took her list and left the kitchen, heading back towards her bedroom. Simon looked up and realized the world had moved on, smiled at Rhea, and returned upstairs.

It was quiet, yet she didn't feel alone even though the room was empty. She felt like she was part of a close-knit, happy family. She heard what she could only assume was Elliot coming down the steps. He entered the kitchen looking haggard but not as bad as he used to look.

"Adam and Simon were up all night talking," he kissed Rhea on the head, "that low bass rumble kept me awake."

Rhea laughed, and as she did, her phone buzzed.

It was Hamish. She read the text.

"It's posted," she conveyed to Elliot.

"Have you read it?" he asked, pouring the remaining coffee into a cup.

"No," she replied. "Hamish literally just sent me the text."

Elliot picked up his phone. "It's funny that he didn't text me."

"Give me a second. I'll send you the link," Rhea looked down at the text and the article. There it was. All of this cat and mouse would end with the mouse sticking its nose out in the open while the cats were chasing their tails in Mexico.

Rhea was fully aware that the next step was making sure some minor cities' evening news picked up on the story and took a chance at breaking it. This is where Hector came in. He tipped off two friends, one from Wichita and the other from Carson City. In the end, it was Wichita who broke the news first, and the tiny internet story took on a whole new life.

Hamish called her that evening just wanting to check on her,

Miles, and the kid. Miles came out to the front porch later, where she was drinking some red wine that Marcia had kept for a special occasion.

"Are we heading to Dallas?" she asked him.

"Yeah," he said, sitting down carefully, holding a glass of whiskey. "Adam's there, and Hamish is heading there."

"I know," she said, "he called me earlier this evening."

"Oh," Miles raised his eyebrows, but then his phone lit up. "It's Mikey," he said as he answered it.

"Hello, Mikey," he said. "I've got Rhea with me as well. What's up?"

"Barton is on his way," she heard the gruff voice.

"Took the bait, did he?" Miles confirmed.

"Like catnip, couldn't stay away," Mikey chuckled. "I'll check in once things are set here."

"Thanks," Miles said to him, but Rhea was pretty sure that Mikey had already hung up.

"What exactly is he setting up?" Rhea asked Miles, hoping for some clarity since it was only the two of them.

"A wild goose chase of sorts," Miles slid his phone back into his shorts. He stretched his legs out in front of him and crossed his bare feet. "Should keep them busy for a long time."

"Won't that be dangerous for Mikey?" She seemed shocked at Miles's demeanor.

"You've not met Mikey." He turned to face her and raised his glass.

Rhea felt uncomfortable with that answer; it was as if Miles wasn't telling her everything, but she let it pass. Marcia came out of the door and told them the local news was about to air a special report. The two of them jumped up and hurried into the house. On the TV sat an older gentleman, dignified and self-serious.

"We begin tonight with a breaking story. Republican presidential primary candidate Marcus Brent is the center of some controversy this evening. A report printed on the internet magazine Truth First has reported allegations that Marcus Brent paid for the abortions of at least six different women. The story goes on to report that most of the women worked with the doctor to fake their abortions and keep their children. The article on Truth First goes on to allege a connection between Marcus Brent and a mother and son, Angela and Dustin Camp, who died of suspicious circumstances in North Carolina early this summer. Other aspects of the story are coming to light, and we hope to have more on this story for you as soon as we can."

"Here we go," Elliot said as he excitedly clapped.

Rhea just sat there. It was a reality now. And there was no going back.

Chapter Thirty-One

The news had trickled throughout the country at first, but by the time they left for Dallas, it had turned into a full-fledged storm. Articles were run with pictures of all of them. Elliot looks rugged, shirtless, at a well in Burkina Faso. They used photos from the university websites for Rhea and Miles. The articles that came out after the Wichita News ran the story were just retreaded information. Hamish was fielding the calls for them. He hadn't released a statement yet, but he would, he said, at a press conference in Dallas the next day.

"Elliot," Rhea was talking to him on the phone, "Miles and I are in the restaurant." She paused for a second and listened. Then she hung up.

"What?" Miles asked as he stared at the menu.

"He ran into Hamish and got held up talking with him," she said.

"Didn't he realize that Hamish was joining us?" Miles asked.

"Who knows," she said and picked up her menu, "but he was pissed that he'd never been introduced to Hamish. Hopefully he's pacified now."

Simon came into the restaurant with Marcia. Jennings had

stayed back at the farm. Hector was en route to Dallas, but he was to be a background figure this time. Hamish was assigned to run this part of the show, everyone else was taking a back seat.

Hamish and Elliot were only a few seconds behind Marcia and Simon. Miles nodded to Hamish, who gave him a thumbs-up. Elliot hugged Miles, like he was prone to do, even though they had seen each other only an hour before. As he was hugging him Elliot whispered into his ear, "This dude is a real dick; you're right to hate him." It wasn't entirely true, but it made him feel better.

They were not a quiet bunch, especially given what they would be doing that evening. Oddly enough, no one seemed to be nervous. The ballroom of the hotel had been set up, and there was a room beside it for them to prepare for the interview. Hamish went over it again and again. Miles would read the press statement that Rhea and Hector had prepared. They would take a few questions, at least four of which were pre-staged. Hamish would call on the reporters. It was all scripted out so to avoid any unwanted surprises. They would exit the stage to the prep room and then wait. Security had been hired by Simon. They were men that Adam had hand-picked for the job, including Adam himself.

Soon, they were moving toward the prep room. There were couches and water bottles. A small TV had been set up that displayed the stage and the table with microphones where each one would sit. Rhea would sit between Miles and Elliot, with

Miles coming onto the stage last. Miles took it all in. Hamish was talking animatedly, and it was clear that Elliot had just said something that made him flinch a bit. They were all there. He'd had a choice in Berlin. It was a choice he didn't want to make, but given what had happened since then, it was the only choice he could have made. Having their names and story out in the public made them safer. It also made them a different type of target now, and he wasn't sure what the ramifications would be for them.

There was a slight commotion at the entrance to the waiting room. Miles looked up to see one of the guards with his hand out, pushing back another man, who also looked like he was working security. Hamish was moving towards the doors, as were Simon and Adam. The press conference wasn't set to start for another 30 minutes, and Miles was worried, over and over, that something would happen to prevent them from speaking to the press.

Hamish stood at the door talking. Miles heard him say to the guard at the door, "Let him in." Miles knew the man who walked through the door from pictures and the occasional image on TV. Saul Traeger was walking towards them with Hamish on one side and Simon on the other. He was shorter than Hamish and Simon, but he carried himself with the ease and grace of someone twice his size. He didn't stop looking at Miles as he entered. He stopped in front of the couch where Elliot sat with Marcia. They all stared at him, waiting for him to speak. He, on the other hand, seemed to be waiting for them to say something, but the room stayed quiet. It was Hamish who finally broke the ice.

"Well, what was so important?" he asked Saul.

"I'm Saul Traeger," he said to everyone, ignoring Hamish's question. "I'm representing the interest of Marcus Brent in this situation. I've come to make you an offer."

"We aren't interested, asshole," Elliot jumped in.

"I can understand if you feel that way right now, but you might not after I make my presentation."

"I can't think of anything you could offer us that would change our mind," Rhea's voice came in. Miles, standing next to her, could sense the determination in her voice. She resolved to stand her ground and seek justice for the Camps and Lillian.

"Let me start by saying this," Saul began, "what I'm about to say neither acknowledges nor denies the possibility that you're Marcus Brent's children. I'm too damn tired to care about that. I just assume you are because, hell, I've worked for him for almost 50 years. I actually pity you, because I wouldn't want to be his child. What I'm here to do is to ask you to stop before this gets out of control."

"It's already out of control," Miles found himself saying. "Your son kidnapped and killed Lillian. Your other henchmen took a shot at Elliot."

"*NO*, she didn't," he said. "Elliot's friend was always the intended target. He had seriously offended a local tribal leader. And as far as anyone knows, Lillian was a victim of a hunting accident, it's a real miracle that they even found her body."

"Bullshit," Elliot said to Saul.

"Maybe you're not understanding this, but everything you say, I have a way to spin it."

"Oh, we understand that," Hamish interjected. "But you can't keep spinning things indefinitely."

"Watch me," he said to Hamish. "You all underestimate the length and grasp of my employer. He doesn't take no as an answer ever." He emphasized *ever*.

"Well, that's too bad because it's a hard no, with a fuck you as an emphasis," Elliot shot back.

"Mr. Sharp," Saul turned to face where Elliot was standing. "How much debt is the company you work for in? Do you know?"

"Why," was all Elliot asked him.

"It's a pretty deep hole, and with that last well not finishing on time, it may be a bit deeper—puns intended."

"So, what does the debt of that company have to do with anything going on here?" Elliot snapped with his arms crossed.

"That backpay they owe you, or, well, let's see, those medical bills from your friend's unfortunate accident, well, currently they can't pay for those things. I can make it go away."

"Like hell you can," Simon said, jumping into the conversation.

Saul just shrugged. "I'm simply here to ask you all to stop, and you'll be compensated for your acquiescence."

They all looked at each other, except for Rhea, whose eyes were fixed on Saul Traeger. Miles was surprised by the fierceness he saw in her glare. She didn't move her lips to say a word, but her face said it all.

"Again, I only lay before you an opportunity to avoid all of the circuses you've made for yourself. You step onto that stage, you step into a realm that none of you has any business being in. You think that you're about to throw a wrench into Marcus Brent's political career when, in reality, there is nothing you can do to stop him. He already has everything and everyone he needs to survive and thrive in this storm."

"If he's so set," Rhea's calm yet determined voice rang out, "then why are you here? Why not let us take the drubbing you're so confident that we'll receive? The only explanation that I can think of is that you're scared."

"Scared of what exactly, Ms. Baker," he tossed a question at her.

"That we can connect Elizabeth Deavers to you."

"And we can say that she was and continues to work of her own free will," he waved his hand. "I've no problem sacrificing her to the wolves. It's obvious to me that since the three of you are sitting here, she didn't do her job well. Even I can admit the horror of how she's dealt with many circumstances."

Miles shook his head. It was their word against a giant spin machine. They were literally at an enormous disadvantage. The only result the article had was to put the spin machine into motion, crafting stories to counteract their own. It was hopeless.

"I have an offer for each of you," a man from Saul's security detail said, bringing three folders to him. "Mr. Trent," Saul held out the folder, but Miles refused to move to take it from him. He placed it on the coffee table. "Ms. Baker," he turned to her and extended the folder to her, but she refused to stand up and just glowered at him. He then turned to Elliot, whose fists were in a ball, and his face raged with anger. "Mr. Sharp, or should I say Vaughn," and Miles braced himself for what was about to come.

"It's Sharp," Elliot seethed, "and the only reason I would take that folder from you is to take it and stick it up your ass and pull it out of your throat you motherfu…" Marcia stood up next to him and grabbed him before he could finish.

"Auntie apparently controls the leash," Saul smirked.

Marcia spun on him. "Your button pushing isn't getting you anywhere. It's only making their resolve greater. Leave!"

Saul raised his eyebrows at this outburst. "I'm going. You have a press conference to attend, but let me leave you with this: inside each of those folders is something that you want. If you would like to walk away from this circus and keep from having the weight of the media and Brent Industries bearing down on you until you're smashed into oblivion, all you have to do is not attend the press conference. I'll be in touch with you, and this will all go away, and that," he motioned to the folders on the table, "well, that will change your lives."

With that Saul Traeger turned on his heels and marched out of the waiting room. Hamish followed behind him and watched him leave and then closed the door that he came in from.

"He's all talk," Simon said to them. "This shows that they're scared. This is exactly how they do what they do, over and over again. They scare you with bullshit theories and then offer you your wildest dreams to walk away from the right you're about to do!"

"Dad," Miles said, "I see that. I've understood that."

"And," Hamish asked as he walked back to the group. "What do you want to do about it?"

"I'm going to fight," Elliot's rage was apparent in the tremor of his voice. "I'm not even looking in that fucking folder."

"Miles," Rhea came closer. "What are you thinking?"

"He's going to fight it, too. Aren't you?" Elliot said.

Miles didn't know, but what he did know was this: "Rhea, I can't be responsible for your decision. You need to make that on your own, and so do you, Elliot. I knew that from the start! This was my biggest fear. I knew that by going up against them, even with the truth, we would be made to look like liars. I sat on my balcony in Berlin and asked myself over and over if it was worth it. I look at you, and I think, yes, for me it was worth it. But now I wonder, is it worth putting you all through this? Then I think of Lillian, Dustin, and Angela, and I know it's worth it. My biggest fear is that what we do won't matter. It doesn't mean we don't do it."

"I agree," Rhea said. "I'm not going to back out now. I've invested too much in this. We have a voice, and we have a story. They can't change that."

"If we're wrong, then we'll all be wrong together," Miles said with a fire in his voice. "If we go forward, we do it together. There's no turning our backs on each other once we walk out on that stage."

Miles noticed that Hamish was getting antsy. "What do you think, Hamish?" Miles asked him.

"I think he's underestimated what we have," he said. "I also think the timing is suspect. He comes to you all seconds before you have to go out there, tries to scare the shit out of you, and never once addresses the biggest piece of this puzzle."

"What's that?" Simon stepped forward.

"That Marcus Brent is your father," he said. "He practically agreed with you! The fact that he has answers to all of your claims tells me they aren't taking this as seriously as maybe the public will take it."

"He doesn't understand that we're building our case based on that truth; a truth that they seem to have accepted. I don't think they realize the impact it will make on the average person who sees this story," Simon said.

"Brent Industries is only concerned about its media presence.

They don't care an ounce about how the average American will look at this because they don't think the average American votes. In their minds, only the people who follow the media religiously vote, and they will only listen to the side of the story that they want to," Hamish added. "They may have seriously miscalculated what we're about to do."

Miles realized that there was some truth to what they were saying, but he also knew that Hamish and Simon were both spinning the situation to give them the courage they needed. Rhea stood up and walked over to the mirror that was in the room. She straightened her blouse and flattened out her skirt.

"Let's do this," Hamish said to them all as he looked at Rhea.

"Marcia," Simon offered his arm to her, "shall we?"

Marcia accepted his arm, and they left the room to head to the back of the ballroom, where they would watch the press conference.

Hamish stuck his head through the door that led to the stage where the table was. He gave someone they couldn't see a thumbs up and turned to them.

"I'll go out, make a statement, and then I'll call you all out."

Rhea and Elliot moved towards Miles. Hamish disappeared through the door, and they heard the drone of the crowd quiet down. They could hear him speaking, a speech that Rhea knew by heart. Elliot stood close to Miles and put his arm around him.

"If we're wrong, we're wrong together," he smirked, "fucking legend."

"Thanks," he said, and he heard Hamish introduce them. Elliot led the way, and Miles followed after Rhea. The crowd in the ballroom was standing room only. He could see his father in the back, standing with Marcia. They looked nervous but not concerned. He scanned the room and recognized a few faces from television newscasts. All the major players seemed to be here: CNN, Fox, MSNBC, AP, BBC, and Al Jazeera. Local as well as national. He wondered if someone out there was covering this for the Frankfurter Allgemeine or Süddeutsche Zeitung.

He got behind his chair, where his name tag was, pulled out the seat for Rhea, and then took his seat. At that moment, Miles was hit with the fact that there should have been five kids at the table, but there were only three of them left.

ଔଔଔଔ

The next few days were a whirlwind. Rhea, Miles, and Elliot were whisked from one interview to the next. It was happening so quickly that he hadn't had time to read what people were saying.

The interviews they'd given since then had almost always focused on what they wanted, not how they had gotten here. No one asked about a candidate who claimed to be pro-life but paid and forced women to abort his children. When the Camps came up, it was as if the press wasn't that interested. The word 'alleged' was used all the time, so much so that Miles suggested they shouldn't bring it up again. Hamish was pretty sure that was what they wanted.

The few interviews, in which they tried to push their ideas, dissolved into quick endings and lukewarm well wishes. The interviewers thanked them on the screen and then, as soon as they cut, dismissed them as if they weren't that important. All the while, and it was often pointed out before any interview commenced, Marcus Brent hadn't made any statement about these children of his showing up on the scene.

They were heading to Philadelphia in the morning. Hamish had stopped the press tour for a few days, waiting to see how things played out. There were a few articles that were to be printed, and Hector was still busy getting ready for his end of the story. Elliot sat down and called Scooper.

"You look good in those interviews," he said as he answered the phone.

"Fuck off," Elliot grinned. "How're you doing?"

"I'm almost done with my PT," he said.

"You feel any stronger," Elliot inquired.

"Strong enough," he said and paused like he was about to say something else, but didn't have the nerve to do so. Most conversations with Scooper since they'd left Burkina Faso had gone like this.

"Well, right now we aren't sure of what's next. I'm hoping to go back to Oklahoma soon. I think we're all waiting to see if there's any official statement from Marcus Brent himself before we make our next move."

"What about that crazy woman who shot me?" Scooper asked. "How does she factor into this?"

"We don't know for sure where she is, but we think that she's in Mexico, or at least Miles says she's in Mexico. I think he set some sort of trap for her."

"Was that wise of him?" Scooper seemed curious.

"Nope," Elliot said, "as a matter of fact, it's one of the only stupid things I've seen him do."

"That surprises me," Scooper responded.

"It only partly surprises me," Elliot continued, but then there was a long pause. "I'm probably not going to go back to Africa," he said, more because he knew that Scooper was looking for a way out, than it actually being true.

"I'm not sure I would be allowed to go back for a long time," he said to Elliot. "What are you going to do?"

"I'm going to move out to Portland with Rhea," he said. "She knows an NGO that's situated there. I might be a good fit for them."

"That's awesome," Scooper said. But even over the phone, Elliot felt an underlying sadness.

"I'm excited," he said.

"Me too," Scooper answered. "I started looking for some positions the other day, but I haven't figured anything out. My Aunt knows someone who she thinks can land me an interview for a job in a marketing department in OKC."

"Use that degree you paid so much for," Elliot's voice was filled with sadness, too.

"Exactly," Scooper said. "I don't want to cut this short, but I need to head to my…" he trailed off. "Elliot, stay safe. Pay attention."

"I will," he said as he smiled. "We should be okay now that people know who we are. They won't be able to kill us, at least, maybe just fuck up our lives."

"That's reassuring," Scooper sighed. "Talk to you soon."

"Yeah, talk to you soon."

He had no sooner put the phone down than Miles came into the hotel room. He looked excited and nervous. "Brent's holding a press conference tomorrow, and it seems he plans to address questions about us."

"Whoa," Elliot said. "Didn't see that coming after this long."

Miles nodded. "Baseball games are on, want to watch one?"

"No," Elliot said. "Let's go out for a drink, I'm tired of being cooped up in buildings. Where are we anyway?"

"Pittsburgh," Miles laughed. "Where do you think we can go where we won't be recognized by someone?"

"Doesn't Hamish know somewhere he can sneak us in, like by the back door?"

"Why don't you ask him?"

"God, I can't stand that asshole," Elliot said as he cued up

Hamish's number.

"Hello, Elliot," Hamish sounded bored already.

"Miles and I want to go and grab a drink. Any place you can get us into where we won't be the center of attention now that we're famous?"

"Miles wants to go out for a drink?" Hamish asked.

"Yep," Elliot answered him. "So where can we go?"

"I know a place," Hamish said. "Give me ten minutes and meet me downstairs."

"You don't have to go with us," Elliot said. "I wouldn't want to disrupt whatever plans you had."

"Elliot, you are going anywhere without me," he shot back.

Elliot's eyebrows arched. "Then we'll see you in ten minutes."

Elliot led the way through the lobby to where Hamish was standing. He was dressed casually, which took Elliot back for a second. He wore shorts and a polo shirt.

"Gentleman," he called out to them.

"Hamish," Miles smiled, "I hope this isn't too much of an inconvenience."

"It beats sitting in a hotel room," he nodded towards the entrance of the hotel, and they all moved towards the taxi that was waiting for them.

Elliot had lost track of where they were as the cab turned into an alley and stopped at a door. They hopped out, and Hamish knocked at a large access door painted with the Irish flag's colors.

"Hamish," a small, slender woman said as she opened the door. "You're looking good on the TV."

"Thank you, Gretchen! You're looking as young and spry as ever," he winked at her as Elliot rolled his eyes and whispered to Miles, "I can sweet-talk women like that, too."

"Well, Elliot," Hamish had heard him, "if I remember correctly, we're here because you called me to take your ass out to a place for a drink."

"Yep, you're right," Miles chuckled. "And Elliot," Miles fixed his gaze on him, "is very grateful and is going to start showing it."

Hamish shook his head as Gretchen let them through the door and led them through a kitchen to a small room at the back of the bar. A curtain divided the room, with two tables and a couch. The walls were decorated with large posters of Ireland.

"It's an Irish Pub?" Miles asked as he looked around.

"Yep," Hamish said, "on the other side of that curtain it is. Back here, it's a private place for the three of us to drink and then go back to the hotel."

Gretchen reappeared with a notepad. "What can I get you, boys?" she asked.

"Scotch and soda," Hamish answered. "Light on the soda."

"And for you, handsome," she asked Miles.

"Double Whiskey on the rocks," he said.

"Crown Royal gonna be okay," she asked him.

"That's Irish," he tossed a question instead.

"It's what we got," she said with a smile. "Got a bunch of assholes out there who have drank all our Jameson and Jack Daniels."

"Then that's gonna be fine," he said with a smile.

"And how about you, smart ass," she said to Elliot. Elliot was impressed. Miles and Hamish just chuckled.

"Same as my brother," he said while patting Miles on the back.

"I'll be right back with your drinks," she said and snuck out of the room through the curtain.

"What's this place called?" Miles asked Hamish.

"McKinley's, her uncle owned the place, now she and her son do," he said. "I love this place, but they've been struggling to make ends meet."

"And she still waits on the patrons?" Elliot asked.

"No, just special ones who she doesn't want to be mistreated."

"Oh, so just you," Elliot shot back at Hamish. "How often are you in Pittsburgh?"

Hamish shook his head, "Elliot, cut the shit. Do you have to act like a petulant teen all the time? I'm getting tired of you pushing my buttons just to get a reaction out of me. I'm on your side."

"I didn't mean to push your buttons," Elliot seemed apologetic, "I was just trying to find the mute button."

"Shut up," Hamish chuckled, "you stole that from a meme."

Elliot laughed out loud and looked at Miles, who had a smirk on his face. Elliot tilted back in his chair, looking back. "Miles was telling me about your time together in Berlin. It sounded downright fascinating."

"Listen," Hamish said to Elliot, "is this why you're on me constantly?"

"I'm on you constantly," Elliot asked him, knowing it would piss him off more.

"Miles," Hamish said, "I'm sorry that I drew you into that whole mess in Berlin. I often don't think about the ramifications of things like that. I sure as hell never thought that I'd be working with you so closely again, or I would have done more to preserve your dignity and mine as well."

Miles's face was a confusing mess of shock and relief, and Elliot almost regretted pushing it that far. He wanted some justice for his brother, but he hadn't thought about what that would dredge up.

"Thank you," Miles said to him after maintaining a few moments of silence. Gretchen arrived with their drinks and placed them in front of each of them. Miles picked up his glass, "To Hamish, who is paying."

Gretchen laughed as she handed Hamish his drink, "Owes you, does he?"

"Penance is a motherfucker," Hamish said.

Gretchen laughed and scurried away. Hamish turned towards Miles again. "I didn't know she …," he paused, "I didn't know that she liked me, and I sure as hell had no idea she was setting up what she did that night."

"You didn't arrange that?" Miles asked as he raised his eyebrow and crossed his arms.

"I think she got her signals crossed," he said, taking a slug of his scotch.

"Wait, what?" Elliot asked. They both ignored him, which made him even more curious.

"Did you get the information that you needed from her?"

"I got the lead that I needed. Yes!"

"So, you two…" Elliot tried one more time.

"Wouldn't you like to know," Miles said and waited for a beat. "And also, no, it's not what you're thinking."

"Um," Hamish said, "It could be what he's thinking."

Elliot suddenly felt left out, but laughed it off. Gretchen came through the curtain, which Elliot noticed had stayed open. He could see that the bar was packed. It didn't look like the type of crowd Hamish would generally hang out with. It reminded him of a bar back home in Oklahoma or the bar where his mother had worked in Nebraska.

Gretchen was bantering with Hamish and Miles when Elliot heard the commotion.

"Yo, Jay, look who's in the back!"

A gruff-looking man with a trucker hat on was climbing down from his barstool. He was wearing a cut-off T-shirt and jeans. He held a bottle of Miller Lite in his right hand. Jay, who looked just like him, turned his head and locked eyes with Elliot. It was obvious from the Brent for President hat where this would go.

"You motherfuckers," Jay yelled as he rushed back to the curtain. Gretchen moved to stop him, but he just blew right by her with his loud friend right behind him, as well as about six other people, men and women. "Who gave you the goddam right to say such shit about God's chosen president for our country! You fucking heathens…" Hamish was up in a flash, standing between the guy and Elliot.

"If Marcus Brent loses this race, some raging liberal is going to win and force us all to be commies!" a worn-out woman with a greasy ponytail shouted over the guy in front of her. "You all need to shut your fucking mouths and stop your fucking lying before you ruin him!"

"God is going to get rid of filth like you," the redneck, whose name wasn't Jay spit at Elliot. "If I had my gun, I'd fucking do it now!"

Elliot knew he looked like a deer in headlights, but Miles was calm and steady. He spoke up over the loud clamor of swearing and hatred, "We're just telling our story. You do know he is lying to you all, right?"

The uproar from that statement reverberated in his chest. If it wasn't for the bouncers coming from out of nowhere, Elliot was sure that Miles would have been hit with that Miller Lite bottle. The men pushed the guys behind the curtain. Hamish looked at the two of them with shock on his face. Miles picked up his drink and downed it. "We should probably pay and go," he said.

Gretchen hurried them out the back and into a cab as quickly as possible. As they exited the other end of the alley from where they'd entered, Elliot peered out the rear window and saw a knot of men milling about at the mouth of the alley. It appeared that they were plotting something.

"I never guessed that we would be trading a trained assassin stalking us for a bunch of good ole' boys."

"Brent's fan base is loyal," Hamish said. "And they don't have a problem vocalizing how upset they are. You'll both have to be careful. We might need to get you some security."

"That won't be necessary," Miles said.

The next day, though, Miles understood why it was necessary. Some of Brent's supporters had found his apartment and camped at the entrance. They had thrown eggs at his windows, which got them arrested for vandalism, but it didn't stop them from showing up again and again.

"I said it before; I'll say it again," Elliot was anxious. "From being hunted by an assassin to being hunted by Marcus Brent supporters. Who would have ever guessed the latter was the scarier of the two."

Miles checked his phone, and Elliot knew why. He was waiting to hear from Mikey. The plan was going to be set in motion soon. Hopefully, by tomorrow, the only threat they would face was the one that kept throwing eggs at their windows, unless something went wrong.

Chapter Thirty-Two

To Elizabeth, Mexico would always be oppressive heat and cabs with no working AC. This trip didn't fail to meet that standard. The driver pulled up to the resort entrance and got out to retrieve her small suitcase. She handed him the fare along with a small tip. He grabbed the money, grunted something, and then drove away.

"See, you still have that special touch," a voice from behind said. She turned to see Mikey standing there. He was dressed in a polo shirt, khaki pants, and flip-flops. She was pretty sure she had never seen him dressed so casually, and she was damn sure he had never looked as handsome as he did at that moment.

"I need a drink," she told him while handing him her bag.

"You're talking to a man who can make that happen," he said as he took her bag. They walked into the reception, and she checked in. Mikey was talking with the bellboy, who was taking the luggage up to her room. When he reached for the briefcase, Mikey told him that she needed to keep that one with her for their meeting. She smiled; she had trained him well.

He led her into the bar area; it looked like everyone there knew him.

"Popular man," she said to him, somewhat irritated.

"Well, I'm the manager at the bar," he said. "It's my retirement dream come true."

"I bet it is," she said as they took a table closest to the beach at the end of the covered bar. A young, dark woman came to the table. She was wearing a light blue polo shirt, and her name tag identified her as Tamar.

"Hello, Mikey," she greeted him. "How are you today?" Her English was accented but not in Spanish; it sounded almost Caribbean.

"I'm well, Tamar," he replied.

"What can I get for you today?" she asked.

"My usual," he said, and she nodded.

"For you, ma'am," she asked Elizabeth.

Elizabeth turned to the young lady, who waited patiently. "I'll have a double bourbon, neat."

"I'll be right back with those," she said, and she sauntered off to the bar.

"Bar manager, huh?" She directed her focus on Mikey.

"It's the second bar I've managed," he said.

"Where else have you been?" Elizabeth asked, but she already knew. Soon after she had contacted him about Hannah's son, she dug up what she could. She realized that Mikey's information was checking out, and Miles's passport had cleared customs in Cancun a day before he called her. As of yet, it hadn't pinged in any airport since, so he must still be there. If she could take him, Esme, and the child out, she would be one step closer to closing the loops and keeping her deadly secret buried. It was that fear that drove her.

As Mikey finished talking about Miami, where he had been before, she asked him, "What made you move here?"

"Have you looked around?" he said while circling a finger in the air. "It's beautiful. The cost of living alone, compared to Miami, is worth it. This resort is amazing to work for. Should I keep on listing?"

"Why not open your own bar instead of managing one?" she said.

"If you think hard, you can answer that for yourself," he responded. She nodded as Tamar came back with their drinks.

"Have you ever run into someone from the past?" she asked him as she picked up her bourbon.

"All the time," he said, "but most of the time, they don't recognize me. Context matters, and no one ever thinks that some old bar manager could have been a goon for someone like Brent."

"Sometimes they do," she said in a neutral tone.

"Once, maybe twice," he said, "but never like in Nebraska."

"Oh," she sighed, "Nebraska. That's reared its head again."

"Really, why?"

"Hannah Vaughn didn't abort that child. Instead, she gave it to her sister."

"No way," he appeared shocked. "You mean that teenager at the funeral, he was…"

"Yes, he was her son with Marcus."

"That's why you called me a while back," he sipped his tequila thoughtfully. "Does the kid know that?"

"He does," she answered. "I missed the chance to take him out a few months ago."

"What, he's just a kid," Mikey protested.

"Like hell he is," she said as she took a sip. "He's close to 25 now. He was hiding out in some godforsaken African country. He's crafty as fuck, too."

"Well," Mikey said with a noticeable hint of shock on his face, "I'm sure there is more to that story, but here you are now. If you don't mind me asking, how did you end up in this mess?"

"Wouldn't you like to know!" She could sense that her response was a bit too harsh for what seemed like a sincere question. The problem was that she wasn't able to explain how she got here without admitting she had fucked things up and now had to take immediate measures to cover her ass and Marcus Brent's as well.

"It's literally why I'm asking," he responded with a straight face.

"It's a long story," she groaned and tried to redirect his attention. "Dr. Abbott lied and hid some important information from me. Namely, that he didn't perform abortions on six women.

On top of that, he helped them hide it from us."

"Thus, Ms. Connors is here with her little one."

"Exactly," she said to him. "I've a question for you," he was one of the few people she could ask this. "Does the timing of her pregnancy seem off to you?"

"What do you mean?" he asked, leaning closer. He hadn't paid much attention to the details, but she thought she'd ask anyway.

"Hadn't Marcus been to have the snip, snip?" she made a cutting gesture with her index and middle finger which didn't seem to faze Mikey one bit.

"No," he said, "He got it a few days later."

"Wow, nothing like sneaking a last one in to keep a broad busy."

"My guess is he didn't even think about it," he said. "I sometimes wonder if he ever knew he got any of these women pregnant."

"He knew about a few of them. Others, we just didn't tell him. Esme would have been one we didn't tell him about," she said while swirling her drink.

"Well, I'm guessing he won't miss her then."

"He probably doesn't even remember her."

"I would imagine there's a good chance of that," Mikey answered her and finished his drink. "So, there are how many of these kids that Abbott let live?"

"God, it sounds horrible when you put it that way."

"How should I put it, our jobs never really gave us a way to put things delicately," he said to her. "Why do you think I prefer tending bar?"

"There are five of them," she said. "There was a sixth one, but the mother, Angela Camp, do you remember her?" Mikey shook his head no. "Well, she sent an email to Abbott, and we intercepted it. I took care of it, but at the memorial service, I ran into Miles, whom you have met, I assume, and the oldest one, Rhea."

A perky middle-aged blonde woman was making her way toward their table. She had on a nice blouse and a pair of dark slacks and high heels. It was apparent that she worked for the hotel. She smiled as she got near the table. Elizabeth was pretty sure she was attracted to Mikey.

"Hi, sorry to bug you," she interrupted. "But Mike, you have a party on the line with reservations tonight, and they wanted to talk to you about changing the cocktail selection."

"Can you take a message?" Mikey asked her politely.

"This is the fourth time they've called," she said.

"Listen," Elizabeth jumped in, "I'll go get settled in my room. You deal with this, and we can meet back down here in fifteen minutes."

The blonde lady smiled at her and nodded.

"That sounds like a good idea. I'm sorry, I need to deal with this," he said. "Lucy, can you make sure that Ms. Deavers here is shown back to this table when she returns?"

"Sure thing," she said cheerfully, making Elizabeth want to slap her. She could never stand the effervescence of the young and particularly hated it when they were young, blond, and beautiful.

"Ms. Deavers, here was my boss many years ago," he told her.

"Oh, at the bar in Miami," she asked her.

"Do I look like I would work in a fucking bar," she spat as she walked by her.

She overheard Mikey say to her, "She was in HR."

"Oh, that makes sense," Lucy said to him. As Elizabeth neared the bar, she could no longer hear what they were saying. Out of the corner of her eye, she caught Mikey walking towards a door at the opposite end of the bar from where she was.

Her room was comfortable. She unpacked the clothing that she needed and prepared the gun and the silencer for later that evening. When she felt ready, she headed down to the bar to catch up with Mikey. Lucy was there to greet her and lead her to their table. The bar had emptied a bit, and Mikey joined her shortly, carrying an envelope with him in one hand and a drink in the other.

"Where were we?" he asked her as he slid into his seat.

"You were telling that perky little bitch I worked in HR."

"Well, you sort of do," he said as he slid the envelope across the table to her. "I'm pretty sure you've done a lot of firing over the years."

"Not you," she hissed as she opened the envelope. "You seemed to have been able to exit the game quite easily."

"I wouldn't put it that way, but I'm lucky to be able to be out of the business, especially given my last employer's penchant for tying up loose ends."

"Well, be glad it isn't his dad running the business."

"Trust me, I am."

"Well, this," Elizabeth pointed to the envelope, "helps me to see whose side you're truly on."

"It's the location, an assessment on how best to enter and leave. You'll find it run of the mill. People turn a blind eye here all the time," he said to her, but she sensed a bit of trouble in his voice.

"Something seems a little off with you just now," she said.

"I've seen the kid," he said. "I know what needs to be done, but if you could just leave the kid alone, please. The government will whisk her off to an orphanage, they won't look into her past. She'll grow up thinking her mother was killed because she was involved in some sort of drug or gang violence, nothing more."

"You've gotten soft, Mikey," she said to him. "Weren't you the one who dropped that teenage boy out of the window in '92?"

"I dropped him onto an awning. And if that had happened today, that would have been in the news."

"Or he would have filmed it with his phone."

"It's not just that," he said.

"Then what is it," she crossed her arms and leaned back.

"You don't know?" his expression was serious as he asked.

"Know what?" she was startled by his question.

"Yesterday, a small gossip website, something or something Truth, posted an article naming names. Saying that Marcus Brent had paid for abortions, that a doctor helped women fake the abortions, and that one of those mothers and her son had died recently of suspicious circumstances. You're running out of time."

It was as though the earth had turned upside down and threatened to throw her off. She couldn't figure out if he was messing with her, but his face showed nothing but concern for her.

"What names?" she asked as she adjusted herself on her seat.

"Elliot Sharp, Rhea Baker, and Miles Trent. It names their mothers and when they could have possibly met Marcus, and it claims that a blood test confirms that they all have the same father."

"Oh, shit," she whispered. It hit her, "Why wasn't Esme Conner's name in that article?"

"Beats me," Mikey shrugged. "Maybe she didn't want to be a part of it."

"She is a part of it," Elizabeth replied. "She doesn't get to choose. Taking her out will send a clear message to the rest of them. Has any other news source picked up on this yet?"

"It gets worse," he replied.

"How could it?" she shook her head.

"They held a press conference today and have given a few dozen interviews," he said. "How haven't you heard of this?"

"I don't watch the news unless I need to," she said to him. "I don't even have a news app on my phone. Why didn't someone from Saul's office…" She trailed off for a second. Mikey looked at her, waiting for her to finish her thought. "Hell, why didn't Saul himself call me," she felt panic rise up in her chest.

"Maybe they don't think it's that big of a deal. Maybe you're running around trying to fix something that doesn't need to be fixed."

"Others have made claims in the past, and nothing has come of it, maybe this will go away too," she said as a way of reassuring herself. This did change things. With their names out there, it would be very difficult to deal with them in the way that she had planned. "Send me the article so I can read it," she demanded.

Mikey pulled out his phone, pressed a few buttons, and she felt the vibration on her phone. "I'm going to my room to read this. I'll talk with you later this evening after I've taken care of things."

"I'll see you then," he said. "You're going to want to watch the interviews as well."

She nodded back and forth. "This just needs to end, and it needs to end on my terms."

"Please reconsider about the kid," Mikey pleaded with her again.

"I'll think about it," she lied, and she got up and headed to her room. She knew that there was no way that she was going to let anyone in that house escape. It was an easy job, a mother and a toddler. In and out, and then she hoped it would all be over, no one would know anything else.

That hope faded as she read the article and watched the interview. The more she read, the more worried she was. The chances of Marcus and Saul not seeing this dwindled with every hour. She turned off her phone, closed the curtains, and lay there in the dark. If Saul hadn't contacted her, then he wasn't going to. She was a liability now, and the only way forward was to deal with this mess here and then disappear.

She shut her eyes for a second and then began reviewing the drawings and pictures in the envelope. No more loose ends. No more mistakes. Once she dealt with Esme, she would also have to take care of Mikey. Then she would disappear for good. The plan was straightforward. No more loose ends were allowed.

⋘⋙⋘⋙

Elizabeth carefully slid out of her hotel room, doing her best not to look too suspicious or draw unwanted attention. Mikey had already hidden a black shirt and pants in the resort's pool house, her first stop. From there, she planned to make her way along the beach until she came across the path that led towards the surf shop. Esme's house, secluded and remote, stood about 300 meters from its nearest neighbors, providing the right privacy Elizabeth needed.

It was a gorgeous night as she walked along the beach. She could understand why Mikey had retired here, though managing a bar hardly felt like retirement. As she approached the last cabin before Esme's, Elizabeth felt the sense she was about to make things right. She would take care of Esme, and from there go into hiding, leaving the clean-up duties to Barton, who had been uncharacteristically quiet since she'd left LA.

She saw a soft glow of light coming out of the bungalow, and she was pretty sure she saw someone moving about inside. Elizabeth walked up to the bungalow. She kept the gun as hidden as possible. She could see the light was on in the front of the room. Her nerves were calm. Slung over one shoulder was a knapsack in which she had everything she needed to make this look like a drug deal gone wrong. She didn't care how cliché that seemed. If she had to get out of there quickly, she would spare the life of the kid, but that all depended on where the kid was. It was an easy choice if she was in a separate room. If she was honest with herself, this seemed too easy.

She carefully climbed the stairs onto the porch and slowly turned the knob to the door. She smirked at the fact that it was unlocked. She pushed it open and glanced quickly inside.

"Hello, Elizabeth," the voice came from behind her. She spun around, bringing up the gun as swiftly as she could. She saw his face and felt the impact of the bullet at the same time. She flew backward, bouncing off the door frame and landing inside the bungalow. The contents of the bag scattered around as the pain seared through her whole body. At first, she couldn't breathe, but sluggishly, she crawled to a sitting position as Barton made his way across the room.

"Nice touch," he said as he looked at the cocaine blocks on the floor. "I'm sure they cost Brent Industries a pretty penny."

"What the hell, Barton?" she managed to stammer.

"It's your retirement party," he declared. "Dad and I felt it best to deal with you now instead of later. You've been lying to me, Elizabeth. Lying!"

"What do you mean?" She could see the hole just above her breast. The pain coursing through her body was making it hard for her to understand Barton.

"I found Abbott, and he was full of information. He played you, too," Barton crouched down near her, "said he was banking on you never checking up on those women. He said that you were so sloppy. He saw it, and more than anything, you made it easy for him. Before I took him out, he had a message for you, it was something like he hoped you burned in hell with Marcus."

Elizabeth gasped for air as he spoke; her gun had flown from her hand, but she had a spare if she could reach it without him noticing. The pain was so intense every time she moved.

"I can't believe," Barton was standing again, "that you, knowing the gravity of what they had on you, didn't pay closer attention."

"You don't understand," she said weakly. "Harlan," but she couldn't get the rest of it out.

"Harlan's dead, Elizabeth. You should have known that a ghost can't continue to run things."

"I was just trying to clean up the mess," she gasped again. Her eyes were blurring. She thought that she could reach for her gun if she just pushed past the pain.

"We'll crush the kids," he said. "We didn't need to kill them. We'll just drag them through the mud, and, well, you'll become a side note and a scapegoat. Every bad thing you've done, or I've done for that matter, will be pinned on you, the vigilante of Brent Industries."

She felt the tears in her eyes. It hurt so badly, and she knew she was losing consciousness. She heard something then—light footsteps; they were there under Barton's mocking voice. She was sure she heard something. It was hard to see anything, but suddenly, she heard Barton's voice trail off. His attention was elsewhere, and with the last bit of energy she had left in her, she pulled out her gun. The last sound she ever heard was a body hitting the floor.

Chapter Thirty-Three

Simon and Hector stood with Rhea as Marcus Brent and Saul Traeger moved toward the podium. As always, Brent was surrounded by at least twenty people on stage, standing behind him, cheering his every move like a rehearsed chorus. She'd checked in with Miles and Elliot, who were safely hanging out in Philadelphia at Simon's place. The presence of Brent's faithful made it seem that Miles would most likely have to move by the beginning of the fall semester.

The general consensus was that Brent would acknowledge that Miles, Rhea, and Elliot were possibly his children. He would acquiesce to a blood test if needed, but he would definitely try to spin the situation to win back some of the Christian right. That constituency had been taken aback by the stories of mothers coerced into abortions. In the last week since they went public, his ratings had taken an unexpected dive as more and more people weighed in on the story. It really was no surprise that he was finally addressing the controversy with a press conference.

Miles and Elliot had stopped reading the press about themselves after the confrontation in the bar, but Rhea had almost developed a religious fervor for reading every news item related to them. They were presented as heroic in the liberal and progressive press, but the vile comments from the more radical right were the loudest and the most disturbing. Never in her life had she been vilified for anything. Even as a professor, the students who didn't gel with her never painted her in such vile terms.

A religious leader, speaking on the parentage of herself and her siblings, called her a feminist whore, who was only interested in destroying a man of valor and morals with her made-up lies. The attack on her mother, who was the only mother that the press was able to dig information on, was horrific. Her dead mother, a writer of young people's fiction, was in the news again. One southern woman appeared on the news and talked about how her mother's books were pushing feminist socialist views and that they should be banned and burned.

"That's exactly what I took away from your mother's books as a kid," Elliot joked when they had heard that on the news report a few days ago. "It's why I swear so much."

"Stop it, Elliot. These people are trying to destroy my mother's legacy."

"Sorry," he said. "God, I wish I still smoked."

"Me too," she said absentmindedly, without realizing what she had just said. When she felt Elliot's eyes on her, she quickly apologized and asked him what he had said.

Elliot decided to not answer her and changed the subject,

"This is why I stopped reading their shit!"

"Rhea," Miles said gently to her. "If you're going to read the news, you have to take it less personally. Brent's people are hoping this will all blow over, and the truth is no one will talk about us by the next news cycle."

"I hope you're right about that," Rhea said.

Rhea's attention was brought back to the present reality. After their bar escapade in Pittsburgh ended up on TikTok and other social media outlets, Hamish had pulled the plug on them attending this press conference. Rhea would go, but she'd have Adam with her, and they would stay out of sight.

Marcus stood off to the side as his press agent opened the press conference. Saul stood just behind him, and as the press agent, Justin Thiel, made his introductory remarks and laid out some directions, Hector moved to the front row. His place with the Post would allow him to ask questions first.

Her phone buzzed, and she looked at it. It was Miles.

"Mikey is safe in the States. Sent us this article from yesterday."

A link to a news article was attached. She saw that Hector was also on his phone, but his eyes were not betraying what he read.

She looked back down at the article, and as she read through it, her body tensed in horror. The police in Mexico reported a drug transaction gone wrong and that two Americans had been murdered.

"WTF? They're dead?"

The three dots appeared and then disappeared.

"Did you know?"

She wrote back without waiting for his response.

"I'm not surprised."

She felt a punch in the gut. Was Miles really aware that they would be killed? She didn't have time to think through that.

"Brent is here to stay!" Marcus Brent said aloud into the microphone.

"It takes more than kids I didn't know about to stop me! You have proven over and over again that you'll stand by my side as I push to change the tide of this country." Marcus paused, and the audience erupted in cheers. "We've dealt with too many liberal ideals that have caused us nothing but pain and problems. They've lied; they've destroyed our morals!" This part made Rhea choke.

"Keep throwing it at me. Nothing will stick!" The people screamed and yelled. The group on the stage pumped their fists and waved their flags, making a giant ruckus.

"Now, I'm going to need to be upfront with you." The uproar died down as he prepared to move to address the talk of the town. "I had a wayward youth and often strayed in my 40s. They're probably my children, but I promise you this…" he paused for dramatic effect. "I had no idea that those women were pregnant, and in no way, shape, or form would I've ever forced them to give up the lives inside of them! That's a fabrication meant to push those of you who find life in the womb sacred far away from me!" The microphone caught the sound of his inhale.

People cheered again, and the press captured photos and videos while waiting for their chance to ask him questions. Rhea was ready to spit. Her anger burned like wildfire. Marcus droned on, pointing out how he was such a paragon of good old-fashioned American values, and if you stood against them, you were only looking to pull this country into socialism and poverty.

Adam suddenly appeared by her side. "We should probably leave, Rhea."

Rhea nodded and turned to leave, but stopped as Marcus Brent launched into a tirade.

"I've no idea who these supposed children of mine are talking about. I've never employed a woman named Elizabeth Deavers!"

She saw Saul's face turn white. That was a stupid lie that even his staunch supporters couldn't spin. There were actual pictures of her with him, and people like Mikey, who could prove it! Marcus must have gone off script as Thiel was at his arm whispering in his ear within seconds.

The press agent stepped in. "It seems it's time for questions."

Justin Thiel stomped off to the podium and pointed at a reporter about six people to the left of Hector. Her questions revolved around Marcus's willingness to take a DNA test to prove parentage.

"I'll do it," he answered dramatically. "But I'll also be willing to admit that I did have relationships with Ms. Baker, Mrs. Trent, and Hannah Vaughn. I'm not proud of how I behaved, but I also had no idea that they were pregnant afterward."

The next question was about what he was willing to do if he found out they were his biological children.

"They don't seem to be asking me for anything," he responded. Seemingly, the first few questions were planted because his answers were canned.

Theil finally picked Hector, who immediately rose.

"Do you have a statement regarding the report out of Cancun that Elizabeth Deavers and Barton Traeger were found murdered in what looks like an apparent drug trade gone wrong?"

Saul's face visibly lost all its color, and Thiel was caught off guard and pissed off at the same time. Hector was to ask about something else entirely! The room erupted in shouted questions, and Marcus stumbled over his words, and then he lied again, "We have never employed anyone by that name!" he yelled over the crowd, and within seconds, Thiel had taken over the podium, and Marcus Brent was being ushered off the stage, quite differently than when he made his entry. The twenty or so people on the stage stood there looking confused. Not sure if they should be celebrating despite the weird turn of events.

Hector shouted after Marcus Brent, and Adam took Rhea by the arm, "Rhea, we need to go now! Simon will keep you up to date with what is going on." She went with Adam and followed him out to the parking lot.

"What the hell just happened in there?" she asked him tensely.

"Miles and Hector had planned that for a few days," he explained.

"What? That wasn't what was supposed to happen! They weren't supposed to die. They were to disappear." Rhea was yelling.

"That's the same thing in Mexico, Rhea," he reasoned. "What did you expect? They would disappear for a few weeks, then reappear safe and sound?"

Rhea sighed, "I don't know what I thought. I hadn't thought through what could happen."

"Miles did," he said, "and, to be honest, it was a good call."

"Miles didn't arrange this hit," she protested.

"No, but he knew it was going to happen. I guarantee that Mikey was very clear about what he was going to do."

"That's why he got Esme to go back to California."

"That and Mikey has friends that will look after her and his child there."

"The article didn't say anything about it being Deavers or Barton," she said as they got into the car.

"Mikey sent them both confirmations that it was the two of them. Mikey was the brain behind this. Don't mess with that dude, especially with his kid." Adam checked out the hallway they were walking down. "He was questioned by the police about the two of them since he was seen meeting with them."

"How do you know that?"

"I've been on a text thread between the three of them," he said. "It's my job since I'm covering security. You don't know about it, so you have plausible deniability if this ever comes back on us. It won't, but just in case."

"How do we know it won't?" she asked.

"Because they won't look into it," he said. "Because, without a doubt, they sent Barton to take care of Elizabeth, and Elizabeth took care of Barton."

Rhea nodded her head as they drove off. She struggled to find solid footing for her emotions. On the one hand, their biggest threats were gone, but on the other hand, that meant that they were dead, and she did not like that she had anything to do with that. It was hard enough to deal with the so-called dirt that the conservative press had dug up on her. It was another, carrying the weight of two lives that were no longer there.

Adam must have sensed that something was bugging her. "You do realize that Mikey had his own beef with them. This wasn't about you, nor was it because of you. He saw an opportunity to solve a whole host of problems at once."

"Will they be able to tie it to him?" she asked.

"Nope, he was at work the whole night."

"At the bar?" she inquired.

"At the bar," he answered.

ೞ౷౷ೞ

As they neared Simon's place, she was scrolling through the aftermath of the press conference. Even the more conservative and sensational news outlets were trying to grab onto what happened with Elizabeth Deavers and Barton Traeger. She felt terrible that Saul Traeger had to find out that way. He might have been a monster and even sent his son to do the dirty work he was afraid to do, but he didn't deserve to find out such heartbreaking news that way.

She tried to consider how this revelation would shift the news cycle. The past few days focused on the three of them, with only a mention or two of Lillian in the more liberal and progressive press. It was also uncanny how the conservative and sensational press ignored Elliot's life in Africa. Benjamin had been interviewed by a reporter from a more conservative paper, and he told them about an attempt on Elliot's life by a woman he identified as Elizabeth Deavers. But no one had pointed that out.

Elliot was brought up on TV as a backward farmer boy who turned into a wannabe frat boy. They pointed out that he was known at OSU for being brooding and often drunk. He had just shrugged when he read it. "It's a fair assessment," he said. The press had the most challenging time finding dirt on her and Miles from their respective universities. They had received supportive texts and emails, and both Portland State and Penn circled the wagons and pointed out that they were beloved professors.

Hamish also found himself under scrutiny, and he hadn't fared as well as the other three. His more complicated past and press-handling abilities were called into question. They hadn't been in the news long enough for them to make any other connections in their lives, or for them to begin to harass Simon, Jennings, or Marcia. Jennings had said that he needed to do some explaining at church that Sunday, "but as a whole," he had chuckled over the phone, "most of them were kind and only talked about us behind our backs." Rhea smiled every time she thought of him saying that to Elliot on FaceTime.

They pulled into Simon's place. The boys were using the basement as their place until they could straighten things out more securely at Miles's apartment. Rhea had taken over the one guest bedroom. Elliot was sitting in the kitchen when they got there.

"Where's Miles?" she asked him.

He looked up from what he was working on, "In the basement I think," he pointed in the direction.

"Where's Hamish?"

Elliot nodded towards the backyard patio, where Hamish could be seen talking on the phone. He had a notepad in front of him, and he was writing something down when he wasn't speaking on the phone.

"Did you watch?" she asked Elliot as she went into the kitchen.

"I did," he said. "That was a real shit show, wasn't it? Did anyone see you there?"

"No," she said, "I was able to get in and out without anyone seeing me."

"What did Miles think?" she was probing him about his reaction to the news.

"He nodded a lot, then he got excited when Brent lied about Ms. Deavers," Elliot said. As if on cue Miles came up from the basement.

"Rhea," he called out to her. "Did anyone notice you?"

"No," she said, "but I've a question for both of you."

"Shoot," Elliot said.

"Did you know that Mikey was going to have them killed?" she asked. Elliot erupted in laughter.

"What's so funny?" she looked serious.

"Wasn't that just assumed when the former bodyguard, not to mention the father of the child, got involved?"

"No," her jaw dropped in disbelief. "I didn't imagine that was going to happen."

"Why not?" Miles countered.

"Because we don't let people be killed," she said.

"So, we just let ourselves be killed," Elliot shot back.

"Rhea," Miles said, "I did not know how it was going to go down, but I had assumed when Mikey came up with the plan that it could go down this way."

"Was it the plan to have Hector ask that question at that time?" She looked at Miles, hoping desperately that he hadn't sacrificed his character through this whole ordeal.

"No," he said, which made her feel relieved. "He was going to ask if they had a comment about the two of them disappearing."

"Again, Rhea," Elliot jumped in, "what did you think was going to happen?"

"I thought he was going to," she couldn't utter a complete sentence. She only thought that Mikey would make them disappear, and she hadn't thought about what exactly that meant.

"Mikey didn't kill anyone," Miles stated. "Barton was there to kill Deavers, and he was going to be arrested as he did it. She just shot him before the police got there."

Rhea stared at him. It felt wrong that two people were dead, but it didn't feel like it was her fault. "I just feel bad," was all she said.

"Why?" Elliot asked with a sense of surprise.

"It's just…" She couldn't find the exact words she was looking for, but it didn't matter because Elliot jumped right in.

"Have you forgotten that this woman tried to shoot me and ended up shooting my friend?"

"No, I haven't forgotten that."

"Or that he kidnapped and killed Lillian?"

"Hell," Miles was worked up too, and Rhea was surprised by the force at which he spoke, "Have you forgotten that she murdered your younger brother and his mother?"

"No, I haven't forgotten any of that, but I also don't feel that justifies their deaths!"

"I disagree," Elliot said. "It doesn't bug me one bit that they're no longer on this earth. It was the justice they deserved, and we know damn well we wouldn't have gotten justice for any of it if that asshole gets elected."

"Miles," Rhea muttered. "Do you feel the same way?" She stood staring at Miles.

"I'm with Machiavelli over there," he motioned to Elliot, "and I say the ends justify the means."

"Machiavelli didn't say that it's just a summary of what he thought," Hamish said, coming in the door. She'd noticed that the three of them had become chummy since their encounter in the bar.

"Hamish," she was now talking to him. "What is your take on this? Is it our fault that Deavers and Barton were killed?"

Hamish looked at her with his head slightly tilted to the side. "Did you pull a trigger?"

"You know what I mean," she was irritated by his question.

"Rhea," the way he looked at her calmed her heart, which also made her automatically suspicious of him. "The decision was made before you were even told about it. You weren't going to stop what Mikey put into motion. This wasn't about revenge for you all; this was a personal vendetta for Mikey, and they put themselves in the crosshairs by coming into his territory."

"He invited them," she said to them all.

"And they took the bait," Elliot added. "You didn't force them to go!"

"I'm not going to win this, am I?"

"There is nothing to win," Miles said. "I'm sorry you didn't understand what was going to happen, but I agree with Hamish; there was absolutely nothing you could do about it. Marcus Brent played his cards and unknowingly played right into the hands of a man who had a serious vendetta against those two. Did we benefit from those deaths?" he paused and shook his head, "We sure as hell did."

"Knowing that they're gone, I feel a whole lot better," Elliot said. "Now I only have to deal with these Brent nut jobs everywhere."

Rhea was unsettled. She knew they had a point, but that didn't mean she had to agree. She didn't pull the trigger or give the green light; that was true, but she knew something was going to happen, and she was upset with herself for not seeing that it was going to lead to murder. She couldn't help but feel like the two dead souls would haunt her dreams for some time.

ᒕᒕ

Elliot was surprised at how quickly the press picked up their story again and then just as quickly dropped them. Marcus Brent took a hit for lying, but not for long. Soon, facts had been spun into lies, and thoughts had been directed away from the truth. What had seemed to him, and everyone around him, as a question of moral integrity had been glazed over or altogether ignored.

Rhea had no desire to do any more interviews. Elliot saw that she was struggling with how things had ended with Deavers and Barton. It plagued her at each interview. Rhea was always relieved when the interview ended, and no one had asked them about the two dead Brent Industries employees found in Mexico. As the attention on them died down, she bowed out.

Elliot didn't want to leave Miles alone to do the interviews, but he noticed that he was also weary. He couldn't understand how such solid evidence of moral depravity could be ignored and swept under the rug in the name of political games. Brent was the candidate, warts and all, and it seemed that suddenly everyone was finding warts attractive. It made Elliot angry. When Miles suggested they take a break from giving interviews, Elliot jumped at his chance to move on.

Miles nodded when he told him. "I understand," he said.

In the next few days, they hashed out a plan. Rhea was going to head back to Portland to get ready for her fall semester, and he would head to Oklahoma, pack up his belongings, and drive out to Portland. The job that Rhea had a lead for had come through, and he was ready to start a new chapter.

It was a somber Thursday evening when he and Miles pulled

up to Simon's house. They would have one last meal together before going their separate ways. Rhea met them at the door, hugging each of them in turn. If Miles was feeling sad, he wasn't showing it. Elliot couldn't show it. He felt like he was letting Miles down. He hadn't been able to put that into words, and so it had gone unsaid and hung between the two of them like the unfinished business it was.

It was mid-way through dessert when Miles finally spoke about the last few months. "I know we didn't get the justice we wanted, but I have no regrets. We did what we had to do."

"Here, here," Simon said. "I am very proud of all three of you."

Elliot nodded and looked over at Rhea. She seemed to be contemplating what was being said.

"Was anyone else surprised," she said, "at how people reacted to the story?"

"Absolutely," Elliot responded. "It was like what he did to our mothers didn't matter. It wasn't a big deal. It was as if people were shocked and then shrugged their shoulders, saying, 'Oh, well, boys will be boys.' Don't even get me started on ignoring the fact that three people are dead. It didn't seem like anyone cared."

"The excuses they've made up have taken compartmentalizing to a whole new level," Rhea said. "I've never seen something like this on a massive scale. It was only three weeks ago since that press conference, and no one mentions us or Deavers and Barton at all. They've moved on. Even the Democrats have picked a different battle. No one cares if Marcus Brent's morally corrupt when he's claiming he can keep the liberals at bay."

"It's bullshit," Elliot said. "They wore us down and then swept us under the rug."

"No," Miles responded, "not completely."

"What do you mean, son?" Simon asked him.

"I don't plan on letting it go."

"Miles," Rhea pleaded, "no one cares anymore."

"I do," he responded. "I care a lot. I'm going to bide my time and then rear my head later. I've already talked to Hamish about it, and we have a plan."

"I hope that isn't the book deal he's been babbling on about," Rhea responded.

"No," Miles said. "It isn't. I don't want that. I want Marcus Brent to think we've disappeared, and then when it can hurt him the most…BAM," Miles punched the air, "we're back!"

"I can't," Rhea said. "I'm okay with you moving forward, but I can't. It's too much."

"Miles," Elliot looked at his brother and changed what he wanted to say mid-sentence, "keep me in the loop."

"It will be an uphill battle, and no one may care," Simon said, "but it doesn't mean you don't do it."

Miles nodded. "I know the world doesn't care about facts or morals. I'm still blown away at how they could paint victims as bad guys. I'm not sure what we can do, but I must do something. If we don't do something, history will look back and judge us."

"Spoken like a bona fide history professor," Elliot smiled. "Just don't forget, we've already done something. Now it's time for someone else to take up the cause."

"Who," Miles stammered. "You can't trust society to listen to reason. They do all sorts of mental gymnastics to support their political sides, even when the evidence shows them their own politicians aren't acting in good faith towards them. Extremism, historically, always means you are believing some sort of lie in order to discredit and vilify your enemy."

"I know," Elliot said, "people vilified us!"

"Moderates are always the villain," Simon chimed in, "because they are always the voice of reason. The bravest thing in this world right now is to be a moderate."

Elliot's heart took on the weight of that statement. He knew his own generation was guilty of extremism. Now, he'd been marginalized by those extremes, and he'd stopped fighting. He looked at Miles, and he saw a hero. He saw the person who understood what was at stake. Elliot was proud to call that man his brother.

Chapter Thirty-Four

The students had about two more weeks until Christmas break. Miles had survived the first part of the semester, where he was either the focus of liberal professors who lauded him for what he did or was the butt of jokes made by those in support of Brent. His students didn't seem to care and had, as he'd expected, hunkered down and worked hard. Many of them did have questions for him.

"Why did you turn down the book deal?"

"Has Marcus Brent ever contacted you personally?"

Miles's students also asked him about the beautiful woman who had shown up to visit him at Thanksgiving, but he would just shrug that question off with a smile. Esme and Esperanza had been there for Thanksgiving at Rhea's request. Rhea had been in California in October and had made it a point to stop in and meet her. They were complete opposites from each other, Esme had said, but she also knew that Rhea was the salt of the earth, and the two had been in constant contact since. Elliot and Rhea had flown out as well. Simon pretended to be overwhelmed but wouldn't have had it any other way. It was the first time that Elliot had met Esme.

Elliot had pulled Miles aside on Wednesday afternoon when everybody was busy shopping or prepping for dinner, "I see why you kept her from me."

"It's not like that," Miles said, but then added sarcastically, "You're right. I knew you would've snatched her up right under my nose."

"It's okay," Elliot said. "I met a girl at church."

Miles was a bit stunned. "At church?"

"Yeah," Elliot said with a grin, "the NGO Rhea got me the job with was doing a presentation at this church in Salem that does tons of missions work. The doctor and his wife, who stitched up Scooper, came from this type of church, so I wasn't as skeptical as usual."

"Go on," Miles said.

"Well, within the first five minutes, this guy comes up to me and tells me he recognizes me. I was ready for him to go off on the whole Marcus Brent, the Christian standard bearer crap," Miles noticed that Elliot hadn't said shit, but instead crap. "Instead, he looked at me, shook my hand, and said that there were so many people that he knew who thought we were all so brave."

"Whoa," Miles was awestruck. "That hasn't been my experience here, though I've not been in church for a long time."

"Well, starts to talk to me, and I don't know what to say, other than most of the Christians I run into think we're evil and liars. I hadn't seen her, but this beautiful girl was standing behind him, and she suddenly said, 'Everyone I know felt grateful that you exposed the truth about his character.''

"Just like Rhea always said," Miles commented.

"Just like Rhea always said," Elliot smiled. "We made a small difference, and it seems we have at least got some people talking."

"So, what's the young lady's name?" he asked Elliot.

"Anna," he said.

"Wow, congratulations, Elliot," Miles patted his back.

☙❧❦❧❧☙

It had been interesting to watch Elliot throughout the weekend. Gone were the hard edges that often made his soft side unnoticeable, except to Miles and Rhea. He may have sworn once or twice, but Miles noticed he didn't need to dread what might come out of his mouth. This was especially welcome since Esperanza was present.

"He's a different kid," Rhea said. "That church has been good for him, I guess."

"Have you met this Anna?" Miles asked her.

"Yes, she's sweet," Rhea responded. "She works for a graphic design firm and has two younger brothers who love Elliot. Jennings and Marcia were out a few weeks ago to visit, and she made the two of them light up!"

"And have you been in touch with Hamish?" he asked her.

She nodded her head in the affirmative. "But I don't hold out a lot of hope for us. He's just a bit too arrogant for me. He could use some humbling."

Miles just nodded and laughed. The world had changed for each of them. Last year, at this time, he was in Berlin, and an only child. Now, he was back in Philly, and his family had grown. Who knew where he'd be next year at this time?

Christmas break came, and with it came a trip out to the West Coast. His first stop was to visit Esme and Esperanza. After that, he'd head up to Portland to spend Christmas Day with Rhea and Elliot. It was a wonderful visit. The time with Esme had gone well, but he could tell that the bond between them was different. It wasn't like it was with his siblings. She had met a young guy closer to her age, and he seemed nice. In many ways, Miles felt that she was taken care of, and he could move on to taking care of his own life.

⁂

It was the middle of January before Miles was back at his desk. He had finished working on his syllabi for the next semester and had just read through the list of students he would teach. It was exciting. His time in California had been amazing, and switching to a West Coast university was an appealing idea. Simon was struggling with that, and they'd just had a bit of a dust-up over it that morning on the phone as he drove to work.

Miles got up from his desk and walked down to the staff kitchen. He wanted a cup of coffee, and they had a Keurig. As he walked, he reminded himself that he should buy one, so he didn't have to make the trek down the hall. He also reminded himself that this meant he would miss out on some of the interactions with his colleagues, which he really did enjoy.

He looked out the window onto the sliver of campus before his eyes. It was cold and gray; the snow had started to melt but then had refrozen. California had been warm and cozy, but there was something oddly reassuring about this type of weather he'd grown up in.

He walked back to his office and thought that he saw a shadow on the door. He hurried his steps, thinking that maybe he'd forgotten a meeting. Instead, he found two tall men standing behind his desk, with another older man sitting in his desk chair. It was Marcus Brent.

"Hello, Miles," he said. "I thought that I'd drop in for a little discussion."

Miles stood there with his mouth open, holding his coffee.

"Come on in and take a seat," Marcus said to him, motioning to one of the chairs where his students would sit.

"You're in my seat," Miles managed to say to him.

"Well, let's switch things up for a bit," Marcus told him. One of the two guards moved from behind the desk, ushered him in, and closed the door. Miles refused to sit down and stood behind the chair.

"Please take a seat, Miles," Marcus said firmly.

"No," Miles responded. "I'm just fine standing."

"Ah, yes," Marcus responded. "You remind me very much of your mother. Obstinate. Defiant. She acted similarly when we broke up."

In Miles's narrative of his mother's relationship with Marcus Brent, she had always done the dumping.

"Harlan was not a fan," he said. "She wasn't the right pedigree for the Brent family. You'll probably agree with me that she is sure a hell of a lot better than the lot I've been hitched to."

Miles just glowered at him.

"I can see you agree," Marcus said as he continued. "I just wanted to meet you face to face. As you know, I don't have any legitimate male heirs. It must be the wrath of God acting upon me and my misdeeds that I have three of them out of wedlock."

"Two," Marcus said to him, "the third is dead."

Marcus nodded at him, "You're right, and I mourn the loss of Dillion."

"Dustin," Miles corrected him.

"Dustin," he repeated. "I, unfortunately, don't remember his mother at all."

Miles knew that he was turning red. A flush crept up his neck and into his cheeks.

"I had nothing to do with that, you know," he said to Miles. "My father hired Elizabeth Deavers years before to clean up my messes. I, of course, had no idea by what means she was cleaning up those messes."

"Yeah, right," was all Miles could think to say.

"Miles," he said as he stood up. "I actually loved your mother."

That hurt so badly. Miles took a deep breath in an attempt to hold back a sob.

"I've known about you for a long time now," he said. "It was shortly after your mother died that I realized that you weren't Simon Trent's son. I knew you were mine." Marcus Brent smiled.

"Like fuck you did," Miles heard it come out of his mouth.

"That sounded more like a response your brother Elliot would give," he said with a chuckle. "You've been on my radar for years. My firstborn son. The child of a woman I actually loved. You'll always be special to me."

Miles felt the tears slipping out of his eyes. He wasn't able to control it anymore. He was broken, which seemed to be what Marcus Brent wanted.

"You lie," Miles stammered. "You didn't know I existed."

"I do lie," Marcus said without a hint of emotion. "All the time. Hell, if a fraction of the people who wanted to vote for me realized how advantageous it is for me financially to be the leader of the free world and what it will actually cost them, I wouldn't have made it out of the primary. Instead, they think the world I'm about to benefit from is against them. Why? Because I know how to fucking lie." He paused for a minute and looked at Miles with eyes that seemed genuine and not evil. "What I won't lie about is that I've known you existed. I figured it out, but I didn't let anyone know. Your success, you owe that to me."

"No way," Miles protested. "I've never been handed anything."

"I'm sure you see it that way," Marcus said, sitting back in Miles's seat. "Between your adoptive father Simon…"

Miles interrupted him before he could complete the sentence. "Simon is my father. It doesn't matter what the genetics say."

"Oh, for sure," Marcus said, "you have his investigative prowess as well as his legal mind. That you got from him, but from me," he shrugged, "you got that grant to study in Belgium in college. The endowment that let you teach in Berlin for three years, that was me too."

"No, it wasn't," Miles's voice cracked. His mind raced to make sense of what was being said. He dug for comebacks, but none came. He stood there staring at the man who had created him with nothing but hatred and contempt, and deep down, his gut told him that it was very conceivable that his life's success was owed to this unscrupulous man.

"You don't need to accept it as a fact. I'm only offering this as a way for you to realize that nothing was ever going to happen to you. You've been protected since I realized you were mine, and literally, no one has ever known."

Miles just stood there; he was furious at himself because he could not muster words to fight back.

"I'm going to leave you in peace," Marcus said. "I'll make sure nothing ever happens to you, Elliot, or Rhea."

"Why?" Miles said. "We're trying to destroy your platform!"

"I'm doing it because I loved Betsy McDonal," he said solemnly, so much so that Miles almost believed him. "And I'll honor the fact that she didn't want me in your life."

"You're evil," Miles whispered.

"I may be, but good luck trying to convince most of the people out there of that fact! I'm their savior! I'm the one to keep this country from descending into socialism, which you and I know will never happen. Those idiots don't, though. I may be evil to you, but I'm a hero to them. I'm God's judgment on the liberal filth of this world."

"Better to be liberal filth than the moral filth that you are," Miles spat at him as he moved around the desk. He felt like a ten-year-old in a shouting match on the playground. He knew he couldn't win, but it made him even more determined to have the last word. His movement sprang the security guard behind him into action. He grabbed Miles firmly. Marcus Brent just chuckled.

"Again, they're all blinded to my moral filth, and all they see is you, an unmarried liberal professor who is trying to drag my name through the dirt. You're the depraved one, not me. Welcome to my America, son!"

"Don't call me…"

"Son," Marcus interrupted him. "I know. But before you get too high and mighty about that, just remember you, not I, are the one pointing out that I'm your father. I'll leave you with that," he said. He left the room with one guard in front of him and one behind.

Miles slumped down in the chair in front of him and cried. He pulled out his phone from his pocket, but didn't know who to call. He typed in Rhea's name but then changed his mind and put in Elliot's. He changed his mind again, not wanting to open up the past they both seemed to have moved on from. He went through Simon and even Jennings for no good reason other than that he listens so well. In the end, he put the phone on his desk and prayed for the strength to forgive for the first time in a long time.

He stood up and moved back to his chair. There was a card on the desk. He didn't recognize the handwriting but opened it to find a note. It was addressed to his mother, and it was from Marcus Brent. There was a sticky note on the other side with barely legible writing on it, "I loved her, that I would never lie about. MB." Under it was a phone number. He closed the card, not able to read what was in it. He didn't need to know. He just needed to move on and be grateful for the things he had gained in the end.

Epilogue

The heirs that remained never inherited the kingdom they were entitled to. Instead, they would walk away from what they legitimately had a claim to. Sometimes, an inheritance isn't worth the connection to the estate.

By the time Marcus Brent was impeached the second time, Rhea had deemed Hamish humble enough to marry, and their first child was born as they watched the vote on the congressional floor.

By the time Marcus Brent had lost his re-election bid, Elliot had returned from working in Thailand and was happy to be an uncle. Anna didn't work out in the end, but Gia did, and their story was written during a tumultuous time in the land.

By the time Marcus Brent had been killed, Miles would be living again in Germany, a refugee from his country of birth. The country that his birth father had ruled and ruined. The kingdom wasn't worth having anymore, and the subjects got what they had asked for.

Acknowledgments

Two sets of eyes have seen every iteration of this novel: my wife's and my Aunt's.

My wife, Sarah, spent so many hours reading, her pencil always ready. I couldn't have crossed the finish line without her. No one has wanted me to realize this dream more than my best friend and wife. She has journeyed and sacrificed much to see this happen.

My Aunt Ruth has always been my champion in telling stories. Her encouragement pushed me on even when I felt like an impostor.

Nicole Baart changed the direction of this novel after having only read a few pages. I'm forever indebted to her advice and careful criticism.

Everyone at Amazon who helped me realize this dream, thank you!

It was springtime in Berlin eleven years ago when the craziest idea sprang into my head. I was running through the city with my dear friend Mike, and I spoke the thought aloud. He looked at me and said, "Yes, *that*!" "*That*" turned into this novel. Mike's friendship and the hours we spent together in bars, living rooms, and running the streets of Berlin formed the zeitgeist of this novel. We both so desperately want to *unstick* this world!

My people, you know who you are. You have prayed, you have held me accountable, and you have loved my family and me so well. I could write paragraphs about the specific ways you have inspired and helped me. I have so much love and gratitude for each of you, but this isn't the right place to spell that out. Please accept your names here as my small way to show that I couldn't have done this without you: Bill and Christie (for all the *time*), Chris and Amber (for making us feel like family), Heather and Ash (for all your encouragement), Mike and Elissa (for caring and not leaving us alone), Mike and Claire (for every minute we get to spend together), John, Lori and Jill (for all the stories), Tyler and Liz (for letting me be the best man), Chris and Rebecca (for the best talks), Tom and Jackie (for showing us how to be decent human beings and even better parents) and Becca (who gives me great books to read).

Finally, Dane and Jenna…My greatest joy has been the two of you, and that joy has pushed me to finish this sprawling book and has motivated me to write even more.

www.ingramcontent.com/pod-product-compliance
Lightning Source LLC
Chambersburg PA
CBHW061032310726
48969CB00004B/933